"Where did you learn to kiss?"

She ran her tongue over her tingling lips, and his eyes darkened further. "Books. I read a lot of books."

He nodded slightly. "I reckon the women in those books always pucker up to kiss."

"Yes, they do," she answered, wondering how he had drawn that conclusion from her simple statement, only one answer quickly coming to her mind. "Perhaps we've read the same books."

"I doubt it," he said, his voice low. He cradled her cheek. "Don't pucker."

Before she could protest, he covered her mouth with his. She'd barely noticed when he'd kissed her before, but now she realized his lips were warm, pliant. She hadn't expected that of a man as hard as he was rumored to be.

By Lorraine Heath

TEXAS GLORY

LORRAINE HEATH

AVONBOOKS

An Imprint of HarperCollins*Publishers*

Texas Glory was originally published in the United States in 1998 by the Penguin Group.

First Avon Books mass market printing: July 2018

Print Edition ISBN: 978-0-06-285232-8
Digital Edition ISBN: 978-0-06-204661-1

Designed by Amy Halperin
Cover illustration by Victor Gadino
Cover photograph by Image 1st LLC (couple); © acceptphoto/ Shutterstock (horses)

For Mom and Dad N.
When your son asked me to become his wife,
you welcomed me as your daughter.
No finer gift could have been given.

A Letter from Lorraine Heath

My Dear Reader:

I began writing *Texas Glory* shortly after my father passed away in 1996, so I don't think it's any coincidence that Dallas Leigh is bigger than life with a gruff exterior and tender interior, doing things for which he takes no credit and seeks no glory. Very reminiscent of my dad.

When I was growing up, the birthday card from my British grandmother always arrived opened, with a dollar nestled inside. When I told my dad I wanted to open the cards myself, he explained that the *post office* was required to open and inspect mail that came from other countries. And my young, innocent self believed him—until I went off to college and my birthday card from my grandmother arrived at my dorm unopened, without a dollar. When I mentioned it, my dad confessed that he'd promised my grandmother, who lived on a very limited income, her birthday cards would always contain a dollar. So he religiously opened every one she sent, and if a dollar wasn't inside, he'd slip one in. Then he promptly pulled out his wallet and handed me a dollar. I don't know which dollars came from him or my grandmother, but I do know each card was filled with love.

Because my dad wasn't overtly demonstrative when it came to affection, I have a soft spot in my heart for heroes who have a difficult time openly expressing their love, but prefer instead to show it in quiet, sometimes secretive, ways. Dallas is very dear to me because he knows he's a hard man and has convinced himself he doesn't need love—but I think of all the Leigh brothers, he's the one who needs it most of all.

He also needed a very special heroine. Cordelia believes it's a woman's lot in life to live within the shadows cast by men, until Dallas guides her onto the path where she can cast her own shadows. I adore Dallas and Cordelia because they manage to bring out the best in each other, and in so doing bring out the best in themselves.

Whether you're new to *Texas Glory* or taking a return trip through the pages, I hope you enjoy Dallas and Cordelia's hard-fought journey toward glorious love.

Wishing you many happily-ever-afters,
Lorraine

Chapter One

May, 1881

*D*reams. Gossamer images that most people carried with them into their sleep, but for Dallas Leigh, they were the incentive that woke him before dawn, the impetus that pushed him toward midnight.

Dreams were the stepping stones to glory.

By pursuing them, he had attained a level of success that exceeded most men's reach and acquired all that he had set out to gain: Land, cattle, and wealth beyond his highest expectations.

Yet, desperation gnawed at him like a starving dog that had just discovered a buried bone, and as he gazed at the stars that blanketed the velvety sky, he felt as though he had achieved nothing.

He was a man with a solitary dream that remained untouched, the one that had served as the guiding beacon for every goal that he had fulfilled. Without the realization of his greatest desire, his other accomplishments meant little, and he feared that they might mean nothing at all—if he never gained a son with whom to share them.

The lingering warmth of the parched earth seeped through his backside as he worked the ridge of his spine into a comfortable position against the gnarled and crooked post that served as one of a thousand anchors for his barbed-wire fence.

He hated the fencing with a passion, but he knew it was destined to become essential to every rancher's survival in the same manner that the railroad had wended its way into their lives. Workers continued to lay the tracks that brought more people farther west. The days of knowing one's neighbor and where his land ended and a man's own land began were dwindling. The barbed wire cut through the questions, marked a man's domain, and left no doubts as to his ownership.

Unfortunately, it was an aspect of the future that only a few men could envision, and those blinded by the traditions of the past were determined that the barbed wire would not stand.

Dallas Leigh intended to make damn sure that it did.

"Dallas?" The hoarse whisper momentarily silenced the nightly serenade of the crickets, frogs, and katydids.

He glanced at his youngest brother, who was stretched along the ground, his arms folded beneath his dark head, his tall, lanky body running the length of the fence. "What?"

"How long we gonna stay?" Austin asked.

"All night if we have to."

"What makes you think they'll come?"

"Full moon. The McQueen brothers like to do their thieving and destroying by the light of a full moon."

"I don't know how you can be sure that they're gonna cut the wire right here," Austin said, exasperation laced through his youthful voice. At twenty-one, he had little patience when it came to waiting for the next moment.

"I don't know where they will cut it, but if you shut your mouth, we'll hear the tinny sound of the cut traveling along the wire, and we'll know in which direction to ride. Just close your eyes and imagine that you're listening for that first twang to come from your violin when you slap your bow on it."

"I don't slap my bow onto anything. I place it on the strings as gently as I'd touch my fingers to a woman's soft cheek or press my lips against her warm mouth. Then I stroke it slow and long, the way I'd stroke—"

"Will you shut up?" a deeper voice growled.

Dallas didn't need to lean forward to see the disgruntled expression he knew he'd find on Houston's face. His middle brother was the only one among them to have a wife, and Dallas imagined right now he'd rather be curled up in bed with her nestled against his side. He appreciated the fact that Houston was guarding the fence instead.

Austin snickered. "You're just aggravated 'cuz you ain't home doing your own stroking."

"Watch your mouth, boy," Houston warned. "You're gonna cross into dangerous territory if you bring my wife into this conversation."

"You know I wouldn't say nothing bad about Amelia. I just figure you'd rather be at home making another baby instead of sittin' out here waitin' on something that might not happen."

"We've already made another baby," Houston

said, pride and a great deal of affection reflected in his voice.

Dallas shot forward so he could see his brother's face limned by the moonlight. Despite the heavy scarring on the left side of his face and the black eye patch that hid the worst of it, Houston looked to be a man who had realized every dream he'd ever dared to hope for. Dallas sometimes envied him that contentment, especially since he'd accomplished it all by stealing Dallas's wife from him.

"When did this happen?" Dallas asked.

Houston tugged on the brim of his hat. "Hell, I don't know. Sometime in the last month or so, I reckon. Amelia just told me tonight before I rode out."

"So Maggie May is gonna have a little brother or sister," Austin said, his wide grin shining in the moonbeams that passed through the clouds. "You ain't planning to name all your young'uns after the month they were born in, are you?"

Houston shrugged. "I'll name them whatever Amelia wants to name them."

Dallas leaned back against the post. "I sure as hell am glad you took that woman off my hands. I wouldn't like living my life around a woman's wants and needs."

"If you loved her as much as I love Amelia, you'd like it just fine," Houston said.

Dallas had to admit that he probably would, but finding a woman to love in a land populated mostly by cowboys and prairie dogs was no easy task.

Hell, he couldn't even find a woman to marry and bear his son, let alone a woman to love.

The absence of decent women in this portion of West Texas was a sharp thorn in his side, a nagging ache in his heart, and a steadfast barrier to the fulfillment of his final glory: a son to whom he could pass down the legacy he had worked so hard to carve from a land known for its disappointments and broken promises.

He had hoped founding a town would attract women to the area, but Leighton was growing slowly. The banker, Lester Henderson, had a wife who easily occupied the entire width of the boardwalk when she strolled to the general store. Perry Oliver, the owner of the general store, was a widower with a lovely daughter. Dallas had considered asking the merchant for his daughter's hand. At sixteen, his mother had married his father, but Dallas couldn't bring himself to marry a woman younger than half his age. Besides, he had a suspicion Austin had set his sights on the young woman. Why else would his brother find an excuse to ride into town every day to purchase some useless contraption from the general store?

Neither the sheriff nor the saloon keeper nor the doctor had brought women with them. The town's seamstress, Mimi St. Claire, was unmarried, but she was on the far side of forty if she was a day.

With resignation, Dallas was coming to the conclusion that, once again, he would need to search beyond his town, beyond the prairie, in order to find a woman who could give birth to his son. At thirty-five, he was beginning to feel the weight of the years pressing in on him. He needed a son.

He wanted a son sitting beside him at this very moment, sharing the anticipation of the night. He wanted to count the stars with his son. He needed to feel the breeze blow over their faces and know that when it no longer touched his face—when Dallas was dead and buried—the breeze would continue to caress his son's face.

The nearby river flowed to the rhythm of Nature's lullaby: the mating call of insects mingled with the occasional swoosh of an owl's wings and the howl of a stalking coyote. Dallas wanted his son to hear that song, to appreciate the magnificence of nature, to tame it, to own it. He imagined his son standing here years from now, looking out over all that they had accomplished, listening to the water lap at the muddy shore, listening to the—

Ping!

The tune of destruction broke into the night. Dallas jumped to his feet as the high-pitched whine came again. "They're to the south."

He and his brothers mounted their horses with an agility that came from years of chasing after stampeding cattle. The moon's silver glow lighted their path along the river's edge.

With a firm grip, Dallas removed the coiled rope from his saddle. He needed only the sure pressure of his thighs to guide the stallion that had helped him herd cattle north. When the shadows of three men emerged from the darkness, the horse didn't falter.

The tallest of the men fired his gun while the two other men scrambled for their horses. Dallas heard shouts and yells. Horses snorted, neighed, and reared up, their hooves slicing at the air.

Raising his arm, Dallas snapped his wrist and threw a loop that whistled through the muggy air and circled Boyd McQueen. Dallas yanked hard on the rope. The gun flew from McQueen's hand as he stumbled to the ground. Without hesitation, Dallas secured his end of the rope around the saddle horn, set his heels to his horse's sides, and galloped toward the precious river.

Dallas glanced over his shoulder. The moonlight

glinted off Boyd McQueen's angry face. Dallas took satisfaction in the man's fury and guided his racing horse into the shallow water that more closely resembled a babbling brook than a full-fledged river.

"Damn you, Leigh!" McQueen yelled just before the horse splashed into the center of the stream.

Water sprayed Dallas's legs. He looked back to make certain McQueen's head was above the surface. He didn't want the man to drown, but he intended to give him a rough ride.

Dallas heard the echo of three rapid gunshots. No responding gunfire sounded. The eerie silence that followed signaled a warning.

Dallas jerked his horse to a staggering halt. His brothers weren't behind him. Three more steady shots bellowed.

Groaning, McQueen struggled to his feet, sputtering obscenities that Dallas didn't wait to address. Releasing the rope from the saddle horn, he urged his horse back toward the fence.

Alarm skittered along his spine when he saw the silhouettes of two men standing and one man kneeling. He dismounted before his horse halted.

He dropped to his knees beside the man sprawled over the ground. "What happened?" Dallas asked.

"Austin took the bullet Boyd fired, and it doesn't look good," Houston said.

"WHERE IN THE hell is the damn doctor!" Dallas growled as he stared through the bedroom window. He'd sent his foreman into town to fetch the physician, but that had been over two hours ago.

"He'll be here," Amelia said softly. While Dallas had brought Austin home, with no help from the McQueen brothers, Houston had ridden to his house and fetched his wife and daughter. With the innocence of a child, Maggie had viewed coming to her uncle's house in the dead of night as an adventure.

Dallas stalked to the bed where his brother lay, his eyes closed, his breathing shallow. He watched as Amelia wiped a damp cloth over Austin's face. She'd stanched the flow of blood, but they needed the doctor to remove the bullet from Austin's shoulder. It hadn't come out the other side so Dallas could only assume it was embedded in his bone. He was lucky the bullet hadn't dropped lower and gone through his heart. "He looks too pale."

Amelia lifted her gaze to his. She had the prettiest green eyes he'd ever seen. He remembered a time when he'd thought he could easily fall in love with those eyes. Perhaps he had.

"I don't think it's as bad as when Houston got shot," she said quietly.

"I'd feel a hell of a lot better if he'd wake up."

She returned to her task of running the cloth over Austin's brow. "He'd only feel the pain then."

Better the pain than death. Dallas glanced at Houston who sat in a nearby chair, holding his own silent vigil, his daughter curled in his lap, asleep.

"I guess you think I should have handled this differently," Dallas said.

"It makes no sense to me to build a town, hire a sheriff, and then *not* use him when you've got trouble."

"I hired him to protect the citizens. I can handle my own trouble."

"You can't have it both ways, Dallas. If you bring the law out here, then you can't be your own law."

"I can be anything I damn well want to be. It's

my land. McQueen is going to learn to stay the hell off it, and I'll teach him the lesson myself."

"But at what cost?"

The words rang out loudly with concern. Dallas turned his attention back to his wounded brother. "Why don't you tuck your daughter into my bed?" he suggested quietly to Houston.

"I'll do that," Houston replied as he easily brought himself to his feet, without waking Maggie. He walked from the room.

Dallas wrapped his hand tightly around the bedpost, searching for answers to his unfortunate dilemma. The McQueens had moved to the area three years ago, thinking they had purchased the land that ran along both sides of the river. Dallas suspected that the person who had sold them the land had been a land grabber. Land grabbing had been a common practice following the war. A man would buy a parcel of land and extend the boundaries as far as he wanted, often posting a notice in a newspaper to validate his claim. Although the practice usually worked, the notice was not legally binding. Dallas had filed claims with the land office for every acre of land he owned. Unfortunately, the McQueens seemed to believe—as many ranchers did—that a gun spoke louder than the law. They had refused to acknowledge Dallas's deed to the acreage and had blatantly prodded their inferior stock into grazing over Dallas's spread.

He wouldn't have minded sharing his water or his grass if he didn't need to control the breeding of his cattle so he could improve the quality of beef his cows produced.

He'd begun to put up his barbed-wire fence. If the McQueens had accepted that, Dallas would have left a portion of the river open to them. But they had torn down the fence before Dallas's men had completed it. Irritating, but harmless. Dallas had paid a visit to Angus McQueen and demanded that he keep his sons tethered. Then Dallas had ordered his men to finish building the fence and to carry it beyond the river.

Two months ago, Angus McQueen's sons had again destroyed a section of the fence, cutting the wire, burning the posts, and killing almost forty head of cattle, most on the verge of calving. Dallas had given Angus McQueen a bill for the damages that the man had refused to pay because Dallas couldn't prove his sons had torn down the fence and murdered the cattle.

Dallas could certainly prove McQueens had cut his wire tonight, but as Houston had stated—at what cost?

Dallas held his thoughts and his silence when Houston returned to the room and took up his vigil in the chair beside the bed.

Dallas swung around as soft footfalls sounded along the hallway. Relief washed over him when Dr. Freeman shuffled into the room. The tall, thin man looked as though he were hovering on death's doorstep himself. His bones creaked as he crossed the room without a word. He set his black bag on the bedside table and began to examine Austin's wound.

"Where in the hell have you been?" Dallas demanded.

"Had to set Boyd McQueen's arm." Dr. Freeman glanced over his shoulder at Dallas and raised a thinning white brow, his steely gray eyes accusing. "Boyd said you broke it."

Twin emotions twisted through Dallas's gut: rage because McQueen had selfishly had the doctor tend to his needs, knowing all along that his bullet had slammed into Austin; and guilt because he hadn't realized he'd broken Boyd's arm when he'd dragged him through the river.

"Did McQueen tell you that he shot Austin?"

Dr. Freeman sighed. "No, I didn't learn that bit of information until I returned home and found your foreman waiting for me." Shaking his head, he began poking his fingers around Austin's ravaged flesh. "You and the McQueens need to settle your differences before this whole area erupts into a range war."

"Is Mr. McQueen going to be all right?" Amelia asked.

"Yes, ma'am. It was a clean break, and I left him in his sister's care."

Dallas stared at the doctor as though he'd just spoken in a foreign language. "Sister? Boyd McQueen has a sister?"

"Yep. Shy little thing," Dr. Freeman said absently as he opened his black bag. "Hear tell, she spent most of her growing-up years tending to her ailing mother. Reckon she spent so much time being forced to stay at home that she never thinks to leave now that she's grown.

"How grown?" Dallas asked.

"What?"

"I mean how old is she?"

"Twenty-six."

"Twenty-six?" Dallas repeated.

Dr. Freeman jerked around and glared at Dallas. "Do I need to check your hearing before I leave?"

"I just didn't know McQueen had a sister."

"Well, now you know. Go get some more lanterns and lamps so I can have enough light in here to dig this bullet out."

A few hours later, Dallas watched his youngest brother as he lay sleeping, his shoulder swathed in bandages. Dr. Freeman had assured Dallas that Austin was in no danger. He'd be sore, weak, and cranky, but he would survive. Still, Dallas decided he'd feel a lot more confident with the doctor's prognosis if Austin would awaken.

Dallas assumed Houston held the same concerns. Houston had convinced Amelia to sleep with Maggie while he sat on the opposite side of the bed, never taking his gaze off Austin.

When dawn's feathery fingers eased into the room, Austin slowly opened his eyes. With a low groan, he grimaced. Dallas eased forward. "You in much pain?"

"That worthless bastard shot me in the shoulder," Austin croaked. "How am I gonna play my violin?"

"You'll find a way," Dallas assured him.

"When . . . I'm strong enough . . . I say we run 'em off their land." Austin's eyes drifted closed. "Dallas?"

Dallas met Houston's troubled gaze.

"Dallas, you've got to do something to stop this feuding. Dr. Freeman is right. Next time, we might not be so lucky, and I don't want my family caught in the middle." Houston shifted uncomfortably in the chair. "I *won't* have my family caught in the middle. If I have to choose—"

"You won't have to choose. I've been pondering the situation, and I think I might have a solution to our problem. I'll schedule a meeting with Angus McQueen and see if we can come to some sort of compromise."

"Good." Houston stood, planted his hands against the small of his back, and stretched backward. "I'm going to get a little sleep." He started walking across the room.

"Houston?"

Houston stopped and turned.

Dallas weighed his words. "Do you think McQueen's sister is as mean-spirited as he is?"

"What difference does it make?" Houston asked.

Dallas glanced at Austin's pale face. "No difference. No difference at all."

"BY GOD, YOU have no right!" Angus bellowed.

Leaning back, Dallas planted his elbows on the wooden arms of his leather chair. He steepled his long fingers and pressed them against his taut lips. Narrowing his dark brown eyes, he glared at the spittle that had flown from McQueen's mouth and plopped onto the edge of his mahogany desk. He could imagine it sliding along the front of his desk like a slug slipping out at night to coat the land in slime.

Slowly, he raised his eyes to his adversary's. "I have every right to fence in my land," he said calmly.

"But you fenced in the river!"

"It's on my land. Any rancher of sound reputation would side with me. None would blame me for stringing up your sons from the nearest tree. We have an unwritten code that most cattlemen honor. Once a man has a valid claim to a river or a water hole, another cowman won't come within twenty-five miles of it—with or without a fence. No one would have questioned my right to take the fence back farther, but I graciously left miles of land open to grazing."

"To taunt us. I don't need grassland, damn you! I need water!"

"You have creeks and rivers on your land."

"I've got nothing but dry creek beds."

Dallas shook his head in sympathy. "I can't help that Nature chose to dry up your water supply and left mine flowing, but I don't part with anything of mine freely."

McQueen's face turned a mottled shade of red. It occurred to Dallas that the man might have an apoplexy fit right here in his office. Then Dallas would never get what he wanted.

"Freely," Angus muttered. "You won't part with your water freely, but you will part with it for a price. Is that what this meeting is about? Is that why you fenced in the river? So you could get something for the water? Isn't it enough that you stole my land?"

"I've owned that stretch of land since 1868."

Angus snorted. "So you say."

"The law backs my claim," Dallas reminded him.

Angus released a harsh breath. "Then name your price for the water, and I'll pay it. What do you want? Money? Cattle? More land?"

Dallas lowered his hands to his lap, the fingers of his right hand stroking the ivory handle of the gun strapped to his thigh. He should have insisted this meeting be held without weapons in tow.

"I have money. I have cattle. I have land. I want something that I don't have. Something as *precious* as the cool water. Something as *beautiful* as the flowing river." Giving his words a moment to echo inside McQueen's head, he tightened his hand around the gun. "Something as *pure* as the sun-glistened water."

Angus shook his head. "You're talking in riddles. I don't have anything that's pure or precious or beautiful."

"I've heard you have a daughter," Dallas said, wishing he hadn't needed to be quite so blunt.

The furrows that ran across McQueen's brow deepened. "Yes, I have a daughter, but I don't see what that has to do with anything."

Dallas was beginning to question the wisdom of holding his meeting with Angus, wondering if it might have been better to discuss the particulars of his compromise with Boyd. "Maybe you haven't noticed, but women are scarce. I need a w—"

"My God! You can't be serious!" McQueen yelled, his eyes bulging from their sockets.

"I'm dead serious."

Angus slumped in his chair. "You'll give me access to your water if I give you access to my daughter?"

With a speed Dallas never would have expected of the rotund man, Angus lunged across the desk and grabbed Dallas's shirt. Dallas brought the gun from his holster and jabbed it into the folds of Angus's neck, but the man was apparently too angry to notice. Spittle spewed into Dallas's face.

"I'll see you dead first," Angus growled.

"That won't get you the water," Dallas said in an even voice.

"I won't give you my daughter as a whore!"

"I don't want her as a whore. I want her as my wife."

Angus McQueen blinked. "You want to marry her?"

"Is there a reason that I shouldn't?"

Angus dropped into the chair. "You want to marry Cordelia?"

Cordelia? He was going to pull his fence back for a woman named Cordelia? Where in the hell had McQueen come up with that name?

"You don't even know her," McQueen said.

Dallas leaned forward. "Look, McQueen, we've been arguing over that strip of land for three years now. The law says it's mine and gives me the right to fence in and protect what's mine. Your sons killed my cattle—"

"You can't prove it—"

"Two nights ago, they damn near killed my brother. I went to war when I was fourteen. I've fought Yankees, Indians, renegades, outlaws, and now I'm fighting my neighbors." Dallas sank into his chair. "I'm tired of fighting. Angus, I need a son to whom I can pass my legacy. I need a wife to give me a legitimate heir. The pickin's around here are slim—"

Angus came out of the chair and pounded a fist on the desk. "The pickin's? If I were ten years younger I'd pound you into the dirt for thinking so lowly of my daughter."

"I think very highly of her because I respect her father. We're both working hard to carve an empire from desolate land, and we're both on the verge of destroying all we've attained. Barbed wire is part of the future. I put it up, you tear it down. I'm going to keep putting it up." He took a deep breath, ready to play his final hand. "But tomorrow at dawn, I'm giving my men orders to shoot to kill anyone who touches my wire or trespasses on my land."

"You are a son of a bitch," Angus snarled.

"Maybe, but I've poured my heart and soul into this ranch. I'm not going to let you destroy it. Marrying your daughter will give us a common bond."

"You don't even know her," Angus repeated, bowing his head. "She's—"

Dallas had his first sense of foreboding. "She's what?"

"Frail, delicate, like her mother." He lifted his

gaze. "I honest to God don't know if she could survive being married to you."

"I'd never hurt her. I give you my word on that."

Angus walked to the window. Beyond the paned glass, the land stretched into eternity. "You'll pull your fence back?"

"The morning after we're married."

Angus nodded slowly. "Deed the land that runs for twenty-five miles along both sides of the river to me, and I'll have her on your doorstep tomorrow afternoon."

Damn! Dallas wondered if Angus had read the desperation in his voice or in his eyes. Either way, Dallas had lost his edge, and staring at the cocky tilt of his neighbor's chin and the gleam in his eyes, he knew that Angus understood he had the upper hand. "When she gives me a son, I'll deed the land over to you."

Angus pointed a shaking finger at him. "All the land that I thought I owned when I came here."

"Every acre."

"ARE YOU OUT of your mind?" Houston roared.

Fighting not to squirm, Dallas stared into the writhing flames burning low in the hearth. Houston of all people should understand his brother's desire to have a wife. Hell, he'd taken Dallas's wife from him. Houston could at least support Dallas in his quest to find a replacement.

"Maybe I am, but the town we're building hasn't done a whole hell of a lot to get women out here. Eligible women, anyway."

"You don't even know her!"

Dallas spun around and met his brother's gaze. "I didn't know Amelia either when I married her."

"You knew her a lot better than you know Angus's daughter. At least you wrote letters to each other. What in the hell do you know about this woman?"

"She's twenty-six . . . and delicate."

"From what I hear, I don't imagine she's much to look at either."

Dallas snapped his head around to stare at Austin. He sat in a chair rubbing his shoulder, his face still masked with pain.

"What have you heard?" Dallas asked.

"Cameron McQueen told me she doesn't have a nose."

"What do you mean she doesn't have a nose?"

Austin lifted his uninjured shoulder. "He said Indians cut it off. Nearly broke her heart so her pa fashioned her one out of wax. He took the wire off some spectacles and hooked it to the wax so she has a nose to wear . . . like someone might wear spectacles."

Dallas's stomach roiled over. Why hadn't Angus revealed that little flaw in his daughter? Because he hadn't wanted to lose the chance to obtain the water and the land. He imagined the McQueen men were having a good laugh right about now.

"Call it off," Houston said.

"No. I gave my word, and by God, I'm gonna keep my word."

"At least go meet her—"

Dallas slashed his hand through the air. "It makes no difference to me. I want a son, goddammit! She doesn't need a nose to give me a son."

Houston picked his hat off a nearby table and settled it low over his brow. "You know, until this moment, I always felt guilty for taking Amelia from you.

Now, I'm damn glad that I did. She was a gift you never would have learned to appreciate."

"What the hell does that mean?" Dallas asked.

"It means for all your empire building, big brother, you'll never be a wealthy man."

Chapter Two

*I*t was a woman's lot in life to live within the shadows cast by men.

Cordelia McQueen knew that unfortunate truth and understood its ramifications only too well.

With her hands folded primly within her lap, she gazed out the window toward the horizon where the sun boldly retreated. She had never blamed her mother for wanting to run toward the majestic blues and lavenders that unfurled across the sky. Her mother had called it an adventure, but even at the age of twelve, Cordelia had recognized it for what it was: an escape.

Her mother packed one carpetbag and told Cordelia and Cameron to bundle up their most precious possessions. She explained that Boyd and Duncan were too old to go on the journey, Cordelia and Cameron too young to stay behind.

They were walking down the hallway when her father trudged up the stairs, his face flushed with fury.

Cordelia pulled Cameron into a far corner, hiding his face within the crook of her shoulder while her father ranted and raved that Joe Armstrong wouldn't be taking his wife—his property—anywhere.

Horror swept over her mother's face. She turned for the stairs, and her father jerked her back. "That's right! I know! I know everything!" He backhanded her across the face and sent her tumbling down the stairs.

Her mother's scream echoed clearly through Cordelia's mind as though she had heard it this afternoon. For ten long years she had cared for the woman who had once cared for her. The accidental fall—as her father referred to it—had left her mother an invalid, with woeful eyes housed within an immobile body, her thoughts trapped by a mouth that could no longer speak. Only when her mother's eyes had welled with tears did Cordelia know for certain that her mother lived within the withering shell that held her prisoner.

Her mother had simply exchanged one prison for another, and now it seemed as though Cordelia would do the same.

"Goddammit, Pa! There are other ways to get the water we need," Cameron said. Six years younger than she was, Cameron had always been her champion. Often his blond hair and pale blue eyes reminded her of the foreman who had disappeared the day her mother was injured. "You don't have to give Cordelia to that man!"

That man. Cordelia had only seen Dallas Leigh once, and then only from a distance. He was taller than she was, broader than she was, and when he'd announced that the land he'd roped off was to be used for a town, the wind had been gracious enough to carry his deep voice to everyone who had gathered around him. She didn't think he was a man who would have accepted less.

Now he was demanding that she become his wife. The thought terrified her.

"This matter isn't open to discussion, Cameron," Boyd said. A tall dark sentinel, he stood behind his father's chair. Since they had moved to Texas from Kansas following her mother's death, her father's health had diminished considerably. Within the family, Boyd blatantly wielded the power. Only his love and respect for his father allowed him to let outsiders think his father remained in charge.

"When I want your opinion on a matter, Cameron, I'll ask for it," her father said.

"I'm only saying—"

"I know what you're saying, and I'm not interested in hearing it. I've already given him my word."

"Well now, you won't be breaking your word if he happens to die tonight, and we can certainly arrange that," Duncan said.

Cordelia kept her gaze focused on the pink hues sweeping across the horizon. She had no desire to see the depth of their hatred for this one man. She had seen hatred that deep once before: when her father had confronted her mother. She knew of no way to stop it. As a child, she'd hidden from it in a shadowed corner.

As a woman she had a strong desire to hide again, in her room, deep within one of her books. She feared Duncan was not in a mood to jest. As her father continued to hold his silence, she became concerned that he thought murder might have some merit.

"Killing him won't get us the water!" her father finally bellowed. "That's what this is all about. The water!"

"Leigh will treat her no better than a whore!" Duncan roared.

Flinching, Cordelia clenched her hands in her lap. She hated the anger and rage, hated the way it distorted faces that she loved—for she did love her brothers—into faces that she feared.

"Cordelia, go to your room. Your brothers and I obviously have a few details to work out," her father barked.

She rose to her feet, her hands aching as her fingers tightened around them. She had considered weeping. She had considered dropping to her knees and begging, but she had learned long ago that when her father and Boyd set upon a path, nothing would deter them. She salvaged what little pride remained, angled her chin, and met her father's glare. "Father, I'm not opposed to this marriage."

Cameron looked as though she'd just pulled a gun on him. "You can't be serious."

She took a tentative step forward. "Try and understand. Father's dream is to raise cattle, and you have always been part of it. I've only ever been able to watch from the window. Now, I have an opportunity to be part of his dream. I am the means by which he can gain the water he needs."

"You've no idea what goes on between a man and woman, Cordelia," Cameron said, his voice low. He abhorred violence as much as she did, and she knew he followed Boyd's orders so his brothers would never question his manhood.

She looked at her father, remembering when she had been six and a nightmare had sent her scurrying to her parents' room. Her mother had been weeping. Her father had sounded like a hog grunting as slop was poured into the trough. He had called her mother a damn cold bitch, and although Cordelia had not known what the words had meant at the time, the force with which her father had spat them had seared them within her mind. "I do know, Cameron," she said quietly.

"Then you should understand why Duncan and I are opposed to this. Dallas Leigh hates us all, and he'll show you no mercy."

"Surely, he's not that unkind."

"Then why did his first wife leave him within a week of their marriage?" Duncan asked.

He stood like a pillar of strength, watching her as though he truly expected her to know that answer. Dark hair, dark eyes, it was only his usually sedate temperament that distinguished him from Boyd.

"I want to do this," she lied, for Cameron's benefit and peace of mind if for no one else's.

Her father slapped his hand down on the table. "Then, by God, it will be done."

FOR AS LONG as she could remember, Cordelia had wanted to be a man, to enjoy the freedoms that men took for granted. She pulled the curtain away from the small window of her traveling coach and gazed at the barren, flat land. How anyone could deem this desolate place a paradise was beyond her. Why men would fight to own it was incomprehensible to her.

But fight they had. Boyd's broken arm served as a testament to one of the battles, and tonight the man who had harmed her brother would come to her bed. She prayed for the fortitude to suffer through his touch in silence, without tears.

A huge adobe house came into view. She could only stare at the massive rectangular structure. A balcony surrounded each window that she could see on the second floor. The crenellated design of the roof reminded her of a castle she'd once read about.

Riding on his horse beside the coach, Cameron leaned down and tipped his hat off his brow. "That's where you'll be living, Dee."

"Are those turrets on the corners?"

"Yep. Hear tell Leigh designed the house himself."

"Maybe after today, you and Austin can be a bit more open with your friendship."

Cameron shook his head. "Not for a while yet. Be grateful you're not riding out here, Dee. The hatred is thick enough to slice with a knife."

"I thought today was supposed to make the hatred go away."

"What you're doing today is like the waves of the ocean washing over the shore. No matter how strong it is, it only takes a little of the sand away at a time."

She smiled shyly. "You're such a poet, Cameron."

He blushed as he always did when she complimented him.

"Listen, Dee, Dallas scares the holy hell out of me—I won't deny that—but I'll try and find a moment alone with him to ask him to show you some gentleness tonight."

She reached through the window and laid her hand over his where it rested on his thigh. "He'll either be gentle or he won't be, Cameron, and I don't think your words will change him, so spare yourself the confrontation. I'll be fine."

She settled back against the seat of the coach and drew the veil forward to cover her face.

STANDING ON THE front veranda, with his brothers flanking him on either side, Dallas watched the approaching procession. It looked like the cavalry, as though McQueen had every man who worked for him coming for the ceremony.

Good. Dallas had all his men here as well as everyone from town. He wanted witnesses, plenty of witnesses.

He'd even managed to locate the circuit preacher. Fate was on his side.

He squinted at the red coach traveling in the center of the procession. He'd seen it once before: the day he had set aside the land upon which he planned to build Leighton.

"Do you think she's inside that red coach?" he asked.

Austin leaned against the beam. "Yeah, that's what she travels in when she's allowed to travel, which isn't often, according to Cameron."

"If you know so much about her why didn't you tell me she was in the area?" Dallas asked.

Austin shrugged. "Didn't figure you'd want a woman who didn't have a nose."

Dallas pointed his finger at each of his brothers. "Don't go gaping at her. Dr. Freeman said she was shy. That's probably why, so don't stare at her."

"I'm hardly in a position to gape at anyone with a disfigurement," Houston said, scraping his thumb over the heavy scars that trailed along his cheek below his eye patch.

Dallas nodded and turned his attention back toward the caravan. "A nose isn't important." Eyes. Eyes were important. God, he hoped she had pretty eyes.

The horses and coach came to a halt. All the men sat in their saddles, glaring, not a smile to be seen.

"Where's your father?" Dallas asked Boyd McQueen.

"He was feeling poorly this afternoon, so I'll be acting in his stead, and I'll be wanting a word with you in private before the ceremony."

"Fine."

Dallas watched as Cameron dismounted and opened the door of the coach. A white gloved hand slipped into Cameron's tanned one. A slender hand. Long fingers. A white slipper-covered foot came into view, followed by a white silk skirt, a silk and lace bodice, and a white veil. The veil covered her face, but beyond it, Dallas could see she had swept up her black hair.

"Stop gaping," Houston whispered beside him, but Dallas couldn't help himself.

The woman was tall. Dr. Freeman had said she was a "shy little thing," and Dallas had expected a woman along the lines of Amelia, a woman who came no higher than the center of his chest. But Cordelia McQueen was as tall as her brothers. He thought the top of her head might be level with the tip of his nose. Slender, she was a fine figure of a woman.

Dallas took a deep breath and stepped off the veranda. He noticed the subtle tightening of the woman's fingers on her brother's hand. The thick veil hid her features from him, but he thought she might have dark eyes. He could live with a woman who had dark eyes. He could tell by the slight jutting of the veil that her father had carved her a tiny nose. He wondered if it melted in summer when the stifling heat dried the land. Maybe he'd whittle her a nose of wood, small like the one she had of wax.

Dallas swept off his hat. "Miss McQueen, it's a pleasure to have you here."

"I hope it will be, Mr. Leigh."

Her voice was as soft as falling snow.

"I'll do all in my power to see that it is, Miss Mc-Queen. Give you my word on that."

It was impossible to tell with the veil covering her eyes, but he had a feeling in his gut that she was staring at him.

"Stay here, Cordelia," Boyd said as he dismounted. "We need a few minutes alone with your future husband."

Turning, Dallas glared at Boyd. Of all the Mc-Queens, Dallas had taken an instant dislike to Boyd the moment their paths had first crossed. "I imagine what you have to say concerns her, so she'll come with us."

"Fine," Boyd said through gritted teeth. "We'll need the preacher as a witness."

Dallas crooked his arm and tilted his head toward Cordelia. "Shall we go inside?"

She glanced at Cameron, who gave her a smile and a nod. Then she released her hold on her brother and wrapped her fingers around Dallas's forearm. He wished he couldn't feel through the sleeve of his jacket that she was shaking worse than a leaf in the wind.

CORDELIA HAD NEVER seen a house with such cavernous rooms. Their footsteps had echoed over the stone floors as they walked to Dallas Leigh's office.

She wondered if he would allow her to spend time in this room. She was in awe of the floor-to-ceiling shelves that lined three of the walls. Empty shelves—save one—but shelves all the same. She imagined all her books could have found a home in here.

Cameron had convinced her to bring only a few of her belongings in the event she decided not to stay. As though she would have a choice in the matter. Watching the man sitting behind the large mahogany desk, she had a feeling that leaving him would not be an option for her once she became his wife.

Just as leaving had not been an option for her mother.

When Dallas Leigh had removed his hat and the shadows had retreated, she had been unprepared for the perfection of his chiseled features. She tried not to stare at him now, but she seemed unable to stop herself. A thick black mustache framed lips that looked too soft to belong to a man.

Over the years, the wind and sun had carved lines into a face that reflected pride and confidence. And possession. Dallas Leigh was a man who not only owned all that surrounded him, but owned himself as well.

Soon he would own her, just as her father had owned her mother.

His brothers sat at the back of the room as though none of this arrangement concerned them, and yet, she was left with the distinct impression that they were poised to change their minds in the blink of an eye.

Boyd stood before the desk, Cameron and Duncan standing just a little behind him. She had always found her brothers a trifle intimidating. It looked as though Dallas Leigh only found them irritating.

Reverend Preston Tucker had kindly introduced himself before they'd entered the room. Appearing amused, he stood near the windows that lined the remaining wall.

Boyd withdrew a sheet of paper from inside his jacket. "Before Cordelia signs the marriage certificate, we want your signature on this contract we've had drawn up. It spells out the two conditions under which my father agreed to give you permission to marry his daughter. We've added a third condition."

Dallas lifted an eyebrow, and she was reminded of a raven's wing in flight. "And that condition would be?"

"If fate should be kind enough to make her a widow, she inherits all you possess on this day and all that you gain from this day forward."

Cordelia watched Dallas's jaw clench. She couldn't say that she blamed him. Had her family lost their minds to think he'd agree—

"It goes without saying that if she's my wife, all that I have goes to her upon my death."

"You don't think those two sitting back there would object?" Boyd asked.

"Not if I tell them not to."

"Not good enough," Boyd said. "We want it in writing and signed."

"My word is good enough for the bank, good enough for the state, good enough for any man who has ever had to depend on it. It had damn well better be good enough for you."

Cameron and Duncan cast furtive glances at each other. Boyd simply pulled his shoulders back. "Well, it's not good enough. If you don't sign the document, we go home, and Cordelia goes with us."

Cordelia thought it would be difficult enough to build a marriage on a foundation of hatred, but to begin it knowing no trust existed . . . She eased forward in the chair. "Boyd, surely this isn't necessary—"

"Shut your mouth, Cordelia," Boyd growled.

Cordelia shrank against her chair as Dallas Leigh planted his hands on the desk and slowly came to his feet. Cameron and Duncan stepped back, and she thought given the choice, they'd gladly leave the room. She wanted to leave herself.

Dallas's brown eyes darkened, and she imagined Satan would look like an angel standing next to this man when he was consumed with rage.

"Never use that tone of voice in my presence when you're talking to a woman and, by God, never talk to the woman I'm going to marry in that manner."

"You won't be marrying her if you don't sign the paper," Boyd said.

Dallas narrowed his eyes until they resembled the sharp edge of a knife. She knew pride kept him from applying his signature to the document. Pride would keep her from becoming a wife today.

Cordelia heard the patter of tiny feet and saw the flash of a blue dress and blond curls as a little girl raced past her. Jostling the small kitten she held securely in her arms, she rushed toward the man standing behind the desk. The woman who walked behind her was obviously ignorant of the seething hatred and anger filling the room. Houston stood, but he seemed hesitant to interfere.

"Unca Dalls?" the little girl said as she tugged on Dallas's trousers.

Cordelia slowly rose from her chair, fearful for the child's well-being, uncertain as to what she could do to prevent Dallas from turning his rage on the child.

Then it was too late.

He glanced down, and the girl pointed her finger toward his nose. "Kitty bit me."

The anger in Dallas's eyes faded into concern. His brow furrowed. "He did?"

She bobbed her head, the blond curls bouncing with her enthusiasm.

"Where?"

She stretched up on her toes, taking her finger higher. "There."

"Ah, Maggie," Dallas said as he reached into his pocket. "Looks bad."

Maggie nodded, although Cordelia could see no blood, and the child had yet to release her hold on the offending animal. Dallas knelt, kissed Maggie's finger, and wrapped his handkerchief around it, giving her a bandage almost as big as her hand. She giggled. He touched his finger to the tip of her nose. "Run along now."

As she hurried across the room and found additional comfort in Houston's arms, Dallas stood, picked up a pen, dipped it in the inkwell, and scrawled his name over Boyd's document. "Let's get this goddamn thing started."

Cordelia wished Boyd had been gracious enough not to smile triumphantly.

"I'm sorry I wasn't outside to greet you when you arrived."

Cordelia swiveled her head at the soft voice. The woman who had followed the little girl into the room smiled at her. "I'm Amelia, Houston's wife. I put Maggie down for a nap and ended up falling asleep myself. I hope you'll forgive me."

"There's nothing to forgive. I truly didn't expect you to be here."

"Why ever not?"

Cordelia felt the warmth suffuse her face. She couldn't very well explain that she hadn't expected Dallas to welcome the woman who had abandoned him back into his house nor had she imagined that the woman would remain friends with a man who had been such a poor husband. "I just . . . well, this arrangement just came about so quickly I didn't expect anyone to be here."

Amelia smiled warmly. "Between all the ranch hands and the people from town, we have quite a gathering. Dallas believes in doing everything in a grand fashion."

Cordelia felt as though a swarm of bees had suddenly invaded her stomach. She had hoped for a small, quiet ceremony, but it appeared her future husband was a man of bold preferences.

She glanced toward Dallas. He wore impatience as easily as she wore her gloves.

Boyd was explaining to Reverend Tucker that he needed his signature to serve as a witness. Reverend Tucker didn't seem inclined to want to give it.

"Goddammit! Just sign the paper," Dallas said, irritation heavily laced through his voice.

Reverend Tucker tightened his jaw and slowly nodded. "If this is what you want." He dipped the pen into the inkwell. "Revenge is mine sayeth the Lord." With a piercing blue gaze, he glared at Boyd. "Keep that in mind."

SIGNING THE DOCUMENT had been a damn stupid thing to do, Dallas decided in retrospect as Reverend Tucker performed the ceremony. Boyd McQueen had given him an honorable way to get out of marrying his sister, and Dallas had been too stubborn to take it.

For her sake, he wished he hadn't insisted she come to his office, wished he'd left her outside so she wouldn't have had to witness all that had transpired. Her hand rested on his arm as they stood before the preacher with everyone they knew standing behind them, and he could feel that she was shaking worse than she had been earlier when he'd first met her.

He'd told Reverend Tucker to use words that had to do with trust, honor, and respect and steer clear of love. He didn't want to make the woman aware of what she wasn't getting.

Reverend Tucker finished his opening remarks. "Would you two face each other and join hands?" he asked quietly.

As Dallas took Cordelia's hands, her trembling increased until he thought it rivaled the shaking of the ground during a stampede.

"Do you, Cordelia Jane McQueen, take this man to be your lawfully wedded husband, for better or worse, through sickness and through health, to honor and to cherish from this day forward?"

A hush settled around them. Dallas resisted the urge to peer beneath the veil and assure his bride that everything would be all right. Why was she wearing a veil anyway? Dallas never closed a business deal without looking a man straight in the eye. A marriage was just as important. It seemed to him that this moment was the one time when a woman shouldn't be shielding her gaze from a man.

The silence became suffocating. Dallas was grateful that Reverend Tucker spoke low enough that only those standing nearby could hear. He was even more grateful that only family stood nearby.

Reverend Tucker leaned forward slightly. "If you're inclined to marry Dallas, simply say, 'I do.'"

"She does," Boyd said.

"Goddammit, McQueen, let her say it," Dallas snarled.

"What the hell difference does it make?" Boyd asked.

"Years from now, it might make a difference to her."

Reverend Tucker cleared his throat. "Could we possibly refrain from using the Lord's name in vain during the ceremony?"

Dallas felt the heat rise in his face. "Sorry, Reverend. Why don't you leave out that part about cherish?"

"That doesn't leave much," Reverend Tucker said.

"Leaves enough."

"Very well. Do you, Cordelia Jane McQueen, take this man to be your lawfully wedded husband, to honor from this day forward?"

She held her silence, and Dallas damned his impatient nature. He should have taken a few minutes to put her at ease, to talk with her. He'd been so worried that he'd lose this opportunity to have a wife that he had rushed into it without considering her feelings. He'd call the whole thing off if he didn't think he'd lose the respect of every person standing in his front parlor.

Reverend Tucker rubbed the side of his nose. "I've had dealings with Dallas off and on for over five years now. I can assure you that it won't be difficult to honor him."

"I do," she said quietly.

Dallas worked hard not to let the relief show in his face.

Reverend Tucker turned to him. "And do you, Dallas Leigh, take this woman to be your lawfully wedded wife, to have and to hold, through sickness and through health, to honor and to cherish from this day forward?"

"I do."

"You have a ring?"

Nodding, Dallas reached into his pocket and pulled out the ring that had once belonged to his mother, had once been worn by Amelia. Awkwardly, he tugged off the glove that covered Cordelia's left hand. Her hand was almost as white as the glove . . . and as cold as a river in winter. He'd heard once that if a woman had cold hands, she had a warm heart. He latched on to that small hopeful thought as he slipped the ring onto her finger. "With this ring, I thee wed."

He glanced at Reverend Tucker. "Sorry, Reverend, I got ahead of you."

Reverend Tucker smiled. "That's all right. We've been here before, haven't we? I now pronounce you man and wife. You may kiss the bride."

Dallas's mouth went dry, and now his fingers trembled worse than hers as he slowly lifted the veil.

She had a cute little chin and the reddest lips he'd ever seen. Perhaps the red seemed more brilliant because her skin was incredibly pale, as though it had never known the touch of the sun. Her mouth reminded him of a ripe strawberry, shaped to torment a man. He could live with that.

He whipped the veil up and against his will, his gaze latched on to her nose. Her tiny, perfect nose.

He narrowed his eyes and glared at Austin. Austin's mouth had dropped open. Austin jerked his gaze to Cameron, who looked as stunned as Dallas felt.

"Your brother has a strange sense of humor," Dallas said quietly as he turned his attention back to the perusal of his new bride. She had brown eyes that reminded him of a fawn he'd once seen. They were shaped like almonds, large . . . frightened.

He hated the fear reflected there and decided if he could make her relax, could fill those eyes with happiness, they would be her most striking feature.

Dallas smiled. "Let's see if your brother likes my sense of humor."

He'd planned all along to give her a quick kiss and be done with it, but he understood that sometimes the circumstances demanded that he change the plans. He decided a long, slow, enjoyable kiss was in order, might even make her brothers squirm.

He cradled her face in his large hands, lowered his mouth the short distance to hers, and discovered what he should have known: she'd never been kissed. She'd puckered her lips as though she'd just bitten into a lemon.

He drew back because he had no desire to initiate her into the proper way to kiss in front of the whole town.

"Ladies and gentlemen," Reverend Tucker's voice boomed. "I present to you Mr. and Mrs. Dallas Leigh."

Chapter Three

~❦~

She was married.

Cordelia stared at the wide band of filigreed silver on her finger. She wasn't surprised to discover that it didn't fit properly. Bending her finger to keep the ring from slipping off, she feared nothing in her life would ever feel right again.

People she had never met introduced themselves, the men smiling broadly as though their happiness for her husband knew no bounds, the few women wiping tears from their eyes as though they knew she was doomed to unhappiness. All called her Mrs. Leigh. She wasn't comfortable with the name, but she couldn't dredge up the courage to ask them to call her Cordelia.

Pumping Dallas's hand, men congratulated him. While women kissed his cheek, he never let his eyes stray from her. Her mind had turned into a freshly painted blackboard, erased clean of all previous thoughts and shared knowledge. She seemed unable to remember the simplest of statements. He was her husband, and she had no idea how to uphold her end of the vows they had exchanged—how to honor him.

When her mother had become incapacitated, Cordelia's world had shrunk until it encompassed little more than her mother's bedroom, her family, and works of fiction. Until this moment, she didn't realize how ill-prepared she was to become a wife.

Like vultures anticipating their prey's final breath, her brothers stood on the other side of the unfurnished parlor, their arms folded over their chests, their gazes locked on to Dallas as though they were waiting for him to make a mistake. She prayed that he wouldn't.

Music began to slowly drift across the room. People shuffled back, leaving an empty space in the center of the floor. At the far edge of the circle, a white-haired man played a fiddle.

Dallas extended his hand toward her. "Would you honor me with a dance?"

She lifted her gaze to his and quickly lowered it. "No. I mean . . . I don't know how to dance."

"It's not hard. I'll guide you."

She shook her head briskly. "Please, not in front of all these people."

"Give me your hand."

Wishing the floor would suddenly crack open and swallow her, she curled her fingers until her nails dug into her palms.

"Trust me," he said quietly.

She thought she heard an edge of desperation in his voice, and only then did she realize how he must appear to his friends, his family—holding his hand toward her while she blatantly ignored it. Since no one else was dancing, she assumed everyone expected that the bride and groom would dance first, no doubt alone, the center of attention. Without looking at him, she took a deep ragged breath and slipped her trembling hand into his. Strong and coarse, his fingers closed around hers.

"We're going to step outside for some fresh air," he announced in an authoritative voice as he addressed the gathering. "Enjoy the music."

Cordelia feared she might weep with relief as he guided her through the doors. As soon as she stepped onto the veranda, she released his hand and walked to the far corner. "Thank you."

The music floated through the open door, laughter and voices mingling with the soft strains. Her husband's footsteps echoed around her as he neared. Her husband. Dear God, what had she done?

"I suppose your father told you that I was a mean-hearted bastard."

Cordelia spun around, her eyes wide. Dallas Leigh studied her, his face grim.

"Yes, as a matter of fact he did."

"What else has he called me?"

"A thief."

He raised a dark brow as though amused, and she was unable to stop herself from throwing the rest at him. "And a cheat."

"Yet he gave his blessing for your marriage."

Humiliation swamped her as tears sprang to her eyes. "Because you offered him something that he valued more than he valued me." She turned away, squeezing her eyes shut, fighting back the burning river of shame. "I'm not certain I can forgive you for that."

"I don't need your forgiveness. You can hate me, for all I care, but it won't change the fact that you are now my wife."

She flinched at the cold, ruthless reminder. He cursed harshly, and she wondered if he might strike her. With his large, powerful hands, he would be able to inflict a great deal of damage in a very short time.

"I don't imagine you ever expected your wedding to go exactly as it did today," he said, his resonant voice enveloping her like a mist at dawn. "I'm sorry for that."

She dared to look at him. "Sorry enough to let me leave?"

"No."

She wouldn't beg, but dear God she wanted to fall to her knees and plead with this man for mercy and freedom.

His gaze dropped to her lips, his brown eyes smoldering with an emotion she couldn't identify. She didn't think he was angry, but her wariness increased.

"Where did you learn to kiss?" he asked.

She ran her tongue over her tingling lips, and his eyes darkened further. "Books. I read a lot of books."

He nodded slightly. "I reckon the women in those books always pucker up to kiss."

"Yes, they do," she answered, wondering how he had drawn that conclusion from her simple statement, only one answer quickly coming to her mind. "Perhaps we've read the same books."

"I doubt it," he said, his voice low. He cradled her cheek. "Don't pucker."

Before she could protest, he covered her mouth with his. She'd barely noticed when he'd kissed her before, but now she realized his lips were warm, pliant. She hadn't expected that of a man as hard as he was rumored to be.

His mustache was soft, reminding her of the fur of a puppy she had once owned, a puppy Boyd had killed.

Dallas slowly rubbed his thumb along the tender flesh beneath her chin. "Relax your jaw," he whispered against her mouth, his breath strangely sweet and warm as it fanned over her cheek. Another thing about him that she had not expected.

"Wh—" She learned the answer before she'd fully formed the question.

His questing tongue slipped between her parted lips and waltzed in rhythm to the lilting music she still heard in the background.

Bold. Strong. Like the wind before a storm, a tempest sweeping across the horizon—

"You couldn't even wait until your guests left to taste her again," Boyd said, his voice rife with disgust.

Dallas drew away from the kiss. Mortified, Cordelia would have stepped away from him but his hand tightened on her neck.

With anger blazing within his eyes, Dallas looked at Boyd. "I don't think anyone would find fault with a husband stealing a kiss from his new bride."

"Well now, you'd be the one to know about stealing, wouldn't you?" Boyd asked.

Cordelia was close enough to see Dallas's nostrils flare. He reminded her of a raging bull. For a moment, when his lips had touched hers, she'd almost forgotten that he was the man her family hated, the man who had broken Boyd's arm, the man who had revealed exactly what she was worth to her father. She started shaking, suddenly feeling cold where she had only moments before felt warmth.

"Please let me go," she whispered, wishing she didn't sound like a starving beggar willing to settle for crumbs.

Dallas looked at her, no anger shining in his eyes, and she wondered how he changed his emotions so quickly. His callused hand slid away from her neck.

When he returned his attention to Boyd, the anger accompanied him. "Because your sister deserves fonder memories of her wedding day than we've given her so far, I'll overlook that remark. You wanted something?"

"A private moment with my sister."

Dallas shifted his gaze between the two of them as though he trusted neither of them. Cordelia didn't know why that knowledge hurt.

"I need to tell our guests to move the celebration outside so they can enjoy the beef my men prepared. If your sister isn't standing in this spot when I get back, my fence will remain where it is."

"Then you'd be going back on your word."

Dallas took a menacing step toward Boyd. Boyd flinched.

"Man to man," Dallas said, his voice low, "you know I want more than words exchanged before I'll pull my fence back. Don't try to cheat me out of what is now mine by right."

He shouldered his way past Boyd and disappeared into the house. Cordelia wrapped her arms around herself and pressed her back against the cool adobe wall. "I can't stay here, Boyd," she whispered.

He crossed the small distance separating them, his eyes hard. "You've got no choice, Cordelia."

She longed for someone to put his arms around her, to hold her close, to comfort her, but her family consisted of men who never expressed themselves with anything but their voices.

Boyd clamped his fingers around the veranda

railing instead of holding her trembling hand. "Believe it or not, I did come out here to talk to you."

He appeared to be on the verge of delivering bad tidings, and she wondered if her father was more ill than she realized. "Is it Father?" she asked.

"No, but since he's not here and Mother is dead, the chore falls to me, and I don't want you going to Leigh's bed not knowing what to expect."

A scalding heat rushed through her body, her heart thundering. "Boyd—"

"It's gotta be said, Cordelia, for your sake. It'll go a lot easier on you if you don't fight him. Just crawl into his bed, lift up your nightgown, and lie as still as you can."

She squeezed her eyes shut to block out the images his words brought to mind. "I can't do this," she whispered hoarsely.

"If you don't, you'll kill Father's dream, and probably him along with it. Is that what you want?"

She opened her eyes. "We've moved before. Why not find land that has more water?"

"Goddammit! We thought we had the land and water when we moved here, but that bastard you married stole it from us. Now we have a chance to get it back if you do your duty."

Her duty. She forced herself to nod and wondered where she would find the strength.

Dallas decided that today was quickly becoming a day in his life that he'd prefer to forget.

Nothing had gone as he'd hoped.

Clutching his arm, his wife spoke only when spoken to. She never offered her opinion on anything, and he couldn't figure out how to make the fear leave her eyes. Everything he said only seemed to deepen it.

He cursed Boyd McQueen for whatever he had told his sister to terrify her.

She seldom raised her gaze to his, but preferred to stare at a button on his shirt. He'd considered yanking it off, but figured she'd just find another button to stare at. He didn't think it would be seemly for a man of his position to greet his neighbors with no buttons on his shirt.

People had wandered outside. He could hear their laughter and the drone of their voices as they ambled to the cookhouse he'd built near the bunkhouse.

Plenty of food and drink awaited them on the planked tables inside. Cookie continued to play his fiddle. The half-dozen women who lived in the area were going to wear out their shoes by the end of the evening.

He watched Amelia waltz with Houston, remembering the first time he'd seen her dance. She hadn't feared him, but then considering the hell she'd gone through to get to him, he didn't think she'd ever feared anything.

He glanced over at his present wife. She looked more nervous than a cat in a room filled with rocking chairs.

"Do you want something to eat?" he asked.

Her gaze darted to him briefly. "No, thank you."

"Something to drink?"

"No."

"Well, just standing here is about to drive me crazy. Let me show you around."

She nodded. "All right."

Turning away from the people who were dancing, Dallas pointed. "That's the house."

Cordelia wondered if perhaps he was teasing her. It had never occurred to her that he would have a sense of humor. She could think of nothing significant to say. "It's big."

"I designed it myself. Hired a fella from Austin to come build it for me when Amelia . . . uh, a few years back."

He began to walk away before she could respond. She tightened her grip on his arm so she could keep up with his long strides.

"It reminds me of a castle," she said, searching for anything to distract her from Boyd's earlier words.

He shortened his strides. "It's supposed to. When I moved here, there was nothing. I wanted something"—he held out his hands as though he thought the words might appear in them—"something glorious."

He shifted his gaze away from her as though embarrassed by his words. "That's the cookhouse."

He pointed to a small stone building. Smoke, carrying the scent of mesquite, spiraled from the chimney.

"During roundup, the cook takes the chuck wagon out to the men. Other times, he just stays here. They either take something with them or come back in to eat. Cookie brings our meals to the house."

She remembered the name "Cookie." He was the gentleman playing the fiddle.

"The bunkhouse. I've got twelve men hired on right now. Come roundup, I'll hire twelve more."

She wished she knew what to say. She didn't know if twelve was a lot. She had no idea how many men worked for her father.

"Corral, barn."

She walked with him until they passed the barn.

He stopped and jerked his head toward a wooden lean-to. "Blacksmith works there."

"Dallas?"

They turned together as Reverend Tucker approached, his long black coat flapping with his movements, revealing the gun he wore strapped to his thigh.

"Dallas, if you've no further need of my services, I need to get about the business of searching for a lost soul."

Dallas smiled warmly, the humor shining in his eyes mesmerizing. For a moment he wasn't the man her family despised, but a man she thought any woman would happily call husband.

"Did you get something to eat?" Dallas asked.

Reverend Tucker rubbed his stomach. "More than I should have, I'm afraid. Gluttony is a sin."

"I know of worse sins."

"Reckon we both do," Reverend Tucker said.

"You know, Reverend, I was serious about building a church in my town where you could preach."

"I know you were, and I wish I could take you up on the offer, but I can't."

Dallas shook his head, his smile widening. "I imagine we have plenty of lost souls around here."

"But I'm looking for one in particular."

Dallas extended his hand. "Then I hope you find him."

"Her," Reverend Tucker said as he shook Dallas's hand. "And trust me, I will. Sooner or later, I will find her."

He tipped his head toward Cordelia. "Mrs. Leigh, I wish you all the best."

Cordelia envied him the freedom to leave. "Thank you, Reverend."

"Would you mind if I had a moment alone with your husband?"

She welcomed the opportunity to escape from her husband's side. If she could just find Cameron, talk with him, she knew he could lay her fears to rest. "No, of course not. I want to talk with Cameron. Excuse me."

Dallas watched his wife practically gallop away. He hoped she wasn't entertaining any notions of leaving with Cameron.

"Things seem a bit awkward," Reverend Tucker said.

Dallas blew out a quick gust of air. "I can count the number of decent women I've known in my life on one hand. I'm not skilled when it comes to talking to them."

"You never seemed to have a problem talking to Amelia."

"Hell, a fence post could talk to Amelia. She has a way about her of making you say things."

Reverend Tucker smiled. "She does at that."

"I can't seem to find the right wording when I'm talking to . . . Cordelia." He grimaced. "Where do you think her father got that name?"

"Jewel of the sea."

Dallas lifted a brow.

Reverend Tucker blushed. "I used to have an interest in names and their meanings. Maybe she'll become your jewel of the prairie."

"She's pretty enough. Hell, she's beautiful. I wasn't expecting that. Maybe that's why I get tongue-tied around her."

"Sometimes you don't need words if the actions are right."

"Still, I'd like to give her words. Hell, I'll give her anything she wants if she'll give me a son."

"You think a son is what is missing from your life?"

"I know it is," Dallas said with conviction.

Reverend Tucker gazed toward the setting sun. "I used to think I knew what was missing from my life." He smiled sadly. "But I discovered too late that I was wrong."

"I'm not wrong."

Reverend Tucker met Dallas's gaze. "You know you signed your death warrant today."

"Boyd McQueen wouldn't be that stupid."

"I know his type. He's a man without scruples. Watch your back."

"I always do."

SITTING WITH HIS back pressed against the side of the house, Austin watched the sun sinking below the horizon. He moved the bottle of whiskey from his mouth and took a moment to enjoy the burning in his gut before passing the pleasure on to his best friend.

Cameron took the bottle and downed his share before handing it back. "I can't believe you told Dallas that story about Cordelia's nose."

"I didn't know you'd lied to me when I asked you why she never came to town."

"I was only funning with you. I didn't think you'd believe it."

Austin took another gulp of whiskey. All the colors of the sunset seemed to be running together. "Why not? You're my friend. You ain't supposed to lie to me."

Cameron grabbed the bottle and took a long swallow. Then he wiped the back of his hand across his mouth. "You know what really bothers me, though?"

Austin shrugged and winced as the pain rolled through his shoulder. They'd already finished one bottle of whiskey. He didn't see how Cameron could be bothered by anything with the world spinning around them the way that it was.

Cameron grabbed his shirt, and they both wavered. "He married her anyway."

Austin snatched the bottle. "Hell, yeah, he married her. She coulda come to him without a face, and he woulda married her." He held up the bottle. "'A woman don't need a face to give me a son,' he woulda said. That's all he wants. A son. Reckon he woulda married her if she didn't have a head."

Cameron chuckled. "She'd a been dead without a head." His eyes brightened. "That rhymes!"

"You're such a poet, Cameron."

Austin jerked his gaze around at the sound of the sad feminine voice. Two women swam before him, then they bumped into each other and became his newest sister-by-marriage.

"Ah, hell," he groaned, feeling a sickness in his stomach that had little to do with the whiskey churning inside him.

"What are you doing, Dee?" Cameron asked, his words slurred.

"I was looking for you. I wish now that I hadn't found you." She spun around and quickly walked away.

Cameron struggled to his feet. "Hell, I'd better . . . go after her."

"Think she heard everything?" Austin asked.

Cameron nodded, stumbled to the ground, and started to snore.

Damn! Austin decided that he needed to go after his best friend's sister and figured as soon as he found his legs he would. Meanwhile, he downed the remaining amber brew. Unfortunately, the burning in his throat didn't ease the ache in his heart.

"There you are."

Austin heard a voice sweeter than any sound his violin could make. Dusk was easing in around him as he squinted at the girl standing before him.

Becky Oliver. Sweet Becky Oliver. With eyes the color of a summer sky. The setting sun turned her auburn hair a shade of red. Her father owned the general store. Austin started to smile at her and then remembered she was the reason he was trying to get drunk. He tipped back the bottle. Two drops were hardly enough to satisfy him.

She knelt beside him, and he could smell vanilla. She always smelled like something he'd like to run his tongue over.

"You're angry at me," she said softly.

He shook his head, then nodded. "You were dancing with Duncan McQueen."

"I would have danced with you, but you didn't ask."

"Only got one good arm," he said as he tapped his shoulder and grimaced.

"You could dance with one arm."

He shook his head. "Like to hold my women close. Need two arms to do that."

She worked the empty bottle from his grip and tossed it aside. "How many women do you have?"

He smiled crookedly. "One. Just one." He touched her cheek. It was softer than a cloud billowing in the sky. "I wanted to play my violin for you, but I can't do that either."

She lowered her gaze to her lap. "Do you need two arms to kiss me?"

"To do it proper." He slid down the adobe wall. He deserved to have his head slam into the hard ground. Instead, she scooted nearer, and he found his head nestled in her lap, a pillow softer than any he'd ever known. He closed his eyes. "Gotta kiss you proper the first time."

She combed her fingers through his hair. The darkness swirled around him. He moved his good arm around her backside, and promised himself that as soon as his shoulder healed, he'd kiss her proper.

CORDELIA WANTED TO hide, to be alone with her thoughts, her sorrow. She wanted to be in her own room, curled in her bed, with a book in her lap.

But here, in this huge house, she had no room that belonged only to her. She had no private sanctuary. No place to call her own.

She closed the heavy front door behind her and held her breath. She heard no voices, no footsteps. Everyone was outside, celebrating her marriage, a marriage she didn't want, a marriage that family obligations forced her to accept.

She tiptoed down the hallway, retracing the steps she'd taken earlier in the day until she reached Dallas's office.

Quietly, she opened the door and peered inside. Early evening shadows lurked in the corners. Slipping into the room, she closed the door. She walked to the chair and sat, pulling her legs onto the soft cushion.

And gave the silent tears the freedom to fall.

Dallas Leigh didn't want a wife. He wanted a son.

She felt like a prized mare chosen for the offspring she could produce. Dallas Leigh cared nothing for her appearance, her wants, her needs, her dreams. She wasn't the person he wanted by his side as he journeyed through life. She was simply the means to an end.

Her thoughts drifted back to the kiss Dallas had begun on the veranda. She wondered where it might have led. She supposed that Boyd had interrupted them because he knew exactly where it would have taken them.

Boyd's horrid words slammed into her, terrifying her . . . unless she held on to the memory of Dallas's kiss. When he had looked at her, before he had kissed her, she had felt . . . touched, as though his hands were on her when they weren't. Perhaps if he kissed her again . . .

She buried her face in her hands. She didn't want to be here. She didn't want to be a wife. She didn't want to give him a son.

She heard a soft crackling. She tensed, her heart beating at a rapid tempo. She lowered her hands and gazed around the room.

She was alone.

The sound came again as though someone were crumpling paper. Slowly, she eased her feet to the floor and stood.

She heard a thump come from his desk, a bump too loud to have come from a mouse. She held her breath, waiting, wondering what sort of animals Dallas kept, wondering if she should find him and let him know that one of his creatures had escaped.

Another bump and crackle.

She studied his desk. Someone had shoved the chair away. The front of the desk spanned its width and nearly reached the floor, where she saw a scrap of blue.

Hadn't the little girl been wearing blue?

Quietly, she sneaked across the room and peered around the desk. A tiny black shoe tapped the air, the foot moving in rhythm to no music Cordelia could hear.

Cordelia knelt and looked into the alcove where Dallas would normally sit. The little girl sat with sacks wadded within her lap. Her eyes widened to form huge circles of green.

Cordelia smiled softly. "Hello. You're Maggie, aren't you?"

The girl nodded, scooted forward, and touched her tiny finger to Cordelia's damp cheek. "You got a sad."

Cordelia swiped at the tears that lingered on her lashes. "No, not really."

"Yes, you do. I can make the sad go away."

"You can?"

Maggie nodded enthusiastically. She crawled out from beneath the desk and struggled to pull open a drawer.

Cordelia eased a little closer to her. "I don't think you should play in your uncle's desk."

Maggie pressed her finger to her lips. "Shh." She pulled out a sack and shoved the drawer back into place.

Smiling brightly, she crawled into her previous hiding place and crooked her finger. "Come 'n."

Folding her body, Cordelia worked her way under the huge desk, wondering if everything in Dallas's life was big.

"Close your eyes," Maggie said.

"Why?"

"Unca Dalls says so."

Dallas had taught the little girl how to make sadness go away? Cordelia lowered her lashes.

"Open your mouth."

Hesitantly, Cordelia obeyed. She heard paper crackle. Then something hard skipped across her teeth and hit her tongue. She tasted sweet and bitter before she spit it into her hand. She stared at the lemon drop.

"When it's gone, so is your sad," Maggie said. "Unca Dalls says so." She reached into the bag. "I gotta sad, too." She popped a lemon drop into her mouth and snuggled against Cordelia's side.

Holding the child close, Cordelia popped the confection back into her mouth. She heard Maggie smacking as she sucked on the candy.

She was surprised to discover that a little of the sadness did melt away.

Chapter Four

$\mathcal{I}$t had been a mistake to leave his new wife alone, but then it seemed to be a day for making mistakes.

After Reverend Tucker left him, Dallas decided to carry her belongings to the house. She had only brought one small trunk, and it didn't take Dallas long to haul it to his bedroom, but apparently it was long enough to lose her.

Darkness was settling in, and people were beginning to take their leave. Without his wife by his side, Dallas thanked them for coming and refused to answer the questions he saw reflected in their eyes.

When the last wagon filled with townspeople rolled into the night, the tension within him increased. He was beginning to think he might know how a length of rope felt when it was being made: stretched taut and wound.

He needed to find his wife, give her the opportunity to say farewell to her brothers, send them on their way, and get to the business of realizing his final dream.

He saw Houston leaning against the corral and didn't waste any time in crossing the space separating them.

"You seen my wife lately?" he asked.

"Nope."

"I took her trunk up to my bedroom, and now I can't find her."

Turning, Houston scanned the dwindling crowd that consisted of the lingering ranch hands. "She has to be here."

"I've looked everywhere. Even in that gaudy thing she travels in."

"I know what you're thinking. Nobody stole her."

"But she might have left."

Houston nodded sagely as though he thought she probably had. "Let's find Austin—"

"Houston!"

Both men turned at the sound of Amelia's frantic voice.

"I can't find Maggie," she said as she skidded to a stop and dug her fingers into Houston's arms.

"What do you mean you can't find her?" Houston asked, panic threaded through his voice.

"I mean she's lost. The men were supposed to take turns watching her, and they lost track of whose turn it was. I should have kept my eye on her. I shouldn't have started dancing—"

Houston leaned down and pressed his mouth to hers to silence her. "We'll find her."

"But what if—"

"I know where she is," Dallas said.

Relief washed over Amelia's face. "You've seen her?"

"No, but I know where she likes to hide out. If I'm right, she's gonna go home with a big belly-ache."

He started walking toward the house, Amelia's peace of mind taking precedence over his own.

"Have you seen my wife?" he asked Amelia as they neared the house.

"Not since you took her walking. Why?"

"I think she's left."

He shoved open the front door.

"Surely not," Amelia said softly.

"I can't find her, and I don't imagine she's hiding under my desk with Maggie."

Dallas walked down the hallway. He quietly opened the door to his office and peered inside. He didn't want to startle his niece if she had a lemon drop in her mouth.

He heard paper rattle and smiled. He so loved that little girl.

With Houston and Amelia following in his wake, he crept across the room and waited beside his desk until her heard the paper crackle again, a sign that she'd finished one lemon drop and was reaching for another. He'd taught her not to put more than one in her mouth at a time.

He quickly moved behind his desk and dropped to his haunches. "Caught you!"

A piercing scream ricocheted through the room. Dallas stared at his wife, hunched over beneath his desk. She screamed again.

Maggie yelled, her tiny hands waving frantically. The kitten hissed and slashed a paw through the air.

Dallas reached for his wife. Drawing back, screaming again, she kicked him in the shin. He grunted. Maggie started to cry. The cat made a puddle on the floor.

Houston shoved him aside, and Dallas landed hard on his backside.

"Shh. Shh. It's all right," Houston cooed in a voice that Dallas had often heard him use to calm horses. "It's all right. No one is in trouble. No one is going to get hurt. Shh. Shh."

Maggie crawled out from beneath the desk and into Houston's arms. Houston passed her up to Amelia.

With tears streaming down her face, Maggie looked at Dallas with accusation in her green eyes. "We had a sad!"

Dallas felt like a monster as he brought himself to his feet. Houston was holding his hand out to Cordelia. "Come on, Cordelia. It's all right. Dallas doesn't mind that you ate his lemon drops."

He watched as his wife cautiously peeked out from beneath the desk. It didn't ease his conscience to see that she'd been crying, too. She allowed Houston to help her to her feet.

"I'm sorry," she whispered as she swiped at the tears glistening on her cheeks.

"It was my fault," Dallas said. "I shouldn't have . . ." He shouldn't have what? Tried to tease his niece? How in the hell was he to know his wife would crawl—

Thundering footsteps echoed down the hallway and Cordelia's three brothers burst into the room, Cameron waving a gun through the air. "Get the hell away from her, you bastard!" Cameron yelled.

"Cameron—" Cordelia began but Dallas held up a hand to silence her.

He moved around the desk and slowly walked toward her brother, putting himself between those behind the desk and the gun, since neither Boyd nor Duncan seemed inclined to try to take the weapon from Cameron.

"Give me the gun, Cameron," Dallas said in a low, calm voice.

He shook his head. "I'm not gonna let you hurt my sister."

"I'm not going to hurt her."

"I heard her scream. I know the sound of her scream."

He waved the gun to his right, and Dallas stepped in front of it. "I frightened her," Dallas said. "It won't happen again."

Cameron turned a sickly shade of green and sweat popped out on his brow. Dallas reached for the gun.

"I won't hurt her," he repeated.

"Give me your word," Cameron rasped, the shaking of his hand increasing.

"I give you my word," Dallas said as he snatched the gun from Cameron's grasp.

Cameron doubled over and brought up his dinner.

As the others in the room gagged and moaned, Dallas leapt back and ground his teeth together. Wonderful. Now he had vomit *and* piss to clean up.

Cordelia rushed past him and pressed her fingers to Cameron's brow. "Oh, Cameron."

"I'm all right, Dee," he said, wiping his sleeve across his mouth and averting his gaze from Dallas.

Dallas glared at Boyd. "McQueen, wish your sister well, gather up your brothers, and get the hell out of my sight."

Cordelia eyed him as though he were a snake. "Cameron can't leave. He's sick."

"He can throw up outside as easily as he can inside."

"You're heartless," she said.

"I'm all right now, Dee," Cameron repeated. He extended his hand toward Dallas. "Can I have my gun back?"

"I'll bring it to you in a couple of days after tempers have cooled," Dallas said. "Right now, it would be best if you left."

Cameron nodded and looked at his sister. "Night, Dee." He eased his way past her.

"Do you have to leave?" she asked.

"Your husband's demanding it," Boyd said. "Let's go."

He spun on his heel and stomped out, with his brothers following like dogs with their tails tucked between their legs.

Not exactly the way Dallas had planned to end the evening.

Maggie padded across the room, placed her tiny hands on Dallas's thighs, and tilted her head back. "We had a bunch of sads," she said. "A bunch of sads."

He lifted her into his arms. "Are they all gone now?" he asked her, although he focused his gaze on his wife who watched him as though she thought he might harm the child.

Maggie nodded and laid her head on his shoulder. "Only now my tummy hurts."

"I'm not surprised." He looked at his brother. "Why don't you take your daughter, and I'll show my wife to her room? Then I'll deal with this mess."

He handed his niece over to Houston and held his arm out to his wife.

"Mrs. Leigh," he said, knowing his voice sounded too stern, but unable to stop it. He'd lost one wife on his wedding night. He didn't intend to lose another.

She stepped toward him hesitantly as though he'd just said he was going to take her to the gallows instead of to her room. Her fingers dug into his forearm, and dammit, she was still trembling.

"This way."

Cordelia followed him from the room, down the hallway, and up a wide flight of stairs. He walked to the last room on the right—the corner room where the door was closed.

"This is our bedroom. I moved your trunk into it earlier so it's waiting for you."

Their bedroom. Not hers, but theirs. She knew he fully intended to share it with her tonight. "I'm sorry we ate all your lemon drops," she said inanely, wishing the sun had never set, night had never fallen.

"Did it work?"

"I beg your pardon?"

"Did it make the sadness go away?"

"Not entirely."

"I'm sorry to hear that."

"I'm sorry I screamed."

"I knew Maggie was hiding beneath my desk. I wouldn't have tried to startle her if I'd known you were there as well."

"I'm sorry I said you were heartless."

A corner of his mouth tipped up. "We could probably stand here all night apologizing for things we said or did throughout the day. Let's just acknowledge we got off on the wrong foot, and we'll go from there."

He put his hand on the doorknob.

"The first two conditions—" she said quickly.

He removed his hand from the door, straightened, and looked at her. She licked her lips.

"The first two conditions that my father agreed to . . . what were they?"

"Didn't he tell you?"

"He said you would share your water with him if I married you. Without the water, he would lose his cattle."

"That was the first condition. I promised to pull my fence back the morning after we were married."

"Was that your idea?" she asked.

"It was my offer."

"And the second condition?"

"When you give me a son, I'll deed a portion of my land over to your father."

"Was that your idea as well?"

He hesitated. "No."

Cordelia felt as though someone had just pulled her heart through her chest.

"Isn't there a name for a woman who trades her favors for gain?" she asked.

"There's also a name for a woman who takes a husband. You're my wife, not my whore."

"In this case, Mr. Leigh, it seems to be a fine line. May I have a few moments alone?"

He nodded and opened the door to their bedroom. "I'll see my brother and his family off, and then I'll come back."

She slipped inside the room, closed the door, and pressed her back against it.

Her father knew the fears she harbored, knew what she had seen as a child. She had been standing in the doorway, terrified, when he'd finally rolled off her mother.

He had promised her that no man would ever touch her. He had traded his promise for a strip of land, knowing full well that what Dallas Leigh expected of his wife was what her father had sworn she would never have to give.

DALLAS LEANED AGAINST the veranda beam and watched as Houston tucked Maggie into the back of the wagon. Amelia had been kind enough to help him clean up his office. He wished she had the power to wipe away his doubts as easily as she had wiped away the kitten's puddle.

Was a son such a terrible thing for a man to wish for?

"Have a safe journey home," he said.

Houston looked up from his task. "We will."

"If you need anything—"

"We'll be fine," Amelia said. "Get back to your wife."

Walking into the house, Dallas closed the door behind him. After a day filled with guests, the house seemed unbearably empty. His footsteps echoed down the hallway. He began climbing the stairs.

His wife was waiting for him. His wife. He'd planned to dance with her, toast her happiness, and charm her.

Instead, she'd seen his temper flare up more than once, and he'd frightened her. Her scream had been one of pure terror.

He stopped outside the door to his room. A pale light slipped into the hallway. She was inside waiting on him.

Tonight he'd have someone beside him, and with any luck, nine months from now, he'd have someone in his heart.

He'd vowed for better or worse. He'd do all he could to make everything better for her, but he'd live with worse if he had to.

He put his hand on the knob, turned it, and discovered she had locked him out.

By God, he had been challenged at every turn today, and he was damn tired of it. With a burst of rage that sent the blood rushing through his temples, he kicked in the door.

She screamed and flew out of the chair by the fire he'd built earlier in the hearth, clutching her brush to her breast.

"Never lock the door against me," he said in a low menacing voice. "Not in my house."

She shook her head and took a step back. "No, no, I wouldn't. I know my duty. I . . . I was just preparing myself for you."

Her duty. The words sounded incredibly harsh, but then what had he expected? She knew less about him than he knew of her because all she knew of him had come from her brothers, and it was obvious after the confrontation in his office and conversations held throughout the day that they had few kind words to say about him.

Her eyes were as large as a harvest moon, and he could see now that her brush was tangled in her hair. Tangled in her thick black hair that cascaded down to her narrow hips like a still waterfall.

She wore a white cotton shift with lace at the throat and tiny pearl buttons running down the front. Something a woman might sleep in.

As he took a step forward, he saw her bare toes curl. For some inexplicable reason, that small action touched him as nothing had all day. He glanced over at the door, hanging at an awkward angle, torn from the top hinges. He looked back at Cordelia. "I'll send someone up to repair the door."

She gave him a jerky nod. He walked from the room, rushed down the stairs, and stormed into the night. He saw Houston, standing by the wagon, kissing Amelia as though he hadn't spent the whole day with her, wasn't sharing the rest of his life with her. "Houston!"

Houston lifted his head and drew Amelia closer to him.

Dallas felt like a fool. A damn fool. "I need you to . . . to fix the door to my bedroom."

"Fix it? What happened to it?"

"A little misunderstanding. I kicked it in, and now it's hanging off the hinges. I thought it might be better if someone else repaired it."

Dallas grunted when Amelia hit him in the stomach.

"Watch our daughter," she ordered.

Amelia and Houston hurried into the house. Dallas walked to the back of the wagon and glanced inside. Maggie lay on a bundle of blankets, the kitten Dallas had given her curled within the curve of her stomach. "Wouldn't you like to have a little boy to play with?" he asked quietly.

He caught sight of a movement out of the corner of his eye. Austin was weaving toward the wagon. "Austin?"

Austin stumbled to a stop. "What?"

"Watch Maggie. I need a drink."

He ignored Austin's groan as he headed into the house.

CORDELIA WAS SHAKING so badly that she didn't think she'd ever be warm. Amelia had added wood to the fire, but Cordelia still felt cold, so cold. Amelia had draped a blanket around Cordelia's shoulders but that hadn't brought any warmth with it either.

"I can't stay here," she whispered.

Amelia knelt before her and took her hands. "It'll be all right."

Cordelia shook her head. "My brother Duncan told me that you had married Dallas and that he had been so cruel that you left after only a week."

Cordelia saw a spark of anger ignite within the green depths of Amelia's eyes.

"Is that what he said?"

Cordelia nodded. "I can understand why you left him."

Amelia began to work the brush free of Cordelia's hair and smiled softly. "No, I don't think you do understand. I was promised to Dallas. A few days after we were married, he realized that I loved Houston, and that Houston loved me, so he gave me an annulment."

"I wish he'd give me one."

Amelia began to brush her hair. "I'll never forget what he said to me that night . . . when he let me go."

Cordelia didn't want to know anything more about the man she'd married, certain she knew all she needed to know. He had a temper worse than any she'd ever seen, that ignited like a piece of kindling.

Yet she remembered earlier in the day how he'd banked his temper when his niece had tugged on his trousers. The lemon drops. His unwillingness to let Boyd speak for her during the ceremony. Against her will, she heard herself ask, "What did he say?"

"'I don't need love, Amelia, but I think you do, and if you find it with a man who dreams of raising horses, know you do so with my blessing.'" Amelia stood and handed Cordelia the brush. "I'll leave you with a little secret. Dallas does need love—more than any of us. I know your marriage hasn't begun under the best of circumstances, but I think if you give him a chance, he will worship the ground you walk on."

HIS ELBOWS DIGGING into his thighs, Dallas stared blankly at the low fire flickering within the hearth in his office. He remembered the day he'd married Amelia. He'd seen disappointment in her eyes, a touch of sadness, but there had also been hope and trust.

He thought about the day she had married Houston. She had glowed with love and happiness.

He hadn't expected the woman he married today to glow, but neither had he planned to fill her with raw fear. What had he been thinking to marry a woman he'd never met? He'd arranged to marry her as though she were little more than a carefully selected brood mare. He couldn't blame her for being offended, wary, and frightened.

"I fixed the door," Houston said.

Without turning his attention away from the fire, Dallas merely nodded. "'Preciate it."

"You scared the hell out of Cordelia . . . again."

Dallas grimaced. "I know." He sighed deeply. "I know how to bed a whore. I've got no earthly idea how to go about bedding a wife."

"You didn't seem to have any problem when you were married to Amelia."

Dallas glanced up at the anger reflected in his brother's voice. He'd offended someone else without trying. "You know as well as I do that we never got that far. With Amelia getting kidnapped on our wedding night and you getting shot when we rescued her, I barely had the opportunity to kiss her. I never saw her standing in front of the fire in some flimsy gown that was little more than shadows. Cordelia has legs that go clear up to her shoulders."

Houston gave him an understanding smile. "I know all about shadows." He cleared his throat. "Look, Dallas, this is none of my business, but there's no law that says you gotta bed her tonight. Knowing her pa, she probably didn't have much say in this marriage. What would it hurt to give her a couple of days to get used to it?"

Dallas stood. "Yeah, I've been thinking the same thing. It's getting late. Did you and your family want to stay here tonight?"

"'Preciate the offer, but there's a good moon tonight and a clear sky. We'll be fine."

Dallas followed his brother from his office and stood at the stairs, waiting while Houston walked through the front door. Dallas glanced up. The stairs had never before seemed so high. As he began to climb them, he started running apologies through his mind, trying to find the right one, the one that would undo all the damage he'd unwittingly inflicted on his wife's peace of mind.

When he reached his bedroom, he tapped lightly on the door and waited an eternity for her to open it.

Cordelia peered out at the formidable man standing in the hallway. She opened the door farther, giving him access to the room, offering him access to her. She watched as his Adam's apple slowly slid up and down.

"Be ready to ride before dawn," he said gruffly and turned toward the stairs.

Stunned, Cordelia stepped into the hallway. "You mean to ride a horse?"

He stopped walking and stared at her. "What the hell else do you think we ride? Cows?"

She shook her head. "No . . . I just . . . I have something to wear. I've just never . . . ridden a horse."

She thought if she released a deep breath, he'd fall over and tumble down the stairs.

"You've never ridden a horse?"

"Father said it was too dangerous. I always traveled in my coach."

"There is no way in hell my wife is going to travel around the countryside in that red contraption. I had your brothers take it with them."

"Oh." She pressed her hand to her throat, trying to think of something to say.

"I've got a gentle horse you can ride, and if you don't want her, you can ride with me."

Quickly she shook her head. "The gentle horse is fine."

"Good. Then I'll see you before dawn."

He spun on his heel and stomped down the stairs. Cordelia slipped back into her room, closed the door, and leaned against it. She pressed her fingers against her mouth. He had made her brothers take the hideous coach away!

Tomorrow, she was going to start riding a horse around the countryside.

She wrapped her arms around herself. He had said he'd see her in the morning. Did that mean she would be safe tonight? She could sleep alone?

She walked to the bed. It wasn't until she reached up to pull the blankets down that she noticed the flowers resting between the pillows.

Wilted now, their fragrance still wafted over the bed. She picked up a yellow flower and trailed her finger over the fragile petal. They grew over the prairie. Easy enough to find. Not much trouble to pick.

Yet tears welled in her eyes. So simple a gesture. She wanted to believe Amelia had left them for her, but somehow she knew they had been a gift from Dallas.

She walked to the far side of the room, drew the

heavy draperies aside, opened a door of windows, and stepped onto the balcony.

In the distance, she saw the silhouette of her husband sitting on the top railing of the corral, his shoulders hunched, as he gazed in the direction of the moon.

Chapter Five

※

Cordelia lay in the massive oak bed listening for her husband's footsteps. Several minutes past midnight, she finally heard them on the stairs. She followed the sound along the hallway until she heard him stop outside her door. She held her breath, waiting for the click of the turning doorknob, the echo that would announce he was coming to claim her as his wife.

But all she heard was the fading tread of his boots as he walked away.

She rolled to her side and watched as the shadows played around the room. Her room.

She wondered how long he would give her before he insisted on making it "their" room.

She slept fitfully through the night and finally crawled from the bed in the early hours of the morning to prepare herself for her first ride on a horse. It was then, in the quietness before dawn, that she noticed the many things she'd overlooked the night before.

She washed her face using the water that filled the heavy oak washstand. She gazed at her reflection in the oval mirror that hung on the wall. She imagined Dallas usually shaved here. His shaving equipment rested on a small table beside the washstand. She knew he was skilled with a razor. His chin and cheeks had been smooth and carried no nicks or scars, save one small one just below his left eye, but she didn't think a careless razor had created it. His mustache had been evenly trimmed.

Using one of the two towels he had set beside the washstand, she patted the moisture from her face. Then she walked to the mirrored dresser, sat in the straight-backed chair, and unraveled her braid.

On the dresser, he had placed a small bottle of bay rum. Her brothers often doused themselves with it, yet it had smelled different on Dallas's tanned skin. He owned this ranch, but she didn't think he spent nearly as much time in his office as her father did. Dallas's features were too brown, too weathered.

She swept up her hair, then quickly donned her red riding habit. She'd only worn it once. The day Mimi St. Claire had delivered it to her, a gift from Cameron in hopes he could convince their father to let her ride. She had admired the woman for traveling to the ranch, unescorted, in a buggy. She had envied the woman the freedom she had to come and go as she pleased because she was not shackled to a man.

Cordelia had asked her father if perhaps she could do the same, but he had forbidden her to travel unescorted, as though he didn't quite trust her to return. No one had found the time to escort her to town after the day Dallas had set aside the land.

She had devoted so many years to caring for her mother that staying at home had become a way of life that she had seldom questioned. She had grown up with her father's adage, "A woman's place is in the home, tending her menfolk."

Cordelia jumped at the rapid-fire knock. Taking a deep breath, she crossed the room and opened the door. She was struck once again with the handsome shape of Dallas's chiseled features. His gaze slowly traveled from the tip of her hat to the tips of her toes.

"We need to go," he said in a voice that sounded as though he were strangling.

She followed him down the stairs and into the early morning darkness. He had tethered two horses to the front veranda.

"This is Beauty," Dallas said as he placed his hand on the mare's chestnut rump. "She's about as docile a horse as you'll ever find. Pull back on the reins to stop her. Give her a gentle nudge in the sides to make her go. For the most part, she'll just follow my horse."

"Sounds easy enough," Cordelia said.

Dallas looked at her and squinted. "You've never ridden?" he asked as though he thought he'd misunderstood her the night before.

She shook her head. "My father considered it unseemly and dangerous for a woman to ride a horse."

He walked backward until he stood by the horse's shoulder. "You just grab the saddle horn, put a foot in the stirrup, pull up, and swing your other leg over."

Although she was tall, she still found the horn to be exceptionally high as she wrapped her hands around it. Dallas grabbed the stirrup and held it steady after her foot missed it twice. She slipped her booted foot into the stirrup, took a deep breath, and bounced up. Dallas grabbed her waist with one hand, pressed his other hand to her backside, and hoisted her over. Heat flaming her cheeks, Cordelia settled into the saddle. No one had ever touched her so intimately.

As the horse shied to the side, Cordelia dug her fingers into the saddle horn. Dallas grabbed the bridle, and the horse calmed.

"Take these," he said, holding the reins up to her.

Cordelia stared at the strips of leather threaded through his fingers. Long fingers that had easily spanned half her waist. She reached out and took the reins. "Thank you."

"You don't have to thank me," he grumbled as he stalked around to his horse and mounted in one fluid movement. "Come on. Give Beauty a gentle kick."

She did as he instructed, and Beauty followed Dallas's horse at a slow pace. She wondered how it would feel to gallop across the plains, the wind blowing in her face. She could feel the breeze now, just a slight breath over her cheeks.

The man riding beside her looked as though he'd been born to the saddle, as though he and his horse were one.

Cordelia glanced around, expecting others to join them. "Where's the escort?"

Dallas stared at her. "What escort?"

"My father always insisted that I travel with at least six men to guard me. I just assumed your men—"

"I protect what's mine," he said in a taut voice.

He didn't have to move his hand to the gun resting along his thigh or the rifle housed in his saddle to convince her that he spoke truthfully.

"What . . . what is your horse's name?" she asked.

"Satan."

The black devil rode Satan. It somehow seemed appropriate.

"I had a devil of a time breaking him," Dallas explained. "In the end, I had to let Houston handle him."

"You sound disappointed."

He shrugged. "That's where Houston's talent lies, taming horses."

"What is your talent?"

He held her gaze. "I build empires."

They rode west for over an hour with nothing but silence and a soft breeze between them.

Dallas fought to keep his gaze focused on the far horizon instead of on his new wife. He'd thought she had looked lovely dressed in white yesterday. In red, she was devastatingly beautiful. The deep shade brought out the richness of her porcelain skin, black hair, and brown eyes.

The combination was almost enough to make him change his mind about what he'd decided to do this morning. But the hesitancy in her voice when she spoke to him and the fear that still resided in her eyes kept him from altering his plans.

He drew Satan to a halt at the top of the small rise and turned the horse slightly. Beauty stopped beside him.

"Why did we stop?" Cordelia asked.

"To watch the sunrise."

He couldn't explain why he wanted to watch the sun ease over the horizon with this woman by his side. Dawn wasn't his favorite time of day. He preferred the night, when the clouds faded away to reveal the stars. The stars had guided him home countless times. As a boy, he'd even wished on them.

He had thought about asking Cordelia to ride

with him last night when he couldn't sleep, but he'd needed time alone to think, to wade through the quagmire he'd inadvertently created. He didn't know if he could untangle the mess, but he was hoping he could give them a smoother trail to follow.

He heard her small intake of breath as the sun began to wash away the darkness. He wondered if she'd ever watched the start of a new day. He knew so little about her. It had all seemed unimportant until last night.

"It's beautiful," she said quietly.

So are you hung on the tip of his tongue, but he couldn't bring himself to say the words, not knowing how the morning would end.

Barely turning her face in his direction, she gave him a hesitant smile. "Thank you."

He grimaced. "I didn't make the sunrise. I just brought you to see it."

She nodded slightly and averted her gaze. He would have taken back the gruffness in his voice if he could. He didn't know why he always sounded angry when he spoke to her. Perhaps because the fulfillment of his final dream rested on her willingness to give it to him.

Reaching out, he grabbed Beauty's reins and turned both horses away from the rising sun.

Cordelia stared at the river, the men lining its far bank, and the barbed-wire fence that stretched along the length of the stream. In the distance, beyond the fence, a cloud of dust rose toward the sky as cattle tromped toward the fence.

She recognized her brothers leading the herd, Boyd with his arm still in a white sling, Duncan and Cameron on either side of him. They brought their horses to a halt, and the cattle wandered to a stop behind them as the men flanking each side cut off the cows that wanted to keep moving.

She heard the babbling of the river and low bawling of the cattle. Her heart tightened in her chest as she realized why Dallas had brought her here: to see exactly what her family had traded her for.

She wished she were skilled enough with a horse that she could simply gallop away.

Beside her, Dallas removed his hat and draped his wrist over his saddle horn. "I've always considered myself easy on the eyes. I've got more land than I know what to do with and enough money that my family will never do without. I assumed any woman would be pleased to have me for a husband.

"Your family and I have been feuding over this strip of land ever since the day you arrived. I want a son. I want the feuding to stop. Marrying you seemed a way to have both. Unfortunately, I failed to take your feelings on the matter into consideration."

He shifted his gaze away from her. "See that man standing by the fence?"

She saw a tall, lean-boned man positioned next to the barbed wire, his horse tethered to a post. "Yes?"

"That's Slim, my foreman. You ride down there, and he'll cut the fence for you, let you go through so you can meet up with your brothers on the other side."

"And you'll still pull your fence back?"

He turned his dark unwavering gaze on her. "This land has soaked up my sweat and blood . . . and that of my brothers. I won't give an inch of it away if I receive nothing in return."

Her hopes plummeted. "And if I stay here?"

"Raise your hand and lower it. Then my men will pull the fence back. Today I'm giving you what your family and I failed to give you yesterday: a choice. Stay or go. It's your decision."

"But we're already married."

"It can be undone easy enough."

"My father and brothers will be furious.'

He held her gaze. "I'm prepared to deal with that."

"You broke Boyd's arm before. What will you do this time? Kill him?"

His gaze never faltered. "If I have to."

Her stomach lurched. She certainly couldn't accuse Dallas Leigh of being dishonest. Her mouth grew as dry as the wind. "You've only given me the illusion of a choice."

"Sometimes, that's all life gives any of us."

A few moments ago, she had marveled at the beauty of the sunrise, and now she was seeing the ugliness of men and their greed.

"Do you want to be married to a woman who hates you?" she asked, realizing with sickening dread that she could very well grow to hate this man.

He settled his hat on his head, throwing shadows over his face. "I don't need your love, but I need your decision. My men have work they need to get to."

She felt the anger seething through her. "My father was right. You are a coldhearted bastard."

He turned his head sharply as though he were as surprised by the vehemence in her voice as she was. She'd never in her life dared to speak so sharply to anyone. She expected him to give her what her father gave her brothers when they used that harsh tone on him: a backhand across the face.

"I'm giving you a choice he wasn't willing to give you," he said.

Hearing the tautness in his voice, she marveled at his restraint.

"I'll gladly take it," she said as she kicked the sides of her horse. She allowed the mare to take a half-dozen steps before she pulled back on the reins. She glanced over her shoulder. Dallas hadn't moved. Not a muscle. She remembered him as she had seen him last night: sitting on the corral, staring at the moon.

What choice had life given him for a wife? She hadn't counted, but she had seen fewer than a dozen women at her wedding. Her brothers were always discussing the absence of women, speculating as to where they might find a wife, going so far as to answer advertisements in magazines.

Perhaps an illusion of choice was all any of them truly had.

Her true choices were limited to living within the shadows cast by her father and brothers or living within the shadow cast by this man. Shadows when she longed for sunshine.

Prison was prison, but at least her current jailer gave her the freedom to ride, an inane reason to raise and lower her hand, but she did, never taking her eyes off her husband. The air suddenly filled with shrill whistles, whoops, and yells.

Dallas urged his horse forward until it was even with hers. "You might as well watch what you've given them," he said, his voice low.

She turned her gaze from him as his men lassoed the crooked posts and began pulling them back across the river. Her brothers removed their hats, waved them in a circle over their heads, and urged their horses forward, the cattle following.

"I want a son," Dallas said quietly.

Cordelia's heart thudded madly in her chest. "I'm aware of that. My family gets the land they want. And what do I get?"

He removed his hat and met her gaze. "Anything you want."

Cordelia considered asking for her freedom, but she knew in her heart that she would never abandon a child she brought into the world. His son would bind her to Dallas more strongly than any vows she had spoken yesterday.

She had never known what it was to hate anyone, but she felt the uncomfortable stirrings now. Her father had sheltered her, protected her, until she had become little more than a possession to be bartered away.

"Love?" she asked.

His eyes darkened. "Give me a son and I'll find a way to give it to you."

AUSTIN DEARLY WANTED to kill the little men who were building a town inside his head. Their constant pounding reverberated between his temples.

He forced himself to sit up and swing his legs over the side of the bed. The pounding grew louder, and he realized a good deal of it wasn't in his head at all.

"Breakfast is ready!"

He groaned at Dallas's booming voice.

"I'm coming," he mumbled. He bowed his head and hoped to God Dallas had let Cordelia sleep late. He didn't know how in the world he was going to be able to look her in the eye.

He shoved himself to his feet, washed up as quickly as he could, changed into a clean shirt, and headed down to breakfast.

Dallas and Cordelia were already sitting across from each other, Dallas chewing his food, Cordelia scraping the eggs from one side of her plate to the other. Austin took the chair between them.

"You look like hell," Dallas said.

"I feel like hell."

Dallas shoved a plate of fried eggs toward him. The yellow yolks quivered, and Austin's stomach roiled.

"Get something into your belly," Dallas ordered.

Austin reached for the coffeepot and poured the steaming black brew into his cup. "I just want coffee."

He planted his elbow on the table and set his chin on his palm to keep his face from falling to the table.

"'Preciate you hauling me to bed last night," Austin said.

"Couldn't very well leave you in the back of Houston's wagon."

He remembered thinking how comfortable Maggie looked curled up in the wagon, and he'd climbed in beside her. His mouth felt as though he'd swallowed the cat's tail.

"What time you gonna pull your fence back?"

"I've already pulled it back."

Grimacing at the censure in his brother's voice, Austin forced himself to meet Dallas's gaze. "Reckon I should have been there."

"Reckon you should have been, but it's done now. You planning to go into town today?"

"I don't think I could sit in a saddle for more than five minutes without puking."

Dallas shook his head. "What in the hell were you and Cameron thinking?"

"We were trying not to think."

Dallas leaned back in his chair. "I'm going to work on my books for a while, and then I need to check on the herd. Will you be able to take care of my wife if she needs anything?"

Austin glanced quickly at Cordelia and nodded.

"Good." Dallas scraped his chair back and picked up his plate.

"I'll clean that for you," Cordelia said softly.

Austin had never seen Dallas look as though he didn't know what to do, but he sure looked hesitant now. They weren't accustomed to having a woman around to see after their needs.

"I don't mind cleaning up after the meals," Cordelia said.

Dallas set the plate on the table. "Fine, then. I appreciate the gesture."

He strode from the room, and Austin wished he could have left with him, but he knew too many things remained unsaid between him and Cordelia, and living in the same house would be hell until everything was settled.

He took a long drag on his coffee, hoping to clear his head. Then he leaned toward her. "Do you mind if I call you Dee? I know Cameron does."

She glanced up, then back down. "That's fine."

"No, it ain't fine, and we both know why." He put his hand over hers, and she snapped her gaze up to his. He gave her a sad smile. "You heard something last night that you were never supposed to hear."

She lowered her gaze. "It doesn't matter."

He squeezed her hand until she looked at him again. "It does matter. When men get drunk, they say things they shouldn't. I won't deny that Dallas wants a son . . . bad. But I also know he'll treat you right, the way a man ought to treat a woman."

"Cameron told you I didn't have a nose?"

Austin grimaced. "Yeah, I don't know why he did that."

"And you told Dallas."

"Yep, and I don't know why I did that."

"And he still married me. He must be desperate indeed."

He took her hand between both of his. "You have to understand our family. You've seen Houston. Men don't come much more scarred than he is. Amelia fell in love with him. After seeing that, I reckon we just don't put much stock in looks."

"WHAT IN GOD's name did you think you were doing this morning?"

Dallas glanced up from the spittle that had landed on his desk and met Angus McQueen's fiery gaze.

"Moving my fence back."

"With my daughter on a horse, on a rise where she could have easily fallen and been killed. I told you she was delicate."

"Your daughter sits a horse well, McQueen. The horse is gentle enough that my three-year-old niece rides her. Your daughter was safe."

"So you say. You've got to protect her—"

"I'll protect her, but I'll do it my way."

Angus dropped into the chair. His sons continued to stand, their arms crossed, although Dallas thought Cameron looked as though he might bring up his latest meal at any moment, a thought he didn't find particularly reassuring.

"You just don't understand," Angus said. "Women can't protect themselves. You've got to keep them close or they'll harm themselves, just as my dear wife did."

Dallas rubbed his brow, trying to ease his headache. He'd wanted an end to the strife, and he'd only managed to reshape it. "Look, McQueen, she's my wife now. I'll take care of her."

"It's not easy to hand your daughter over to another man's keeping."

"Seemed easy enough yesterday. You couldn't even bother to drag yourself over here to be with her when the very devil himself took her as his wife."

McQueen narrowed his eyes. "I wasn't feeling well—"

"My guess is you'd spent the night before drowning your guilt, and a hangover kept you at home." When the man started to rise from his chair, Dallas held up a hand. "I don't want to hear it, McQueen. Your excuses, your worries, your concerns. I don't give a damn about any of them. You want to visit with your daughter, fine. Visit with her. But don't lecture me on how to care for her. You gave that right up when you traded her for my water. She can ride bareback, buck naked across the plains for all I care."

Dallas was certain the man was going to keel over from heart failure, his face turned so red, his mouth worked, but no words spewed forth.

Dallas stood. "I'll let her know you're here."

He walked from the room and up the stairs. Austin had told him Cordelia had retired to her room after they had finished breakfast. He had a feeling he hadn't accomplished all he'd planned to this morning. She was still too wary of him.

He knocked lightly on her door. He heard her quiet footsteps on the other side. She opened the door and peered out as though she expected to find a monster on the other side.

"Your family is in my office. They'd like to visit with you . . . if you want to see them."

"Yes, I'd like to see them."

"I need to check on my herd. I won't be back until after dark. Austin will be here if you need anything."

"Thank you," she said softly.

Not exactly what he wanted to hear. *Be careful. Hurry back. I'll wait up for you.* Any of those would have pleased him

He slapped his gloves against his palm. She flinched.

Not caring much for the sting in his chest that her reaction caused, he turned to leave, stopped, and glanced over his shoulder. "Do you want me to stay while you visit with them?"

"No. I prefer to see them alone."

He headed down the stairs, knowing he hadn't accomplished a damn thing that morning.

CORDELIA STOOD OUTSIDE Dallas's office, gathering her courage. She had hoped her family would wait to visit, would wait until the ache in her heart had lessened. Taking a ragged breath, she walked into the room.

Cameron sat in a chair holding his head. She supposed the whiskey, and not illness, was responsible for that. Austin had looked much the same when he'd joined them for breakfast that morning.

Boyd and Duncan flanked her father. Her father brought himself out of the chair. She wished he didn't look so old.

"How are you, daughter?"

She eased farther into the room and sat in a nearby chair. "Fine. I'm fine."

Her father lowered himself into his chair and leaned forward. "Did the bastard hurt you last night?"

It suddenly occurred to her that she had never heard Dallas refer to any member of her family with such loathing. He never called them derogatory names. He never hinted that their parentage might be questionable or that they might not be men of honor.

"No, Father, my husband did not harm me."

"He didn't hurt you at all?" Boyd asked.

She glanced up and met Boyd's baffled gaze. "No, Boyd. Did you expect him to?"

"Did he bed you?" Boyd asked.

Cameron snapped his head up. "I don't see where that's any of our business."

"She came to him a virgin," Boyd said. "A virgin always feels pain. Did he or did he not bed you last night?"

Cordelia could not believe the words Boyd threw at her as though she had no feelings, no privacy. She had thought her heart would break last night when she'd heard the conditions of her marriage. At this moment, she felt her heart shatter. She wished she had the courage to ask them all to leave.

"Answer him, girl," her father said.

She stared at these men, wondering if she knew them at all. She didn't think she could have answered them if her life depended on it.

"Sweet Lord, you better not have denied him his rights last night," Boyd said.

"Do you think he would have pulled the fence back if she had denied him?" Cameron asked.

"I just want a simple answer, Cordelia. Yes or no," Boyd demanded. "Did he bed you?"

"That is absolutely none of your business."

Cordelia jerked her head around. Houston stood in the doorway, his hand resting on the gun housed in his holster. He tilted his head toward Cordelia. "Didn't mean to barge in. I was looking for Dallas."

"He . . . he had to check on the herd," Cordelia said.

"Well, then, I feel confident in speaking for him. You *gentlemen* need to be headin' out."

The way he said "gentlemen" made Cordelia realize he didn't consider them gentlemen at all.

Boyd glared at Houston. "That sounded like an order. This ain't your house."

"I'm gonna do you a favor, McQueen. I'm not gonna tell Dallas what I just heard in this room. Now bid your sister good day and head home."

Her father stood. "We were leaving anyway." He patted her head as though she were a trained dog. "We'll keep in touch."

Her father shuffled toward the door. Houston moved aside, leaving ample room for her father and brothers to file past.

Cameron stopped at the doorway and glanced at her before leaving. She thought he looked miserable.

Houston crossed the room and took the chair her father had vacated. "Are you all right?" he asked.

Nodding, she pressed her trembling fingers to her lips, fighting to hold back the tears.

"Think there are any lemon drops left in Dallas's desk?" he asked.

She shook her head. "I don't think they could take away a sad this big."

She didn't know how it happened, but suddenly his arms were around her and her face was pressed against his shoulder.

"Go ahead and cry," he said quietly.

The sobs came hard and heavy. "They don't care about me. They only want the land. Dallas only wants a son."

His arms tightened around her. "I can't deny it looks that way, but sometimes things aren't always the way they seem."

Stifling her sorrow, she worked her way out of his embrace. He handed her a handkerchief, and she wiped the tears from her face. She took a deep shuddering breath. "How is Maggie this morning? Is her tummy all right?"

"She's right as rain."

She handed his damp handkerchief back to him. "Thank you."

"You're more than welcome. I take it things aren't much better this morning."

She shook her head. "Dallas frightens me."

"I know. He frightens me, too, sometimes."

His words startled her. If Dallas scared his brother, what chance did she have of ever feeling comfortable around him? "Yesterday, when we were all in here, and Maggie ran to him, I was so afraid . . ." She sniffed. "You were here. You knew how angry he was, but you let her approach him anyway." She studied him, remembering how slowly, calmly he had come to his feet. "You knew he wouldn't harm her."

"With the exception of doors, Dallas isn't one to direct his anger at the innocent."

He wrapped his hands around hers, just as Austin had earlier. The small gesture was incredibly comforting. What she would have given if her father or brothers had done the same for her instead of badgering her for knowledge about her wedding night.

"It's probably not my place to say this," Houston

said quietly, "but it might help you to understand Dallas a little better if you know . . ." He lowered his gaze.

Alarm rushed through her, and she scooted up in the chair. "Know what?"

He gave her an awkward smile. "I can talk to Amelia about the war, but I'd forgotten how hard it is to talk to others about it."

"The War Between the States?"

"The War of Northern Aggression is how Dallas refers to it. I was twelve, he was fourteen when our pa enlisted us."

"Fourteen?"

"Yep. I was Pa's drummer, and Dallas . . . Dallas was his second in command. A lot of the men resented that a boy was giving them orders. In the beginning they gave him a hard time, seemed to take delight in doing the opposite of what he told them to do. It bothered him, bothered him a lot. One night, I heard Pa giving him a dressing down because he'd discovered some men hadn't followed the orders Dallas had given. Pa told Dallas, 'They don't have to like you, but they gotta respect you and they gotta obey you.'"

Houston shook his head. "Dallas stopped caring whether or not they liked him. He stopped asking them to do things, and he started telling them. The habit stayed with him, even after the war ended."

He leaned forward. "I guess what I'm trying to say is that he doesn't mean to sound angry or hard, but a lot of people depend on him . . . and he's simply forgotten how to ask."

He released her hands and stood. "Well, I need to find Dallas and head back home. Will you be all right now?"

She liked the way he said "home." As though he knew of no finer place in the whole world.

"I'll be fine."

For long moments after he left, she simply sat in the chair and remembered the comfort of his touch, the calming resonance of his voice. She could certainly understand why Amelia had overlooked his scars and fallen in love with him.

Chapter Six

As a clock downstairs chimed twelve times, Cordelia eased from the bed. Dallas hadn't come to her room. She wasn't even certain if he was home.

She wished she had brought her books. She had expected to be busy as a wife. She'd thought she would have no time for reading, but she found she had nothing but time.

She remembered the half-filled shelf in Dallas's office. She slipped on her night wrapper, increased the flame in the lamp, and headed into the dark, quiet hallway.

She crept toward the stairs, holding the lamp high. Careful of her step, she descended the stairs, walked to Dallas's study, and opened the door.

Her breath caught at the sight of Dallas sitting behind his desk. His head came up, and like a doe that scented danger, she couldn't move. The lamp on his desk burned low, so low that much of the room remained in shadow. He had the drapes drawn aside so the wide windows gave her a view of a thousand stars twinkling in the night sky.

He scraped his chair across the floor and stood. She waved her hand. "No. Don't get up. I'm sorry. I didn't mean to disturb you. I didn't know you were here."

He angled his head. "You needed something?"

"I couldn't sleep. I remembered that I saw some books on your shelves. I thought I might borrow one."

"Help yourself."

She licked her dry lips. "Houston was looking for you this afternoon."

"He found me. His lumber came in. I'll be going to his place on Sunday to help him build an addition onto his house. You're welcome to come."

She thought of Maggie, Houston, and Amelia. She thought she would enjoy spending the day in their company, with people who weren't always angry. "I'd like that."

"Good. How was the visit with your family?"

"It was fine. Just fine." She walked quickly to the bookshelf. "I'll just be a minute."

"Take your time."

Only a half-dozen books stood at attention on the shelf. The covers were frayed and worn. She lifted the lamp higher until she could make out the title of the first book: *Whole Art of Husbandry.* The book nestled beside it was entitled *The Practical Husbandman.*

She trailed her fingers over the spines. Out of the corner of her eye, she saw her husband move in beside her. "Have you read these?" she asked.

"Every word," he said, his voice low, his breath skimming along her neck.

"You read books on how to be a husband?" she asked in awe.

She turned her head to find him staring at her. "I didn't know," she explained. "I didn't know books had been written on this subject. Do you think someone has written a book on wifery that I could read?"

He laughed. Deeply, richly. Smiling broadly, he touched his fingers to her cheek. The warmth that swirled through her body startled her, and she shrank back, her heart beating hard, her breath lodged in her throat.

His smile withered away, and he returned to his chair behind his desk. "Feel free to read any of my books."

She grabbed *The Practical Husbandman.* Surely the advice offered to a husband would apply to a wife. Clutching the book to her breast, she scurried across the room and stopped at the door. She swallowed hard before looking over her shoulder at her husband. He was watching her, but no humor remained in his dark eyes. "Will . . . will you be coming to bed soon?"

"Do you want me to?" he asked.

She tightened her fingers around the book. Was he giving her a real choice or only another illusion? "I'd rather you didn't."

"Then I won't." He dipped his pen into the inkwell and began to scrawl in his ledgers, dismissing her in the process.

"Thank you."

She hurried into the hallway and rushed up the stairs to her room. Setting the lamp on the bedside table, she removed her wrapper and slipped beneath the blankets. She put the pillows behind her back, brought her knees up, and opened the book, anticipating all the secrets it would unlock.

It was not the key she had hoped for.

WITH THE EARLY morning sunlight streaming through the window at the end of the hall, Dallas stood outside the door to his bedroom, knowing he had the right to simply walk into the room, knowing it was a right he wouldn't exercise. Not yet anyway.

He hated the fear he saw in his wife's eyes every time she looked at him. The few times he'd touched her, the fear had intensified. What the hell did she think he was going to do: ravage her?

He despised the way she opened the door and peered out as though fearful of what she might find on the other side, but he knocked anyway. She opened the door, and he bit back his frustration at the apprehension reflected in her eyes.

"I'm sending one of my men into town this morning to pick up some supplies. If you'll give me a list of things you need, I'll have him pick them up for you."

"Oh, thank you. I'll only be a moment."

He stepped into the doorway as she hurried to the bureau and tore a piece of paper from a book. He supposed she kept a journal. He knew so little about her, but he discovered he liked the shape of her backside when she bent over and began to write on the piece of paper. She straightened and turned sooner than he would have preferred. Hesitantly, she held the paper toward him. He took it from her.

"Thank you," she said softly.

He hated her gratitude as well. He stalked from the house and crossed the yard to where a young man was waiting beside the wagon. He extended the slip of paper toward Pete. "Need you to pick these up for my wife."

Pete dropped his gaze and started kicking the ground with the toe of his boot.

"Come on, boy, I ain't got all day." Dallas shook the list under his nose. "Take the list and git."

Pete looked up, his freckled face redder than the hair that his hat covered. "I can't read."

"What do you mean you can't read? I give you a

list every week, and you take it into town and pick up my supplies."

Pete shifted his stance. "Nah, sir. Cookie reads the list to me. I remember everything on the list, but I didn't know you were gonna have another list for me, and Cookie's gone out with the herd today, but you can tell me what she wrote and I'll remember it. I got a good memory."

Dallas figured over half his men probably couldn't read. They were smart men he could depend on to get the job done, and that job seldom required reading. His son would need a tutor if the town didn't have a school in a few years. Dallas would see to it that the tutor also taught any of his men who wanted to learn. Meanwhile, they'd do the best job they could with what they had.

Dallas unfolded Cordelia's list and stared at the single word she'd written.

Pete cleared his throat. "You don't read neither?"

Dallas met the young man's earnest gaze. "No, I read just fine, but this is something I'll need to take care of myself. You go on to town and get the supplies I need."

"Yes, sir."

Not until Pete had climbed on the wagon and started to roll toward town did Dallas dare to look at his wife's list again. He shook his head in bewilderment, wondering if he'd ever understand how a woman's mind worked, convinced he'd never understand his wife.

He headed into the house, searching through every room, certain she wouldn't still be in her bedroom. She'd been dressed when he'd knocked on her door earlier. Surely she didn't stay in the bedroom all day.

But when he knocked on her bedroom door, she

opened it as hesitantly as she always did. He held up her list. "Flowers? You wanted my man to go into town and purchase you some flowers?"

She blinked, clutching her hands before her. "I was thinking he could pick them on his way back to the ranch."

"Why can't you pick them?"

Her brown eyes widened with alarm. "They're outside."

"I know where flowers are."

"I'm not allowed outside. The dangers—"

"Jesus Christ! Were you a prisoner in your father's house?"

Tears welled in her eyes. "In Kansas, I cared for my mother. Here . . . here, my father thought it was in my best interest to stay inside. He said there were dangers. Renegades. Outlaws. A woman wasn't safe."

Dallas repeatedly swept his thumb and forefinger over his mustache, trying to make sense out of what she had just said. "Have you been staying in this room all day?"

She nodded. "Is there another room I should stay in?"

He slammed his eyes closed. She wasn't just afraid of him. She was afraid of everything. Good Lord, could he have married a woman who was more opposite than he was?

Heaving a sigh, he opened his eyes. "You don't have to stay in any room. You don't have to stay in the house. If you want flowers, go out and pick them."

She looked aghast. "But the dangers—"

"I'm not leaving you alone here. My men are about. If you need them all you have to do is holler. They'll be by your side before your mouth closes, so go get your flowers."

He turned to walk away.

"Where will you be?" she asked.

"Checking on my herd." He wished he hadn't seen relief plunge into her eyes.

CORDELIA STOOD ON the front veranda, enjoying the feel of the warm breeze as it riffled through her hair, gently working the strands free from her bun. She inhaled deeply and imagined that she could smell freedom. The freedom to roam from the house to the barn, to walk in the fields that lay beyond the house.

She could hear the steady clanking of iron on iron. She stepped off the porch and walked toward the lean-to on the other side of the barn. A man worked bellows to heat the coals.

"Hello," she said softly.

He turned his dark gaze toward her. He was powerfully built, his black skin glistening with his labors. "Ma'am."

"I was just taking a stroll," she told him.

"Nice day for it. 'Nother month or so and it'll be too hot to enjoy."

She gnawed on her lower lip. "I think I saw you at my wedding, but I don't remember your name."

"Samson."

She blushed self-consciously at the sight of his muscles straining against his shirt, the arm hanging at his side that still looked as if it were gripping something. "Samson? The name suits you."

"Yes, ma'am, that's what my master thought when he named me."

"You were a slave?"

"Yes, ma'am, surely was."

She allowed her gaze to roam past him to the

open land that stretched toward the horizon. "Freedom is a little frightening, isn't it, Samson?"

"Yes, ma'am, it surely is, but it brings with it a measure of glory. I remember the first breath of air that I took as a free man. I thought it smelled so much sweeter than anything I'd ever breathed before."

She linked her fingers together. "I was thinking of picking some flowers."

"You do that, and when you get out where the flowers are the brightest, you just stop a minute and take a deep breath."

She smiled shyly. "I will."

She walked around the side of the barn just as another man was walking out of the barn. She remembered his name because it described him so well and because he had been waiting at the barbed-wire fence for her decision.

"Hello, Slim," she said hesitantly.

He came to a quick halt and doffed his hat. "Mrs. Leigh."

Cordelia's stomach tightened. She thought she might never get used to having that name directed her way. "Is Beauty inside the barn?"

"No, ma'am. I took her back to Houston."

Disappointment reeled through her. She had so liked the horse.

"You want me to saddle up another horse for you?" Slim asked.

Cordelia shook her head. "No, I'm just going to walk today."

"Well, you let me know if you want to ride, and I'll find you a horse."

"Are you married?"

Beneath his dark tan, his face flushed. "No, ma'am."

"Is anyone around here married?"

"Dallas is married, but then I reckon you knew that."

He smiled as though they were sharing a private joke.

"Yes, I knew that." She waved her hand before her. "I was just going to walk out there and pick some flowers. Do you think it's safe?"

"Oh, yes, ma'am. Just watch out for prairie dog holes. Wouldn't want you to turn your ankle."

"Thank you for the warning."

She walked through the tall prairie grasses, enjoying the feel of the sun warming her face.

Before her accident, her mother had tended a flower garden, the only time she had seemed truly at peace. Years had passed since Cordelia had thought about her mother's garden, the sweet lilt of her mother's voice as she had hummed while she tended the flowers, the sharp fragrance of freshly turned soil on her mother's hands, and the beautiful blossoms that had always adorned each room.

Cordelia bent and plucked a wildflower. She wondered if Dallas would mind if she planted flowers near the veranda. Surely not, if he didn't mind if she walked beyond the house.

She glanced over her shoulder. The house wasn't so far away that she couldn't see it. She could still hear the steady pounding of the blacksmith as he worked.

As though she were a child, she sat on the ground, tilting her head back, and closed her eyes. She had spent long hours reading books to her mother. They had taken Cordelia everywhere that she wasn't allowed to go while taking her mother to places where she could no longer go.

After her mother had died, Cordelia had continued to retreat into her books. It had been easier than trying to step beyond the boundaries her father had established over the years.

Until she had married Dallas, she had been content with a life that revolved more around fiction than reality. But now she wondered what she may have missed, what did lie beyond her small world.

She only knew that she had no skills when it came to talking to a husband. Each time she looked into his dark brown eyes, her heart sped up, her palms grew damp, and her breath would slowly dwindle away to nothing.

If only he didn't always seem so angry.

"Well, now, what are you doing?"

She opened her eyes and was greeted with Austin's smiling face as he hunkered down beside her. He had the most beautiful blue eyes she'd ever seen, eyes the shade of the hottest flames that writhed within a fire.

She held up her solitary flower. "I was picking flowers."

"There are prettier ones farther out." He stood and held his hand toward her. "Come on."

She slipped her hand into his, and he pulled her to her feet. As they began to walk, her hand remained nestled within his. She wished she could feel this comfortable around her husband.

Cordelia heard a small bark. She glanced around, but couldn't see any sign of a dog. The bark came again, a tiny yip.

Austin released her hand and withdrew his gun from its holster.

"What is it?" she asked.

"A prairie dog," he said as he picked up his pace. "You stay here."

She had never disobeyed a man's order before, and she didn't know what possessed her to disobey now . . . perhaps it was the pitiful cry that sounded so much like a hurt child or the fact that Austin reminded her of Cameron and she had yet to think of him as a man.

She saw the small brown animal before Austin did, whimpering as its tongue darted out beneath its long snout to lick its paw.

"Oh, no," she whispered as she rushed forward, knelt beside the small creature, and studied the iron trap that had captured its paw. "Who would do such a thing?"

Austin crouched beside her. "Head on back to the house. I'll put it out of its misery."

She snapped her head around. "I don't think her leg is broken. Her bone isn't sticking out like Boyd's did when Dallas broke his arm."

"What's that got to do with anything?" Austin asked.

Cordelia furrowed her brow. "If you can pull the metal sides apart, I could remove her paw from the trap. Then I could take her to the house and tend her wound."

Austin could do little more than stare at the woman. "It's a prairie dog," he reminded her.

Cautiously, she brushed her fingers over its head. "It's just a baby. Please help her."

Dee was looking at him with so much hope in her big brown eyes that he couldn't do what he knew needed to be done. He slipped his gun into his holster. Thank God, she was married to his brother and not to him. Dallas could break her heart. Austin wouldn't.

NEAR DUSK, DALLAS brought his horse to a halt in front of the corral. The flowers he'd pulled from the ground along the way had wilted in his hand. He dismounted, trying to decide if his wife would want them anyway.

"Boss?"

He turned at Slim's irritated voice.

"We got trouble," the lanky man said.

Dallas sighed, not at all surprised. One of his wells had run dry, and he had cattle dying on the north end. "What kind of trouble?"

"Prairie dog. Austin took your wife walking, and they found a prairie dog. He let her keep it."

"He what?"

"He let her take it into the house to doctor it up. Said she was gonna feed it some milk. You ever hear of anything like that? I dadgum guarantee that ain't gonna sit well with the men. Thought you oughta know."

The flowers fell from Dallas's hand. "See after Satan, will you?"

"You'll get rid of that prairie dog, won't you?" Slim asked.

"I'll get rid of it."

Marrying a woman he didn't know hadn't sounded like such a bad idea until he'd done it. What in the hell could she want with a prairie dog?

Dallas strode toward the house. Austin sat on the steps, one long leg stretched out before him, the other serving as a resting place for his violin as he plucked the strings.

Dallas ground to a halt, and Austin tilted his head back, his blue eyes looking as innocent as a newborn babe's.

"Tell me that we're having prairie-dog stew for supper," Dallas commanded.

Austin smiled. "I'd be lying if I said that. Learned long ago that lying only brings trouble."

"Then what in the hell were you thinking to let her take a prairie dog into the house?" Dallas bellowed.

Austin lifted a shoulder in a careless shrug. "She ain't my wife. Didn't think it was my place to tell her she couldn't keep it. Figured that decision was yours to make."

"There's no decision to make. A prairie dog isn't a pet. It's a varmint."

"You gonna tell her that?"

"Damn right I am."

"You gonna tell her she can't keep it?"

"Hell, yes, I'm going to tell her she can't keep it."

Austin shook his head. "I sure wouldn't want to walk into that house wearing your boots."

"You couldn't if you wanted. Your feet are too big. Where is she?"

"Last I saw her, she was in the kitchen."

He marched through the house and strode into the kitchen. With the creature squirming in her lap, Cordelia fidgeted in a straight-backed chair. She jerked her head up.

"Oh, thank goodness," she said on a rushed sigh with obvious relief.

The anger drained right out of him at the sight of her lovely face with no fear in her eyes.

"Here," she said as she stood and held the varmint toward him. "Hold her."

"What?"

"Hold her," she repeated as she shoved the animal into his hands, grabbed his arm, and pulled him to the chair. "Sit down."

Stunned by the urgency in her voice, Dallas sat.

"I cleaned her wound and put some salve on it, but I was having a terrible time trying to wrap her leg," she explained as she picked a strip of white linen off the floor. "Hold her paw for me so I can dress it. Otherwise, she'll lick off the salve."

Dallas fought to hold the animal motionless while Cordelia wound a piece of good clean linen around its wound.

Her hands suddenly stilled, and she looked at him. "Someone set a trap on your land. What sort of cruel person would do that?"

Guilt had him clearing his throat. "Someone who recognized that a prairie dog is dangerous."

Her hands once again stilled. "How is she dangerous?"

"Because it lives underground and burrows holes across the prairie. A horse drops a leg into that hole, he usually breaks his leg and has to be shot."

"Then the hole is dangerous, not the prairie dog."

"That's like saying a gun is dangerous, not the man holding it."

"It's not the same at all." She finished wrapping the bandage around its paw. "Austin thought I should name her Trouble, but I like the name Precious. What do you think?"

He thought he could get used to carrying on a conversation with her that wasn't guided by fear, but he had to deal with this unpleasant task first. "Prairie dogs are a cowboy's worst enemy. You can't keep it."

"Why? I'll keep Precious with me. I won't let her dig any holes."

"I need to take the prairie dog outta here."

She grabbed the animal from his hands and scurried to the corner, hunching her shoulders as though to protect herself and the animal. "What are you going to do with her?" she asked, the apprehension plunging into her eyes.

The dog released a high-pitched yelp. Dallas couldn't tell the woman he was going to shoot the varmint. He shoved himself to his feet with such force that the chair teetered and toppled to its side. His wife flinched.

"I'll make it a damn leash, but if it gets off the leash I won't be responsible for it."

Dallas stormed through the kitchen door at the back of the house and headed into the barn. He jerked the reins off the wall and stalked to the workroom at the back of the building. He set the leather strips on the scarred table, unsheathed his knife, and started cutting.

If he ever had any daughters, he was going to teach them how to deal with a rough world. They could cuss, chew tobacco, and drink like a man for all he cared, but they sure as hell weren't going to be docile creatures afraid of their own shadows or their husbands' voices.

He heard the muffled footsteps and carved more deeply into the tanned hide.

"So did you break the news to her?" Austin asked as he leaned against the doorway.

"Yep," Dallas ground out through his clenched teeth as he drilled a ragged hole into the leather with the point of his knife.

"How did she take the news?" Austin asked.

"She took it just fine."

Austin shook his head. "Sure wish I had your skill with people. I couldn't think of a way to tell her without breaking her heart."

He ambled into the room and looked over Dallas's shoulder. "What are you doing?"

"Working."

"I can see that. What are you making?"

Dallas tightened his jaw until it ached. "A leash."

"A leash? For what? That's so tiny . . . Good Lord! You're letting her keep it."

Dallas spun around and brandished the knife in front of his brother's face. "Don't say another word. Not one word. If you value your hide, you'll wipe that stupid grin off your face and get the hell out of here."

Holding up his hands, Austin began to back away. "I wouldn't dream of saying anything."

But when he was out of sight, his laughter echoed throughout the barn.

Chapter Seven

"Ain't never seen a prairie dog on a leash before," Houston said.

Dallas slammed a nail into the fresh lumber, hoping that his brother would choke on his strangled laughter.

"A man of vision would open himself up a store in Leighton that sold leashes especially designed for prairie dogs," Austin added, grinning.

Dallas stopped his hammering and glared at his youngest brother. "If you don't want *your vision* hampered by two swollen eyes, you'll discuss something else."

"I think Austin has a valid point," Houston said. "With all the prairie dogs around here, selling leashes could be a booming business, particularly for a man interested in building empires."

"No doubt about that," Austin said, "and it doesn't take Dallas long to put a leash together. The one he made Dee only took about ten minutes, and he wouldn't have needed that much time if he hadn't carved the dog's name into it."

Houston started to chuckle. "You gotta have the dog's name on it just in case he loses it. How else would you know who it belongs to?" The laughter he'd been holding in exploded around them.

Austin's guffaws filled what little space remained for noise. Dallas failed to see the humor in the situation.

"Thought you wanted to add onto your house?" he asked.

He could see Houston struggling to stifle his laughter. He had a strong desire to come to his brother's aid and hit him up side the head with his hammer.

"I do," Houston finally managed to say.

"Then we need to stop jawing and get the frame up."

"You're right," Houston admitted, his face growing serious a brief moment before his laughter erupted again. "Good Lord, Dallas, a prairie dog on a leash. I never thought you'd let a woman wrap you around her finger."

"I'm not wrapped around her finger, and I liked you a lot better when you never laughed."

Houston's laughter dwindled. "But I didn't like me. Didn't like me at all."

Dallas knew Houston had held himself in low esteem until Amelia had wrapped herself around his heart. He also knew no wrapping would take place between him and Cordelia . . . not around his heart, not around her finger. It wasn't his way.

He unfolded his body. "Let's get this frame up."

"It's so GOOD to hear them laughing, to know they're enjoying each other's company," Amelia said.

Cordelia glanced at the woman standing beside her, her fingers splayed across her stomach, a contented smile on her face.

"When I first came here, they seldom spoke to each other and they never laughed," Amelia confided quietly.

"Why?" Cordelia asked.

"Guilt and misunderstandings mostly." As though drawn to painful memories of another time, Amelia released a long, slow sigh before walking to the open mesquite fire where the beef was cooking.

Cordelia watched as the men began to raise the frame that would serve as the structure for the addition to Houston's house. She was rapidly discovering that Dallas did everything as though he were on a quest for success.

Along with Austin, they had begun their trek long before dawn and had arrived at Houston's homestead just as dawn whispered over the horizon. Dallas helped her dismount before taking the cup of coffee that Amelia offered him as she stepped onto the porch.

"You know what you want?" he asked Houston as his brother slipped his arm around Amelia and kissed her cheek.

"Yep," Houston said, handing Dallas a scroll.

Dallas unrolled the parchment and held it up so the day's new light could shine on it. "Looks like you want to add two rooms to the back and put a loft above them."

"That's what Amelia wants."

"Then let's get to it."

And they had. The measuring, the sawing, the pounding of hammers against nails, nails into wood, had echoed over the prairie.

When they finished setting the frame in place, Dallas took his first break. Cordelia held Precious more securely within her arms and watched as

Dallas jerked off his hat, pulled his sweat-soaked shirt over his head, and shook like a dog that had just come out of a river. He tossed his shirt over a nearby bush, settled his hat into place, and returned to work. Although he had not spared her a glance since their arrival, she could not take her eyes off him.

His bronzed back glistened, his muscles bunching and stretching as he hefted a board. His long legs made short work of the distance between the pile of lumber and the newly erected frame. He laid the board against the frame and crouched, one hand holding the board in place while the other searched through the grass for his hammer. His trousers pulled tight across his backside. She didn't think she'd ever noticed how lean his hips were. He reminded her of the top portion of an hour glass: his broad shoulders fanning out, his back tapering down to a narrow waist—

"I wish they hadn't done that," Amelia said on a sigh.

Her cheeks flushed, Cordelia glanced at Amelia. "What?"

"Taken off their shirts. I'm trying to prepare dinner, and all I want to do now is watch them work."

Cordelia turned her attention back to the men. She didn't know when Houston and Austin had removed their shirts, but their backs didn't draw her attention the way Dallas's did, didn't make her wonder if his skin was as warm as it looked.

She watched as Maggie ran toward the men, her blond curls bouncing as much as the ladle she carried. Water sloshed over the sides. Cordelia didn't think more than a few drops could have remained in the ladle when the little girl came to an abrupt stop beside Dallas and held it out to him.

A warm smile spread beneath his mustache as he took the ladle, tipped his head back, and took a long, slow swallow. As Maggie clasped her hands together and widened her green eyes, Cordelia had a feeling Dallas was putting on a show for his niece. When he moved the ladle from his mouth, he touched his finger to the tip of her nose and said something Cordelia couldn't hear. Maggie smiled brightly, grabbed the ladle, and ran back to the bucket of water.

Breathless, she looked up at her mother. "Unca Dallas said it was the sweetes' water he ever had the pleasure of drinkin'. I'm gonna git him some more." She dunked the dipper into the bucket before running back to her uncle, the water splashing over her skirt.

"Poor Dallas. She adores him. He won't get any work done now," Amelia said.

"The feeling seems to be mutual," Cordelia said, wishing he would bestow that warm smile on her.

"You're right. He spoils her. I shudder to think how he will spoil his own children."

The heat fanned Cordelia's cheeks at the reminder of her wifely duties. "I . . . I meant to thank you earlier for the flowers you placed on my bed the day I was married."

Amelia smiled. "I didn't place any flowers on your bed."

"Oh." Cordelia looked back toward Dallas. They had finished raising the frame and securing it in place. The men had begun to lay the wooden planks for the floor. Dallas was holding a nail while Maggie tapped it with a hammer. After a few gentle taps, Dallas took the hammer from her and slammed the nail into place.

She didn't know what to make of Dallas Leigh.

He seemed as hard as the nails protruding from his smiling mouth, hardly the type of man to pick flowers . . .

Knowing for certain that he was the one who had placed the flowers on her—their—bed made it difficult for her to dislike him, much less to hate him. Yet still she did not relish the thought of the marriage act.

Maggie scrambled over the frame they had laid across the ground—the frame that would support the floor—and began to hold nails for Austin. Although he carried his arm in a sling, he was managing to pull his share of the load. Something Cordelia had to admit she wasn't doing. "Amelia, what can I do to help?"

"I left several quilts on the porch. Why don't you place them around the tree so we can sit under the shade?"

Cordelia set Precious on the ground, and with her pet tagging along on her leash, hurried to the porch, grateful to have a task, although she didn't think it would stop her mind from wandering to thoughts of her husband.

FROM THE CORNER of his eye, Dallas watched his wife scurry toward the front of the house. He was having a hell of a time keeping his mind focused on the task at hand—building Houston's house.

He kept finding his thoughts drifting toward his wife. It hadn't helped that during the week she had laundered his clothes and when he had begun to sweat earlier, her lavender scent had risen up around him. He'd thought he might go insane, having her fragrance surround him while she stood incredibly far away.

He had made a mistake not exercising his husbandly rights on their wedding night. Now, he had no idea how to approach her and let her know that her reprieve was over.

He knew if he knocked on her door, she'd open it with terror in her eyes, and he couldn't stand the thought. She reminded him of the way too many soldiers had looked at him during the war. They'd followed his orders and gone into battle, fearing him more than they had feared the enemy or death.

He didn't believe in living with regrets, but sometimes he wondered how many men his hard nature had sent to their deaths.

He didn't want his wife looking at him with that same fear in her eyes when he came to her bed. Only he didn't know how to erase it. For a short time while they had tended the prairie dog, the fear had left her eyes, but Dallas couldn't see himself bringing her a wounded prairie dog every night.

He brought himself to his feet and went to fetch more boards and nails. When he neared the pile of lumber, he stopped long enough to admire his wife's backside as she bent over and laid quilts on the ground.

He wished he knew how to keep the fear out of her eyes—permanently.

They ate their meals in silence except for the conversation Austin provided. Dallas could never think of a single thing to say to his wife. It reminded him of when he had first started writing to Amelia. His first letter had only been a few lines. By the end of the year, he had been sharing whole pages of his life with her. He'd thought about writing a letter to Cordelia, but that seemed the coward's way out. He needed to learn how to say the kind of words that put a softness in a woman's eyes, the kind of softness Amelia wore every time she looked at Houston.

He carried several boards to the frame structure, set them in place, knelt beside one, and removed the nails from his mouth. "Houston, when you and Amelia were traveling here . . . what did you talk about?"

Houston pounded a nail into a board that would serve as flooring and shrugged. "Whatever she wanted to talk about."

Dallas clamped down on his frustration. "What did she want to talk about?"

Houston tipped his hat up off his brow. "You, mostly. She was always asking questions about the ranch, the kind of man you were, the house."

"You must not have told her the truth about the house if she came anyway," Austin said.

Dallas swung his gaze around. "What's wrong with my house?"

Austin wiped the smile from his face and looked at Houston. Houston shook his head and gave him a "you should have kept your mouth shut this time" look. Then he started pounding a nail into the board.

"What's wrong with my house?" Dallas asked again.

"Uh, well, uh . . . it's big," Austin explained.

"Of course it's big. I intend to have a large family."

"Well, then, there's nothing wrong with it," Austin said. He handed Maggie a nail. "Maggie May, hold it right here for your Uncle Austin."

Dallas glared at his brother, trying to make sense out of what he'd just heard. "Your comment had nothing to do with the size of my house. I want to know what you meant."

Austin slammed his eyes closed and blew out a quick breath before meeting Dallas's gaze. "It doesn't look like a house. It's . . . it's . . ." He shifted his gaze to Houston, who had stopped his hammering.

Dallas thought his brother might be searching for courage. He knew his house was unusual.

Austin looked back at Dallas. "I think it's downright ugly. There, I said it, but that's just what I think. Houston might think otherwise."

Houston narrowed his eye. "Keep me outta this conversation, boy."

Dallas felt as though a herd of cattle had just trampled him. "Do you agree with him?" he asked Houston.

Houston clenched his jaw. "It's different. That's all. It's just different. It's not what I'd want to live in—"

"Food's ready!" Amelia called.

"Thank God," Houston said as he stood. "I'm starving. How about you, pumpkin?" Maggie squealed as he swung her into the air.

Dallas unfolded his body and grabbed Austin's arm before he could escape. "Why didn't you ever say anything before?"

Austin's face burned bright red. "You were just so proud of it, and what we think isn't important. What matters is what Dee thinks of it. Maybe you ought to ask her."

Ask her if she hated the house as much as she hated her husband? Not if he lived to be a hundred would he ask her.

"I like the house," he stated flatly.

Austin gave him a weak smile. "Then there's no problem. Let's go eat."

AFTER TETHERING PRECIOUS to a nearby bush, Cordelia watched with growing trepidation as the men approached. Each had quickly washed at the water pump before slipping back into his shirt. For that small act, she was extremely grateful. She didn't think she could eat if Dallas's chest had remained bare.

She had laid three quilts around a wooden box. Amelia had set platters of beefsteak strips and potatoes on the box, plates and utensils on the quilts.

Amelia sat on one quilt. Houston dropped beside her, Maggie nestled in his arms. "Looks good," he said.

Cordelia knew it was pointless to hope that Austin would sit on the quilt beside her, but she found herself wishing anyway. He gave her a smile before he took his place on the opposite quilt.

On the small quilt, Dallas seemed incredibly large as he sat beside her.

"This isn't one of my cows, is it?" Dallas asked.

Houston smiled. "Probably. He wandered onto my land. What was I supposed to do?"

"Send him home."

"Not on your life."

Austin held out his arm. "Will you lookee here? I'm the only one without a woman to share my quilt. Maggie May, come sit with me."

Her face bright with excitement, Maggie jumped up, crossed the small area, and rammed into Austin. Hissing sharply, Austin moved her aside with his good arm.

Houston snatched his daughter back into his arms. "You all right?" he asked Austin.

Austin had paled considerably, but he nodded. "I'm fine."

"Sorry," Maggie said, her bottom lip trembling.

He smiled. "It's all right, sweetie. I'm still a little sore." He patted his thigh. "Just come sit beside me, not on me, all right?"

Ever so carefully and slowly, she crawled over the quilt and sat beside him.

"What happened to your arm?" Cordelia asked.

A hush fell over the gathering as everyone looked at Cordelia. The heat rushed to her face. "I'm sorry. I didn't think to ask before."

Austin appeared uncomfortable as he answered, "I got shot."

"Dear Lord. Outlaws?" she asked, horrified at the thought.

"Cattle rustlers," Dallas said as he slapped potatoes onto his plate. "But they won't be bothering us anymore."

"I'm grateful to hear that," Cordelia said. She cut her meat into tiny pieces, eating sparingly.

"You don't eat enough to keep a bird alive," Dallas said.

She glanced up to find him glaring at her plate, his brow deeply furrowed. She couldn't very well tell him that whenever he was around her stomach knotted up so tightly that she could barely swallow.

"I've never been a big eater," she said quietly and dropped her gaze to her plate.

"Guess I'm just used to watching men eat," Dallas said gruffly.

"I never eat as much as my brothers," she said.

A desperate silence surrounded them. Cordelia wished she could think of something—anything—to say.

"When do you think the railroad will get here?" Amelia asked.

Dallas reached for more potatoes. "Sometime next year."

"Things should change then," Amelia said quietly.

"Reckon they will. With any luck, Leighton will start growing as fast as Abilene. I'll be wanting to build a school. Do you want to be in charge of finding a good teacher?" Dallas asked.

Amelia smiled. "I'd love to. Besides, I have experience at placing advertisements, and we'll definitely want someone from the East."

"Give me a list of everything you'll need so I can tally up the costs before I go talk to Mr. Henderson at the bank."

Amelia leaned forward and took Cordelia's hand. "Dee, would you like to help me?"

Cordelia glanced at Dallas. He was studying her as though waiting for her answer. Surely if he had wanted her to help, he would have suggested it.

"I don't know anything about schools. I had a tutor."

"Then we'll learn together," Amelia said.

Cordelia shook her head. "No, I don't think I can—"

"Our son will do his learning at this school," Dallas said. "You ought to have a say in it."

Cordelia nodded quickly. "All right, then, I will."

"Good," Dallas said brusquely.

Amelia squeezed Cordelia's hand. "It'll be fun."

Yes, she imagined it would be, and it would give her something to do besides wash dishes and clothes. Dallas and Austin were seldom inside the house and maintaining it required so little of her time that she thought she could quite possibly go insane.

The conversation turned to other aspects of Leighton, but it made little sense to Cordelia. She had not visited the town since the day the land had been set aside. She'd asked several times for someone to take her, but none of her brothers had ever had time. She had always thought it would be exciting to watch something grow from nothing . . . like watching a child grow into an adult.

Her husband had planted the seeds for the town the day he had set aside the land. She remembered that Boyd had called him a greedy bastard that day . . . one of the nicer names he had for Dallas. She knew little about business, but she didn't see how a school or the church he'd offered to build for Reverend Tucker would bring him much money.

As a matter of fact, in the short time she had been his wife, she had seen no evidence of his greed except for the morning he'd refused to pull his fence back if she left him. But even then, he had gained nothing but a reluctant wife while her family gained access to the river. Eventually, he would gain a son while her family would gain land.

She was beginning to think that Dallas hid his greedy nature well . . . so well that she wondered how Boyd had ever discovered it to begin with.

"The new addition to the house seems to be coming along fine," Amelia said, shifting the conversation away from talk of Leighton.

"Ought to have the first floor and most of the walls in place before nightfall," Dallas said.

"It means a lot to me that you and Austin would give up your day of rest to build onto our house."

"That's what family is for," Dallas said.

"But we won't be able to return the favor. I can't imagine that you'll ever need to add onto your house."

"Speaking of Dallas's house," Austin said. "Dee, what do you think of it?"

Cordelia snapped her gaze to Austin, then to Dallas who watched her with such intensity that her breath almost stopped. Meaningless words scrambled through her mind.

"We need to get back to work," Dallas said, setting his empty plate on the quilt.

Houston groaned and rubbed his stomach. "I'm too full. I intend to sit back and relax for a while."

"Thought you wanted these rooms," Dallas said.

"We do, but we can finish them up next Sunday."

"It'll be that much hotter next Sunday," Dallas said as he stood. "I'm going back to work."

Cordelia watched her husband jerk his shirt over his head as he stomped back toward the house.

"One day, Austin, you're gonna learn when to keep your mouth shut," Houston said.

DALLAS HEFTED A board and carried it to the far side of the house. He'd grown tired of hammering the floor into place. Houston and Austin could finish it when they woke from their naps. They'd both fallen asleep beneath the scraggly boughs of the tree—Houston with his head nestled in Amelia's lap, Austin with Maggie curled up against him.

Cordelia simply sat in the shade, her hands folded in her lap—looking beautiful.

He wondered if she'd given everyone, except him, permission to call her Dee. Not that he had asked . . . nor would he, but Dee sure rolled off his tongue a lot easier than Cordelia. He thought Dee suited her better, was softer.

He set the board upright against the side of the

house and nailed it into place. Sweat rolled along either side of his spine. He was looking forward to a good hot bath this evening.

He set another board into place and began to pound the nails into the wood.

A good hot bath in his house. In his big house.

He spun around and froze. Cordelia stood beside him, holding a ladle of water. Fear plunged into her eyes.

"Amelia thought you might be thirsty."

"Not very neighborly of her to send you into the lion's den, but I appreciate the water."

He took the dipper from her trembling hand and downed the clear liquid in one long swallow. His gaze riveted on hers, he wiped the back of his hand across his mouth before handing the dipper back to her. "Thanks."

He lifted another board and set it against the frame.

"About your house—" she began.

"I'll build you another one," he said as he lined up the board. "Makes no difference to me."

"Actually, I rather like it."

He glanced over his shoulder. She was gripping the ladle tightly enough to make her knuckles turn white. "You do?"

She nodded jerkily. "Uh, I think it's a bit stark . . . uh, I mean, I think it would seem more friendly if you had some decorations—"

"You mean like knickknacks?"

"And perhaps some paintings or wall hangings. Maybe a flower bed in the front. I could give you a list of ideas—"

"No need. Just do it." He crouched and set a nail against the board.

"What if you don't like what I do?"

"Apparently my taste in things isn't to everyone's liking." He hit the nail. "I'll trust your judgment. I've got a Montgomery Ward catalogue in my office. Order what you need from there or go to Oliver's general store and get it from him."

Standing to position another nail, he looked over his shoulder, expecting her to comment, but she was staring, eyes wide, at the area where they'd eaten their meal. Dallas peered around the edge of the board. Houston had apparently woken from his nap, angled his body over his wife's, and was enjoying his dessert: Amelia's sweet lips.

"It's not polite to stare," Dallas said as he pounded another nail into place.

"But they're . . . they're . . ."

"Kissing," Dallas said. "They're just kissing."

Cordelia turned away, her face red. "But they're so close to each other."

"It's more fun that way. Didn't that book you borrowed tell you that?"

He didn't think her blush could grow any deeper, but it did.

"That book is misnamed," she said in a hushed whisper as though afraid someone might hear. "It has nothing at all to do with being a husband."

He couldn't stop himself from smiling. "But it has everything to do with husbandry."

Confusion clouded her eyes. "I don't understand."

"Husbandry is a polite word for breeding and taking care of livestock."

"You might have explained that to me before I took it."

He shrugged. "You married a rancher. Figured it wouldn't hurt for you to read the book. It'll give us something to discuss at dinner."

Her eyes widened. "We wouldn't!"

His smile thinned until it disappeared into a hardened line. "Not if you can think of something else to talk about during our meals. I'm getting tired of eating in silence. If I wanted that, I'd stay out on the range and eat."

"I didn't realize you wanted to talk while we ate. At home, I wasn't allowed to speak during meals."

"Seems your pa and mine had the same attitude: children were to be seen and not heard, but you're not a child any longer."

"No, women . . . women were to be seen and not heard."

Dallas shook his head in disbelief. "I spend all day listening to bawling cattle and the rough voices of men. In the evening, I'd like to hear the soft voice of a woman."

"I'll . . . I'll try to think of something we can discuss during meals."

"Good." He turned back to his task. "Before we leave, you need to tell Houston to let you pick out a horse. Beauty belongs to Maggie. Reckon it's time we stopped borrowing her."

WITH THE EARLY evening shadows moving in, Dallas leaned against the wooden beam of Houston's front porch and stared at Cordelia, standing at the corral, talking with his brother. Talking, smiling, occasionally laughing.

He'd never before heard her sweet laughter. It sounded as innocent as she was.

"Would you like something to drink?" Amelia asked him.

Without taking his eyes off his wife, Dallas wrapped his fingers around the glass of lemonade

Amelia offered. "My brother seems to have become quite the ladies' man."

"He's not a threat to her," Amelia said softly.

Dallas jerked his head around. "And you think I am?"

"*She* thinks you are."

"Christ, I don't know how she can think that. I haven't touched her since the day I married her."

"How often have you called her by name since you were married?"

"What's that got to do with anything?"

"You've been here since dawn, and never once did I hear you speak her name. A woman likes to hear her name from time to time."

"Her name gets tangled in my tongue."

"Her name isn't that much different from mine, and you never have any trouble with it."

"It's a hell of a lot different. Your name is soft. Her name is . . . hard . . . like a stack of wood."

"I like her name."

"Well, I don't."

She hit his arm, and the lemonade sloshed over the glass onto his hand. He stepped back. "Goddammit!"

She hit him again. "Then call her something else."

"Like what?"

"Sugar bunch."

He grimaced.

"Sweetheart, darlin'."

"I can't see words like that rolling off my tongue."

"Then find a word that will, but call her something."

"Why? She's never said my name either."

"You're acting like a two-year-old."

He felt like a fool, watching his wife with another man, looking as though she was enjoying herself when she'd never enjoyed a single moment of his company.

Amelia rubbed his arm. "I'm sorry. It's really none of my business. I just want to see you happy."

"I will be as soon as I get my son."

A sadness washed over her features. "Is a son so important to you?"

"Yes. It's the only unfulfilled dream I have left."

"Why did you have love and cherish removed from your marriage vows?"

He shifted his gaze to the glass of lemonade, the truth as bitter as the drink in his hand. "I'm not an easy man, Amelia. I know that. Love isn't something she's likely to give me. Didn't see any point in asking her to take a vow she couldn't keep." He handed the glass back to her. "We need to get going before darkness settles in." He stepped off the porch.

"You don't give yourself enough credit," she said softly.

With a sad smile, he glanced back at her. "Seems I gave myself too much. If I told her she could leave and I'd still keep my fence pulled back, she'd be gone before the first star came out."

Chapter Eight

Dallas crossed his arms over the top railing and stared at the stars. Spending the day with his brother's family had sharply brought home just how much was missing from his own life: not only his son, but the warm glances Houston and Amelia had exchanged throughout the day that had revealed the depth of their love for each other without a single word being spoken.

He didn't expect Cordelia to ever look at him the way Amelia looked at Houston: as though he hung the moon and stars. If he were a kind man, he'd set Cordelia free, send her back to her father without ever knowing the complete taste of her mouth, the feel of her flesh within his palms, the sound of her cries as he poured his seed into her.

But he wasn't a kind man. He wanted to kiss her again, more deeply than before, his mouth devouring hers. He wanted to skim his hands over her breasts, across her narrow waist, and along her slender hips. He wanted to hear her gasps, sighs, and moans.

He wanted her in his bed—he groaned in frustration. She was already in his bed. His problem was that he didn't know how to get himself back into his bed without knocking on her door and seeing the fear reflected in her eyes.

He'd thought about slipping into her room in the dead of night, nuzzling her awake, trailing kisses—

"Dallas?"

He swung around at the hesitant lilt of Cordelia's soft voice. She had come to his study shortly after they had returned home to get his catalogue. He had hoped she would browse through it in his office, but she'd just grabbed it and scurried out like a frightened rabbit. He hadn't seen her since, had assumed she'd gone to bed—without him once again.

He crossed his arms over his bare chest and wished to God his feet weren't bare. He felt naked and chose to clothe himself in anger. "What are you doing out here?"

"Austin told me to come talk to you."

First Amelia. Now Austin. It seemed his whole family was intent on nudging the woman toward him. Unfortunately, he wanted her to come of her own accord.

Cautiously, she eased closer to the corral and ran her finger along the railing. "I see you out here often. Do you have trouble sleeping?"

"I've just got a lot on my mind."

"Like what?"

How pretty your eyes are. How soft your skin looks. How sweet you smell. How much I want to hold you.

"My brand. I need to change it."

"Why?"

Because I haven't held a woman in years, not since Amelia.

"Because the symbol isn't right anymore."

"What happened to change it, to make it wrong?"

Destiny.

"When I first bought this land, I used a *D* for Dallas. When Amelia agreed to marry me, I added an *A*. I made it lean against the side of the *D* so the letters were joined. Only she and I aren't joined. You and I are, so I need to change the symbol, but your name doesn't lend itself well to leaning against the D. A *C* and *D* just look like two *D*'s back to back so I'm trying to figure out how to put the *C* and *D* together so they look like themselves and not other letters." *And rambling like an idiot in the process.*

She held his gaze in the moonlight. "Did you love her?"

"Who?"

She lowered her lashes. "Amelia. Did you love her?"

He brushed his thumb and forefinger over his mustache. He'd never stopped to ask himself that question. Maybe he should have. "I was fond of her. She added a grace to my life while she was here, but no, I didn't love her. Not the way Houston did then; not as deeply as he does now."

"They seem happy."

"I reckon they are."

She stepped on the bottom rung of the fence. Her toes curled around the wood. He thought about touching his bare foot to hers, rubbing his sole along her delicate ankle.

Pulling herself up, she leaned against the corral. Within the shadows of the night, he could see the curve of her breasts pressing against her wrapper. He ached to slip her wrapper off her shoulders, cup her breasts, and feel her satiny skin against his roughened palms. He dug his fingers into his arms to keep them from reaching for her when she looked so serene.

"I think back to back would work," she said softly.

Back to back? The woman was incredibly innocent. Back to front might work, although he'd prefer front to front. He'd never known a woman as tall as she was. Pressed against her, he imagined he would find very little of himself not warmed by her flesh. Thigh to thigh. Hip to hip. Chest to breasts. His shoulders might come a little higher than hers, but he could live with that.

She glanced over at him. "Cameron calls me Dee. I prefer it to Cordelia, so you see, two *D*'s back to back might work."

"Two *D*'s? Back to back?" He snapped his head back, gasping for breath. "My brand. You're talking about my brand."

"What did you think I was talking about?"

He gave her a jerky nod. "My brand. I thought you were talking about my brand."

She angled her head as though she didn't quite believe him and wanted to figure out exactly what he had been thinking. He shoved his sweating hands into his trouser pockets. "Why does he call you Dee?"

"When he was a baby, Cordelia was too hard for him, so he just started calling me Dee. I never liked Cordelia but we don't get to choose our names . . . or our families."

He imagined in the last week, she'd learned more about her family than she'd care to know. Houston had told him what he'd overheard in Dallas's office, and it had taken every bit of restraint Dallas could muster not to pay the McQueens a visit. He'd cursed Houston long and hard for making him give his word he'd pretend he didn't know what had transpired before Houston had ever told him what had.

"I heard Austin and Amelia call you Dee. I could call you that if you want."

"I'd like that."

"Fine. I'll see about putting two *D*'s on our brand."

She tilted her face toward the stars. "What happens to your men when they get married?"

Like the length of her body, her throat was long and slender. He stepped closer to the corral and rested his elbow on the top railing so he could see her more clearly. "They don't get married."

"Never?"

"Not a ranch hand. If a man wants a family, he's gotta save up his pay, purchase some land, and start his own spread so he's got a place for his family to live."

"Doesn't that seem sad to you?"

"Never thought much about it. That's just the way it is. A cowboy knows that from the beginning."

She seemed to contemplate his answer. He wished he knew what she was thinking, wished he knew what she would do if he put a foot on the railing, cupped her fragile face in his wide hands, and kissed her.

He had the right—

She diverted her attention away from the stars. "Austin is going to town in the morning. Can I go with him?"

He ignored the jab to his pride because she preferred to travel into town with his brother. He would have happily taken her if he'd known she wanted to go. "You're not a prisoner here. You can do anything you want. You don't have to ask my permission."

"I can do *anything*?" she asked.

"You can't move back home," he quickly answered, certain her thoughts were about to head in that direction.

She jerked her chin up slightly, almost defiantly. "You claim to give me freedom, but then you limit the choices, which takes away the freedom."

She stepped off the railing. "Thank you for giving me permission to leave with Austin tomorrow."

She strolled away. He wanted to grab her braid, wrap it around his hand until he'd brought her face even with his . . . and kiss her until neither one of them had any choices.

STUDYING THE WORDS she'd written before she'd gone to sleep last night, Cordelia slowly chewed on the biscuit. She knew freedom was an illusion. She could come and go as she pleased as long as she didn't go where she wanted—someplace where she could cast her own shadow.

Still, she intended to enjoy the day. Even Dallas's apparent lack of interest in her topics wasn't going to spoil her mood. She glanced up from her notes. "Why do you suppose the leaves change color in autumn?"

With his egg-laden fork halfway to his mouth, Dallas stilled. "Because they die."

"I see." She looked at Austin. "Are you of the same sentiment?"

Peering at her over the brim of his cup, steam rising from the coffee, humor in his eyes, he nodded.

She returned her attention to her list. She had been incredibly pleased with herself last night for walking to the corral to ask Dallas for permission to ride to town with Austin. Of course, Austin had shoved her out the door and locked it, forcing her to find the courage to face her husband, but still she had found it . . . eventually.

"What is your favorite color?"

"Brown."

She lifted her gaze. "Brown? Of all the colors in the world, why do you like brown?"

Dallas couldn't bring himself to tell her the truth. He favored brown because her eyes were brown. The one time he had seen them without fear or wariness clouding them, they had mesmerized him. "I just do."

"Oh."

She looked at her scrap of paper, and Dallas bit back a scathing expletive. He had threatened her with a discussion on husbandry if she didn't talk, and she had brought a list of topics to the table this morning and kept running her finger over it, looking for things to discuss.

Wind. Rain. The shape of clouds. The entire time she prattled about things, he discovered that he wanted to talk about her. What she had feared as a little girl. Her dreams. If she was lonely.

He shoved his chair back, and she jerked her head up. He stood, walked to her end of the table, and set an envelope beside her plate.

"What's this?" she asked.

"Spending money." For over an hour, he had contemplated how much to give her, fearing too little or too much might offend her. He had no idea how much money ladies needed and had settled on twenty dollars. "If it's not enough, you can put your purchases on my account, and I'll take care of it the next time I go to town."

She trailed her fingers over the envelope, and he wondered what it would feel like to have her slender fingers skim over his chest.

She peered up at him. "Thank you."

"You're my wife. I'm supposed to see that you don't do without." He glared at Austin. "Take care of her, or I'll hang your hide out to dry."

He stalked from the room, wondering why he couldn't have simply leaned down, kissed her on the cheek, and told her to enjoy the day.

CORDELIA TOOK GREAT delight in riding with Austin. He possessed much more patience than his older brother. He had already taught her how to send Lemon Drop into a trot. She loved the feel of the wind brushing across her face, the movement of the golden mare beneath her, and the knowledge that she was in control of the beast.

If only she could control her husband as easily. If only he would set her free.

She slowed her horse to a walk. Beside her, Austin did the same.

"You did that real well," he said, smiling broadly.

She felt the warmth fan her cheeks. "She's a good horse."

"That's the only kind Houston raises."

"Do you think we'll go back and work on their house this Sunday?"

"I'm sure we will. Dallas ain't one to leave a job half-done."

"No, I don't imagine he is at that." She shifted her backside over the saddle. "Why did your parents name you and your brothers after towns in Texas?"

"According to Houston, our pa had a wandering streak in him and named us after the town he was living in at the time we were born. I don't remember our pa, but Houston says Dallas is a lot like him, says that's the reason Dallas purchased so much land. He could wander far and wide and still be at home."

His answer gave her pause for thought. She wondered if Dallas had longed for roots while he was growing up as much as she'd longed to leave. She brushed a fleck of dirt off her riding skirt. "I was wondering . . ."

Austin tipped his hat off his brow. "Yes, ma'am?"

"My father sends someone into town every week for supplies. Wouldn't it save you considerable time if you brought a wagon so you wouldn't have to go into town every day for supplies?"

Austin's face turned beet red as he tugged his hat down. "I ain't goin' into town for supplies. Dallas sends Pete in to get the supplies."

"Then why do you go every day?"

He cleared his throat. "I just like to."

"Dallas doesn't mind?"

"Long as I get my work done, he don't mind at all."

She contemplated his answer. Her days were long, her nights even longer. She wondered if she could find something in town to help her pass the time.

Tightening her hold on the reins, Cordelia stared as Leighton came into view. Half a dozen wooden buildings checkered the wide dusty street. On the outskirts of town, it looked as though people had haphazardly thrown up tents.

Workers were hammering on the frame of a building. The scent of sawdust filled the air. She had never seen anything like it.

The day Dallas had announced that he was setting aside the land for a town, she had seen nothing but open prairie. She hadn't returned since.

She had known the town had acquired a dress-maker and a general store. She hadn't known about the saloon or the bank or the jail.

"What are they building?" she asked Austin as he led their horses down the center of town.

"A livery and a blacksmith shop."

"It really is going to be a town," she said in awe. "Boyd had said it would never happen. That Dallas was a fool."

"Boyd's the fool," Austin said. "I've never seen Dallas fail at anything."

Austin brought their horses to a stop in front of a false-fronted building that proclaimed OLIVER'S GENERAL STORE. He dismounted, tethered both horses, then reached up and helped Cordelia dismount.

A whole town to walk through. Well, not quite a whole town, but it would be someday, and her husband was responsible. An empire builder.

Perhaps he was more. A builder of dreams.

How did one even go about knowing where to begin?

Austin opened the door that led into the general store. As soon as he entered the building, he swept his hat from his head and an easy smile played at the corners of his mouth.

Becky Oliver stood on a ladder, placing canned goods on a shelf. She glanced over her shoulder, her blue eyes growing warm.

Cordelia thought she might have discovered Austin's interest in coming to town every day.

"What can I do you for?" asked a balding man standing behind the counter.

Cordelia remembered being introduced to Perry Oliver at her wedding.

Becky rolled her eyes and climbed down from

the ladder. "Oh, Pa, you got the words all mixed up again."

He winked at Cordelia. "Young'uns. They ain't never happy with what their parents do." He looked at Austin. "Well, young man, what brings you into town today?"

"Dee needs something so I just brought her into town."

Cordelia fought to keep the surprise off her face. She didn't need anything, but Austin gave her an imploring look that begged her to play along. How could she resist the plea in those blue eyes?

"What do you need then, Mrs. Leigh?" Mr. Oliver asked.

Mrs. Leigh? She thought she'd never get used to that name. "I . . . uh . . . books . . . I need some books."

Mr. Oliver's eyes widened. "You already read those books your husband came in and purchased last week?"

Cordelia glanced at Austin. He simply shrugged. She had no idea what books her husband had bought. No doubt more on husbandry. "No, he didn't share them with me," she finally confessed.

Mr. Oliver rubbed his palm over his shining bald pate. "That's odd. He said they were for you. Said you liked to read." He squinted his pale blue eyes and puckered his lips. "Let's see. I had *A Tale of Two Cities* and *Silas Marner*. He bought them both."

Words failed her. If Dallas had purchased the books for her, wouldn't he have told her? If he hadn't purchased them for her, why had he told Mr. Oliver that he had?

"They were all I had in stock," Mr. Oliver continued. "He told me when I got more books in, I was to set them aside until he'd had a chance to look at them."

The bell above the door tinkled as a young boy walked hesitantly into the store. His black hair was in dire need of a cut and his face a good scrubbing. His bare feet shuffled over the wooden floor as he neared the counter and dug his hand into the pocket of his coveralls. One strap trailed down his backside since he had no button on the front of the coveralls to hold it in place. It looked as though the button on the other side wasn't going to stay with him much longer.

Perry Oliver leaned over the counter. "Well, Mr. Rawley Cooper. What can I do you for today?"

The boy slapped some coins on the counter. "My pa's needin' some cig'rette makin's."

"I've got some right back here," Mr. Oliver said as he disappeared behind the counter.

The boy gazed at the jars of colorful candy that lined the counter. Cordelia didn't think he could be much older than eight. His black eyes shot back to Mr. Oliver when the man set a pouch of tobacco and some papers on the counter.

"Obliged," the boy said as he slipped the supplies into his pocket and turned to leave.

"Hold on there a minute, Rawley. You gave me too much," Mr. Oliver said as he placed a pudgy finger on a copper penny and slid it across the counter.

Rawley looked doubtful as his gaze darted between Mr. Oliver and the penny. Hesitantly, he placed his grubby hand over the penny.

"I'm selling licorice for a penny today," Mr. Oliver said. "Don't reckon your pa would miss a penny."

Rawley shook his head, grabbed the penny, and hurried out the door.

"You should have told him it was free," Austin said.

Mr. Oliver shook his head. "Tried that. The boy has too much pride to take something for nothing. Beats anything I've ever seen. Considering who his pa is, I don't know how he managed to latch on to any pride."

"Who is his father?" Cordelia asked.

"One of the workers putting up the buildings, although calling him a worker is giving him the benefit of the doubt. Mostly he just draws his pay and gets drunk."

"Where is Rawley's mother?" Cordelia asked.

"Dead, I reckon."

Austin pulled two sarsaparilla sticks out of a jar. "Put these on my account," he said as he headed toward the door.

"He won't take them," Mr. Oliver called after him.

Austin flashed a disarming grin. "I can be quite charmin' when I want to be."

As the door closed behind him, Cordelia backed away from the counter, feeling self-conscious without Austin by her side. "I'm going to look around."

Mr. Oliver nodded. "You let us know if you need anything."

Cordelia walked to the far side of the store, not certain what she should do if she did find something she wanted to purchase. She felt vulnerable and lost, like a child who had let go of her mother's hand in a crowd of people.

She was twenty-six years old, and she had no idea how to purchase a ribbon for her hair. Her father and her brothers had gotten into the habit of bringing everything to her while she had tended to her mother. The habit had remained long after her mother had passed away.

Where once she had felt pampered, she now felt afraid.

She had allowed herself to become dependent on the kindness of her family, and they had pulled that kindness out from under her. She turned toward the soft footfalls.

Becky smiled at her. "Did you find something that you wanted?"

Cordelia wrung her hands together. She supposed she should begin turning Dallas's house into a home. "I was looking for some rugs."

"We have some over here," Becky said.

Cordelia skirted barrels and boxes as she followed Becky to the other side of the store. Becky patted a stack of rugs.

"This is all we have. Just look through them and let me know if you want one."

Careful not to disturb the pile, Cordelia removed one rug at a time and examined it. She wanted something with brown woven through it, Dallas's favorite color.

"I sure was surprised when I heard Dallas was going to marry you," Becky said.

Cordelia glanced up from the selections and smiled. "I guess you didn't know my brothers had a sister."

"Oh, I'd heard the rumors," Becky said. "I was just surprised Dallas would marry you after Boyd shot Austin."

Cordelia's heart rammed against her ribs, and she could feel the blood draining from her face.

Becky's eyes widened. "Oh, my goodness. Didn't you know?"

Cordelia lowered her gaze to the floor. Why wouldn't it crack open and swallow her whole?

"I'm sure Dallas has forgiven him, otherwise he wouldn't have married you."

The door swung open, and Austin sauntered

into the store, a sarsaparilla stick jutting from his mouth. "Well, I did it. Got the boy to take one of the sticks."

He strolled over to Cordelia, confidence in his step. "What you got there, Dee?"

"R-rugs. I thought . . . I thought I'd purchase one for the house."

"That'd be fine," Austin said, talking around the sarsaparilla stick. "Which one?"

Cordelia quickly searched through the stack and pulled out a brown rug. "This one."

Becky took it from her. "I'll wrap it for you and put it on Dallas's account. You can pick it up on your way out of town."

"Can we go home now?" she asked Austin.

"Thought you wanted to see the rest of the town?"

"Oh, yes, I forgot." She couldn't bring herself to look at Austin, knowing her brother had shot him.

Austin took her arm. "Come on, Dee, you're looking pale. Let's get some air."

She allowed him to lead her outside. Then she broke away from him, crossed the small board-walk, and wrapped her trembling hands around the railing.

Austin studied the woman clinging to the railing as though she were afraid she'd drown in the dust without it. He took the sarsaparilla stick out of his mouth. "What happened, Dee?"

She looked at him, with hurt and anger mixed in her eyes. His stomach dropped clear to the ground, and he fought the urge to reach out and touch her, to wipe the hurt and anger away. "What did I do?" he said, his voice low.

"Boyd shot you."

He furrowed his brow. "Yeah?"

"You said it was cattle rustlers."

"Dallas said it was cattle rustlers."

"Why?"

Austin shrugged. "Maybe he didn't think you'd believe him, or maybe he was trying to spare you some hurt. Sitting in that shade, eating our meal, it just didn't feel right to me to say Boyd had shot me. I reckon Dallas felt the same way."

"But Boyd did shoot you."

"Becky tell you that?"

She nodded.

"Dang, that girl has a big mouth."

"Why did he shoot you?"

"Don't think he meant to. He was just shooting, and I got in the way."

Tears welled in her eyes. "I don't have any friends, Austin. I need a friend right now. Be my friend."

"Sure. Whatever you want."

"Friends never lie to each other," she said.

With his thumb, Austin pushed his hat off his brow, wishing he'd been a little slower in agreeing to be her friend. "What do you want to know?"

"Do you know what happened the night that Dallas broke Boyd's arm?"

"Yep. That's the night I got shot."

"Was Boyd guarding his cattle? Did you, Dallas, and Houston attack him?"

Austin jerked off his hat and looked at the sky, wondering where wisdom came from.

"I want the truth," she said. "Am I married to a man who sneaked up on my brother in the dead of night and broke his arm?"

He lowered his gaze to hers. Within her brown eyes, he saw a sparkle of hope, and he wondered which would hurt her the least—the truth or a lie.

"The truth," she whispered as though understanding his hesitancy.

"No, you're not married to a man who'd sneak up on anyone. It's not Dallas's way. It never has been. He meets every problem head-on. Your brothers were gettin' into the habit of cutting through Dallas's fence and killing off his cattle. That night, we were waiting for them. When the pain ripped through my shoulder, everything went black, but Houston told me that Dallas had dragged Boyd through the river. I reckon his arm must have hit a rock or something and got busted, but I do know Dallas didn't do it on purpose."

"Dallas frightens me, Austin."

Austin couldn't stop himself from stepping closer and wrapping his arms around her. "I know. I see it in your eyes every time you look at him. He sees it, too, and it makes him mad, which scares you more and makes him furious. It's a circle you can't seem to get out of."

"The things Boyd told me . . . I don't know what to believe anymore."

Austin leaned back and cupped her chin. "Well, you might try by not looking at him through Boyd's eyes, but look at him through your own. Pretend you just met him and had never heard anything about him."

"I think he'd still frighten me."

Austin laughed. "He scares the hell out of me. Out of Houston, too." He grew somber. "But he'd never hurt you, Dee. I know that."

"But he won't set me free."

"If he did, what would you do? Was living with your family better than what you have now?"

"I need something more, Austin. I don't know

what, but I know I need something more than what Dallas or my family has the power to give me."

He drew her close, pressing his cheek against the top of her head. "Then I hope you find it, Dee. I truly do."

Chapter Nine

$\mathcal{D}$allas stepped out of the bank and wished to God that he hadn't desperately searched for an excuse to come into town. He'd hoped to casually cross his wife's path, perhaps walk through the town with her.

He hadn't expected to see her on the boardwalk wrapped tightly within his brother's arms.

Austin looked up and his blue eyes widened. "Dallas!" Like a snake wrapped around a low-lying tree branch, Austin slowly uncoiled himself from around Cordelia. "Didn't know you had plans to come to town."

"Obviously." Dallas balled his hands into fists and clenched his jaw, his gaze darting between his brother and his wife. The terror had returned to her eyes, and he imagined right now she had good reason to fear him.

With a loose-jointed walk, Austin approached him. "Dee found out that Boyd shot me. She was a little angry at us for not telling her outright, for saying it was cattle rustlers. I was just trying to cool her temper."

Dallas glared at his brother. "You don't hug me when I'm angry."

Austin barked out his laughter. "I will if you want me to because I can sure tell that you're fit to be tied right now." Stretching out his arms and tilting his head, he flashed an infectious grin that Dallas was certain he would use to charm the ladies if there were any ladies around. "Want a hug?"

Dallas stepped back. "Hell, no." Dallas shifted his attention at Dee. She was studying him as though he were a stranger, which he realized he was. What did she really know about him? What did he know about her?

"How did she find out?" he asked.

Austin jerked his head toward the general store. "Becky." He rubbed his hands on his thighs. "Listen, Dee's never visited Leighton. Would you show her the town while I talk with Becky for a while?" Austin swiveled his head around. "You don't mind going with Dallas, do you, Dee?"

Dallas watched his wife grow pale before she finally nodded. "That would be fine."

"Thanks. I'll catch up with you."

Austin disappeared into the general store. Dallas wished he had been the one to whom Dee had turned, the one who had held her when she'd learned the truth.

"You've never been to town?" he asked.

She shook her head. "Not this town. Not after the day you set the land aside. My brothers never had time to bring me."

"Well . . ." He stepped off the boardwalk, suddenly self-conscious with all that remained undone. "It's nowhere near finished." He pointed straight ahead. "The general store." He moved his hand to the left. "The bank."

"What were you doing at the bank?" she asked as she walked to his side.

"I wanted to talk with Mr. Henderson about a loan for another building."

"What sort of building?"

He cleared his throat. "A man—cabinetmaker— wrote to me. He wants to move here, but he hasn't the means to finance his own business. I think he would be a good investment."

"Do you have the means to finance him?"

"With the assistance of the bank, I'll help him get his start. Eventually, he'll own his business outright, but the more people I can get to Leighton, the more we'll grow."

"How do you determine which businesses would be a good investment?"

He studied her, not expecting the questions she was asking, but pleased that she knew enough to ask them. He crooked his elbow and watched as she swallowed before placing her hand on his arm. Together they walked slowly along the street.

"I try and figure out what people need," he explained to her. He pointed toward the clothing store. "Houston was always going to Fort Worth to purchase clothing for Amelia. He'd visit Miss St. Claire's dress shop. The idea of a new town intrigued her, so she moved her business here, hoping the town would prosper and more women would come. Until then, she sews clothing for men and women."

"There aren't many women from what I've seen."

"A half dozen if that many. I haven't figured out how to attract them to Leighton. I've been thinking of running an advertisement for brides, similar to the one Amelia placed for a husband. Only I'd want a whole passel of women to come, and I'd need to have husbands waiting for them. I've got to give some thought to the best way to handle that. I don't particularly relish the thought of being a marriage broker."

She slowly nodded, and Dallas almost imagined that he could see wheels spinning in her mind. He wanted to ask her what she thought of the town. He wanted Leighton to be more than just a town . . . he wanted it to be a place that drew people in and gave them a reason to stay.

They neared the saloon. Hesitantly, she glanced at him. "Can I look inside the saloon?"

"Sure."

Cautiously, Cordelia neared the swinging doors and peered inside. The smoke was thick. The odors not entirely pleasant. She could see a few men sitting at a table playing cards. One of the men was her brother.

"What is Duncan doing here?" she asked.

Dallas glanced over her shoulder. "Playing cards."

"I mean why isn't he out working with the cattle?"

"I guess he's just taking some time off."

Stepping back, she studied her husband. "When do you take time off?"

He led her away from the saloon. "Saloons don't appeal to me. I never could bring myself to let the draw of a card take away the money I'd worked so hard to earn."

"But you must relax sometime."

"When I need to relax, I ride out at night and visit one of my ladies."

Cordelia was unprepared for the pain that slashed through her. Why had she expected him to remain faithful to her just because they had exchanged vows? Incensed for reasons she could not begin to fathom, she strode off the boardwalk. "I think I've seen all I want to see of the town."

He grabbed her arm, and she jerked free. "Please don't touch me. Not after you've just thrown your mistresses into my face."

"My mistresses?" He drew his brows together over eyes mired with confusion, then he started to laugh. "My ladies."

"I don't see that it's funny."

"I wasn't thinking."

"Obviously not. A gentleman doesn't mention his other women to his wife. I think we'd both be a good deal happier if you'd married one of them instead of me." She spun on her heel and started to walk away.

"Dee?"

She wanted to keep walking, but a longing in his voice touched her, reached for her, forced her to turn around. No longer smiling or laughing, he watched her as though searching for something.

"The ladies are my windmills," he said quietly. "I enjoy listening to them in the quiet of the night. It brings me peace. I'd like to share that with you sometime."

Incredibly embarrassed, she slammed her eyes closed. "I'm sorry. I acted like a shrew."

"You should get angry more often."

Her eyes flew open. The one time her mother had gotten angry her father had struck her down. "Why?"

"Anger puts a fire in your eyes. I'd rather have the fire than the fear."

"Dallas!" a man yelled.

Cordelia watched as a slender man rushed toward Dallas.

"Tyler, you got a problem?" Dallas asked.

The man skidded to a stop. "Not a problem."

As though he suddenly noticed her, Tyler jerked his hat from his head. He swept the blond locks from his brow and smiled at Cordelia. "Mrs. Leigh, we met at your wedding although you probably don't remember me. Tyler Curtiss."

"I'm not very good with names," she confessed.

"I'm not very good with faces except when they're beautiful like yours." He blushed as though unaccustomed to flirting, and Dallas scowled.

"Tyler designs the buildings and manages the construction," Dallas said, his voice taut.

She smiled with interest. "So you're building the town?"

"With a great deal of help. I'd like to get your husband's opinion on a few things if you can spare him."

"Yes, that's fine."

Dallas seemed to hesitate. "Can you find Austin?"

She nodded. "I'm sure he's still at the general store."

"I'll see you at home then."

She watched him walk away. She could tell from his stance that he was listening intently as Tyler prattled.

Why had it hurt so much when he'd mentioned his ladies with such affection? Why was she relieved to discover he had been visiting windmills?

She began strolling toward the horses tethered to the hitching post in front of the general store. She had erupted with anger and instead of retaliating, he had told her to get mad more often. She decided his suggestion might have some merit. She had found the burst of fury . . . emancipating.

STANDING ON THE balcony outside her bedroom, Cordelia stared at the night. She heard the steady clack of the nearby windmill—one of Dallas's ladies.

He was so unlike her father, her brothers. He angered easily, the rage flashing within his dark eyes, but he kept his temper tethered.

Where the men in her family concerned themselves only with their wants and needs, Dallas broadened his horizons to include others. People were coming to his town because he gave them a chance to share in a corner of his dream, and in sharing, his dream would grow.

She was certain Boyd would have referred to his actions as selfish and greedy, but how could she fault Dallas Leigh with wanting to build a future for his sons . . . a future grander than anything she had ever dared to dream?

A town. A community. A community of men.

She frowned, surprised to discover that she wanted a part of his dream as well. She wanted to accomplish what he had yet to achieve. She wanted to find a way to lure women to Leighton.

She didn't see her husband standing by the corral. She hadn't heard his footsteps echoing along the hallway.

She wondered where he was—if he was in his office. If the two books he'd purchased were waiting there as well.

She didn't want to fear Dallas, but more she didn't want to be dependent on him. She had once coveted freedom, but now she realized without independence, freedom didn't exist. The first step toward independence was conquering her fear.

She walked into her bedroom and retrieved the book she had borrowed from him—*The Practical Husbandman*.

She remembered the depth of his laughter, that night and this afternoon. The spontaneity of it. The way it had reached out and struck a corresponding chord deep within her.

Holding the lamp, she made her way to Dallas's office. She saw the light spilling out from beneath the door and almost changed her mind. Instead, she forced herself to knock.

"Come in," boomed from the other side.

Her heart quickened. She took a trembling breath and opened the door. Dallas sat at his desk, the ledgers spread out before him. He came to his feet.

"Oh, no, don't get up," she said as she slipped into the room. "I just wanted to return your book."

"Fine."

She took a step closer to the shelves. "Do you always work on your ledgers late at night?"

"Usually."

She licked her lips, her mouth suddenly dry, her determination withering. "My father . . . my father works on his books during the afternoon."

"He has three sons to watch his spread. I only have me."

"And Austin."

"It's not his responsibility. Someday, he'll figure out what he wants from life and he'll leave."

When Austin left, she'd be alone with this man. This man who wanted sons.

"Please don't let me disturb you." She held up the book. "I'll just put this back."

He sat and she hurried across the room. She slipped the book into place, then she trailed her fingers over one of the new books on the shelf: *A Tale of Two Cities.*

She glanced at Dallas. He was writing in his ledger as though her presence made no difference to him . . . and yet, he also seemed to be waiting.

She took the book off the shelf. "I've never read *A Tale of Two Cities*," she said quietly.

"It's yours," he said gruffly. "Along with the other one. Just don't thank me for them. Should have put books in here a long time back. Not much point in having shelves if you don't put books on them."

"That's what I thought the first time I saw this room. I fell in love with it."

He snapped his head up and stared at her, his eyes incredibly dark.

"I thought—" She cleared her throat. "I thought these shelves might hold a thousand books."

He leaned back in his chair. "A thousand?"

She nodded. "Or more."

"Let me know what the tally is when you get the shelves filled up." He went back to writing in his ledgers.

Holding the book tightly, she began to walk across the room, then she stopped. The room was quiet except for the occasional scratch of his pen across the paper.

"I used to read to my mother before she died," she said softly.

He lifted his head and looked at her.

"I miss reading to her," she added. "I miss her."

He propped his elbow on the desk and rubbed his thumb and forefinger over his mustache. She remembered its softness as he had kissed her.

"Dr. Freeman mentioned something about your mother being an invalid."

She had never spoken the words. After all these years, acknowledging the truth was still painful. "She and my father had an argument. In the scuffle, she lost her balance and fell down the stairs.

She couldn't move after that, but she wasn't dead. So I cared for her."

"The scuffle? You mean your father struck her?"

She nodded, wishing she'd kept the incident locked away. It sounded incredibly ugly spoken aloud. Had he risen from his chair, had he come toward her, she thought she might have taken flight and rushed back to her room.

Instead, he remained perfectly still. "No matter how angry I get, Dee, I would never hit you. I give you my word on that."

Filled with conviction, the quietly spoken words left her no choice but to believe him.

"Can I read to you?" she asked.

She almost laughed at the startled expression that crossed his features, as though she had spoken the very last words he had ever expected to hear. He looked as though she'd thrown a bucket of cold water on him.

"I know you don't have a lot of spare time. I could read while you work on your ledgers."

As though unable to determine her motive, he nodded slowly. "That'd be fine."

She set the lamp on a small table and sat in the stuffed chair beside it. Bringing up her feet, she tucked them beneath her. She felt him watching her and tried not to be bothered by his scrutiny.

She turned back the cover and several pages before clearing her throat. "'It was the best of times, it was the worst of times . . .'"

She glanced up. His pen was poised above the ledger, his ink dripping onto the paper.

"Can you work while I read?" she asked.

He nodded and dipped the pen into the inkwell again. When he began to write in his ledgers, she filled the shadowed room with the story.

Dallas wasn't certain of the exact moment when his wife had come to regret her decision to read to him, but he thought it might have been sometime after midnight.

Her eyes had been drifting closed, her words becoming softer, less frequent. He had asked her if she wanted to go to bed. She'd snapped her head up and claimed she wasn't tired.

He figured she just didn't know how to stop reading and announce she was going to bed without leaving the door open for him to join her.

So she had read for two more hours, her voice growing hoarse, her eyes crossing from time to time until eventually they had closed and her head had dropped back.

She looked damned uncomfortable propped up in the chair, her head tilted at an awkward angle, and incredibly lovely with all the worry and fear slipping away for the night.

He wished he knew how to keep the worry and fear out of her eyes when she was awake. He'd considered being blunt and simply explaining to her what he expected and what he would settle for.

But he imagined that a woman needed more than a man's view on the subject. She probably wanted tender words that he didn't know how to give.

As quietly as he could, he pushed his chair back, rose to his feet, and walked to the chair where she was slumped. Gingerly, he eased the book from her grasp and set it on the table beside the chair.

Then he slipped one arm around her back, the other beneath her knees, and cradled her against his chest. Sighing, she snuggled her cheek into the crook of his shoulder.

He hadn't expected her to be as light as a summer

breeze, to feel so dainty in his arms. As tall as she was, he had expected her to weigh more. She was little more than soft curves and warmth.

He carried her to her bedroom and gently laid her on the bed. She rolled onto her side, drew her knees up toward her chest, and slipped her hand beneath her cheek. He brought the blankets over her, crouched beside the bed, and watched as she slept.

He had enjoyed the spark of temper that his reference to his ladies had ignited in her eyes that afternoon.

Knowing what he now knew about her mother's ailment, he realized that her outburst, small as it was, had been a form of trust. Perhaps she was beginning to test her boundaries, to see how far he would allow her to go.

He thought about telling her, but he didn't think she'd believe him. He'd simply have to show her.

CORDELIA AWOKE WITH a start. A faint glimmer of sunlight shadowed the room. She pulled the blankets up to her chin trying to remember when she had come to bed.

Dallas had been in her room. Somehow she was certain of it. His presence lingered like a forgotten scent. Had he brought her to bed and then left her alone to sleep?

She thought she might never understand him.

He had wanted a wife to give him a son, and yet, with the exception of their first night, he had made no overtures toward her. She wondered if he regretted marrying her, if perhaps he would never truly become her husband.

She eased out of bed, walked to the balcony

doors, and drew the curtain aside. She could see Dallas standing by the corral talking with his foreman. When Slim walked away, Dallas mounted his black horse and looked up. His gaze locked with hers.

Her breath caught and her heart pounded. His mouth moved, forming words she couldn't hear.

She unlatched the door and stepped onto the balcony. "What?" she asked.

"Get dressed to ride!"

"Now?"

"Yep."

As he dismounted, she hurried back into her room, closed the balcony door, drew the curtains together, and wished she'd never ventured from her bed.

DALLAS WASN'T CERTAIN what had possessed him to invite his wife to ride with him, although he had to admit that she probably hadn't considered his words an invitation.

It wasn't in his nature to ask. Perhaps it had been when he was a boy, but the war had driven it from him. At fourteen, he'd issued his first order. When the war had ended, he'd continued to issue orders. It was the easiest way to accomplish what needed to be done. Tell a man. If he didn't like it, he could move on.

Unfortunately for Cordelia, if she didn't like the way he issued orders, she had no freedom to move on. A marriage contract bound her to him, whether she liked it or not.

He'd hoped they were making progress toward an amicable relationship when she'd offered to read to him last night, but now she rode beside him with her back as stiff as the rod of a branding iron, her eyes trained straight ahead, and her knuckles turning white as she held the saddle horn.

The horses plodded along as though they had all day to get to where they were going.

"How good are you at keeping your word?" he asked.

She swiveled her head toward him, her brow furrowed. "I don't lie, if that's what you're implying."

"My pa taught me that a man is only as good as his word. I've never in my life gone back on my word. I'm just wondering if your pa taught you the same."

Cordelia was at a loss for words. She couldn't recall her father teaching her much of anything except her place within a man's world, a place she had never questioned until she had discovered that it didn't fit very well within her husband's world. "I know how to keep a promise," she finally admitted. "I suppose it's the same thing."

He nodded. "Then I need you to give me a promise."

"What sort of promise?"

He drew his horse to a halt. She did the same. Removing his hat, he captured her gaze.

"I want you to promise that if something should happen to me you won't give my land to your brothers."

"What would happen to you?"

"Anything could happen to a man out here. I just don't want your brothers to benefit from my death."

His death? The words echoed through her mind, through her heart. "Why would you die?"

His lips curved into a slight smile. "I'm not planning to. I just want your word that if we have a son, you'll hold on to the land for him."

"And if we don't have a son?"

"Then hold on to the land for yourself or sell it. Just don't give it to your brothers."

"I wouldn't know what to do with the land," she confessed.

He looked toward the distant horizon. "Give me your word that you won't give the land to your brothers, and I'll teach you how to manage it."

She swept her gaze over the land. He was entrusting her with his legacy. She realized that if something did happen to him, she would need to know how to manage the ranch so she could teach their son. She glanced at him as he steadfastly watched her. "I could destroy everything you've built."

"If I thought there was the slightest chance in hell of that happening, I wouldn't have made the offer."

The force of his words slammed into her. He trusted her with the empire he had built, trusted her to honor her word, just as she had vowed to honor him.

He was giving her the opportunity to level the shaky foundation upon which they had begun to build their marriage. "I give you my word."

A slow smile spread beneath his mustache. "Good."

In the days that followed, she came to know his men and their respective jobs. She had assumed that they simply watched the cattle. She could not have been more wrong. Men constantly rode the fence line, mending the cut or broken wire, replacing posts. The mill rider visited the windmills to grease the bearings and repair anything that had broken. Bog riders searched for cattle that had become tangled in the brush or trapped in mud. The numerous types of riders and their various tasks astounded her.

It seemed everything always needed to be checked and checked again: the fence, the windmills, the cattle, the water supply, the grazing land. Decisions had to be made as to when and where to move the cattle.

By the end of the week, Cordelia was overwhelmed with the knowledge she had attained.

She also had a greater respect and understanding of her husband and his achievements.

DALLAS POUNDED THE nail into the floorboard. This Sunday was turning out to be much the same as last Sunday.

He worked on the loft while his brothers lollygagged. He was surprised they'd managed to get the walls put in on the first floor.

He heard the deep rumble of laughter, followed by the gentler giggles. Against his better judgment, he unfolded his body and carefully walked across the beams until he got to the edge of the second floor. He leaned against the open frame.

Cordelia stood at one end of the yard. Everyone else was positioned in different places. She turned her back to them, and everyone moved up. Houston took one big step and stopped. Amelia took three tiny steps. Maggie skipped and fell to her knees. Austin ran.

Cordelia spun around. Austin staggered to a stop. She pointed a finger at him. "I saw you running."

"The heck you did!" he yelled while everyone else laughed.

She wagged her finger at him. "Go back to the beginning."

He stomped to a rope stretched along the ground several yards away from Cordelia. Cordelia pivoted, giving them her back, and everyone started moving again.

Dallas shook his head. No doubt another one of Amelia's games. The woman had more games than a tree had leaves.

Dallas smiled as Maggie and Houston got sent back to the rope. Houston lifted his daughter onto his shoulders.

Cordelia turned her back, and Austin's legs churned faster than the blades of a windmill when a norther blew through. Dallas clamped his teeth together to stop himself from yelling a warning.

Cordelia spun around too late. Austin scooped her off the ground. Dallas's chest tightened as she threw her arms around Austin's neck and laughed. Austin twirled her around, his laughter mingling with hers.

Maggie yelled that she wanted to play again. Austin set Cordelia on her feet. She glanced toward the house and her gaze slammed into Dallas's, her smile withering like all the flowers he'd pulled for her over the week and never given her. Dallas turned away and walked to the other side of the room, wondering when he'd grown so old.

A few minutes later he heard the footsteps on the stairs—the stairs he'd built that morning. He couldn't fault Houston. If he had a wife who looked at him the way Amelia did and a daughter who adored him, he wouldn't be up here pounding nails into wood either.

"I thought you might like some lemonade."

He glanced up at Cordelia. She stood uncertainly in the doorway, holding a glass. He crossed the short space separating them, took the glass, and downed the drink in one long swallow. He handed the glass back to her. "Thanks."

He walked back to his corner, lined up the board, and hammered the nail into place.

"You put me to shame," she said softly.

Furrowing his brow, he glanced over his shoulder. "Why?"

She walked across the floorboards he'd already nailed into place and knelt beside him. "I have a clearer understanding of how you spend your days now. All week long you manage a ranch, you oversee the building of a town, and on what should be a day of rest, you're building an addition onto your brother's house while I'm playing silly games and purchasing rugs—"

"I like the rugs."

She tilted her head sideways. "Do you?"

He regretted that he hadn't mentioned it earlier. "Yeah, I do. I like the quilt you hung on the wall in the parlor and those curtains."

"I thought they made the room seem more cozy. I've ordered some furniture for the parlor."

"Good."

Since the night she had first begun to read to him and the day he had first started explaining the managing of the ranch to her, the wariness had slowly faded from her eyes. She watched him now with no fear. He considered leaning over and kissing her, but he discovered that it wasn't enough that the fear had left. He wanted to see a warmth reflected in her gaze when she looked at him. He wanted her to want him as much as he wanted her.

A damn foolish thing to desire.

She dropped her gaze and scraped her fingernail over the nail he had just hammered into place. "Is it hard to build a floor?" she asked.

"Nope." He extended the hammer toward her. "Do you want to do it?"

A sparkle lit her eyes. "Can I?"

"Sure."

She took the hammer, and he handed her a nail.

"You want the nail to go through the top board and dig into the beam running lengthwise. That holds it in place. Keep your eye on the nail and tap gently."

"It always sounds like you hit the nail hard."

"I have experience behind me so I'm less likely to hit my thumb."

"Oh."

He watched with amusement as she set the nail in place and gripped the hammer. Her brows came together to form a deep furrow. She pulled her bottom lip between her teeth.

He swallowed, remembering the feel of that lip against his.

Her eyes darkened with concentration. He wanted to see them darken with passion.

Gently, she tapped the nail, the furrow deepening, her teeth digging into her lip, her knuckles turning white. He thought about giving her some more instruction, but some things in life were better learned through trial and error. After a dozen hits, the nail had settled into its new home.

She rubbed her fingers over the nail. "Is that what building a town feels like?" she asked.

He'd never thought about it, didn't know how to answer her question.

She looked at him with wonder in her eyes. "Children will crawl over this floor. Then they'll walk over it and run across it. If this house remains for a hundred years, what you have done today might touch children you'll never meet. It's the same with your town and your ranch. Everything that you do reaches out to touch so many people. The things I do touch no one."

She laid the hammer on the floor and rose quietly to her feet.

He fought the urge to grab her ankle and halt her steps away from him.

"I could use some help," he growled. "Tell Houston to get his butt up here."

She disappeared through the doorway. He pressed his thumb against the nail she had embedded in the wood, and damned his pride. He hadn't wanted her to leave. He didn't want to hear her laughter and not be part of it. He didn't want to witness her smiles from a distance.

He hadn't been able to bring himself to ask her to stay, to share the task with him, to lighten his load with her presence.

If he couldn't ask her for something as small as that, how in the hell did he think he was going to ask her to welcome him into her bed?

Chapter Ten

With the flowers wilting in his hand, Dallas walked through the house. Every room was empty. Every room except the kitchen, and there, he only found the prairie dog.

He'd come in from the range early with the thought of asking his wife to take a ride with him, and he couldn't find her.

He stalked out of the house and headed to the barn. It didn't ease his mind any to see the empty stall where Cordelia's mare should have been.

"Slim!"

His foreman came out of the back room. "Yes, sir?"

"Do you know where my wife is?"

"Yes, sir. She went to town with Austin."

"Thought she went to town with him yesterday."

"Yes, sir, she did, and the day before that as well."

Trepidation sliced through Dallas as remembered moments rushed through his mind: Austin holding Cordelia outside the general store. Austin lifting Cordelia into his arms and spinning her around at Houston's house.

Cordelia talking to Austin during meals without the aid of her topic list.

In the evening, Austin had begun to come into Dallas's office and listen to Cordelia read. Dallas would occasionally look up from his ledgers to find Austin gazing at Cordelia as though she were the most wonderful woman in the world.

Dallas hated himself for resenting Austin's intrusion. Austin had been five when their mother had died, and he'd grown up with no other women in his life. Dallas knew he shouldn't begrudge Austin the pleasure he found in Cordelia's soft voice—but he did.

"You want me to stop saddling her horse?" Slim asked.

"No," Dallas answered quickly. "No, she's free to come and go as she pleases." He tossed the flowers into the empty stall and strode back to the house.

Dusk had settled over the land before they returned.

Sitting at the head of the table in the dining room, Dallas heard their hushed laughter in the hallway. His gut clenched at the delightful sound she never made in his presence.

He forced himself to his feet when they entered the dining room, looking as guilty as two children who had sneaked away to go fishing before they'd finished their chores.

"Sorry we're late," Austin said as he pulled Cordelia's chair out for her.

Smiling shyly at Austin, she sat. Austin took his place beside her and began to ladle stew into both their bowls. "We lost track of the time."

"I figured that," Dallas said as he took his seat. "I fed your damn prairie dog."

Cordelia glanced up, then quickly lowered her gaze to her bowl of stew. "Thank you."

"It was yapping so loud I couldn't concentrate on my work," Dallas said.

"I'm sorry. I'll take her with us next time."

With us next time. The words hung heavy in the air. Dallas's stomach tightened. "How was your trip into town?"

Cordelia snapped her head up. She looked at Austin. Austin opened and closed his mouth.

"Fine," Cordelia said. "Just fine."

Dallas scraped his chair across the floor. As though consumed with guilt, Cordelia and Austin jerked back from the table.

"I'll leave you to enjoy your meal," Dallas said.

He wasn't surprised that neither of them protested.

He walked to the corral, knowing himself to be a fool. He'd asked Amelia to marry him, then he'd sent Houston to fetch her, and she'd fallen in love with his brother.

He'd married Cordelia, and he'd told Austin to keep her company. What in the hell had he expected to happen?

Reaching into his pocket, he withdrew the watch Amelia had given him as a sign of her affection when she had first arrived at his ranch. He didn't expect Cordelia to give him anything as a symbol of her affection, but he was certain she was going to leave him.

He considered arguing that too many years separated Cordelia from Austin, but he figured love didn't put a lot of stock in the passage of years. Besides, he was several years older than Cordelia and his heart didn't seem to notice.

He'd build them a house on a distant corner of his land because he didn't think his pride could tolerate seeing the two of them together knowing at one time she was supposed to be his. Then he'd see about finding himself another wife. He could run an advertisement in the newspapers back East or maybe he could—

"Dallas?" Austin's voice came from behind him. "Dallas, I need to talk to you."

He jammed the watch back into his pocket and wrapped a wall of indifference around himself. Shoving the part of himself that could be hurt back into a dark hole, he turned to face his youngest brother.

"Figured you did," he said as he crooked an elbow onto the railing of the corral.

Austin looked down and scuffed the toe of his boot into the dirt. "I don't rightly know how to say it."

"Just come straight out with it. That's usually the best way."

Austin nodded and met his brother's gaze. "Dee asked me not to say anything to you, but I figured you ought to know."

Dallas swallowed past the knot that had formed in his throat. "I appreciate that."

Austin shoved his hands into his pockets. "Remember when you took me to that circus when I was seven?"

If Austin had hoped to lessen Dallas's anger, he had succeeded. Christmas, 1867. The Haight and Chambers New Orleans Colossal Circus and Menagerie had pitched tents in San Antonio. Dallas and Houston were still recovering from the war, with little spare change clinking in their pockets, but they had wanted to give Austin a Christmas he wouldn't soon forget. Dallas couldn't stop himself from smiling at the fond memories. "Yeah, and you pestered me all day with questions. I threatened to pay that sword swallower to stick one of his swords down your throat just to shut you up."

Austin chuckled and rubbed the side of his nose. "I thought you were serious."

"The threat didn't work, though, did it?"

Austin shook his head. "Nope, and that's the way Dee is when I take her to town. She's got so many questions and everything amazes her. They never took her into town, Dallas. Never."

"But you did, and I reckon she's grateful for that."

Austin took a step closer. "I wasn't paying any attention to the questions she was asking. I was just answering them. The whole while I'm answering the questions, she's working this idea up in her head. Today, she finally gets the courage to do something about it . . . and Mr. Henderson laughed at her. What made it worse is that Boyd was there and the bastard—"

"Whoa. Hold your horses." Dallas held up his hand. "What are you talking about?"

"I'm trying to tell you what happened in town today. See, Dee figured when the railroad comes through here, people are gonna need a place to sleep. So she was thinking of building a hotel. She knew you had talked to Mr. Henderson about a loan for the cabinetmaker so she figured that was where she needed to start—by getting a loan. Yesterday she stood outside the bank all day. Couldn't get up the courage to go inside.

"Today she reaches deep down, gathers up that courage, and heads into the bank. Only Boyd is inside, and he tells her the saloon has all the spare rooms this town is ever gonna need. Then he and Mr. Henderson start to laugh. Boyd tells her that your bed is the only bed she needs to be concerned with."

"What did she do?" Dallas asked through clenched teeth.

Austin smiled. "You woulda been proud. She just thanked Mr. Henderson for his time and walked out with her head held high."

"Who else was in the bank?"

"A couple of ranchers and the teller. Anyway, she's feeling lower than a snail's belly. I've been trying to tell her funny stories to make her laugh, but that ain't what she needs. I thought maybe tonight you could sweet-talk her, make her feel special."

"Sweet-talk her?"

"Yeah, you know, say those words women like to hear. The words that make them shine brighter than a full moon."

Dallas nodded. "I'll do that."

Austin's face split into a wide grin. "I'm glad I told you. She was afraid you'd be mad at her for wanting to do something on her own."

"I'm not mad at her."

"I knew you wouldn't be." Austin backed up a step. "Reckon we ought to get to the house. She'll be wanting to read soon. I sure do like listening to her read." He turned toward the house.

"Austin?"

Austin stopped and looked back over his shoulder.

Dallas weighed his words. "Don't ever tell her that you told me what happened today."

"Oh, I won't. You just be sure you give her some good sweet-talkin'."

Dallas nodded. "I will."

SWEET-TALKING. WHAT DID he know about sweet-talking?

Not one damn thing.

Dallas pounded on the door until the hinges rattled. He heard the hesitant footsteps on the other side.

"It's Dallas! Open up!"

The door opened a crack. Dallas reined in his temper.

Lester Henderson opened the door wider. "Dallas, good Lord, you scared me to death. Is something wrong?"

"I don't know, Lester. I heard a rumor, and it's keeping me from sleeping. I'm just hoping it's not true."

Always eager for gossip, Lester Henderson stepped onto the back porch of the second floor. Like most of the newcomers to Leighton, he lived above his business and his business was the bank. "What rumor?" he asked.

"I heard my wife came into the bank and asked for a loan today."

Lester laughed with a high-pitched squeal that grated on Dallas's nerves. "Oh, that. Don't worry, Dallas, I turned her down. Boyd was there, and he explained to her the foolishness of her request. She's supposed to be giving you a son, and Boyd spelled that out loud and clear."

Dallas balled his hands into fists to keep them from circling the little weasel's throat. "Could you come out a little farther, Lester?" Dallas asked.

"Sure."

Lester walked to the edge of the porch. Dallas pointed to the far horizon. "What do you see out there, Lester?"

Lester shrugged. "Moon. Stars. Land."

"My land," Dallas said. "As far as you can see, I own it. I don't have a son, Lester. If I get gored by a bull tomorrow and die, all that land goes to my wife." Dallas tilted his head. "Come to think of it, the land already belongs to her because she honored me by becoming my wife."

He tore his hat from his head and lowered his face until he and Henderson were staring eye to eye. Lester backed up, and Dallas stalked him until the man had nowhere else to go and no choice but to bend over the railing like a sapling in the wind.

"If my wife comes into your bank, I don't want her to have to ask for a damn thing. I want you to jump out of your chair and ask her what you can do for her. If she wants a loan, then by God, you give her a loan."

"But . . . but collateral," Henderson stammered.

"I just showed you her goddamn collateral!"

"But Boyd said—"

"I don't give a damn what Boyd said or what any other member of her family says. If she wants the moon, by God I'll find a way to give it to her. Right now all she wants is a loan from you, and I'd appreciate it greatly if you'd think on her request tonight and decide in the morning that it would be in this town's best interest to give it to her."

Dallas stepped back.

Henderson straightened and puffed out his chest. "Are you threatening me?"

"No, Henderson, I'm not," Dallas said in a voice that rang out as deceptively mild. "I never threaten, but I'll give you my word that if you ever embarrass my wife like you did today, I'll build a bank next to yours and put you out of business. Wherever you go, I'll follow until the day I die, and you'll never again work in a bank, much less own one."

Dallas spun on his heel and started down the steps. He stopped and turned. "Henderson, I never want my wife to know of this conversation."

Henderson nodded mutely, and Dallas stomped down the steps. He didn't figure Lester Henderson would ever accuse him of sweet-talking.

THE FOLLOWING MORNING at breakfast, Dallas watched as his wife slowly trailed her finger over her list of topics.

"Dee?"

She looked up, disappointment etched over her features.

"You don't have to talk to me if you don't want to. I won't discuss husbandry at the table."

She nodded grimly, glanced quickly at Austin, then looked back at her notes.

Dallas could feel Austin's blue glare boring into him. Apparently, Austin had figured out that Dallas had not sweet-talked his wife last night, and it didn't sit well with him.

Cordelia shifted her gaze back to Dallas and gnawed on her bottom lip. "What would you have done if Mr. Henderson hadn't given you the loan for the cabinetmaker?"

Dallas leaned back in his chair, incredibly pleased with her question, more pleased that she wasn't planning to let Henderson or her brother stop her from reaching for her dream. He wondered what other questions she'd written on her list. "I'd go to a bank in another town, convince them to give me the loan."

"What town?"

"Fort Worth would probably be best."

"How far away is—"

A pounding on the door interrupted her question, but he had a good idea where she was headed with the questions, and he hoped she wouldn't have to travel there. "Austin, why don't you go see who's at the door?" Dallas asked.

Austin shoved his chair back and stalked from the room. A few minutes later, disbelief mirrored on his young face, he escorted Lester Henderson into the dining room.

Cordelia gracefully swept out of her chair. "Mr. Henderson, what a pleasure it is to have you in our home. Would you like me to get you some coffee while you speak with my husband?"

Dallas didn't know if he'd ever met anyone as gracious as his wife, and at that moment he was damn proud she was married to him.

Henderson turned his hat in his hand. "Actually, Mrs. Leigh, I'm here to speak with you."

Dallas scraped his chair across the floor. Henderson looked as though he'd almost come out of his skin. Dallas stood. "You can use my office. I need to check on the herd."

He walked out of the house, headed to the barn, and saddled Satan. By the time he rode the horse out of the barn, Henderson was climbing into his buggy.

"I hope you know what you're doing," Henderson snapped, his lips pursed.

Dallas smiled with satisfaction. "I wouldn't be as successful as I am today if I didn't know the value of a good investment."

"Women know nothing about business," Henderson said.

Dallas tipped his hat off his brow. "They know how to manage a home. They know how to manage a family. Why in the hell don't you think they can manage a business?"

Sputtering, Henderson slapped the reins and sent the horse into a trot, the buggy rolling back to town.

Dallas heard his wife's excited squeal as she called Austin's name.

He ignored the ache in his chest because she hadn't chosen to share her joy with him, and he pretended that it didn't matter because sooner or later, she'd have no choice.

She would have to come to him.

When she did, she'd learn that nothing in life came without a price. In order to have what she wanted, Dallas would have to get what he wanted.

AT THE GENTLE tap on his office door, Dallas turned from the window and the night sky. "Come in."

Cordelia opened the door and peered inside. "Can I talk to you for a minute?"

He heard the tremble in her voice. "Sure."

Like someone about to confront an executioner, she walked into the room and stood before his desk. She waved her hand toward his chair. "You can sit."

"Is that what you prefer?"

She gave him a jerky nod.

In long strides, he crossed the room and dropped into his chair. He planted his elbow on the desk and slowly rubbed his thumb and forefinger over his mustache. He lifted a brow.

She dropped her gaze to the floor. "I . . . uh." She cleared her throat. "I thought it would be nice if your town had a hotel. I managed to get a loan and Mr. Curtiss is drawing up the plans for the building—"

"Dee?"

She glanced up.

"You should always look a man in the eye when you're discussing business."

She visibly swallowed. "It makes it harder."

"The man you're doing business with knows that. He'll respect you for it, and he's more likely to give you what you're asking for."

"Do you know why I'm here?"

"I've got a good idea."

"And you're still going to make me ask?"

"Everything in life worth having comes with a price."

"And your price?"

Distrust and fear lurked within the dark depths of her eyes. He hated them both. "Ask."

She took a deep breath and balled her hands into fists at her sides.

"I have the money. I have someone to build it." She clenched her jaw and angled her chin. "But I need the land. When you announced that you had set aside land for a town, in my ignorance, I assumed that meant it was free for the taking. This afternoon, Mr. Curtiss explained to me that you still own the land, and that merchants must purchase the lots before he can build on them." Resignation ripped through her voice. "Without the land, I can't build the hotel."

Dallas shoved his chair back. She jumped. If he had to tie her down, he was going to make her stop jumping every time he moved.

He went to a corner and picked up a scroll. He placed it on the desk and gave it a gentle push. It rolled across the flat surface, revealing the layout of his town: the planned streets, the building lots. He set his inkwell on one end of the scroll to hold it in position and placed the lamp on the other end.

"Where do you want your hotel?" he asked.

Curiosity replaced the fear as she leaned over the map. She trailed her finger along the widest street.

"Main Street," she said quietly. "I suppose I'd want it on the same street as the bank and general store. Where will the railroad be?"

"I'm expecting it to come through at this end of town," he said, touching the southernmost point.

"What are these smaller blocks of land for?" she asked, touching a section set back from the town.

"Houses, if we get enough people moving in."

She gnawed on her lower lip. "The hotel should be near the railroad." She lifted her gaze to his. "Don't you think?"

He wasn't prepared for the shaft of pleasure that speared him. She wanted his opinion. He swallowed hard. "That's where I'd put it."

She nodded and placed her finger on a parcel of land just down from where he'd said the railroad would be. "How much would this piece of land cost me?"

He felt the glory of success surge through him. Her dream was to build a hotel. He understood dreams. His dream was to have a son. A simple trade: one dream for another. They could both have what they wanted. But without trust, without affection, the price suddenly seemed too high.

"A smile," he said quietly.

She jerked her gaze up. "I beg your pardon?"

"The price is a smile . . . like the ones you give Austin or Houston . . . or that damn prairie dog of yours."

She blinked her eyes and straightened. Then she pulled her lips back to reveal a tortured grin that more closely resembled a grimace.

The lesson learned was a painful one: he couldn't force affection. He couldn't force a smile. And he imagined if he crawled into her bed and took what was his by right, he'd feel emptier than he did now.

He dipped his pen into the inkwell and scrawled "Dee's Hotel" across the blank square on the map of his town. Then he walked to the window, placed his hands behind his back, and gazed at the moonless sky, trying to fill a void that only seemed to deepen with each passing moment.

"That's it?" she asked behind him.

"That's it."

"That block of land is mine?"

"It's yours."

"Oh, Dallas."

He turned from the window. In obvious awe, she touched the words he'd written on the map. Tears glistened in her eyes as she looked at him and smiled . . . a glorious smile that stole his breath away.

"I've never owned anything in my whole life, and now I own this little piece of land—"

"You own a lot more than that. In truth, you didn't even have to give me a smile. It was yours all along."

"I don't understand."

"When you married me, you became my partner not only in my life, but in everything—my ranch, the town . . . everything, and I became your partner."

As he'd known it would, her smile retreated like the sun before a storm.

"Then the hotel . . . it will be yours as well?"

"Ours. But I'll be a silent partner."

"What does that mean?'

"You're free to do whatever you want with the hotel. Make it into whatever you want it to be, and I'll keep my mouth shut. But if you ever want an opinion on something, I'll be here."

Sitting, she folded her hands in her lap and stared at them.

"Nothing has changed, Dee."

"Everything has changed," she said quietly. She lifted her gaze to his. "What if I want the hotel to take up two of these spaces on the map?"

He raised a brow. "Two spaces?"

She nodded. "I want it to be a grand hotel. When people pass through here, I want them to talk about it."

He walked back to the desk. "Then mark off another block."

Smiling, she dipped the pen into the inkwell and with deliberate strokes, wrote her name in a space on the map. She peered up at him. "What if I want three?"

"I have some plans for the town, too."

She leaned forward. "What are your plans?"

Her question echoed through his heart. He'd felt slighted when she hadn't shared her plans with him before, and what had he shared with her? Not one damn thing.

He sat, placed his elbow on the wooden arm of the chair, and brushed his mustache. He'd only ever told people what they needed to know in order to get the job done. He couldn't recall ever telling anyone everything he hoped for.

"Uh, well, I've got a newspaperman interested in coming to Leighton."

Her eyes widened. "A newspaper? We'll have a newspaper?"

He liked the way she'd said "we."

"Yeah, we'll have a newspaper. He'll be able to do announcements and post bulletins for people."

"What will the paper be called?"

"The Leighton Leader."

"What else?"

"A mortician."

She visibly shuddered.

"People die," he said.

She looked back at the map and traced her finger along the lines that represented streets.

"McGirk, Tipton, Phillipy . . ." Her voice trailed off, leaving the names of so many other streets unspoken. "Who did you name these streets after?"

He stopped stroking his mustache. His mind suddenly filled with the sounds of cannons, explosions, and gunfire. "Men I sent to their deaths," he said quietly. "They were boys really, more afraid of me than they were of the enemy." He lifted a shoulder. "Naming the streets after them is my way of remembering them, honoring them."

"You weren't very old during the war."

"Few soldiers were."

She scooted up in her chair. "I know so little about you."

"What do you want to know?"

"Everything." She averted her gaze as though embarrassed. "Did you know I wanted to build a hotel?"

"I'd heard the rumor."

She peered at him. "Do you think it will be successful?"

"Absolutely."

She placed her hands on the desk, fear etched within the dark depths of her eyes, but he didn't think it was fear of him.

"Dallas, I want to do something different with the hotel."

She stood and began to pace. So graceful. So elegant. He wondered if he'd ever truly watched her walk.

"What do you want to do?" he asked.

She stopped and grabbed the back of her chair. 'I want to use the hotel to bring women to Leighton."

He furrowed his brow. "What?"

She scurried around the chair, sat, and leaned forward, an excitement in her eyes, the likes of which he'd never seen. "You mentioned placing an ad to get women to come to Leighton as brides, which seems so unfair to me. A woman has to promise herself to a man she's never met—just as Amelia promised herself to you. What happens if she falls in love with someone else? Not every man will be as generous as you were. Not every man will give up his claim. Or what happens if she meets the man and doesn't like him?"

She hopped out of the chair and began pacing again. Dallas was fascinated watching her, as though he could actually see her thoughts forming.

"I want to give women a reason to come to Leighton that has nothing to do with marriage. I want to have a nice restaurant inside the hotel where men will meet to discuss business. I want women to manage the hotel and work in the restaurant. We'll bring women from all over the country here. Train them. Give them the skills they need to work in our hotel. If they happen to meet a man and get married, it won't be because they had no choice."

Her words rammed into him with the force of a stampeding bull. She'd had no choice. He wondered who she might have chosen to marry if she'd been given the choice.

She stopped pacing, placed her palms on his desk, and met his gaze. "What do you think?"

That you should have had a choice.

He held his thoughts, stood, and walked to the window. In the distance, he could hear his windmill. Behind him, he could feel Dee's tenseness as she waited for his answer.

He had not given her a choice when the decision was made that they would marry, but he could give her a choice now. He would stay out of her bedroom until she wanted him there.

Turning, he captured her gaze. "I think you're about to build an empire."

Chapter Eleven

$\mathcal{W}$ithin Dallas's office, Cordelia shifted in the chair and scribbled more notes across what had once been an unmarred sheet of paper. She was quickly discovering that building an empire was no easy task. Details abounded.

In the morning she worked quickly to clean away any evidence that they had eaten breakfast. She tidied the house and made beds.

It occurred to her one morning that if Dallas would truly become her husband, sleep in her bed, she would only have to spend time making two beds, instead of three, washing sheets for two beds, instead of three.

She'd considered discussing the arrangement with him, but she couldn't quite gather enough courage. She was certain he would want to do more than sleep in her bed, and she wasn't altogether ready for what the "more" might entail.

Although with each passing day, she found herself thinking of Dallas with increasing frequency.

After she finished her chores around the house, Austin would escort her to town. She constantly thought about Dallas as she viewed the plans that

Mr. Curtiss was drawing up. She would wonder if Dallas was tending his cattle. She would hope that a reason would surface for him to come into town as well.

It seemed their paths continually crossed. She enjoyed walking through the town with him, listening as he explained the strengths and weaknesses in the buildings or discussed the other businesses that were coming to Leighton: the sign maker, the baker, the cobbler, and the barber.

But she anticipated the evenings most of all. She would curl up in the stuffed chair in Dallas's office and discuss her plans with him: the wording of her advertisements that would bring women to Leighton to work in her hotel, the type of furniture she wanted to place in the hotel rooms, the variety of meals she wanted to serve in the restaurant.

He had offered to give her a discount on beef. She had reminded him that she didn't need a discount. As his partner, she could simply take the cattle she wanted.

He'd laughed, deeply, richly, and she had realized that she loved his laughter, loved the way he listened to her, loved the approval of her suggestions that she saw reflected in his brown gaze.

"What's bothering you?"

Cordelia looked up from the notes she'd been making regarding the restaurant. She tucked her feet more securely beneath her. "Nothing. Everything is fine."

Sitting behind his desk, Dallas narrowed his eyes. "Have you got a problem with the hotel?"

She gnawed on her lower lip. "It's not a problem really. Mr. Curtiss finished the design of the hotel . . . and it's just not exactly what I had in mind."

"Then tell him."

She shifted in the chair. "He worked so hard on the design that I hate to hurt his feelings."

"But it's not what you want. You're paying him to give you what you want. You are paying him, aren't you?"

"Yes."

"Then go into town tomorrow and tell him."

She drew Dallas's latest brand at the edge of the paper. It reminded her of a heart more than it did two *D*'s back to back. All it needed was Cupid's arrow. She drew his brand again, biding her time, wanting to ask him to go with her—

"Do you want me to go with you?"

She glanced up, drawn by the intensity of his gaze. Once she had been uncomfortable with his scrutiny. Now she recognized it for what it was: simply his way of looking at everyone, everything.

She smiled softly. "No, I can handle this matter on my own."

His gaze grew warm, and her heart fluttered like butterflies in the spring. Her answer had pleased him, and she wondered when it was that she had begun to care whether or not she pleased him.

THE NEXT MORNING, with the sun barely easing over the horizon, Dallas guided his horse through the village of tents. Someday they'd all be gone and nothing but wooden buildings would remain. People would come. His town would grow. His son would have a good future here.

He saw Tyler Curtiss standing outside his tent, his suspenders dangling as he shaved in front of a mirror strapped to the tent pole. Dallas drew Satan to a halt.

"Tyler?"

Tyler turned from the mirror and smiled broadly. "Dallas, you're out and about kinda early this morning."

Nodding, Dallas leaned on the saddle horn. "You're making good progress on the town."

"Every time I think my job is nearing completion, I get a request to design and construct another building. I have a feeling this town will be forever growing."

Dallas smiled. "I hope so. Things should boom once the railroad gets here." The saddle creaked in the predawn stillness as he shifted his weight. "Tyler, my wife is going to come by this morning. She's not happy with the plans you drew up for the hotel."

Tyler furrowed his brow. "Yesterday, she said they were fine."

Removing his hat, Dallas studied the distant horizon. With featherlight touches, the sun stroked the dawn with soft hues, much as his wife gently brought sunshine to his days. "You ever been married?"

"No, sir, can't say I've had the pleasure."

"I don't know how much of a pleasure it is. Women are contrary. When Dee says something is fine, it's not fine at all. When it's fine, she gives you a smile . . . a smile that will steal your breath away." Dallas settled his hat on his head. "When she comes to see you today, make certain you do whatever it takes to give her that smile."

Tyler nodded. "I'll do that."

"I'd appreciate it." He turned his horse.

"Dallas?"

He glanced over his shoulder.

"What should I do with the plans I drew up a few months back for the hotel you wanted to build?"

Dallas shrugged. "Do whatever you want with them. This town only needs one hotel."

CORDELIA HAD NEVER in her life been as nervous as she was now. She stood back and watched as the surveyor team pounded markers into the ground and roped off the lots where the hotel would one day stand.

Mr. Curtiss had finished the blacksmith shop and the livery. He was ready to begin construction on the hotel.

She squeezed Dallas's arm as he stood beside her, dressed much as he had been the day she married him: brown trousers, brown jacket, a brown satiny vest. He looked like a successful businessman, not the cowboy who rode in at dusk, covered in sweat and dust. He glanced at her.

"It's really going to happen, isn't it?" she asked.

His lips spread into a warm smile, a smile that touched his deep brown eyes. "Yep."

Holding Precious close within the nook of her arm, she looked over her shoulder. People were gathering behind them, watching the surveyors with interest. She could see all of Dallas's ranch hands.

She saw Houston weaving his way through the crowd, holding Maggie, her arms looped around his neck. Amelia trudged along beside him, her arm entwined through his. As they neared, Amelia released her hold on Houston and hugged Cordelia close. Precious barked. Amelia laughed.

"This is so exciting," Amelia said.

Cordelia couldn't contain her smile. "Mr. Curtiss thinks he can have the hotel completed by October."

"Four months?" Houston asked. "He thinks he'll need that much time?"

Cordelia nodded. "It's going to be a large hotel, a grand hotel." She squeezed Amelia's hand. "That's what we're going to call it. The Grand Hotel." She glanced at Dallas. "Aren't we?"

"We'll call it whatever you want to call it," he said.

Houston chuckled. "Sounds like naming a hotel is sorta like naming children."

Dallas scowled at his brother. "Ain't nothing like it at all."

In long strides, Austin walked up to Dallas and whispered something in his ear. Dallas nodded. "Good."

Austin smiled at Cordelia. "Hard to believe it's been less than three weeks since you walked into Henderson's bank. I think you work faster than Dallas when you get an idea burning."

She blushed and lowered her gaze. "I think this will help the town grow. It will give people a nice place to stay when they visit Leighton." She glanced at Amelia. "We thought we'd have a special room where the schoolteacher could live."

"That would be wonderful," Amelia said, "although much to my shame I haven't done anything to see about securing one for the town."

"I haven't helped you either."

"That'll have to be our next order of business," Dallas said.

Cordelia's breath caught when she saw her brothers striding toward her. Only Cameron smiled at her. He reached out and took her hand. "Hi, Dee, you're looking well."

She felt well, felt happy. "I wasn't expecting to see you today."

"Dallas sent word that he had an announcement to make," Boyd said. He dropped his gaze to her stomach. "Reckon we all know what that announcement is since your husband seems to think everyone cares about his business."

The animosity surprised her. She hadn't realized until this moment that she'd grown accustomed to living in a house where anger didn't always reign supreme. "Where's Father?"

"He couldn't make the trip," Boyd said.

"Is he ill?" she asked.

"Age just catching up with him."

She looked at Dallas. "I really should go see him soon."

"I'll make the arrangements."

One of the surveyors approached. "We're done."

Dallas nodded and turned his attention to Cordelia. "Do you want to walk around the edge of the property before the ceremony begins?"

"The ceremony?" Boyd asked.

With obvious satisfaction, Dallas smiled at her brother. "The groundbreaking ceremony. Our announcement involves the hotel Dee plans to build in Leighton."

Boyd visibly paled. "Hotel? You're not announcing that she's carrying your child?"

"Nope."

Boyd's eyes narrowed. "What's the matter, Leigh? Aren't you man enough to get her with child?"

Cameron shoved his oldest brother back. "That's uncalled for, Boyd."

Boyd held his shaking finger in front of Cameron's nose. "Never do that again. Never."

Cameron shook his head. "This is Dee's moment. Don't ruin it for her."

"You knew she was building a hotel?"

Cameron's gaze darted to Austin before returning to his brother. "Yeah, I knew."

"I don't give a damn about any hotel. All I care about is the land that bastard stole from us." Boyd stormed away.

Cordelia looked at her two remaining brothers. They shifted from one foot to the other as though uncomfortable.

Duncan finally grinned. "I hear there's gonna be dancing, free food, and free whiskey. I plan to stay."

"Me, too," Cameron said with less enthusiasm.

"We're glad to hear that," Dallas said. He turned to Cordelia. "A quick walk around the edge? People are getting anxious for us to begin."

She was anxious for it to end. It always came back to the land, to her giving Dallas a son.

Yet, the man who wanted the son, the man who should be angry because she had not shared her bed with him, was the one standing beside her now, walking around the property that had cost her little more than a smile.

The day she had met him, she had deemed him to be a man of little patience. Yet in the past month, he had never badgered her for what was his by right. He had patiently listened to her plans for the hotel, offered advice, and given her the chance to reach for something that she wanted.

He had asked for nothing in exchange.

"What do you get out of all this?" she asked as they rounded the first corner and walked along the side that would be the back of the hotel.

He seemed surprised as he glanced over at her. "I like to see you smile. Building the hotel seemed to give you plenty of reasons to smile."

"It's that simple?" she asked.

"It's that simple."

They walked around the next corner. "It's going to be big, isn't it?" she asked as her gaze stretched from one taut rope to the other.

"Biggest building in town."

They returned to where they had begun. Mr. Curtiss was standing at the corner, holding a shovel. Dallas and Mr. Curtiss stepped over the rope and walked to the center of the property.

Cordelia felt Amelia slip her hand around hers and squeeze gently. Houston stood behind Amelia. Maggie wrapped herself around Cordelia's legs. Austin moved in beside Cordelia and put his arm around her shoulder.

Cameron and Duncan stood off to the side. With a mixture of sadness for the family she seemed to have lost and resounding happiness for the family she had gained, she turned her attention to her husband.

He swept his hat from his head and a hush descended over the gathering. Pride rang through her heart at the sight of the man she had married standing so tall, so bold before the crowd.

She wanted the women who came to Leighton to have a choice. As for herself, she was no longer certain if she would have chosen differently if she had been given a choice.

"A little over a month ago," Dallas began, the deep timbre of his voice reverberating around him, "I had the pleasure of sharing with you— our friends and neighbors—my joy as Dee became my wife. Today, we want to share with you the beginning of what will be a landmark building in Leighton. Dee's vision for her hotel will set the standard by which all future buildings in Leighton will be judged." He held his hand toward her. "Dee, the dream is yours. The land is yours to break."

Cordelia's breath caught, her heart pounded, and her knees shook. Surely he didn't mean for her to join him in front of all these people. She stepped back and rammed into Houston's hard body.

"Go on, Dee," Houston urged her quietly, gently.

Austin squeezed her shoulder and smiled broadly. "If you can walk into the bank and ask for a loan, you can walk into your own hotel."

Her own hotel.

She looked at Amelia, whose eyes were filling with tears. "I told you," she whispered, "that given the chance, he'd worship the ground you walked on."

Cordelia snapped her gaze back to her husband. His hand was outstretched as he waited for her. She clutched Precious more closely, took a deep breath, and stepped over the rope.

The crowd clapped and cheered, Dallas's smile grew, and her shaking increased. She walked across the plot as quickly as she could and slipped her hand into her husband's, surprised to find his trembling as well.

Mr. Curtiss held the shovel toward her. "You'll need this," he said, grinning brightly.

"Give me the damn prairie dog," Dallas grumbled past his smile as he released her hand.

She handed Precious off to him and took the shovel. Mr. Curtiss helped her to position it. She tightened her hold on the handle, pressed her foot on the shovel as he instructed, and flipped aside a small portion of dirt.

She glanced at Dallas. "How big should I make the hole?"

Shaking his head, he took the shovel and handed

it to Mr. Curtiss. "That's all you need to do." He crooked his elbow. She placed her hand on his arm, and he led her toward the waiting crowd.

She clung to Dallas's arm as people surrounded her, asking her questions.

"I won't leave you," Dallas whispered near her ear.

She relaxed her fingers. No, he wouldn't leave her. Had she ever noticed how often he was there when she needed him?

"How many rooms will the hotel have?" someone asked.

Cordelia smiled. "Fifty."

"I hear it's gonna have a restaurant."

"A very nice restaurant," Cordelia assured them. "The finest food in town."

"Speaking of fine food," Dallas interjected, "we've got beef cooking near the saloon. You're all invited to enjoy it."

As people wandered away, Cordelia turned her attention to Dallas. "Why didn't you tell me I was going to have to dig a hole in front of all these people?"

"Figured it would just make you nervous, and you might decide not to come. I didn't want you to miss your moment."

Her moment.

"Mrs. Leigh?"

She turned. A young man stood before her, holding a pad of paper. "Mrs. Leigh, I'm a reporter with the Fort Worth *Daily Democrat*. Since the same railroad that touches our town will eventually touch yours, I was hoping you could spare a few minutes to answer a few questions about your hotel."

Cordelia looked at Dallas. He smiled. "Your moment."

As he walked away, she began to answer the earnest young man's questions about The Grand Hotel. She explained the fact that women would manage the hotel and work in the restaurant. When she answered his final question, she began to walk toward the other end of town where people were congregating. She could hear the sweet strains of a waltz. She saw Austin standing in the back of a wagon, playing his violin. Houston and Amelia danced, as did Becky and Duncan. Several men danced together.

"Dee?"

She stumbled to a stop and smiled at her youngest brother as she took his hand. "Cameron, I'm so glad you were here today."

"You look happy, Dee. Is Dallas treating you right?"

She glanced toward the saloon. She could see her husband leaning against the wall, Precious nestled within the crook of his arm as he talked to Mr. Curtiss.

"He treats me very well." She squeezed his hand. "You should come visit us. I think you would like Dallas if you stopped looking at him through Boyd's eyes."

Out of the corner of her eye, she caught a flash of black streaking by. "Excuse me," she said to her brother as she scurried away. "Rawley! Rawley Cooper!"

The boy staggered to a grinding halt and dropped his gaze to the dirt. She knelt in front of him.

"Hello, Rawley. I don't know if you remember me. I saw you at the general store one day."

"I 'member."

"I was wondering if you could do a favor for me."

His black gaze darted up, then down. He started digging his big toe into the dirt. She wanted to wrap her arms around him and hug him fiercely. She wondered if anyone ever had.

"I'll pay you," she said softly.

His gaze came up and stayed focused on her, but she could see the doubt and distrust swimming in his eyes.

"How much?" he asked.

"A dollar."

He bit into his bottom lip. "What I gotta do?"

"Take care of my prairie dog so I can dance with my husband."

"Fer how long?"

"Until tomorrow morning."

He narrowed his eyes. "You gotta pay me first."

"All right." She rose and held out her hand. "Let's go talk to my husband."

With his fingers curled, he reached for her hand, then quickly drew it back. "Holding hands is fer sissies."

She wondered briefly if her brothers were of the same opinion. As far back as she could remember, Cameron was the only one who had ever touched her, and then his touch had always been hesitant. She didn't want that for her children.

She walked toward the saloon with Rawley shuffling along behind her. She knew the exact moment Dallas saw her. His attention veered away from Mr. Curtiss, and although the architect and builder continued to talk, she felt as though she had Dallas's undivided attention.

As she stopped in front of her husband, Precious yipped and Dallas shifted her in his arms.

"If you'll excuse me, I want to talk with Miss

St. Claire," Mr. Curtiss said. "She's thinking of expanding her business into an emporium."

"Appreciate your help today," Dallas said.

"My pleasure." He tipped his hat toward Cordelia before walking away.

"How did the interview go?" Dallas asked.

"If I didn't sound knowledgeable, I think it's safe to say I was at least enthusiastic about the new hotel."

Precious barked again and began to squirm. Cordelia touched Rawley's shoulder, and he jerked away. She hoped she wasn't making a mistake.

"This is Rawley Cooper. He's going to watch Precious for us."

Dallas lifted a brow. "Is that so?"

Rawley jerked a nod. "But you gotta pay me. A dollar. Up front."

"That's a bargain," Dallas mumbled as he reached into his pocket and withdrew a dollar. He laid it in Rawley's palm.

Rawley looked at the coin as though he hadn't really expected to receive a dollar. He pocketed the money, held out his dirt-covered hands, and took Precious. He glanced at Cordelia. "Where you want me to meet ya tomorrow?"

"Where do you live?"

He dropped his gaze. "Around."

"We'll find you," Dallas said.

Rawley nodded and slowly scuffled away as though he carried something fragile.

"Now, why did you do that?" Dallas asked.

Cordelia turned her attention to her husband. "Precious was in the way." She stepped onto the boardwalk. Her gaze was nearly level with Dallas's. She could hear the gentle strains of another song fill the air. Her heart began to pound, her stomach to quiver. "The day we were married, you told me that it wasn't hard to dance, and that you would guide me. I was wondering if your offer was still open."

He shoved away from the wall and held out his hand. "It's always open for you."

She placed her hand in his. His palm was rough, his pads callused, his fingers long, his skin warm as his hand closed around hers. She walked with him to an area where only a few others danced.

When he placed his hand on her waist, it seemed the most natural movement in the world to place her hand on his shoulder. He held her gaze. When he stepped in rhythm to the music, she followed.

The melody swirled around her. Beyond Dallas's shoulder, the muted hues of the sky began to darken, lengthening the shadows of evening. He guided her through the waltz as easily as he had guided her toward this day.

"How did you know that I wanted to build a hotel?"

His gaze never faltered. "Austin told me about your visit to the bank."

"Did you tell Mr. Henderson to give me the loan?"

"I simply explained to him that you had collateral—"

"Your land."

"Our land. He had no reason not to give you a loan."

"And if the hotel fails?"

"It won't."

"How can you be so sure?"

His hold on her tightened as he drew her closer. Her thighs brushed against his.

"I've seen you terrified. You stayed when I have little doubt that you desperately wanted to leave. A woman with that much fortitude isn't about to let a business flounder."

"I was a fool to fear you."

He shook his head slightly. "I was the greater fool. I never should have forced our marriage. I should have taken the time to court you."

She watched as he swallowed.

"I should have given you the choice that you want to give other women."

She swayed within his arms, now knowing beyond a doubt that if he had courted her, if she had been given the choice, she would not have chosen differently.

DALLAS WAS NOT a man prone to doubts, but this evening as Dee rode beside him back toward the ranch, doubts plagued him.

Her lips were curved into a soft smile, her face serene as the moon guided them home. She seemed happy and content, more so than he'd ever seen her.

Like a hopeful litany, her words echoed through his mind: *I was a fool to fear you.*

A warm breeze blew gently over the land, and in the distance, he could hear the constant clatter of his newest windmill. He held his silence until the windmill came into view, a dark silhouette against the prairie sky.

"I want to show you something," he said quietly, hoping none of his actions tonight would put the fear back into her eyes.

She glanced over at him. "What do you want to show me?"

He brought his horse to a halt beneath the windmill. She drew her horse to a stop and smiled. "Oh, one of your ladies."

Dallas dismounted and wiped his sweating palms on his jacket before helping her off her horse.

"I've never been so far from home at night," she whispered as though someone might be lurking nearby to overhear her words.

"This is my favorite time of day," Dallas said. "I like to view it from up there."

He pointed to the top of the windmill and her eyes widened.

"How do you get up there?"

"This windmill has a ladder and a small platform." A platform he had built in anticipation of this night. He held out his hand. A warm jolt of pleasure shot through him when she placed her hand in his.

He led her to the windmill. "Just one foot at a time," he said. "Hold on to the railing. The ladder will take you to the platform at the top."

He followed closely behind her until she crawled on the platform. He climbed on after her. The platform was small, barely enough room for the two of them to stand.

Dallas had thought about this moment a hundred times, all the things he would tell her: the things he felt, the things he wanted, the dreams left unfulfilled.

He wanted her to see all that he saw: the vastness of the sky. The canopy of stars. The land that stretched out before them. In the far-off distance, he could hear the lowing of cattle. He could smell the soil, the grass, the flowers that had bloomed throughout the day.

He could smell the night. He could smell her sweet fragrance.

And he knew that no words he could utter would do justice to the magnificence that lay before them, to the future they might share. If she couldn't envision it of her own accord, he couldn't describe it so she would. If she didn't understand it, he couldn't explain it.

"It's beautiful."

Her soft voice, laced with reverence, wrapped around him, increased tenfold the majesty of all he'd acquired, all he had worked so hard to attain.

He had never felt as close to anyone as he felt to her right now, standing high above the earth, with the night surrounding them, and he somehow knew that if he had misjudged the moment, his dream would crumble into dust.

"I want a son, Dee."

She turned her head and met his gaze, and he prayed that it wasn't a trick of the moonlight that made it seem as though she harbored no fear in her eyes.

"I want a son that I can share this with. I want to bring him up here at dawn, at sunset, at midnight. As grand as all this is, I want him to know that it pales in comparison to all that he will be." He swallowed hard. "But I won't take what you're unwilling to give."

He watched her gaze slowly sweep over the land as though she were measuring its worth.

"I want to give you a son," she said softly.

His heart was thudding with such force that he was afraid he might not have heard her correctly. "You do?"

She nodded, and he could have sworn she blushed in the moonlight.

"So if I come to your room tonight, you won't be afraid?"

She shook her head. "Nervous, but not frightened."

He thought about kissing her. He thought about making love to her beneath the windmill, but he wanted everything perfect.

He wanted to give her in one night the courtship he should have given her before he ever married her.

Chapter Twelve

❧

Becky Oliver had never known terror, but she found herself fearing everything now: the rough hands, the fetid breath that stank of too much whiskey, the strong fingers clamped around her wrists holding them behind her back. His mouth missed its mark and skid across her cheek, leaving a slobbery trail.

"Duncan, stop!"

He shoved his thigh between hers. "Come on, Becky, you know you want a little kiss."

She wanted nothing of the kind, at least not from him. She wanted to scream, but she thought she might die if anyone saw her like this: pressed against the back wall of the general store with this man wrapped around her.

"Duncan, please let me go," she pleaded.

"Kiss me first."

She felt the tears threaten to surface. Somehow, she knew that he would enjoy watching the tears fall, so she held them back. "Duncan—"

"She's not interested."

She heard Austin's voice and relief swamped her. Duncan grunted and she was suddenly free of his hold. She cowered beside the boxes that lined a portion of the back wall and watched as Austin slammed his fist into Duncan's face. Duncan cried out and stumbled back.

Oh, she was glad, so glad, even though she knew whiskey had made him mean, had made him frighten her.

Austin stood with legs akimbo, his hands balled by his side, waiting . . . waiting.

"Come on, McQueen, get your ass up out of the dirt so I can hit you again."

Groaning, Duncan rolled over and came to his knees. "You broke my nose!"

Duncan looked over his shoulder, and Becky could see his blood glistening in the moonlight. She rushed from her hiding place and wrapped her fingers around Austin's arms. "Don't hit him again."

Austin snapped his gaze to hers. The anger burning in his blue eyes frightened her almost as much as Duncan had. She'd never seen Austin angry.

"He hurt you."

"No, he didn't. Not really. He just scared me."

Austin pointed his finger at Duncan. "Stay away from Becky or next time I'll kill you."

She knew without a doubt that he meant it, and that knowledge terrified her. He turned to her then, and she could see the worry etched in his face, along with the anger.

"Let me take you home," he said.

Leaving Duncan struggling to his feet, Austin walked with her to the side of the general store and followed her up the stairs. On the landing, he said quietly, "Are you all right, Becky?"

She wasn't and she had hoped to slip into the

house without his ever knowing, but his voice was filled with so much concern that she couldn't stop herself from turning to him, with the tears slipping past her defenses.

"Ah, Becky," he said softly as he welcomed her into his embrace and pressed her cheek against his shoulder.

"He said he wanted to show me something," she rasped through the thick knot in her throat. "I didn't know—"

"Shh. How could you know, sweet thing?"

"You're angry with me."

"No, I'm not." He cupped her face and tilted her head back slightly. "Well, maybe a little. Why couldn't you have danced with Cameron?"

"Duncan asked." She lifted her shoulder. "I really wanted to dance with you."

He stroked her cheek with his thumb, over and over, the anger fading from his eyes, leaving them the blue of a flame writhing within a fire. "I can't dance and make the music. Did you like the music?"

"I thought you played lovely. I would have been happy to just sit and listen to you all evening."

"You looked beautiful dancing, Becky, even if it was with Duncan. I couldn't take my eyes off you." A corner of his mouth curved up. "I could sit and look at you all night." He dipped his head slightly, and her heart sped up. "Tell me to stop, Becky, and I will. Otherwise, I aim to kiss you."

"You gonna do it proper?"

"Proper, the way you deserve."

She had dreamed about his kiss at night while she slept, beneath the blankets, and during the day while she worked, on top of a ladder stacking canned goods. But none of her dream kisses were as wonderful as the reality.

He touched his mouth tentatively to hers, briefly, then brushed his lips over hers, reminding her of the way he had tuned his violin before he had ever begun to play the first song. Testing, teasing, searching for the right sounds.

Waiting for the right moment.

Then the moment came when he settled his mouth over hers and struck a resonant chord within her heart.

DALLAS CRINGED WHEN he looked in the mirror. Like some young buck shaving for the first time, he had three tiny nicks embedded in his chin. Squinting he leaned closer, wondering if he should even out the sides on his mustache a little more.

He'd bathed and trimmed everything on him that could be trimmed: his hair, his nails, his mustache.

He'd never been so damn nervous in his entire life.

Wearing only his trousers—new trousers, never before worn—he examined himself, wondering if Dee would find him lacking. He fought the urge to squirm as his reflection glared back at him.

He jerked his shirt off the bed and slipped it over his head. He started to button it and stopped. Dee would only have to unbutton it—or he would—and his fingers were shaking so badly he didn't know if he'd be able to release the buttons without sending them flying across the room.

Better to leave it unbuttoned.

He yanked his shirt over his head and threw it on the bed. Better not to wear it at all.

They both knew why he was coming to her room. No need to pretend otherwise.

Taking a deep breath, he grabbed the bottle of wine and two glasses. He'd never gotten to open the bottle when he was married to Amelia. He had begun to fear he'd never get a chance to open it.

Only this evening Dee had told him she wanted to give him a son.

The odd thing was as much as her words had thrilled him, they'd also left him wanting. He just wasn't sure exactly what it was he wanted from her anymore.

Her smiles. Her laughter. Her feet tucked beneath her as she considered business decisions.

Her body curled against his.

He opened the door to his bedroom and the sound echoed down the hallway. Had he ever noticed how everything echoed in this house?

In bare feet, he crept toward her room, his heart thundering harder than it had when a bull had stampeded after him in his youth. He wanted to smooth down his hair and run his fingers across his mustache, but his hands were full so he simply took another deep breath and rapped his knuckles on her door.

Immediately the door opened a crack, and he wondered if she'd been waiting for him on the other side. She peered out, her brown eyes large, her smile tremulous. Then she opened the door wider and stepped back.

He walked into the room. Her lavender fragrance permeated the air, along with the lingering scent of her bath.

She clicked the door closed, and his mouth went dry. Sweet Lord, he hadn't been this nervous when he had visited a whorehouse for the first time, not really certain what to expect.

And he realized with sudden clarity that he had

no idea what to expect tonight. He only knew that he wanted to give to her as much as he had to give, wanted to ease the way for her, wanted to keep the fear out of her eyes.

He turned and looked at her. She was wearing the white gown she'd been wearing that first night. Every tiny button was captured snugly within its corresponding loop, clear up to her throat where the lace rested beneath her chin. Why did he find that bit of innocence more alluring than any half-clothed woman he'd known in his youth?

He held up the bottle and glasses. "I brought some wine. I thought it might help you relax."

She smiled timidly. "I'm incredibly nervous."

"Yeah, me, too."

Her eyes widened in awe. "Are you?"

He nodded and walked to the dresser, setting his offering down before the bottle and glasses slipped from his sweating hands. He wiped his palms on his trousers and pulled the cork. Then he filled each glass halfway.

He picked up the glasses, turned, and handed one to her. He clinked his glass against hers. "To our son."

Her cheeks turned a lovely hue of crimson, reminding him of the sunset. Staring at his chest, she touched the glass to her lips and took a small sip. She released a tiny gasp and lowered her gaze to his bare feet.

"Dee, look at me."

She lifted her eyes to his. "I'm sorry. I forgot this is business."

He took the glass from her hand and set their glasses on the dresser.

"It's hardly business." Threading his fingers through the black hair she had brushed to a velvety sheen, he braced the heels of his palms on either side of her face and lowered his mouth to hers.

He skimmed his tongue over her lips. So soft. He tasted the wine that lingered and felt the tiny quivering of her mouth beneath his, wondering if she could feel the tremors racing through him. Like a cowboy with a trick rope, he swirled his tongue over hers in a figure eight.

She took a step nearer, her gown brushing against his chest. An unexpected pleasure shot through him with a gesture that coming from her was as bold as brass.

He angled her head, running his tongue along the seam of her lips, teasing her mouth until it parted slightly. The he plunged his tongue into the welcoming abyss of warmth and flavor unique to her.

He felt her hands moving between them. He continued to plunder her mouth, waiting for the moment when her hands would touch him, his breath locked in his chest, his body straining for her touch.

But all he felt was the strange knotting and un-knotting of her hands.

He drew away from the kiss and glanced down. Raised above her knees, her gown was bunched in her fists.

"What are you doing?" he asked.

Confusion plunged into her eyes. "Boyd told me I was supposed to lift my nightgown for you. I . . . I wanted to do this right."

He slammed his eyes closed and hurled silent curses at her brother.

"I've made you angry," she said quietly.

Opening his eyes, he brushed his knuckles along her reddened cheeks. "No, you haven't made me angry, but your brother is a fool. I want you to forget everything he ever told you."

Reaching down, he pulled her gown free of her clutched fingers, watched as the white linen fell back toward her bare ankles, and wished he were a man of tender words.

He lifted his gaze to hers and could see that she was fighting the fear lurking in the corner of her heart. He cupped her face in hands that were too rough for her smooth skin. "Dee, when a man and woman come together . . . there is no right, no wrong. It's simply a matter of doing what each of us is comfortable with." He stroked his thumbs beneath her chin. "If I do something you don't like, all you have to do is tell me and I'll stop."

"And if you do something I like?"

He smiled warmly. "Then you can tell me that, too."

"How will I know what you like?"

His smile deepened. "You'll figure it out." He trailed his mouth along her throat, up her neck, until his lips were near her ear. "But I guarantee I don't want you lifting your gown for me. When I truly make you my wife, I don't want you wearing anything at all."

She gasped and stiffened. He ran his tongue along the delicate shell of her ear. "I've spent a month wondering if your body is as lovely as your face. Tonight I intend to find out."

"Are you going to be wearing anything?" she asked breathlessly.

He dipped his tongue inside her ear before taking a quick nibble on her earlobe. "I wasn't planning on it."

"Is that the way it's done?" she asked.

He lifted his head and met her gaze. "That's the

way we're gonna do it. And if it takes me all night to get you comfortable with the idea, then we'll take all night."

She smiled warmly, her large brown eyes aglow like a thousand candles burning in the night. She placed her palm on his chest, her fingers splayed just above his heart, her hand steady. The only tremors he felt were those running through his body as he held his urges in check, not wanting to frighten her. He never again wanted to see fear of him reflected in her eyes.

"I don't think it'll take all night," she whispered.

"Thank God for that," he rasped as he again took possession of her mouth.

She ran her hands up his chest, and twined them around his neck. Groaning, he wrapped his arms around her and pressed her body flush against his. Their bodies met exactly as he'd imagined it a hundred times: perfectly, the way the sky dipped down to touch the land at the horizon, blue against green, soft against hard.

He thought he could feel her heart pounding in rhythm with his, beating against the cloth that separated her body from his. Slowly, he moved his hands around to the lace that decorated her throat.

With a patience he hadn't known he possessed, he worked the first tiny button free and trailed his mouth down to press a kiss to the newly exposed flesh.

Her arms fell away from him as he worked another button free and then another, his lips following the virgin trail that the parted material revealed. Her breath hitched as his knuckles skimmed the inside swells of her breasts. He planted a fervent kiss in the valley between her breasts as his fingers gave freedom to the last of the buttons.

He straightened and slipped his hands beneath the material at her throat. He could feel the slight tremors cascading through her, and feared they had little to do with passion.

"Look at me. Dee."

Her eyes met his. "I think Boyd's way was easier," she whispered.

"His way would have cheated us both. I give you my word on that." He raised his hands to cup her cheeks. "But I won't force you to share your body with me."

She pressed her fingers to her lips, tears welled in her eyes, and his heart sank. Boyd's way may have been easier but he'd be damned before he'd only know a portion of her when he wanted to know all of her, from the top of her head to the tips of her toes, inside and out.

"Share?" she asked. "I never thought of this as sharing." She lowered her hands and smiled softly. "It's not so frightening when I think of it as sharing."

"I want to know all of you, Dee. Not just your face and the shape of your toes, but all of you." He glided his hands down her face, her neck, and along her shoulders. Then he slipped the parted material off her shoulders.

The gown slid down her body and pooled at her feet, taking his breath with it. He scooped her into his arms and carried her to the bed.

Gently he laid her down. He began to unbutton his trousers. Her almond-shaped eyes rounded.

"Don't be afraid, Dee."

"I won't be," she said.

"You can close your eyes if you want."

"Don't you think I've wondered what you look like?"

He suddenly wished he'd doused the flame in the lamp, that the room was clothed in darkness. Being self-conscious wasn't something he was accustomed to feeling, but after putting her through the ordeal of baring her body, he couldn't very well deny her the chance to see him. Holding her gaze, taking a deep breath, he dropped his trousers.

"I won't hurt you," he said, his voice low.

"I know."

Her gaze dipped down, then shot back up to his.

"Don't be afraid," he pleaded gently.

"I'm not afraid."

He eased onto the bed. She jumped when his thigh touched hers.

Cupping her face with his palm, he placed his mouth near her ear. "I can't stand it when you're afraid of me, Dee."

"I'm just nervous."

He trailed his mouth along her neck and dipped his tongue into the hollow at the base of her throat. She tasted fresh, pure, and unused—unlike any woman he'd ever tasted.

"Don't be nervous," he said.

He lowered his face until his mouth touched the swell of her breast. She gasped. Without moving his mouth, he glanced up to find her watching him. He moved lower. His tongue circled her nipple.

"Dallas?"

"Shh. Every night I dreamed of tasting you." He closed his mouth around the taut bud and suckled gently.

Closing her eyes, she moaned. He skimmed his mouth over the valley between her breasts and swept his tongue over her. He glided his hand along her stomach, a stomach as flat as the prairie.

Months from now, it would swell, swell with the son he might give her tonight.

He nestled his hand between her thighs, and when she might have protested, he covered her mouth with his, his tongue delving deeply, devouring her sighs, her moans.

Not until she twisted her body toward his, did he give himself the freedom to move his body between her thighs. Then as gently as the wind blew across the plains, he eased his body into hers.

She stiffened and he held still, knowing as fact what he'd only before known as rumor. He had no choice but to hurt her.

"I'm sorry, Dee," he rasped as he blanketed her mouth with his, plunged deeply, and swallowed her cry.

Cordelia wrapped her arms more tightly around him, the plea for forgiveness she heard in his voice bringing tears to her eyes. He stilled above her, his body taut. He continued to kiss her, only to kiss her, as though he couldn't get enough of her.

His mouth blazed a scorching trail along her throat. "It'll get better, Dee."

She plowed her fingers through his hair, cradling his head, turning his gaze toward hers. "I want this," she whispered. "I want to give you a son."

He released a guttural sound low in his throat, and she felt his chest vibrate against her breasts. He returned his mouth to hers, kissing her deeply, his tongue plunging, sweeping, caressing.

He moved against her, slowly, almost hesitantly. The pain receded, and a warmth deep inside her began to unfurl.

He slid his hand beneath her and lifted her hips. "Follow me, Dee," he pleaded in a ragged voice near her ear.

As though she had any other choice. He raised himself above her, his thrusts growing deeper, faster. She watched the shadows within the room play over his chiseled features.

And then as he had done from the beginning, he began to guide her toward the sunlight. To a place where no shadows hovered. She cried out his name as a myriad of sensations exploded within her.

Dallas felt Dee's body tighten around him as she arched beneath him. Pressing deeply, he followed where she had gone.

Glory had never felt so sweet.

DALLAS AWOKE. HE had turned down the flame in the lamp before he'd fallen asleep beside Dee. Now only moonlight spilled in through the parted drapes. He rolled to his side and reached for her.

All he found was the fading warmth of her body. Squinting through the shadows, he saw her standing beside the window, peering into the night, her arms wrapped around herself.

He eased out of bed and joined her. "Dee, are you all right?"

She glanced at him and smiled timidly. "I just wanted to hold it."

"Hold what?"

"The baby you gave me tonight."

He trailed his fingers along the curve of her cheek. "I might not have given you a baby."

She furrowed her brow. "But we—"

"It doesn't always happen the first time."

"Then what do we do?"

"Well, we have two choices. We can wait and see if you have your woman's time or"—he smiled warmly—"we can assume you're not carrying my son and we can keep trying. The choice is yours."

She averted her gaze, and his heart sank. "You shouldn't feel any pain the next time. It hurt tonight because you were a virgin."

She nodded quickly. "I think we should wait and see."

He'd given her the choice and she'd taken it. He didn't know which hurt worse, his pride or his heart.

"Fine, then."

He walked to the bed and snatched his trousers off the floor. "You just let me know."

He strode from the room, closed the door, and headed for his cold empty bed. He wished he'd bedded her as Boyd had suggested.

It'd be a hell of a lot easier to stay away from her if he didn't know how perfectly her body aligned with his, how snugly she fit around him, how wonderful she felt.

Chapter Thirteen

*C*ordelia wondered how in the world a wife looked at her husband the morning following the night that they had made love.

How did she meet his gaze without remembering the hint of wine that had lingered on his lips, the bronzed shade of his skin, the muscles that had tensed as he'd risen above her, the sweat that had beaded his throat and chest as he'd rocked against her, the groans, moans . . .

She splashed more cold water on her face, trying to drown the images of Dallas's clenched jaw and his smoldering gaze.

She couldn't face him. She would simply stay in her room until she knew if she was carrying his son. She would . . . miss out on so much of life.

Last night had been an unexpected gift. It had been unlike anything she had witnessed between her parents. It had not resembled anything Boyd had hinted at.

The knock resounded against her door. She hoped it was Austin, but even as she strolled across the room, she recognized the steady staccato rap as belonging to her husband.

She bundled more snugly within her wrapper and opened the door. His gaze darted around the door frame before finally settling on her, and she wondered if he found it as difficult as she did to speak of mundane, inconsequential things after the intimacy they had shared.

"You didn't come down to eat breakfast," he said gruffly. "I just wanted to make sure you were all right."

She couldn't bring herself to admit that she experienced a slight tenderness when she walked. "I'm fine. Just fine."

He narrowed his eyes. "Are you hurting?"

The heat flamed over her cheeks as she lowered her lashes. "A little."

"I'm sorry for that. I'll . . . I'll do what I can to make it better next time."

She dared to lift her gaze. "If there is a next time. Maybe we were lucky last night."

If she didn't know him as well as she did, she would have thought she'd hurt his feelings from the expression that had flitted across his face.

"Yeah, maybe so," he said. He shifted his stance. "Are you going into town to get your damn prairie dog or do you want me to fetch her?"

The brusqueness in his voice hurt more than a dull-bladed knife plunged through her heart. After his abrupt departure last night, she had feared that she had somehow disappointed him. Now, she knew without a doubt that she had. She swallowed her tears. "I'll fetch her."

"Fine."

He turned on his heel, took two long steps, halted, and glanced over his shoulder. "I need to talk with Tyler today. I'll ride into town with you if you have no objection."

Like a pebble thrown onto still waters, the joy rippled through her. "I'd like that. It'll just take me a few moments to get ready."

"Take your time. I'll saddle our horses."

She slipped into her room, pressed her back against the closed door, and splayed her fingers over her stomach. She wanted to give to Dallas as much as he'd given her. If only fortune had smiled on them last night.

Dallas had shared so much of himself with her, had given her such immense gratification, that she didn't see how he could not have given her a child as well.

As DALLAS RODE beside Dee, he took pleasure in the smallest of things: the graceful slant of her back as she sat her horse, the loose strands of hair that toyed with the wind, the anticipation that sparkled within her eyes as they neared town.

Dallas had decided in the early hours of the morning, as sleep eluded him, that he would steer clear of his wife until she knew whether or not they had *gotten lucky*.

That resolution had lasted until dawn's fingers crept into his room, and he awoke alone with the thought of a day not shared with Dee stretching out before him.

He couldn't deny that he wanted to be in her bed every night, buried deeply inside her, but he also recognized that he wanted more than that.

He wanted her warm smiles at breakfast, her laughter as she galloped across the prairie on Lemon Drop, the squeeze of her hand, the joy in her eyes, her soft voice when she spoke to him.

If he couldn't share her nights, he had decided

sitting at the breakfast table with no one but Austin for company that he would content himself with sharing her days and evenings.

She fairly stood in the saddle as the site for the hotel came into view.

"Oh, Dallas, they've started building it."

"Of course they have. That's why you broke the ground for them yesterday."

"Still, I didn't think it would happen so fast."

She turned to him with such a radiant smile that it was all he could do not to reach across and plant a sound kiss on her mouth.

"Can we go in closer and watch?"

"It's your hotel, Dee. You can hammer the nails into the wood if you want."

"Can I?"

"Sure."

As they brought their horses to a halt, Tyler Curtiss left the throng of workers, smiling broadly. "Morning!"

Before Dallas could dismount and assist his wife, Tyler was enjoying the privilege, his hands resting easily on Dee's waist.

Jealousy, hot and blinding, shot through Dallas like molten lead, catching him off guard. Even when he'd suspected Houston had harbored feelings for Amelia, he'd never felt jealous. Anger, certainly, but nothing that made him want to snatch a man's arm off simply because he'd helped his wife dismount.

Tyler stepped away from Dee and waved his hand in a wide circle. "What do you think?"

"It's wonderful. I can't believe you already have a portion of the frame up."

"The bonus Dallas offered the men if they get the hotel finished within three months had the men sawing and hammering at daybreak," Tyler explained.

Dee turned her attention to Dallas. He shifted his stance, uncomfortable with her scrutiny.

"You're paying them a bonus?" she asked.

"Figured the sooner they finished, the sooner you could get your ladies here, get them trained."

Tyler looked as though a good strong wind might blow him over. "What ladies?"

"Dee plans to have women managing her hotel and lady waiters serving food in the restaurant."

"Lady waiters?" He grinned crookedly. "You wouldn't have had to pay a bonus if you'd told the men that."

"These are respectable women," Dallas said, "not whores. Any man who doesn't treat them properly will answer to me."

"Marriageable women?" Tyler asked.

Dee glanced quickly at Dallas, then at Tyler. "They're not coming with the express purpose to marry, but I expect a few of them might decide marriage is in order."

"Where are they going to live?"

"In the rooms we're putting above the restaurant."

"Then I need to get the men back to work and get this hotel finished."

Dee stepped forward. "Mr. Curtiss?"

He spun around. "Yes, ma'am."

"Can I hammer a nail into place?"

"Yes, ma'am. You can do anything you want. Women waiters. Who would have thought . . ."

Standing back, Dallas watched as his wife confidently walked around the construction site, greeting each man individually. She hardly resembled the woman who had stood in his parlor, hesitant to pledge herself to him.

He wondered if she ever looked at the men she was coming to know and wished she had been given the opportunity to choose the man who would be her husband.

A man handed her a hammer while another gave her a nail. Two other men held a board in place. She pounded the nail into the wood, satisfaction spreading over her lovely features.

He wondered if she might have invited another man to return to her bed last night, if once with Dallas was enough; if once with another man might have never been enough.

He despised the doubts that plagued him because he would never know if given the choice, she would have chosen another.

SQUATTING IN THE tall prairie grasses, Rawley Cooper held the prairie dog close and watched as the lady walked through the skeleton of the newest building.

She was the most beautiful thing he'd ever seen. He figured she looked like an angel—if angels existed. He harbored a lot of doubts about things like angels and heaven . . . and goodness. But the lady made him want to believe.

She stepped through a hole in the frame and backed up a few steps, holding her arms out, as though she couldn't believe how big it was.

Then she turned, smiled softly, and began walking toward him.

His heart started beating so hard that he could hear it between his ears, and it hurt to take anything other than a little breath. He stood, clutching the critter close against him. It yelped and struggled to get free, but he held it tight.

"Hello, Rawley Cooper."

She had the sweetest voice. He wished he had a hat so he could tip it at her like he'd seen some men do yesterday.

She knelt in front of him. She smelled like she'd brought a whole passel of flowers with her, but he couldn't see that she was holding or wearing any. She took the prairie dog out of his arms. "How's Precious?"

"Fine."

Her smile grew. "I appreciate your watching her for me."

He wanted her to hug him the way she was hugging the prairie dog, but he knew she wouldn't, knew no one ever would. He backed up a step. "I gotta go."

As fast as his legs would churn, he ran toward the buildings where he could hide in the shadows.

SITTING IN A rocking chair on the veranda, Cordelia closed her eyes and listened as the music circled her on the wind. The crescendo rose, grew bolder, louder until she could envision a man galloping across the plains, dust billowing up behind him . . .

"Dallas," she said softly and peered through one eye at Austin.

Smiling broadly, he stilled the bow. "Yep."

She closed her eye. "Give me another one."

Dallas had escorted her home and then gone to check on his herd. Austin had joined her on the veranda, the violin tucked beneath his chin as he played tunes of his own creation, melodies that he based on the characteristics of people whom he knew.

She had guessed every song correctly so far—Houston, Amelia, Maggie, Dallas—but this melody was different. It carried no pattern. Strong for one moment, weak, weak, growing weaker with each note.

She opened her eyes, jumped to her feet, rushed to the edge of the veranda, and waved at her brother as he approached. "Cameron!"

"That's right," Austin said as he stopped playing.

Cordelia jerked her head around. "What?"

"That worthless song was Cameron." He shot to his feet and turned toward the house.

"Austin!" Cameron cried as he brought his horse to a halt and dismounted.

Austin swung around. "What?"

Cameron placed a foot on the step, then returned it to the dirt as though he wasn't certain if he was welcome. His gaze darted to Dee, then back to Austin. "I know you're angry."

"Damn right, I'm angry. When I can't be with Becky, you're supposed to take care of her for me. That's what friends are for."

Cameron blushed beneath his hat. "She was dancing with my brother. How was I supposed to know—"

"You should have known, that's all. The minute he took her off to the shadows you should have known. She won't be seventeen until next month. Duncan has to be on the far side of thirty—too old and too experienced for her."

Cordelia stepped cautiously across the porch. "What happened?"

"Nothing happened," Austin said, "because I stopped it." He pointed his bow at Cameron. "And you can tell your sorry excuse for a brother that if he touches her again, I'll kill him."

"Think he figured that out when you broke his nose."

"You broke Duncan's nose?" Cordelia asked in shock.

"I would have broken his whole face, but Becky stopped me." Austin stalked into the house.

Cameron plopped onto the step, planted his elbow onto his thigh and his chin against his fist. Cordelia sat beside him and took his hand.

He turned his palm over and threaded his fingers through hers before looking at her with such a baleful expression that she nearly wept.

"You ever wonder how our family came to be the way it is? Pa ain't feeling poorly. He's drunk most of the time. Boyd's got so much hatred in him that he gets downright ugly for no reason. I think Duncan's straddling a fence. He can't decide whether to set out on his own or follow Boyd."

"What did he do last night?"

"Took Becky out behind the general store and tried to force his affections on her. Austin was playing music for folks—" Cameron shook his head. "And I was a girl."

"A girl?"

"Yeah, there ain't enough girls around so we had to draw bandannas out of a hat. If we pulled a red one, we had to tie it around our sleeve and be the woman. I nearly got my boots danced off."

She pressed her cheek against his shoulder. "Is that why you weren't watching Becky? Too busy dancing?"

"Maybe."

She rubbed the back of his hand, remembering the many times she'd done so as a child, wondering now when he had acquired the hand of a man. Even relaxed the veins bulged, the muscles appeared strong.

"Are you happy, Dee?"

Sighing, she closed her hand around his. "Yes, I am. Dallas is . . . fair."

He jerked his head back. "Fair?"

"I don't know if I can explain it. He never expects more of his men—of anyone—than he's willing to give. He's up before dawn, working, and he labors into the night. He talks to me, but more he listens. I don't know if I've ever had anyone truly listen to what I had to say."

"Do you love him?"

She shrugged and spoke as wistfully as her brother had only moments before. "Maybe."

She glanced up at the pounding hooves of an approaching rider. Dallas drew his horse to a halt beside Cameron's.

Cameron leapt off the steps. "I need to go," he said, bussing a quick kiss across Dee's cheek.

"Can't you stay for supper?" she asked.

"No, I—"

"Your sister wants you to stay," Dallas said, his voice echoing over the veranda.

Cameron nodded quickly. "Then I'll stay."

"Doesn't anyone in your family eat?" Dallas asked as he watched Cameron and Austin ride away from the ranch, heading for the saloon in town. The hostility between the two that he'd first noticed when they'd sat for dinner had abated during the meal. "Your damn prairie dog eats more than he does."

"He was just a little uncomfortable—"

Dallas turned toward her and raised a dark brow.

She dropped into the rocking chair and folded her hands in her lap. "You terrify him."

Dallas hitched a hip onto the railing. He needed a porch swing with a bench that wasn't too wide so he could sit next to Dee and enjoy the evening breeze as night moved in. As soon as the cabinet maker set up shop, Dallas would order one, specially made with his new brand carved into the back.

"Reckon you understand that feeling."

She smiled. "I also know what it is *not* to fear you."

He couldn't argue with that. If she still feared him, maybe she wouldn't have been so quick to kick him out of her bed.

He liked the sight of her sitting on his veranda. It felt right, like the breeze that turned his windmill. The gentle wind that blew her little chimes.

Reaching up, he touched the various lengths of barbed wire that Dee had strung together and hung from the eaves of the veranda, the eaves of the various balconies. They clinked in the wind. She had touched his life with an abundance of small gestures.

"Walk with me," he said.

She rose and followed him down the steps. In companionable silence, they strolled toward the setting sun.

He thought about taking her hand, but after last night, he wasn't exactly sure where he stood, and it would gouge his pride if she didn't welcome his touch.

He had spent thirty-five years sleeping alone, and suddenly he desperately wanted something that he couldn't even put a name to: the filling of an emptiness that he'd discovered within himself last night only after it had overflowed with contentment as he'd lain in her bed, holding her within his arms, listening to her soft breathing.

He almost found himself hoping that he hadn't given her a son.

"I'M NOT CARRYING your son."

Dallas snapped his head up and looked across the table at his wife, her gaze locked on her cold eggs. Austin had left only a few moments before, leaving a heavy silence in his wake, a reticence shattered by her words.

"Are you sure?"

She gave a brisk nod. "I knew several days ago. I just thought it would be better to wait until . . . until now to tell you." Her gaze darted up, then down, and her cheeks flamed red.

He stood and walked to her end of the table, a thousand sentiments thundering through his mind like stampeding cattle. He wanted to kneel beside her, take her hand, kiss her brow, her nose, her chin. He wanted her to look at him, but she just stared at the damn eggs so he spoke words that conveyed little of what he was feeling.

"I'll come to your bed this evening then, if that's agreeable to you."

She nodded brusquely. "I'm sorry."

"Maybe we'll have better luck tonight."

"I hope so."

With a purpose to his stride, Dallas stormed from the house, yanked Satan's reins off the corral post, mounted the black stallion, and kicked him into a gallop. He rode fast and hard over the plains until his brother's house came into view. The past ten days had been hell: wanting to hold Dee, knowing she had no interest in his touch.

It was strange but he had to admit he wasn't disappointed that Dee wasn't yet carrying his son.

He still desired a son, but the urgency of his dream had lessened. What he wanted now was a few more nights stretched out in Dee's bed, with her nestled against him.

Houston was working with a mustang in the corral when Dallas drew his horse to a halt at the house and dismounted.

Amelia sat on the porch, churning butter. Maggie scrambled to her feet and ran down the steps. She squealed as Dallas lifted her toward the clouds.

"I see freckles popping out," he said.

"No!" she cried as she rubbed her nose. "Kiss 'em off! Kiss 'em off!"

He obliged her by quickly raining kisses over her face until she giggled. Lord, he loved her fragrance. She smelled of flowers dug from the earth, kittens, and sweet milk. Her innocence always humbled him.

She crinkled her nose. "Did you git me a boy to play with?"

"Not yet. I'm still working on it."

"Where's he gonna come from?"

Dallas jerked his gaze to Amelia. Shaking her head, she smiled.

Dallas slipped a lemon drop out of his pocket and handed it to his niece. "Why don't you go suck on this for a while?"

"I don't got a sad."

"I do and I need to talk to your ma about it."

He set Maggie on the porch. She plopped the candy into her mouth and began to suck vigorously. Dallas removed his hat, draped an arm over the porch railing, and studied Amelia. He thought she looked pale.

"How are you feeling?" he asked.

"Just a little sick in the mornings, but it'll pass."

"You gonna give Houston a son this time?"

"He's partial to daughters."

"It's a wonder to me that the two of us are related."

"You and Houston are more alike than you think."

He shook his head. "With his skill with horses, he could have himself a thriving business. I'd never settle for less."

"It's not a question of settling for less. It's a matter of knowing what you want and finding contentment in that," she said softly.

"Do you have all you want?"

"As a matter of fact, I think we do. Would you like to tell me about your sad?"

"It's not a sad really. I just said that for Maggie's benefit."

Amelia angled her head as though she didn't believe him. Damn the woman, she'd always seen and figured out too much. He turned his hat in his hands, studying it, searching for the right words.

"Do you remember when we were married?" he asked.

Amelia smiled warmly. "A woman isn't likely to forget her first marriage."

"When I kissed you . . . did you like it?" he asked gruffly.

She glanced up quickly as though the answer rested within the eaves of the porch before returning her gaze to his. "I thought it was nice."

"Nice? The weather is *nice*. A kiss should be—" He stopped abruptly at the flush racing up her cheeks. "What about when Houston kisses you?"

Her blush deepened. "My toes curl."

"Is that why you chose him over me?" The words were spoken before he could take them back. Amelia had always had a way of making a man say what was on his mind. It had charmed and aggravated him at the same time.

She rose to her feet, crossed the porch, and wrapped her hand around his. "When it comes to the heart, choice is seldom involved. I don't know why I fell in love with Houston and not with you. I only know that I did."

"I don't begrudge you that," he said.

She squeezed his hand. "I know you don't."

"I just . . . damn." He forced the bitter words past his tight throat. "I don't know how to please Dee in bed . . . and I want to."

"That's the first step, isn't it? Wanting to please her?"

"Apparently, it's a damn little first step. What does Houston do when he kisses you?"

"I don't know. He just kisses me. Maybe you should ask him."

He glanced over his shoulder. Houston was slipping through the slats of the corral. Dallas had never in his life asked another man's opinion on anything. It stuck in his craw that he was having to ask now—especially about something as intimate and personal as bedding his wife.

"I appreciate your being honest with me," he told Amelia.

She patted his shoulder. "Go talk to Houston."

His stomach reeling worse than the blades of a windmill when the sucker rod had snapped in two, Dallas approached his brother.

"What brings you out today?" Houston asked as he buttoned his shirt.

Dallas shoved down his pride. "How do you kiss Amelia?"

Houston's fingers stilled over the last button, and he furrowed his brow. "What?"

Dallas heaved a deep sigh of frustration. "Amelia says when you kiss her, you make her toes curl."

Houston's mouth split into a distorted grin that moved one side of his face while leaving the scarred side immobile. "She said that, did she?" He peered around Dallas and looked in the direction of the porch where his wife had taken up churning butter again.

Irritated, Dallas stepped in front of him. "Yeah, she said that. So how do you kiss her?"

Houston shrugged. "I just sorta latch my mouth on to hers like there's no tomorrow."

"That's it? Don't you do something special?"

"Like what?"

"If I knew I wouldn't be asking!"

Houston narrowed his eye. "I learned how to kiss watching you. How could you forget how to do it?"

"I didn't forget, but I only ever kissed whores except for Amelia." He grimaced as her description of his kiss resounded through his head. "She says I kiss nice." He stepped forward and crossed his arms over the top rail of the corral. "Nice, for God's sake. I'm surprised Dee didn't gag."

Houston eased up alongside him. "Maybe it has nothing to do with the way you kiss her. Maybe it has everything to do with what you're feeling when you kiss her."

Dallas shifted his gaze to his brother. "What do you mean?"

Houston rubbed the scarred side of his face, his fingers grazing his eye patch. "You'll get angry if I tell you."

"No, I won't."

"Give me your word."

"You got it."

Houston released a deep breath. "The first time I kissed Amelia, we had just crossed that flooded river—"

"You kissed her before you got to the ranch?"

"You said you wouldn't get angry."

"I'm not angry, I'm aggravated. I trusted you—" Dallas reined in his temper. Five years ago, he'd made a decision that had left him without a wife. He didn't plan to repeat his mistake. "Finish your explanation."

Houston gave his throat a sound clearing as though contemplating the wisdom of his words. "Well . . . I was furious because she'd jumped into the river to save me, I was damn grateful she hadn't drowned, and it hit me harder than a bucking mustang that I loved her. I couldn't tell her so I tried to show her. I poured everything I felt into that kiss, and I've been kissing her that way ever since."

"And making her toes curl."

Houston smiled broadly. "Apparently so."

Dallas shoved himself away from the corral. "Thanks for the advice."

"Maybe in time, once your feelings for Dee deepen—"

"That's my problem, Houston. I think I've fallen in love with her and I've got no earthly idea how to make her love me."

Chapter Fourteen

Dallas stood outside Dee's room. He had decided that if he was only going to have one night with her each month, he was going to make the best of it.

He wouldn't leave her bed this time until dawn eased over the horizon, and if she didn't want him to make love to her again, he'd content himself with simply holding her within his arms through the night.

He knocked on the door and waited an eternity for her to open it. He stepped into the room and slammed the door.

"You're early," she said as she drew the brush through her silken black hair.

"Didn't see any point in waiting." He took her in his arms and latched his mouth onto hers like there was no tomorrow, wishing to God that there would be, that her toes would curl, and she would want him in her bed every night.

Her brush clattered to the floor, and she wound her arms around his neck tighter than the noose on an escaping calf. She pressed her body flush against his, and her soles crept over his toes.

He groaned, she moaned, and need rushed through him like a raging river. Holding her close with one hand, his mouth devouring hers, he used his other hand to release the buttons on her gown, hearing several clink as they hit the floor.

He pulled down her gown and bathed in the glorious sight of her bared body as he yanked off his trousers. He lifted her into his arms and carried her to the bed. He laid her down, then draped his body over hers, raining kisses over her face, her throat, her breasts.

He touched her with his hands, his mouth, his eyes, all the while marveling at her beauty, the pink glow of her skin, the deep brown of her eyes.

When he joined his body to hers, he heard no sharp intake of breath, no cry of pain, only a sigh of wonder. He rocked his hips until her sighs became gasps and her body writhed beneath his. He thrust harder, deeper, reveling in the moment when her soft voice echoed his name and she shuddered within his arms.

With a guttural groan, he threw his head back, clenched his teeth, and with a final thrust hurled himself into an abyss of pleasure.

Breathing heavily, he sank onto her quivering body. He could still feel her body pulsing around him. He pressed a kiss to her throat, her chin, her cheek . . . and tasted the salt of her tears.

Self-loathing replaced the blissful replete. He hadn't given her any of the tenderness he'd planned. He'd charged into this room like a rampaging bull, with one thought, one purpose on his mind: burying himself as deeply and as swiftly as he could into her glorious warmth until they were so close that a shadow couldn't have slipped between them.

She would share her body with him once a

month. Instead of savoring the moment, he had
taken her offering and used it as quickly as light-
ning flashed against the sky.

He pressed his lips against the corner of her eye
where her tears glistened, fresh and warm. "I'm
sorry, Dee," he rasped. "I didn't mean to hurt you."

"You didn't hurt me," she whispered.

He lifted his head and met her gaze. He could
see the pain he'd caused swirling within the dark
depths of her eyes. He might not have harmed her
physically, but he had little doubt he'd bruised
her woman's heart, the part that longed for more
than a man satisfying his lust. He threaded his
fingers through her hair. "I did hurt you, and I
regret that."

She shook her head. "No, you didn't hurt me. It
was wonderful."

Wonderful? She thought that hasty mating was
wonderful? "Then why are you crying?"

She touched her trembling fingers to his jaw.
"Because it always hurts you so much."

He stared at her, unable to make sense of her
words. "What?"

Her cheeks flamed red as she lowered her lashes.
"I watch you," she confessed, her voice barely above
a whisper. "You grunt and groan. Your muscles
tense and strain. You clench your teeth." She lifted
her lashes. "The agony must be unbearable. Is that
how Nature evens things out? Since childbirth is ex-
cruciating, women receive a gift of pleasure while
making the baby and men only receive pain?"

"You thought I was in pain?"

She nodded shyly. Hope flared within him like
the crude skyrockets he and Houston had made
out of carpet scraps as boys.

"Is that why you wanted to wait and see if you

were carrying my son? To spare me the suffering of trying when it might not be necessary?"

She trailed her fingers along his cheek, her thumb brushing over his mustache. "I can't stand to see you hurting like that."

"Oh, God." He flopped onto his back, dropped one arm over his eyes, and burst out laughing. His shoulders shook forcefully, and the bed trembled with his outburst.

"What's so funny?"

Fighting to stop his laughter, he peered at Dee's concerned face. She had risen on an elbow, her black hair a silken curtain draped over her shoulders. Wearing a broad smile, he reached out, wove his fingers through her hair, and brought her sweet lips closer to his. "You're precious, you know that? So damn precious."

He brushed a light kiss over her tantalizing mouth. "I wasn't in pain."

Her dark brown eyes widened until they were larger than any full moon that had ever guided his journey through the night. "Not at all?"

"No, quite the opposite in fact."

He eased her onto her back, tucking her body beneath his, unable to wipe the grin off his face. "So Nature gave you no trade-offs."

"That hardly seems fair." She smiled warmly, her blush creeping beneath the sheets she'd drawn up to cover her breasts. "But I'm glad."

His grin slipped away as he swallowed. "Does that mean you wouldn't mind trying again? Just in case we didn't get lucky?"

Burying her face against his throat, she nodded and pressed a kiss just below his Adam's apple.

Joy shot through him. He leaned back, cupped her cheek, and lowered his mouth to hers, kissing her deeply as he worked the sheet aside so he could feel the length of her limbs pressed against his.

Several long minutes later, he dared to peer down at her feet. Distracted, he slid his mouth across her chin.

"What are you doing?" she asked.

Grimacing, he considered returning his mouth to hers and kissing her until she forgot the question and his strange behavior, but he had to know the truth. Dammit, he had to know. "Amelia told me that her toes curl when Houston kisses her. I was just trying to see if your toes curl when I kiss you."

She turned a lovely shade of rose and rolled her shoulders toward her chin. "My whole body curls when you kiss me."

"Your whole body?"

She nodded quickly. "Every inch."

"Well, hell," he said as he settled his mouth greedily over hers with plans to keep her body tightly curled for the remainder of the night.

"SUSAN REDD," DEE said.

Dallas glanced up from his ledgers. Dee was sitting in his office, curled in her chair, a stack of letters on the table beside her. "Susan read what?" he asked.

She threw her head back and laughed. Lord, he loved her laugh, the ivory column of her throat, the glimmer of joy in her eyes.

"Susan Redd, R-E-D-D. That's the name of the woman I'm thinking of hiring to manage the hotel. She runs a boardinghouse back East, which I think gives her wonderful experience. Don't you agree?"

He planted his elbow on the desk and ran his thumb and forefinger over his mustache. A small thrill always raced through him when she asked his opinion, when she shared a corner of her dreams with him. "What I think . . . is that we need to go to bed."

Her eyes widened, not with fear but with wonder and anticipation. "Dallas, it's not even dark yet."

He scraped his chair across the floor, brought himself to his feet, and stalked toward her. "I made love to you this morning, and it wasn't dark then either."

"That was different. We hadn't gotten out of bed yet."

"A mistake I can remedy." He took the letter from her fingers, tossed it onto the table, and scooped her into his arms.

Laughing, she nuzzled her nose against his neck as he carried her out of his office. The front door opened and Austin sauntered into the house.

"Where are you going?" Austin asked.

"To bed," Dallas said as he started up the stairs.

"What about supper?"

"Go see the cook."

"Go SEE THE cook," Austin said. "That's what Dallas said. Then he and Dee start giggling like a couple of coyotes drunk on corn whiskey."

Houston looked across the table at Amelia and smiled. "So you decided to come help yourself to our meal?"

Austin shrugged. "Better than waiting on those two. They might never come back downstairs." He winked at Amelia. "Besides, Amelia's meals taste better than the cook's."

Reaching around the pot of beans, Amelia patted his hand. "I appreciate the compliment. It sounds as though things are better between Dallas and Dee."

"Strange is what they are," Austin said as he cut into the beefsteak.

"In what way?" Houston asked.

Austin planted his elbow on the table and pointed his fork at Houston. "Dee reads to us every evening. Dallas is supposed to be working in his ledgers. Only he ends up watching her. Then she'll look up and forget all about reading. They'll just stare at each other for a few minutes, then Dallas will say it's time for bed, and they'll leave, and I'm left to wonder what's going on in the story. Dee started reading *Silas Marner* to us over a week ago and she hasn't finished the first chapter yet."

"You might have to start reading to yourself," Amelia suggested.

"It isn't the same hearing the story in my voice." Austin continued to cut his steak. "I just need to be patient. I reckon things will get back to normal once Dallas gets his son."

"I wouldn't count on it," Houston said, meeting his wife's gaze. He knew from experience that when the woman a man loved brought his child into the world, the bond only deepened and grew stronger.

"MR. CURTISS?"

Cordelia stuck her head inside the tent where Tyler Curtiss worked. She had awoken at two in the morning with a thought about the hotel that she wanted to share with him, but she couldn't find him anywhere.

Stepping into the tent, she decided to wait.

Large sheets of paper littered his desk, and she couldn't stop herself from looking at them. She saw the new plans for the newspaper office and the apothecary. Small businesses. Large businesses. They would find a home in Leighton.

Moving the papers aside, she saw a drawing of a building with a great many rooms. Bold letters across the top proclaimed it to be a hotel.

Sinking into a chair, she studied the drawing. It wasn't her hotel, and yet the layout seemed incredibly familiar, reminded her of Dallas. Bold. Daring. The rooms were large, designed for comfort not convenience. Not practical for a town where a great many people would simply be passing through. Yet a portion of it appealed to her, particularly if—as she suspected—her husband had been responsible for the plans.

"Mrs. Leigh. What a pleasure!"

She jumped out of the chair with a start. "Mr. Curtiss, I wanted to speak with you." Her gaze drifted back to the drawing. "Whose hotel is this?"

"Oh, that." He gave her a guilty grin. "Uh, well . . . uh." He swept his blond hair off his brow.

"Dallas asked you to draw up plans for a hotel, didn't he?"

"Yes, ma'am. Some months back, as a matter of fact."

"What are you going to do with the plans now?"

"He told me to ignore them. Said this town only needed one hotel."

"Thank you, Mr. Curtiss." She began to walk out of the tent.

"I thought you came to discuss something."

She smiled. "I just realized that I need to discuss it with my husband first."

As SHE RODE into the ranch, she saw Dallas standing by the corral. A broad smile spread beneath his mustache as she drew Lemon Drop to a halt and dismounted.

She strode to him, entwined her arms around his neck, and kissed him, deeply, soundly. From the moment he had made her his wife, he had been secretly placing gifts within reach, gifts that came without wrapping or bows, gifts whose worth could only be measured by the heart.

He drew back, his brow furrowed. "What was that for?"

"I saw the plans for your hotel."

He grimaced. "Oh, that. It was just an idea I was toying with. It never took hold, not like your plans."

She combed her fingers through the hair that curled at the nape of his neck. "I woke up this morning with a thought. I want one of the rooms to be special, but I wasn't exactly sure what I wanted. I was going to talk with Mr. Curtiss about it, and then I saw your drawings. Your rooms were so much larger than mine."

"I wanted to give a man room to stretch out."

"I want to give a man and woman a place to make love."

She broke away and began pacing, the idea little more than a seed. "I truly believe that many of the women who come to work at The Grand Hotel will eventually marry. Some will marry men like Slim, and you'll have to provide your men with a different type of living quarters."

"Is that so?" Dallas asked, intrigued as always with the way Dee set the wheels of an idea spinning inside her head, like a windmill built in the path of a constant breeze.

Her steps grew quicker as the excitement burned brightly within her eyes. "For the most part, they'll marry men of modest means, men who are content to let others dream. They'll get married in the church that you'll one day build, and then they'll go to the house where they'll probably live for the remainder of their life.

"Most won't be able to take a wedding trip, but I want to give them a place where they can go for one night and feel special. A room as beautiful as their love, as grand as their hopes for the future, where a man can make love to his wife for the first time in a huge bed with flowers surrounding them." She stopped pacing. "What do you think?"

That I should have taken you someplace special. He had never stopped to consider exactly what a wedding meant to a woman, what the first night of her marriage should have heralded.

Certainly not her husband kicking in the door as she prepared herself to please him.

He couldn't undo the mistakes he'd made in the past, but he could ensure he didn't repeat them in the future.

She stood on the tips of her toes, her hands clasped tightly before her, waiting on his answer. He could do little more than share the truth with her.

"Think you might need more than one special room."

She grabbed his hand. "Two rooms, then. Will you help me design and furnish them? I want a room where a cowboy would feel comfortable taking off his boots, and a woman could feel beautiful slipping out of her wedding dress."

"Then you should definitely have a bootjack in the room."

A faraway look crept into her eyes. "I should

have a bootjack in every room." She shook her head. "I've completely ignored the details."

"I don't think you've ignored anything. I'm the one who has overlooked things." He brushed the errant strands of her hair back from her face. "I don't think I ever bothered to tell you that you're beautiful."

A lovely blush rose high over her cheeks, her eyes warmed, and her lips parted.

He lifted her into his arms. "Slim, see after my wife's horse."

She snuggled against him as he carried her toward the house.

LIFE WAS A series of changes, and Cordelia knew that after tonight her life would forever be different. She could no longer put off the inevitable.

Joy and sorrow wove themselves around her heart as she read the final words of the story and closed the book.

"I liked that story," Austin said. "What are you gonna read next?"

"I'll find something," she said quietly as she turned the ring on her finger. She could feel Dallas's gaze boring into her, but she couldn't bring herself to look at him—not yet.

She would gain so much tonight . . . and lose even more.

Austin unfolded his body and stood. "Reckon I'll head on to bed."

"We'll see you in the morning," Dallas said.

She listened as Austin's footsteps echoed through the room and the door closed.

"You haven't looked at me all evening," Dallas said.

"I know." She set the book aside and lifted her gaze to his. "I went to see Dr. Freeman today."

Deep furrows marring his brow, he came out of his chair. "Are you sick?"

She smiled uneasily. "No."

He walked around his desk and knelt before her. "Then what's wrong?"

I'll be sleeping alone again when I've grown accustomed to sleeping with you.

"We finally got lucky. I'm carrying your child."

He dropped his gaze to her stomach. "Are you sure?"

She splayed her fingers across her waist where their child was growing. She had suspected for two months, but she had wanted to be certain before she told him, before she gave him hope and took away his reason for coming to her bed. "Your son should be here in the spring."

He intertwined his fingers with hers until their joined hands resembled a butterfly spreading its wings. "My son." He lifted his gaze to hers. "Our son." He touched his free hand to her cheek. "How are you feeling?"

"Fine. Just fine." Tears welled in her eyes. "Except that I want to cry all the time, but Dr. Freeman said that was normal."

With his thumb, he captured a tear before it fell from the corner of her eye. "I've wanted this for so long, Dee, I don't hardly know what to say. Thank you doesn't seem like enough."

"For God's sake, don't thank me." She shoved hard on his shoulders, and he tumbled over, his backside slamming against the stone floor. She rose to her feet and glared at him. "This is why you married me, isn't it? Why my family gave me to you? I'm just doing what I was brought here to do!"

Ignoring his stricken expression, she hurried from the room before he could see the tears streaming down her face. She wanted to give him a son, a chance to realize his dreams, but she didn't want his gratitude.

She wanted his love.

A SON.

He was going to have a son.

Standing at the corral, Dallas grinned like an idiot while the winds of change circled him, bringing the cooler weather that heralded the arrival of autumn. When the warmer winds arrived in the late spring, he'd be holding his son in his arms.

And until then . . . he'd be sleeping alone.

Dee had made that painfully clear.

The smile eased off his face. She'd been letting him into her bed because she'd felt an obligation. He'd begun to think he slept there because she wanted him there.

He shivered as the wind howled and drove all the warmth from his flesh. He'd been looking forward to winter for the first time in years. He'd imagined waking up with Dee nestled beside him, the warmth they shared beneath the blankets growing.

He'd miss so many things. The way she burrowed her nose into his shoulder. The way she rubbed the sole of her foot over the top of his. The way she smelled before he made love to her; the way she smelled afterward.

He groaned deep within his throat.

At one time, he'd thought he had only one dream left: to have a son. A sad thing indeed when a man his age realized he'd settled for a small dream when he might have possessed a larger dream: to have a woman who loved him give him a son.

He pounded his fist against the corral railing. He didn't need love, but damn, he suddenly wanted it desperately. How in the hell could he make her love him, a man who knew nothing of tenderness or soft words or any of the gentle things women needed?

He didn't know how to ask. He only knew how to command. His father had taught him that.

He turned from the corral and walked slowly back to the house. He had no desire to sleep in his cold bed alone. He'd work on his books for a while. Then he'd ride out to look at his herd, to check his windmills, to search for something he might never find.

He opened the door that led into the kitchen and stumbled to a stop. Dee was holding a log in one arm, bending over to retrieve another one.

"What the hell do you think you're doing?" he roared.

"The fire in my room is almost gone, and I could hear the wind. I thought it would be colder in the morning."

"Give me that," he said, taking the log from her arm. He crouched and stacked more logs into the crook of his arm. "You don't need to be hauling stuff."

"I'm not helpless," she said, hands on her narrow hips.

He wondered if he'd ever noticed how slim she was. He knew he had, he just hadn't considered how that might affect her when it came time to deliver his son.

"I didn't say you were," he said gruffly as he stood. "But I don't want you carting wood or anything else that's heavy. If you need something, you let me know."

"You weren't here."

"Then get Austin."

She looked like she wanted to argue more, but she simply stalked past him. When did she get so darn ornery? He'd have to go see Houston tomorrow and find out what other little surprises were waiting for him in the next few months.

He followed her to her room. She sat on the edge of the bed while he rekindled the fire in her hearth. He stood and brushed his hands over his trousers. "There. I'll come in every couple of hours or so and check on the fire. No need for you to get out of bed."

"Fine."

He glanced at her. Her hands were balled in her lap, her bare feet crossed one on top of the other.

"You didn't even have sense enough to wear shoes while walking over these cold stone floors?" he asked as he knelt before her and planted her heels on his thighs. "Your feet are like ice."

She shoved the balls of her feet against his chest and sent him sprawling over the floor.

"They're fine," she said.

He narrowed his eyes and slowly, deliberately came to his full height. "Get under those blankets and get under them now," he said in a low even voice.

She opened her mouth as though to protest. When he took a menacing step toward the bed, she snapped her mouth closed and scrambled under the blankets. He jerked his shirt over his head.

"What are you doing?" she asked.

He dropped to the edge of the bed and yanked off his boots. "I'm gonna warm your feet."

Standing, he pulled off his trousers before slipping into her bed with one quick fluid movement. "Put your feet between my thighs."

Her eyes widened. "But they're freezing."

"I know that. Now, do it, dammit!"

She pressed her lips together and shoved her feet between his bare thighs. He sucked in a deep breath between his teeth.

"Is that what you wanted?" she asked, glaring at him.

"No, but I want you warm," he answered, glaring back.

Tears welled in her eyes, and she averted her gaze. "It wasn't supposed to be like this when I told you. We were supposed to be happy."

Cradling her cheek, he gently guided her gaze back to his. "I am happy, Dee. Happier than I've ever been in my life."

She placed her hand on his chest and he jumped.

"Sweet Lord! Even your hand is cold." He took her other hand and pressed her palms against his chest, laying his hands over hers. "How can you be so cold?"

"You were outside. How can you be so warm?" she asked.

"I've got more meat on my bones."

She ran her tongue along her lower lip. "I'm sorry that I shoved you before—in your office and in here. I don't know what came over me—"

"It doesn't matter. I want a son, Dee, more than I've ever wanted anything."

"I know. I want to give you this child. I hope he'll look like you."

He touched her cheek. "I never gave any thought to what he might look like. I reckon he'll have no choice but to have black hair and brown eyes."

"He'll be tall," she said.

"Slender."

She nodded slightly and gave him a soft smile. "It'll be a while before he has a mustache."

"I reckon it will be at that." His thumb drifted back and forth over her cheek. "I know you don't want my gratitude, and I know you're not helpless, but I want to take care of you while you're carrying my son."

She didn't protest when he reached down, fisted his hand around the hem of her gown, and slowly lifted it over her head. She didn't move when he pressed his mouth against her stomach.

"Our son is growing here," he said in awe, wondering why he had ever thought he would be content to let just any woman bring his son into the world, why he hadn't realized that he needed a woman he could respect and cherish, a woman like Dee.

She threaded her fingers through his hair. He swallowed the lump in his throat and peered up at her. "I'm glad you'll be his mother."

Fresh tears shimmered within her eyes. Easing up, he kissed her as gently as he knew how. Then he drew back and smiled at her. "Your nose is cold. I might have to sleep in here just to keep you warm."

"I wish you would."

"If you want me to, I will. I'll give you anything you want, Dee."

Because she was carrying his son. Cordelia's heart ached with longing as much as with joy. The bond that joined them would forever be a wall that separated them.

But walls could be breached, and tonight, she wanted—she needed—him to scale the wall for her.

"Make love to me. I know there's no reason to now that I'm carrying your—"

He stroked his thumb over her lips as a wealth of tenderness filled his eyes. "I'm thinking there might be more of a reason to now."

He lowered his lips to hers, and with a whispered sigh, she welcomed him, his warmth, his flavor, his gentleness as his tongue slowly swept through her mouth.

The urgency that had seemed to accompany all their lovemaking before melted away like frost upon the windowpane as the sun reached out to touch it.

The goal that had once brought him to her bed was now a spark of life growing inside her. Her breasts had already begun to grow tender, and soon her belly would swell.

With their purpose achieved, she had expected a chasm to widen between them as they waited for the birth. She hadn't expected to bask in the glory of his appreciation.

With infinite tenderness, he touched her as though she were a rare gift, his fingers trailing over her flesh, taunting, teasing until his mouth moved in to satisfy.

She felt as though her body had turned to warm liquid, the sensations a swirling mist as they traveled from the top of her head to the tips of her toes. No matter where his mouth lighted, it felt as though he touched all of her.

She glided her palms over his shoulders, pressed her hands along his back, threaded her fingers through his hair, relishing the different textures of his body: the light sprinkling of hair that covered his chest, the hard muscles that rippled each time he moved, the warm breath that left a trail of dew over her flesh as his mouth continued its sojourn over her body.

Nothing they had shared before had prepared her for this: the ultimate joy of being wanted, of feeling cherished.

When he lifted himself above her and captured her gaze, her breath caught. When he entered her with one long, slow stroke, her body curled tightly around him.

She moved in rhythm to his sure, swift thrusts: giving, taking, sharing. His power. His strength. Her determination. Her courage. The life they had created.

Where once she had feared him, now she understood that she loved him.

Her body arched against his, and in his eyes, she saw reflected the glory and the triumph, and welcomed it as her own when he shuddered and buried his face within the abundance of her hair, his breath skimming along her neck and shoulder.

Lethargically, she lay and listened to his deep breathing.

Had he loved her in return, she didn't think he could have given her more.

With his child growing within her, hope spiraled anew within her heart that one day he would come to love her.

Chapter Fifteen

⁂

*T*he cold winds whipped down Main Street as Cordelia hurried along the boardwalk, drawing Dallas's sheepskin jacket more closely around her. He had given it to her when he'd noticed her two middle buttons were undone on her coat to accommodate her swelling stomach. He had pulled an older jacket out of a trunk for himself.

Lifting the collar, she inhaled Dallas's bay rum scent. A definite advantage to borrowing his coat was that she always felt as though he were near.

She went into the general store, removed her gloves, and rushed to the potbellied stove to warm her hands.

"Thought you had one of them in your hotel," Mr. Oliver said.

Cordelia smiled. "I do. I was warm when I left the hotel, but I got cold so I thought I'd drop in here. Besides, I need to see if my order arrived."

"Sure did. Set of Shakespeare. Twelve dollars."

Her Christmas gift for Austin, not only the books, but the reading of them to him through the next year. "I'll pick it up when we're ready to leave town."

She began to slip her hands back into her gloves. Mr. Oliver motioned her over.

"This has been my best year yet, what with them women waiters you got working in the restaurant. You better plan on putting a Christmas tree up in that hotel so them cowboys have a place to put all the presents they've purchased for them gals."

The first group of women had arrived in October. When they had completed their training, Cordelia had opened the restaurant and the first and second floors of the hotel. She was still furnishing the third floor, but business was good. Leighton was expanding. She squeezed Mr. Oliver's hand. "Wait until next year. I'll have another group of women arriving in the spring."

"Lordy, we're gonna be a real town. I had some doubts in the beginning—"

"Faith, Mr. Oliver. You had faith in Dallas's judgment or you wouldn't be here."

She swept out of the general store. The wind buffeted her as she walked across the street to the clothing store. Bells tinkled over her head when she opened the door and stepped into the shop.

A robust woman with flaming red hair, Mimi St. Claire thrust aside the curtains that led to her sewing room, making a grand entrance into her own establishment.

"You are here for zee beautiful red dress with zee big belly. Yes?"

Cordelia laughed at the description of the dress. She was rapidly losing her waistline and cared not one whit. "Yes. Is it ready?"

"Of course, madam. Your husband pays me too well to make certain your clothes are ready on time."

"He wasn't supposed to know about this."

"He does not know." She lifted a shoulder. "Still, he would expect me to add a little extra to his bill."

"We wouldn't want to disappoint him, would we?" Cordelia teased.

"Of course not. I finished zee coat for Rawley, too. I gave it to him yesterday when zee winds began to blow. It is too cold for a little boy who has no meat on his bones."

Reaching out, Cordelia squeezed her arm. "Thank you. Double the extra that you add to our bill."

Mimi waved her hand in the air. "Zat I do for nothing except zee cost of zee materials which you can afford and I cannot."

"Fair enough. Wrap up the dress. We'll be taking it with us when we leave."

Mimi wagged her finger at Cordelia. "But you cannot wear it until Christmas, no matter how tempting it becomes to please your husband before zen—because zis will please him."

"I know it will. Thank you for having it ready."

Bracing herself for the onslaught of cold, she opened the door, rushed outside, and scurried along the boardwalk until she reached the tanner's. She slipped inside. Dallas turned away from the counter.

Smiling, he opened his coat. She burrowed against him as closely as she could, hampered by the child growing within her.

"Glad you dropped by," he said. "I need to know what we're going to name our son."

"You need to know right this minute?"

"Yep. I'm gonna have his initials put right here on this saddle."

In disbelief she stared at his blunt-tipped finger pressing into the corner of a small saddle resting on the counter. "Tell me you did not purchase that saddle."

"My son's gonna need it."

"Not for years."

He kissed the tip of her nose, a habit he'd acquired when he wanted to distract her from pointing out the purchases he was making too soon. Pint-size boots with intricate stitching and a tiny black Stetson hat were already waiting in the nursery.

"Your nose is cold. There's a hotel up the street. We could get ourselves a room. I could warm you—"

"Dallas, we're not visitors here. We live—"

"An hour away in the cold. It would only take us a minute to get to the hotel. Come on, Dee. Let me warm you."

She caught a movement out of the corner of her eye and turned her head slightly. A heavyset man leaned against the door frame that led into his work area. "Hello, Mr. Mason."

"Mrs. Leigh."

"We're gonna go discuss names, Mason. I'll come back and tell you what initials to put on that saddle."

The man's face broke into a hearty grin as he shook his head in obvious amusement. "You do that, Dallas."

With his arm snugly wrapped around her, his body protecting her from the wind, Dallas escorted Cordelia outside. They walked briskly up the boardwalk and to the far end of town where the red-brick hotel stood.

Dallas shoved open one of the doors, and Cordelia rushed inside.

She took a moment to enjoy the aromas filtering out from the restaurant, the scent of fresh wood, the sight of new red carpet, the candles flickering in the chandeliers in anticipation of dusk.

She looked at Dallas. "You aren't really going to register us for a room are you?"

His eyes grew warmer than the fire blazing within the hearth at the far side of the lobby. "Let's stay the night."

"I didn't bring any clothes."

"You won't need any."

Anticipation and joy spiraled through her. She had never expected him to lavish as much attention on her as he did: his touch was seldom far away, his gaze constantly seeking hers as though he needed her as much as she needed him. Every night she slept within his arms. Every morning she awoke to his kiss.

"I want to check on the restaurant while you get the room," she said.

With a smile that promised no regrets, he kissed her lightly on the lips before he strode to the front desk. The child within her kicked. She slipped her hand within the coat and stroked the small mound. If only Dallas would love her as much as he already loved this child.

Turning, she walked into the restaurant. "Mrs. Leigh!"

She smiled warmly at the restaurant manager. "Hello, Carolyn."

With rosy cheeks, Carolyn James carried excitement within her hazel eyes. "I was wondering if you would mind if we held a Christmas celebration here Christmas Eve. I thought it might be nice for the girls, ease the loneliness of being away from family."

"I think it would be lovely."

She blushed prettily. "Perhaps your brothers would like to come."

"I'm sure they would. Is everything else going well?"

Carolyn nodded. "Very well, although I'll be glad when additional girls arrive in the spring. Some of these cowboys eat four and five meals a day."

Cordelia smiled, knowing their appetites had little to do with the need for food, but with the desire to simply watch a woman. "We'll discuss the details of the Christmas celebration next time I come to town."

"Don't leave it too long. Christmas will be here in two weeks."

Two weeks. As Cordelia walked back into the lobby, she thought it hardly seemed possible that she had been with Dallas for seven months, carrying his child for almost five. She hadn't decided what to give him for Christmas. He had everything he wanted. Maybe she would simply tie a big ribbon around her belly.

At the absurd thought, she bit back her laughter as she approached the front desk where Tyler Curtiss was talking with Dallas. Dallas slipped his arm around her. "This is the woman you need to talk to."

"About what?" Cordelia asked.

Tyler looked at Susan Redd as she stood behind the counter, her chin angled.

"Red, here—"

"It's Miss Redd to you," she said, her voice smoky.

The moment Cordelia had met her hotel manager, she had liked her. Her auburn hair was swept up, curling strands left to frame her face.

"Miss Redd," Tyler said, "isn't inclined to give my workers a discount on the rooms. With this cold spell blowing through, I thought they might enjoy a few nights in the warmth of the hotel, sleeping in a real bed instead of on a cot. Since they built the hotel, it only seemed fair to offer them a special rate."

"I've seen your workers. Most are filthy. No telling what sort of bugs they'll bring with them," Susan said.

Cordelia placed her hand on the counter. "Offer them a discount, half the normal rate, on the condition that they visit the bathhouse before they register. That should satisfy both of you."

Tyler smiled warmly. "Thank you, Mrs. Leigh. I'll work out the details with Miss Redd and let the men know."

She patted his arm. "See that you get one of the nicer rooms."

Dallas secured her against his side and began walking toward the stairs. "I think working out the details with her is what he intended all along," he said in a low voice near her ear.

Cordelia jerked her head back. "You think he has an interest in Susan?"

"Yep."

Before she could turn around to observe that interest, Dallas was escorting her up the stairs. At the landing, she stepped into the hallway. "Which room?"

He scooped her into his arms and carried her up the next flight of stairs.

"Dallas, this floor isn't ready."

"You sure? Thought it was."

"Only the bridal—" Her voice knotted around the tears forming in her throat.

In long strides, he walked to the end of the hallway, bent his knees, and inserted the key into the lock. "Seemed right that you should be the first to use your special room." He gave a gentle push and the door swung open.

A fire was already burning lazily in the hearth, and she realized his real reason for coming into town was not to talk with the tanner as he'd told her that afternoon, but to bring her to this room.

"You deserved something better than what you got on our wedding night so this is a little late in coming."

"What does it matter when you've given me so many special moments since then?"

"I plan to give you more . . . a lot more."

Because she carried his son. What did the reasons behind his thoughtfulness and kindness matter? His generosity was directed toward her.

But the reasons did matter. In a shadowed corner of her heart, they did matter.

CONTENTMENT SWEPT THROUGH Dallas as gently as dew greeting the dawn. He'd never before experienced this immense satisfaction, not only with himself, but with his life, because always before, no matter how much he had—something was always missing.

That something was now draped over half his body, her breathing slowly returning to normal, a glow to her warm skin that spoke of her enjoyment as eloquently as her gasps had only moments before.

He combed his fingers through the ebony hair fanned out over his chest. He loved the silken strands. He loved the brown of her eyes and the tilt of her nose. He loved the tips of her toes, even though they were growing cold.

She started rubbing them along his instep. He loved that as well.

He loved her.

And he didn't know how to tell her. Sometimes, he would mention that he was happy, and she would smile at him, but something in her eyes made her look sad, as though she didn't quite believe him.

He thought all his contentment might seep out like a hole in the bottom of a well if he told her what was in his heart and the silent disbelief filled her eyes.

He'd brought her here to tell her, to share his feelings in the special room she had envisioned for women to spend their wedding night, but she'd given him that look before he'd ever spoken the words, so he'd shoved them back and tried to show her his feelings instead.

He smiled with satisfaction. If her moaning and shuddering were any indication, he'd successfully shown her.

Still, he'd like for her to hear the words . . .

Where her stomach was pressed against his belly, he felt the slight rolling of his son. His contentment increased. He slipped his hand beneath Dee's curtain of hair and splayed his fingers over her small mound.

Dee wasn't growing as round as Amelia was. He figured it was because Amelia was short, and her baby had nowhere to go but out. Dee was tall, giving their child a lengthier area in which to grow.

He enjoyed watching the changes to her body. The darkening of her nipples where his son would nurse, the slightest widening of her hips, the hint of an ungainly walk.

Sighing, she wriggled against him, opened an eye, and peered up at him. "Mmmm. I knew this room was a good idea. It'll be hard to let people I don't know sleep in here now."

"Then don't."

Her other eye popped open, and she lifted her head. "That's the purpose of a hotel."

He trailed his thumb along the side of her face. "Nothing wrong with the owners having a private room that they can use at their convenience, anytime they want."

She narrowed her eyes in suspicion. "Is that why you told me I'd need two rooms—"

Leaning up, he began to nibble on her lips. She shoved him back down. "You planned to use this room all along, didn't you?"

He shrugged. "Seemed like a good idea at the time, an even better one now that we've tried it out."

Laughing, she snuggled into the crook of his shoulder, trailing her fingers over his chest, each stroke going a little higher, a little lower. "Maybe I'll give you this room as a Christmas present."

"Give me something I already own for Christmas? What kind of gift is that?"

She lifted her face. "You have everything."

"No, I don't."

"What else could you possibly need?"

Your love. He swallowed hard. "Something that can only be given if it isn't asked for."

She stared at him. "What does that mean?"

"Hell if I know. Get me a new saddle."

"Oh!" She rolled off him.

He came up on an elbow. "What?"

She looked over her shoulder as she began to gather her clothes off the floor. "I just thought of something."

"Something to get me?"

She waved her hand dismissively through the air. "No, silly. I just thought of something I need to tell Carolyn."

"Can't it wait?"

"No, she wants to have a Christmas celebration here. I want her to go ahead and have Mr. Stewart at the newspaper office make up invitations and announcements that we can send out over the area."

Dallas flopped back onto the pillow. "That can wait until the morning. Come to bed."

She was hastily donning her clothes. When she got an idea she was like a dust devil kicked up by the wind.

"It'll just take me a few minutes." She hurried to the door. "Besides, I'll no doubt get cold when I get downstairs, and you can warm me up all over again."

"Count on it!" he called out to her as she slipped from the room.

Good Lord, she was more obsessed with empire building than he'd ever thought about being, or maybe she simply enjoyed it more.

He'd be content these days to do nothing more than sit on the veranda in their bench swing. That gift had pleased her so much that he'd had a smaller one made—one that he'd hung on the balcony outside their bedroom.

He shoved his hands beneath his head and stared at the ceiling. He'd tell her that he loved her when she got back, whisper the words in her ear just before he joined his body to hers. If she didn't distract him with all those glorious sounds she made and the way her body moved in rhythm to his.

Smiling, he let his eyes drift closed and began to plan his seduction. Seducing her was so easy. Pleasuring her carried rewards he'd never known existed.

A scream shattered his thoughts. A scream of terror that he'd heard once before—on his wedding night.

He leapt from the bed and jerked on his trousers, buttoning them as he rushed down the stairs, his heart pounding, his blood throbbing through his temples.

On his way down, he met Susan Redd on her way up, her brown eyes frightened. "There's been an accident."

"Dear God." He tore past her.

"She's behind the restaurant!" Susan called after him.

He raced through the lobby, the restaurant, and out the kitchen. Wooden crates that had once been stacked outside now lay helter-skelter. Tyler Curtiss was lifting one off Dee's sprawled body.

Oblivious to the cold winds hitting his bare chest and feet, Dallas knelt beside his wife and touched his trembling fingers to her pale cheek. The cold numbed his senses. He couldn't feel her warmth or smell her sweet scent. "Dee?"

She looked like a rag doll a child had grown tired of playing with and thrown aside.

"She swore she heard a child cry," Carolyn wailed, her voice catching. "I didn't hear anything . . . but she came outside . . . I heard a crash, her scream . . . is she dead?"

"Go find the goddamn doctor!" Dallas roared and the people surrounding him ran off in all directions.

He needed to get her warm, needed to get her inside. Gently, he slipped one arm beneath her shoulders, the other beneath her knees.

It was then that he felt it, and fear unlike any he'd ever known surged through him. He'd carried too many dying men off battlefields not to recognize the slick feel of fresh blood.

HE HAD BROUGHT her home, thinking he could somehow protect her better, keep her safe.

But as she lay beneath the blankets, bathed in sweat, her face as white as a cloud on a summer day, her hand trembling within his, he feared nothing he did, nothing anyone did, would keep her with him.

With a warm cloth, he wiped the glistening dew beading her brow. He didn't want her to be cold.

If she died, she'd be cold forever. He couldn't bear the thought, but it lurked in a distant corner of his mind like an unwanted nightmare, keeping company with the sound of her scream.

He would forever hear her scream.

She moaned and whimpered, a pitiful little sound that tore his heart into shreds.

Where was the damn doctor when he needed him? He was going to find another doctor for Leighton, a doctor who knew how to keep his butt at home so he was there when he was needed, not a doctor who gallivanted around the countryside caring for people Dallas didn't even know.

Dee released a tiny cry and tightened her hold on his hand. He'd never in his life felt so utterly useless.

He had money, land, and cattle. He'd bathed in the glory of success and what the hell good was it doing him now? He'd trade it all for a chance to turn the clock back, to keep her in that room with him.

"Dallas?" Amelia placed her hand on his shoulder. "Dallas, she's losing the baby."

"Oh, God." Pain ripped through him so intensely, so deeply, that he thought he might keel over. He bowed his head and wrapped his fingers more firmly around Dee's hand. He'd never known what it was to need, but he needed now, he needed Dee's quiet strength.

"Just don't let me lose her," he rasped.

"I'll do what I can. If you want to leave—"

"No. I won't leave her."

And he didn't. He stayed by her side, wiping her brow when she released a tortured cry, holding her hand while her body twisted in agony.

Words failed him, became insignificant. He considered telling her that the loss didn't matter, that they would have other children, but he couldn't bring himself to lie to her, and he knew she'd know his words for the lie they were.

No other child, no matter how special, how precious, would replace this first child.

So he did all that he knew how to do. He remained stoic, held her, and wished to God that somehow the pain could be his and not hers.

And he watched as she wept silently when Amelia wrapped the tiny lifeless body in a blanket. Dallas forced himself to his feet. "I'll take him."

Amelia glanced up, despair sweeping over her face. "Dallas—"

"I'll see after him while you finish taking care of Dee."

He took the small bundle and left the room. It was the dead of night, but he did what needed to be done.

He built a small coffin and padded it with the delicate blankets Dee had bought to keep the child warm. Then he laid his tiny son inside the wooden box.

With the cold winter winds howling around him, he dug a grave near the windmill beside the house and laid his son to rest.

As gentle as an angel's soft tears, snowflakes began to cascade from the heavens.

A shudder of despair racking his body, Dallas dropped to his knees, dug his fingers into the freshly turned soil, and wept.

CORDELIA FORCED HERSELF through the fog of exhaustion and pain. Every inch of her body protested, her heart protesting most of all for it remembered the loss and the grief on Dallas's face as he'd taken his child from Amelia.

She bit back a cry as fingers poked and prodded. She opened her eyes. Hadn't she suffered enough? Why was Dr. Freeman torturing her now?

He pulled down her gown and brought the blankets over her, seemingly unaware that she had awakened. Through half-closed eyes she watched him walk across the room to the window where Dallas stood gazing out through the paned glass.

"She gonna live?" Dallas asked.

"She should," Dr. Freeman said, "but she's going to need a lot of rest. Pamper her for a while." Dr. Freeman put his hand on Dallas's shoulder. "And find a way to tell her gently that she's not going to be able to have any more children."

Cordelia's heart constricted, and she pressed her hand against her mouth, biting her knuckles to keep herself from crying out. Dallas jerked his head around and stared at the doctor.

"Are you sure she can't have any more children?"

Dr. Freeman sighed heavily. "She's lucky to be alive. She got hurt inside and out. Her injuries were extensive, and there's going to be a lot of scarring.

Based on my experience, I don't see how she could possibly get pregnant."

He walked quietly from the room. Dallas placed a balled fist on the window and bowed his head.

Cordelia's heart shattered with the knowledge that he'd lost his dream.

Chapter Sixteen

Before she was fully awake, before she'd opened her eyes, she was aware of his warm fingers threaded through hers. Her eyelids fluttered, and she could see Dallas sitting in a chair beside the bed, his dark head bent, his face unshaven.

Tears clogged her throat and burned behind her eyes. He looked to be a man in mourning. She used what little strength she had to squeeze his fingers.

He snapped his head up and leaned forward. His eyes were bloodshot and red-rimmed. Gently he brushed wisps of hair from her face. "How are you feeling?" he asked in a voice that sounded as rough as sandpaper.

He became blurred as her tears surfaced. "Was our baby a boy?" she asked.

He squeezed his eyes shut and pressed his lips against the back of her hand. Then he opened his eyes and held her gaze. She watched his throat work as he swallowed.

"Yeah, yeah he was. I, uh, I laid him to rest near the windmill. I . . . I always liked the way the blades clack when the wind comes through, and I didn't know what else to do."

She wished she had the strength to sit up and wrap her arms around him, to comfort him. The tears welled. "I overheard what Dr. Freeman said—that I won't be able to have other children. Dallas, I'm so sorry—"

"Shh. You're gonna be all right and that's what matters. I thought I was gonna lose you, too."

At that moment she didn't think she could love him more—for the lie he had spoken with such sincerity. She knew the truth. If she had died as well, he could remarry—any of the women who had recently moved to Leighton—and have the son he so desperately wanted.

He eased up in the chair. "Dee, I want to know what happened."

Sniffing, she furrowed her brow. "What happened?"

"You left the room. I heard you scream—"

She squeezed his hand, pieces of images racing through her mind. "Oh, Dallas. Rawley."

"Rawley?"

"The little boy. I heard a child cry. I went behind the hotel, and I saw him pressed into a corner. Then someone shoved me and the boxes fell . . . Oh, Dallas, he could have gotten hurt, too. Did you see him?"

"I only saw you."

"Dallas, we have to find him." She tried to sit, and he placed his hands on her shoulders.

"You've got no business getting out of bed. I'll send Austin to find him."

"Have him bring Rawley back here so I can see that he's all right."

RAWLEY COOPER KNEW he was in a heap of trouble. Had known it for days and knew sooner or later his mistake would catch up with him.

He would have preferred later.

He sat staring at the red and orange flames as they danced and warmed the room. The man who had brought him to this big house sat with his feet propped on the desk, his spurs dangling over the edge.

The man had told him his name was Austin. Once Rawley had gone through a town named Austin. He figured this man was pretty important since he had a town named after him.

Important men scared Rawley. They could do anything they wanted and nobody would stop them.

Rawley nearly jumped out of his skin when Austin pulled open a drawer.

"Dallas has some lemon drops in here. You want one?"

He peered over at Austin, saw the bag he held in his hand, the yellow ball he was rolling between his fingers. He remembered the man had given him a sarsaparilla stick once and hadn't hurt him when he'd taken it. But that was a long time back. He shook his head and turned his attention back to the fire.

He knew all he wanted to know about taking gifts. Sooner or later, they always came with a heavy price.

"You don't talk much, do you?" Austin said.

Rawley wondered if he ran into the fire if it would swallow him up. He thought about that sometimes. Finding a way to disappear so no one could touch him, no one could hurt him.

"Where's your ma?" Austin asked.

"Dead I reckon."

"Don't you know?"

Rawley lifted a shoulder.

The door opened. Austin dropped his feet to the floor and stood. Rawley stood, too, his legs trembling. Better to face the man who wanted him.

"You found him," the man said.

The man was big. Rawley had seen him with the pretty lady.

"Yep. His pa was passed out in the saloon. I told the barkeep to tell him the boy was here when he woke up."

"Good."

The man sat in his chair at the desk. Austin hitched up a hip and planted his butt on the corner of the desk. Rawley tried not to look scared but he had a feeling he wasn't having much success at it.

The man leaned forward. "Do you know who I am?"

Rawley nodded. "Yes, sir. You belong to the pretty lady."

A corner of the man's mustache lifted as he smiled slightly. "I reckon I do at that. My name is Dallas Leigh. The pretty lady is Mrs. Leigh." His smile quickly disappeared, leaving his mouth looking hard. "She got hurt a few nights back."

Rawley's heart started pounding so fast he thought it might escape through his chest. "Did she die?"

"No, but she's hurt . . . bad. She said someone pushed her. Do you know who pushed her?"

Rawley shook his head quickly and dropped his gaze to the floor so Dallas Leigh couldn't see that he was lying. Silence stretched out between them. Rawley heard the logs crackle as the flames devoured them. Soon they'd be nothing but ashes. He wished something would turn him into ashes.

"Would you like to see her?"

His gaze shot up. Dallas Leigh was looking at him like he could see right through him. He figured anyone who lied to Mr. Leigh came away with a blistered backside.

He nodded hesitantly, wondering what it would cost him to see the pretty lady, hoping she wasn't hurt so badly that she wouldn't be able to smile at him. He dearly loved her smiles. Her smiles weren't like the smiles most people gave him, smiles that hid something ugly behind them.

Mr. Leigh came to his feet and looked at Austin. "Dr. Freeman is getting a bite to eat in the kitchen. Fetch him upstairs."

Austin walked out of the room with his arms swinging. Mr. Leigh put his hand on Rawley's shoulder. Rawley shrank back.

Mr. Leigh studied him for a minute, his brown eyes penetrating. Rawley figured he could see clear through to his backbone.

"Follow me," Mr. Leigh said and walked in long strides toward the door.

Rawley would have swallowed if he'd had any spit, but his mouth had gone dryer than the cotton he'd picked one summer.

He followed Mr. Leigh into the hallway. He'd never seen a house so big nor stairs so wide. He figured ten men could walk side by side down those stairs without bumping into each other. At the top of the stairs, he wanted to take a moment to look down, to pretend he was the king of the world, but he didn't dare. He didn't think Mr. Leigh was a man of patience and would understand his desire to look down at a world that always looked down on him.

Mr. Leigh opened a door. "In here."

Rawley's heart jumped into a rapid-fire beat. The pretty lady would smile at him, maybe hold his hand, and talk to him in a voice that sounded as soft as the wind. He wiped his hands on his britches, not wanting her to feel his sweat, and stepped into the room.

His heart dropped to the floor.

His gaze darted around the room, searching for a sign that he hadn't been tricked, but with a knowledge a boy his age shouldn't possess, he understood all too well the truth of his situation.

He knew better than to trust, better than to hope, better than to want.

He heard a shuffling and turned. A man who looked like he ought to be lying in a coffin stood in the doorway.

"This is Dr. Freeman," Mr. Leigh said. "He's gonna have a look at you."

Rawley swallowed the bile burning his throat. "The pretty lady—"

"You can see her as soon as Dr. Freeman is done with you."

"Does she want me to do this?" he asked.

"Yep." Mr. Leigh nodded slightly at the doctor and stepped into the hallway, closing the door.

Rawley fought off the bitter disappointment of betrayal and began to carry himself away to a place where the sun kept him warm, the grass was soft beneath his feet, and the breeze always smelled like flowers.

DALLAS HAD LITTLE doubt that the boy knew who had pushed Dee, who was responsible for the harm that had taken away their child.

But he'd also seen what he was too familiar with plunge more deeply into the boy's eyes: fear.

The boy wouldn't tell Dallas what he wanted to know because the boy feared whoever had been behind the hotel more than he feared Dallas.

"It seems to be taking Dr. Freeman a long time," Dee said softly.

Dallas turned from the window and looked at his wife. He had propped pillows behind her back so she could sit up in bed. He was bringing her meals, making certain she had plenty to drink, and had started reading to her in the evenings. She seemed to have little interest in anything but the welfare of the boy, and it had taken Austin two days to find him.

"It just seems that way because we're waiting. Time passes differently when you're waiting." She still looked so pale. "Want me to brush your hair again?"

"No." She studied her clasped hands.

She'd barely looked at him since she had lost the baby. He couldn't blame her. He hadn't listened to her father, hadn't believed she was delicate. He had let her walk out of the hotel room unescorted while he had lain in that bed thinking about what he wanted to do with her body when she returned.

Shame rose within him. He hadn't held her as precious as he should have, and his lack had cost them both, not only a son, but a chance at a future together. She had wanted to give him a son, and for a short time it had appeared that she had wanted him as well. She had laughed so easily while she carried his son, glowed with anticipation, and smiled constantly.

Late into the night, they had whispered silly things: the books she would read to him, the ranching skills Dallas would teach him, the building skills Dee would share with him. They would take him to the top of a windmill and teach him how to dream—big dreams.

So many planned moments that in one night had crumbled into dust to be blown over the prairie and lost.

The door opened, and Dr. Freeman poked his skeletal face into the room. "Dallas, I need to speak to you for a moment."

Dee furrowed her brow. "Is Rawley hurt?"

"He's fine," Dr. Freeman said. "I just need to talk to Dallas."

He disappeared into the hallway. Dallas walked out of the room and closed the door.

Dr. Freeman was standing beside a window, looking out, his hands balled into tight fists at his side. "There are times when I regret taking an oath to cause no harm," he said through clenched teeth. "That boy has more scars than the parched earth has cracks. Do you know what he thought I wanted to do?" Dr. Freeman shook his head fiercely. "No, of course you don't."

When he turned, Dallas was surprised to see tears shimmering in the man's eyes.

"I think that sorry excuse of a man who calls himself the boy's father has been selling him."

Dallas jerked his head back. "Selling him? To whom?"

"Men. Men who prefer boys to women."

Dallas's stomach roiled. "Are you sure?"

"I can't swear to it, but I'd stake my life on it."

"In Leighton?"

"Perversion doesn't come garbed any differently than you or me. You can't look at a man and tell what's in his head or on his mind. I have seen the most upstanding men in other communities do things that would turn your stomach, and I only learned about them because they went too far and needed my services."

Dallas felt the impotent anger swell within him. "Is there anything you can do for the boy?"

Dr. Freeman shook his head. "The hurt he's had on the outside is healing, but it's the deep pain that he's gotta be feeling on the inside that concerns me, the scars he'll carry with him for the rest of his life."

"I won't be taking him back to town," Dallas said with determination.

"I'll let his father know—"

"You leave his father to me."

RAWLEY COOPER KNEW he had made a big mistake. All the doctor had wanted to do was look at him.

Rawley couldn't remember what he'd said, but he knew the exact moment that the doctor figured out what Rawley thought he wanted to do to him.

He'd thought the skinny man was going to puke on the floor, and Rawley knew they wouldn't let him see the pretty lady now. They knew he was dirty on the inside and out.

He heard the door open. He bundled up his shame the same way that he'd bundled up his clothes. He turned from the window.

Mr. Leigh filled the doorway. "Put on your clothes, boy."

Rawley nodded and did as he was told. He'd thought about putting them on before, but the doctor hadn't told him to so he'd decided to wait. He was forever doing what he wasn't supposed to do.

When his fingers had skipped over the two buttonholes in his shirt that no longer had buttons

belonging to them, and he had buttoned the top
button at his throat, the button that nearly gagged
him but made him feel protected, he lifted his gaze
back to the towering man.

Mr. Leigh stepped into the hallway. "Come with
me, boy."

Taking one last look at all the fine and pretty
things in the room, he slowly walked into the hallway. Mr. Leigh was standing beside an open door
that led into a corner room.

"Stop dragging your feet. My wife is anxious to
see you."

Rawley's heart felt like the fluttering wings of a
butterfly he'd once cupped in his hands. Mr. Leigh
knew the truth about him—he could see it in his
eyes—and he was still going to let him see the
pretty lady. He hurried into the room before Mr.
Leigh could change his mind.

Then he stumbled to a stop.

The lady was sitting in the bed, looking like an
angel. She smiled softly and held out her hand.
"Rawley, I'm so glad you could come visit me."

He edged closer to the bed, and she waved her
hand. "Give me your hand."

He shook his head. "I ain't clean."

"That doesn't matter."

He knew she thought he was talking about dirt,
but he was talking about something so filthy it
touched his soul. Tears burned his eyes when he
shook his head this time.

Mr. Leigh walked to the other side of the bed
and stood near his wife. "It's all right, Rawley."

Rawley dared to lift his gaze. Mr. Leigh nodded.

He took a step closer and touched his fingers
to the lady's hand. She closed her hand around
his. Her hand was warm and soft and swallowed

his. He wondered if his ma's hand had been like this.

The lady tugged gently and he moved closer. She brushed her fingers over his brow. He'd never been touched with such gentleness.

"Are you all right?" she asked.

He nodded. "The boxes didn't fall on me."

"I'm glad."

He suddenly remembered all the screaming that had been going on, all the blood, all the yelling about the baby. "Where's your baby?"

Tears welled in her eyes, and Mr. Leigh dropped his gaze to the floor.

"He's in heaven," she said quietly.

"I'm sorry," Rawley croaked as the tears he'd been fighting to hold back burst through. "I'm sorry."

She drew him close and pressed his head against her bosom. "It wasn't your fault."

But he knew it was. If only he hadn't cried out. He knew better than to cry out.

The lady rocked him back and forth while he cried. He didn't know he had so many tears. When he stopped crying, her gown was wet but she didn't seem to care.

For the longest time, he simply stood beside her and let her hold his hand.

When the lady fell asleep, he helped Mr. Leigh bring the blankets up to her chin. Through the window, he could see that night had fallen. He followed Mr. Leigh through the house, through big rooms, until they came to the kitchen.

Austin sat at a small table, slurping stew.

"Sit down, boy," Mr. Leigh said.

Rawley slid into the chair. He was embarrassed when his belly growled like an angry dog. Austin smiled at him. Mr. Leigh put some stew into a bowl and placed it in front of him.

"Go on, boy, eat," Mr. Leigh said.

Rawley squirmed. "Ain't got no way to pay for it."

"What happened to that dollar I gave you?"

"I buried it. They built a hotel on top of it. Didn't know they were gonna do that till it was too late."

Mr. Leigh rubbed his mustache. "That must be why the hotel is such a success. Maybe we ought to change the name to the Lucky Dollar Hotel."

Rawley shrugged.

"Go on and eat, boy. You made my wife smile. That's worth more than a dollar to me."

Cautiously, Rawley brought a spoonful of stew to his mouth. Normally he ate whatever his pa left behind, which usually wasn't much. He'd never had his own bowl before. His own food. His mouth and belly wanted him to eat fast, but he forced himself to eat slow, to pretend he had his own food every night and could eat as much as he wanted.

When he finished eating, Mr. Leigh made him take a bath and put on some of Austin's old clothes. He told Rawley that Austin had been eight years old when he'd worn the clothes. Since the clothes fit him, Rawley wondered if that meant he was eight years old. He wondered if it meant that he'd grow to be as tall as Austin.

Because he knew he couldn't outrun or outfight Mr. Leigh, Rawley followed him back up the stairs to the room where he had been earlier, where the doctor had looked at him. Mr. Leigh stopped and held something toward Rawley.

"Do you know what this is?" Mr. Leigh asked.

"A key."

"Do you know what it's used for?"

"You lock the door so I can't get out."

Mr. Leigh walked into the room and inserted the key in a hole on the other side of the door. "From now on, this is going to be your room. You close the door and turn the key so no one can come in this room unless you want them to."

"Not even you?" he asked suspiciously.

"Not even me. Give you my word."

Mr. Leigh walked out of the room and closed the door. Rawley shoved the key farther into the hole and turned it. He heard the echo of a click.

He waited and listened hard. He heard Mr. Leigh's boots hitting the floor of the hallway. He heard them on the stairs. Then he heard them not at all.

Moonlight streamed in through the window, guiding him. He walked to the bed, removed his boots, and crawled beneath the blankets.

They smelled clean and fresh, just like he did, and crackled beneath him.

He stared at the door for the longest time, at the shadow of the key in the lock. When his eyes drifted closed, for the first time in his life, he slept without fear.

DALLAS WALKED THROUGH the swinging wooden doors of the saloon. The scent of freshly poured whiskey and stale cigarette smoke assailed his nostrils.

Come Saturday night, he wouldn't be able to walk through the saloon without bumping into someone, but tonight only the dregs of his town were here.

Several men played cards at a table. A man sat alone at a corner table nursing a whiskey. Another man stood at the bar, his arms folded across the top.

"Come on, barkeep, give me a whiskey," he said, his voice raspy.

"I don't sell liquor on credit," Beau said as he dried a glass, then held it up so the candles in his chandelier could dance over the glass. "Why don't you head on home, Cooper?"

"'Cuz I ain't drunk enough."

Dallas strode to the bar and slapped a coin on the counter. "Whiskey."

Beau set a glass in front of him and poured a long drink, then walked to the other end of the bar. Cooper's black gaze darted to the glass. He ran his tongue over his chapped lips.

"Wouldn't consider buying me a drink, would ya?"

"Nope, but I want to talk to you about your son."

"Rawley?" His lips spread into a distorted grin. "You don't hardly look the type to be interested in Rawley, but then what a man is on the inside don't always show on the outside." He leaned closer and his rancid breath billowed out like a cloud of dust. "Five dollars for twenty minutes. Twenty dollars you can have him all night."

Dallas had hoped, prayed, that Dr. Freeman had been wrong. He made no attempt to keep the loathing out of his voice. "Can we discuss this outside?"

Cooper sneered. "Sure. You don't want people knowing your pleasures. I can respect that. Know how to keep my mouth shut, too."

He staggered out of the saloon. Dallas found him beside the building. A lantern hanging from a pole sent a pale glow over the man as he held out his hand.

Dallas had never hit a man. He'd never used anything but his voice to make a man listen and obey, to make a man squirm when necessary, to make a man regret he'd chosen differently.

But tonight, his voice just didn't seem to be enough. He brought his arm back and slammed his knotted fist into Cooper's nose.

Cooper squealed like a wild hog and reeled back, blood spurting through his fingers as he covered his face. He hit the ground and cursed as he staggered to his knees.

Dallas waited until Cooper was again on his feet before burying his fist in the man's paunchy gut. When Cooper bent over with a grunt, Dallas drove his fist into the man's chin.

He heard the satisfying sound of bone cracking. Cooper landed flat on his back, moaning and crying. "Don't hit me! Don't hit me again!"

Dallas crouched beside the pitiful excuse for a father, grabbed his shirt, and jerked him upright. Cooper cried out. "No more!"

Dallas glared at the bloody carnage. "Stay the hell away from Rawley or the next time I'll use my gun."

"He's my boy!"

"Not anymore," Dallas said as he shoved the man back to the ground. "Not anymore."

DALLAS WATCHED AS Rawley shoveled the eggs and biscuits into his mouth. It had taken Dallas ten minutes to convince the boy the food was for him, that he was being given another meal.

Once convinced, Rawley had plowed through a plate of eggs and four biscuits, as though afraid the offer would be rescinded. Dallas had little doubt the boy had been offered a lot in his life that was quickly taken back.

Dallas planted his elbows on the table and slowly sipped the black coffee from his cup. That morning, when he'd taken Dee her breakfast, he had told her that the boy was going to be staying.

"I want him to stay, Dallas, but we can't go about deciding what's best for people. Rawley might have been happy where he was. I don't think he was, but you can't take him away from it without knowing."

She was right, of course. Dallas had taken her away from her home without knowing—or caring—if she wanted to leave. He seemed to have a habit of deciding what people should do with their lives. Asking never entered his head.

When Rawley had shoved the last bite of biscuit into his mouth and downed his glass of milk, Dallas set his cup aside. He glanced at Austin before shifting his gaze to Rawley. "Rawley, I have an offer for you."

Distrust plunged into the boy's eyes, and he looked like he might bring up his breakfast.

"I need a helper," Dallas hastily added.

Rawley furrowed his brow. "A helper?"

"Yep. I've got a big ranch, a lot of responsibilities. Sometimes, I don't have time to do everything. I need someone who can help me take care of things."

"Like what?" he asked.

Dallas's stomach knotted. A boy Rawley's age shouldn't know enough about life to have suspicion marking his gaze.

"Take care of the damn prairie dog, for one thing."

"I'm good at that."

"I know you are. I also need someone who can oil my saddle, brush my horse, someone to keep my wife company while I'm checking on the ranch. For your trouble, you get to sleep in that room upstairs, eat all the food your belly will hold, and you get a dollar a week."

Rawley's black eyes widened in wonder. "You mean a dollar a week to keep?"

"To keep, to spend. It's up to you. Just don't bury it. If you want to save it, we'll put it in the bank."

Rawley's brow furrowed, and he gnawed on his bottom lip. "My pa—"

"I talked with your pa last night. He said it's fine if you want to stay here and work for me."

Rawley nodded vigorously, his black hair slapping his forehead. "I do. I can work hard."

"I know you can, son." A sharp pain stabbed through Dallas's chest. He hadn't meant to call the boy that. His son was lying in the cold ground. He shoved the chair back and stood. "When you've finished eating, you go on upstairs and ask Mrs. Leigh to read to you. She likes reading out loud."

In long strides, he left the house before he changed his mind about letting the boy stay. The boy couldn't replace his son—no one, nothing could.

Chapter Seventeen

Standing at her bedroom window, Cordelia gazed at the land that looked as cold as her heart, as empty as the place inside her where a child had once grown.

Sometimes, she imagined that she could still feel him kicking. She would press her hand to her stomach, remembering all the times Dallas had laid his large hand beneath her navel and waited, his breath held, for the moment that would join the three of them. The tender smile he had bestowed upon her when the movement came. The warmth of his lips against her flesh as his mouth replaced his hand, kissing her gently, making her feel precious.

Precious because his dream was growing inside of her.

The tears surfaced and she forced them back. She was tired of crying, tired of the ache in her chest that she knew would never leave, tired of longing for the dreams that would never be.

With the baby, she'd held hope that Dallas would come to love her—if not for herself, for the fact that she had given him a son, through her he had acquired his dream.

But the hope had died with their son.

Dallas came to her room each evening to ask after her health, but he never came to her bed. He never held her. He no longer looked at her as though she hung the stars.

And she missed that most of all.

A knock sounded on her door, and she turned from the gray skies. "Come in."

Dallas stepped into the room. "You're not ready."

She glanced at the red dress he'd brought her from town. How could she wear red when she was in mourning? Or did a child who had never lived receive no mourning period?

"I'm just not up to seeing people."

"You've been in this room for two weeks, Dee. If you can't walk down the stairs, I'll carry you, but Christmas Eve has always been a special time for my family. It's about the only tradition we have." His Adam's apple slowly slid up and down. "It'd mean a great deal to me if you'd join us—if not for me, then for Rawley. I'm not sure the boy even knows what Christmas is."

Rawley. She thought of the way he sat as still as stone and listened, barely breathing, when she read to him. "I'll be downstairs in ten minutes."

He nodded and left the room. Quickly she washed up in the warm water he'd brought her earlier. She brushed her hair and swept it up off her neck. Then she donned the red dress—for Dallas—a small inconsequential gift to him because she knew he preferred her in red.

She stepped into the hallway, surprised to find Dallas leaning against the wall, his head bowed. She had noticed so little about him before, but she noticed everything now.

The shine on his boots, the red vest beneath his

black jacket, a red that matched her gown, the black tie at his throat.

Slowly, he lifted his gaze. At one time, she knew he would have smiled at her. Now, he only looked at her with uncertainty, a woman to whom marriage vows had chained him, a woman who couldn't fulfill his heart's solitary desire.

He stepped away from the wall and crooked his elbow.

Always the gentleman . . . even now honoring his word when she could no longer honor hers.

She braved a smile and placed her arm through his. Slowly they descended the stairs, a wall of silence shimmering between them. How could a child that she had never held in her arms, patted on the head, or kissed good night leave such an aching chasm in her soul?

They walked into the parlor and the world was transformed into gaiety. In a far corner, with red ribbons, strung popcorn and raisins, and brightly painted horseshoes decorating its branches, an expansive cedar tree brushed the ceiling.

Austin sat on the floor beside the tree, Maggie curled against his side. He took a package from beneath the tree, placed it between their ears, and shook it. Maggie's smile grew as the rattle bounced around them.

"What do you think?" he asked.

"A puppy!"

Austin chuckled. "I don't think so." He put the package down and reached for another.

Houston and Amelia sat on the sofa, their fingers intertwined, whispering to each other without taking their eyes off their daughter.

Rawley stood beside an empty chair, wearing a miniature version of Dallas's jacket, vest, and tie.

With his black hair slicked down, his face scrubbed almost raw, and his hands knotted at his sides, she wondered if he knew Christmas came with gifts.

Maggie squealed. "Aunt Dee, you came!" She hopped up, ran across the room, and wrapped her small arms around Cordelia's knees. "I'm so glad." She looked up at Dallas. "Now?"

He touched the tip of her nose. "In a minute."

Awkwardly, Amelia brought herself to her feet with assistance from Houston. Pressing a hand to her protruding stomach, smiling softly, she waddled across the room. With tears in her eyes, she hugged Cordelia. "Merry Christmas," she whispered.

Cordelia fought back her own tears. She had expected a Christmas filled with joy, not sorrow. As Amelia drew back, Cordelia squeezed her hands and gave her a quivering smile. "How are you feeling?"

Amelia smiled brightly. "I woke up this morning and wanted to clean the house from top to bottom. I'm so glad Christmas Eve is today when I'm not tired."

"Me, too," Houston said. "She wanted me to help her clean." He leaned over and pressed a kiss to Dee's cheek. "Merry Christmas, Dee."

"Why don't you sit over here?" Dallas said as he escorted her to the chair where Rawley stood, a silent sentinel.

Sitting in the chair, she smiled at Rawley and touched a finger to the lapel of his jacket. "You certainly look handsome."

Twin spots of red colored his cheeks. He looked down at his boots—new boots, as shiny as Dallas's. She had been so wrapped up in her grief that she hadn't considered the child might need—might want—new clothes. She glanced up, wanting to thank Dallas for making certain the child was dressed as nicely as everyone else on this special day.

But he had moved away and was standing by the tree. He cleared his throat. "Our mother believed in tradition. She didn't have many, but the ones she had always seemed special." He met Houston's gaze. "Austin didn't remember the traditions because he was so young when our mother died, but Houston and I remembered them. We gave our word that we'd share them with Austin, and in time with our families. It always makes us feel as though our mother is still with us." He cleared his throat again. "Anyway, she always sang a song before we opened the gifts."

Houston stepped up beside him. Austin picked up his violin, placed it beneath his chin, and set his bow upon the strings. With one long, slow stroke, he brought the beautiful music into the room.

Then Dallas and Houston added their deep voices to the lyrical strains of the violin.

"Silent night, holy night . . ."

Dallas's voice was a rich resonance that seemed to reach out and touch every corner of the room. Houston sounded as though cattle had taught him to sing, but it didn't matter. The words journeyed from their hearts and their memories. Cordelia sat in awe, listening as three men, three brothers, paid their special homage to the woman who had brought each of them into the world.

Dallas faltered at the words "mother and child," and fell into silence. He looked at her, and for a brief moment she saw the raw pain he'd been hiding from her. Then Amelia's voice filled the room as she nestled against Houston's side and he wrapped his arm around her.

Cordelia wanted to get out of the chair, cross the room, wrap her arms around Dallas, and tell him that everything would be all right. She would find a way to make it right again, but she saw a family standing before the tree, four people who loved each other. She couldn't find the courage to walk into their midst, to ask them to accept her as she was—broken.

A small hand found its way into hers. Smiling softly at Rawley, she wondered if he felt as though he didn't belong as much as she did.

The voices rang out with the final words of the hymn, and as they died away, Austin took his time, allowing the last strains of music to fade.

Maggie walked up to Dallas and tilted her head back. "Now?"

He smiled warmly. "Now."

She squealed and dropped to the floor, clapping her hands. "Now, Unca Austin, now."

Austin set aside his violin and pointed a finger at her. "No peeking, no opening anything until they are all passed out."

Nodding her head, she scooted up. Houston and Amelia returned to their places on the sofa, and Dallas leaned against the wall, his arms crossed over his chest.

Cordelia squeezed Rawley's hand. "Don't you want to move closer to the tree?"

He shook his bowed head, but she could see him peering beneath his lashes at the tree.

Austin dropped to his knees and reached for a gift. "All right, let's see what we've got here." He turned the wrapped box over and over, frowning. "Mmmm . . . oh, wait, I see it." He smiled broadly. "Maggie May."

She clapped, took the gift, and shuffled her bottom over the floor.

Austin reached for another box and lifted a brow. "Maggie May."

Maggie had six gifts beside her before Austin furrowed his brow and glared at her. "How come you're gettin' all the presents?"

She smiled brightly. "I was too good." She glanced over her shoulder at Rawley. "Wasn't you good?"

Cordelia felt Rawley's hand flinch within hers and saw his jaw tighten. "He was very good," she said in his defense, wishing she'd been well enough to travel to town to purchase him a gift, wondering what she might have in her room that she could give him.

"Well, I reckon he was," Austin said. "Lookee—here. This one's for Rawley." He handed the gift to Maggie. "Run it over to him, Maggie May."

Maggie popped up and brought Rawley the gift. She held it out to him, but he only stared at the small oblong box.

"Don't you want it?" Maggie asked.

"I'll take it," Cordelia said and set the gift at his feet. She read the tag, grateful to Austin for remembering the child.

"I'll be darned," Austin said. "Rawley again."

"Oh!" Maggie cried as she took the large flat gift from Austin and ran it back to Rawley.

"And here's one for me," Austin said as he started to untie the ribbon that held the paper in place.

Maggie screeched and grabbed his hand, her brow deeply furrowed. "Gotta wait."

"Then let's get the rest passed out fast."

She helped him, laying presents at the grown-ups' feet. Cordelia looked at her two gifts. One from Austin. One from Houston and Amelia. She had lost her enthusiasm for the season when she'd lost her child, but judging by the number of gifts appearing, she assumed Dallas hadn't. Watching him as he stood apart from the gathering, she thought she could tell when a gift from him was handed off to someone. A warmth touched his eyes, as though he were pleased that he could give abundantly to those he loved.

Yet she received no gift from him.

"What in the heck is this?" Austin asked as he pulled a large wrapped box from behind the tree. Maggie's eyes widened and her mouth formed a large circle. "Goodness gracious, it's for Rawley," Austin said. "Help me shove it over to him, Maggie May."

They both made a great show of pushing the package across the room. When they stopped, Maggie planted her hands on the box and leaned toward Rawley, tipping her head back. "You musta been gooder than me."

Austin clasped his hands together. "That's it. Let's see what we got."

Austin hurried across the room and began to tear into his presents as though he were the same age as Maggie.

Cordelia heard quiet footsteps and glanced up. Dallas stood before her, holding a small wrapped box with a tiny red bow on it.

"It's just a little something," he said. "I was afraid it might get lost under the tree."

With trembling fingers, she took the gift, carefully untied the red ribbon, peeled back the paper, and opened the box. A heart-shaped locket was nestled between cotton. Tiny flowers had been engraved over the gold. Tears burned the back of her throat as she looked up at Dallas. "I . . . I didn't get anything for you," she whispered.

"Under the circumstances, I didn't expect you to." He crouched in front of Rawley. "You gonna open your presents?"

Rawley stared at Mr. Leigh, and then dropped his gaze to the wrapped boxes, trying to believe they were really for him, wondering if it wouldn't be better to leave them as they were, carefully wrapped with his name on them, the only true gifts he'd ever received in his life.

"I always start with the smallest," Mr. Leigh said as he picked up the first gift Rawley had received and held it toward him.

Rawley's mouth went dry. He had to confess first. They'd take the presents away, but he had to tell Mr. Leigh the truth. "I wasn't good."

Mr. Leigh rubbed his thumb and forefinger over his black mustache. Rawley had figured out that he did that when he was thinking hard.

"There's a difference between being good and doing bad things. Sometimes, a person does something because he doesn't have a choice. He might not like what he did . . . but it doesn't make him bad."

Rawley had done a lot that he didn't like. Mr. Leigh shook the box beneath his nose. It rattled something fierce. "Austin, did you put a rattlesnake in here?" Mr. Leigh asked.

Austin was shoving his hand into a new glove. He looked up. "Don't tell him. It'll ruin the surprise."

Mr. Leigh lifted a brow. "What do you think?"

Rawley wrinkled his nose. "Thought rattlers slept in winter."

"Maybe you'd better open it and see."

Rawley nodded and took the gift. His fingers were shaking so badly that he could barely grab the tiny piece of string. He pulled the bow free and moved the paper aside. Then holding his breath, he lifted the lid and peered inside. "Holy cow," he whispered.

He'd never seen so many sarsaparilla sticks in his whole life—except at the general store. He didn't know much about counting but he knew a hundred was a big number so he figured he had at least a hundred sticks in that box. He'd be an old man before he finished eating them.

"You can eat them anytime you want, Rawley," Austin said, wearing a big grin.

"Can I eat one now?" he asked.

"You don't have to ask," Mr. Leigh said. "They're yours to do with as you want."

His. A hundred sarsaparilla sticks. Maybe more. His mouth watered as he took one from the box and slipped it into his mouth. The tangy flavor washed through him. He looked at the lady. She had tears in her eyes. He figured she wanted a sarsaparilla stick, too, but it didn't look like her boxes were the right size to hold one. He knew what it was to want—and to never have. He held the box toward her. "Want one?"

More tears filled her eyes along with the glorious smile she gave him as she reached into his box. "Thank you."

He'd done that. Made her smile. He'd never in his life had anything but misery to share with people. He felt warm inside knowing he had something good he could share, even if it meant he wouldn't get to eat them all. He shoved the box toward Mr. Leigh. "Want one?"

Mr. Leigh smiled, too, as he took a stick and put it in his mouth. Rawley wondered if Mr. Leigh's mustache would smell like sarsaparilla after he'd eaten the candy.

Gathering his courage, he went around the room, offering to share his gift with everyone, even the bratty girl, watching their smiles grow, wishing he had more to give them. When he returned to his place, he glanced at the two unopened boxes. He didn't figure they could hold anything better than what he'd already gotten.

He set his box of candy aside and opened the next present, saving the biggest for last. His heart plummeted when he looked inside the box. A blanket. A blanket he could use when they took him back to town, and he was sleeping beside buildings again. He'd been working so hard, hoping they'd keep him forever, but he hadn't worked hard enough.

"Gonna open the last one?" Mr. Leigh asked.

Rawley nodded, even though he didn't want to open it, to see what else they'd given him. He pulled the bow apart and peeled back the paper, opened the box, and stared.

Stared at the fine brown leather that shone like someone had spit on it over and over. Mr. Leigh reached into the box and pulled out the saddle.

Mrs. Leigh touched her fingers to a corner of the saddle. "Those are your initials."

He didn't know what his initials were but he sure knew good carving when he saw it, and someone had carved little designs all along the saddle, except for the place where he'd put his backside.

"Well, now, if that ain't the stupidest gift I've ever seen," Austin said as he walked over for a closer look. "What were you thinking, Dallas?"

Cordelia wondered what Dallas had been thinking. He'd planned to give that saddle to his son, a son he would never have.

"What good does a saddle do him, if he ain't got a horse?" Austin asked.

"But we brung him a horse!" Maggie slapped her hand over her mouth and turned round green eyes to her father.

Houston scooped her into the air, and she squealed. "You kept that secret longer than I thought you would," he said, grinning.

Dallas unfolded his body. "Let's go outside."

He held his callused hand out for Cordelia. She slipped her hand into his, relishing the strength she felt, the warmth, remembering the feel of his hands touching her intimately as they would never touch her again.

He pulled her to her feet. Austin tossed Dallas a coat from a nearby chair. He draped it around Cordelia. The others shrugged into their coats before walking through the doors that led onto the veranda.

Rawley had put on his jacket, but now he stood like a statue, staring at the door, gasping for breath. Cordelia extended her hand toward him. "Come on, Rawley. It sounds as though this last gift was too big to wrap."

He shook his head vigorously. "I don't want a horse. I don't want to have to leave."

"You don't have to leave, son," Dallas said.

Cordelia's heart lurched at the word—*son*—spoken with such ease.

"Then why you givin' me a horse if you don't want me to ride it outta here?"

"How else are you gonna ride over my range and count my cattle for me?"

Panic delved into Rawley's dark eyes. "I don't know how to count."

"Can you tie a knot in a rope?"

Rawley nodded vigorously.

"Then I can teach you to count."

Cordelia slammed her eyes closed. Dallas would teach Rawley as he'd once planned to teach his own son. She wondered if he was even aware that he was saying to Rawley things that he'd planned to say to his own son.

But Rawley didn't carry Dallas's blood; he wasn't a Leigh. Yet, she couldn't help but wonder if this child of misfortune could possibly fill the gaping hole in their hearts.

Opening her eyes, she wrapped her hand around Rawley's. "We'd better look this horse over before you start making plans. You might not even want to keep him."

Rawley nodded enthusiastically. "Oh, I wanna keep him. Even if he's butt ugly."

Dallas cleared his throat and a smile tugged at the corner of his mouth. "You're too easy to please, Rawley."

They walked to the porch, hand in hand, a family that might have been, a bittersweet reminder of what would never be.

Tethered to the veranda railing, a brown-and-white spotted horse nickered.

Rawley released Cordelia's hand and walked to the edge of the veranda. Dallas continued to hold her hand tightly. She ached to have his arm come around her, to find again the intimacy they had shared as they had anticipated the birth of their child.

Rawley spun around, disbelief in his eyes. "He's mine?"

"He's yours," the three brothers said at once.

They exchanged looks, and Cordelia saw a bond between them that didn't exist between her brothers.

"Because he looks like someone splashed paint on him, he's known as a paint or pinto," Amelia explained. "You'll need to give him a name."

"Spot!" Maggie cried as she wrapped her hands around the veranda beam and leaned back. "Spot's a good name."

Rawley looked at her as though she'd lost her mind. "Spot? That ain't no name for a horse."

She crinkled her nose and stuck out her tongue. "What then?"

Rawley furrowed his brow. "My ma was Shawnee. Could I call him Shawnee?"

Amelia released a small cry and stumbled against Houston, her hand pressed against her stomach.

"I don't got to call him that!" Rawley yelled. "You can name him!"

Houston wrapped his arms around his wife as she began gasping for air. Dallas's hand tightened around Cordelia's.

"What's wrong?" Houston asked, a thread of panic in his normally calm voice.

"Ma? Ma?" Maggie said weakly, tears welling in her eyes as she reached for her mother. Austin snatched her into his arms, the blood draining from his face.

Amelia's breathing began to even out. She glanced around the stunned crowd, her smile quivering, her hand pressed below her throat. "I'm sorry, but we're going to have to go home now."

Houston stared at her incredulously. "Are you having the baby?"

"I think so. We need to go home."

"The hell with that," Houston said as he scooped her into his arms. He looked at Dallas. "Which room?"

"Dee's room. The corner room."

"I don't want to have the baby here," Amelia said.

"Too damn bad," Houston said gruffly. "Austin, fetch Dr. Freeman."

Houston swept into the house, his protesting wife in his arms. Austin handed Maggie off to Dallas.

"Hell," Austin grumbled. "December. Could she have picked a worse month? I refuse to call any relation of mine Something December."

"Just go get the doctor, and we'll worry about what we're gonna call the baby later," Dallas told him.

Without another word, Austin ran toward the barn. Dallas touched his finger to Maggie's nose. "Your ma's gonna be all right."

"Promise?" she asked in a shaky voice.

"Give you my word." He looked at Cordelia. "Houston can probably manage until the doctor gets here, but why don't you go see if they need anything? We'll put Shawnee in the barn, then we'll come inside."

She gave him a shaky nod and walked into the house, praying that everything would be all right. Outside her room, she took a deep breath of fortitude before opening the door.

Houston had a fire burning low in the hearth, the drapes pulled back on the windows, and his wife lying in the bed. Her outer clothing was draped over a chair.

Cordelia gave them both a tremulous smile. "Would you like to borrow a nightgown?"

"Yes," he said.

"No," she said.

With a sadness in her eyes, Amelia held her hand toward Cordelia. Cordelia rushed across the room and wrapped both her hands around Amelia's.

"I'm so sorry," Amelia said. "I've been having little twinges all day, but I thought they'd pass. I know this is hard on you. I didn't want to have my baby here."

Cordelia brushed a wisp of blond hair from Amelia's brow. "Don't be ridiculous. You can't stop having babies just because I can't have them. Let me get you a nightgown. It'll probably swallow you up, but you'll be more comfortable."

Amelia nodded slightly in acquiescence. Cordelia walked to the bureau. She heard a gasp and spun around.

Amelia's face was contorted in pain, her hand squeezing Houston's, her breathing ragged. "Try and relax," he said in a soothing voice.

"You try and relax," she snapped. She fell against the pillows, breathing heavily. She smiled at her husband. "Don't take anything I say from this room." She released a long slow breath. "This baby is going to be here too quickly."

Too quickly turned out to be not soon enough as far as Cordelia was concerned. She felt as though the hours dragged by while she helped Dr. Freeman, wiping Amelia's brow, holding her hand, reassuring her that everything would be all right—until she heard that first lustful cry a few minutes after midnight. Tears filled Cordelia's eyes as Dr. Freeman placed the baby in Amelia's arms.

"Oh, isn't she beautiful?" Amelia asked in a hushed voice.

Cordelia patted the glistening sheen of sweat from Amelia's throat. "Yes, she is."

Amelia looked at her. "Go get Houston."

"Not yet, girl," Dr. Freeman said. "We're not

through yet. Don't know why it is you women think we're finished the minute you're holding that baby."

"Maybe because that one minute is the one we've been waiting for," Amelia said as she brushed her fingers over her daughter's dark hair.

"Hand her over to Cordelia for a minute," Dr. Freeman ordered, "while you and I finish up here."

Cordelia took the precious child and wrapped her in a soft blue blanket she had planned to wrap around her own child. So tiny. With deep blue eyes, the child stared up at her. "Should I wash her?" Cordelia asked.

"Give her some time to get used to being outside," Dr. Freeman said. "You can wash her while Amelia sleeps."

"I want to see Houston first," Amelia said.

Dr. Freeman brought the blankets over her. "Then I'll fetch him. My job is done tonight so I'm gonna head on home, but I'll see you tomorrow afternoon." He pointed a gnarled bony finger at her. "You stay here until I say you can go home."

She smiled softly. "Thank you."

"Don't thank me, girl. This is the part of being a doctor that I enjoy the most." He wrinkled his brow. "Come to think of it, it might be the only part I enjoy." He patted her head. "See you tomorrow."

Cordelia placed the baby back into Amelia's arms. "You'll want to show Houston his daughter."

Amelia grabbed her hand. "Thank you. I know it was difficult for you—"

Cordelia squeezed her hand. "I didn't want to be anywhere else."

She stepped back as Dr. Freeman shuffled across the room and opened the door.

"Reckon you're waiting to get inside here," Dr. Freeman said.

"She all right?" Houston asked as he made his way past Dr. Freeman.

"Course she is."

Houston crossed the room and knelt beside the bed, his gaze focused solely on his wife. Smiling, she folded the blanket back. "We have a daughter."

"A daughter," Houston said in awe as he touched a large finger to the tiny fisted hand. "She's as beautiful as her mother." He lifted his gaze to his wife's. "I'm never gonna touch you again."

Amelia looked at Cordelia. "Will you take her now?"

Gingerly, Cordelia wrapped the child within her arms.

"I mean it this time," Houston said.

"I know you do," Amelia said as she touched his cheek. "Now, come hold me."

Carefully, he climbed on the bed, lay beside his wife, put his arms around her, and pressed his cheek to the top of her head. "I love you."

"I think that's our signal to leave."

Cordelia snapped her head around. She hadn't heard Dallas come into the room, but he was looking at her with an intensity that had her heart beating faster than thundering hooves. "I need to wash the baby."

He nodded. "I've warmed up the kitchen."

She followed him from the room, and he closed the door quietly.

"Are you all right?" he asked as they walked down the stairs.

"Just tired."

"Houston figured they had a couple more weeks, or he wouldn't have brought them over today."

"I'm glad they came. I'd like to think they needed us."

They walked through the dining room. "Where are the children?" she asked.

"I put them to bed shortly after sundown." He opened the door into the kitchen.

A warm cozy feeling settled around Cordelia, and she held the child closer to her bosom. Dallas removed a kettle from the low fire and poured water into a bowl. He'd already set towels and blankets on the table. "You've done this before," Cordelia said quietly.

He glanced up at her. "When Maggie was born. Houston is pretty useless worrying about Amelia the way he does."

"And when your son was born?"

She watched as his Adam's apple slowly slid up and down. "Yeah, I bathed him, too." He set the kettle down. "Why don't you lay her on the towels there. I'll hold her while you wash her."

She laid the child down. Dallas slipped his large hand beneath the child's dark head.

"We'll wash her hair first. She won't like it, but it's gotta be done," he said.

As Cordelia sprinkled the first drops of warm water over the child's head, the baby scrunched up her face and released a wail.

"Do you think I'm hurting her?" Cordelia asked as the wail intensified.

"Nah, she's just exercising her lungs." Gently, he turned the child, cradling her on her side so Cordelia could wash the back of her head.

"She's so tiny," Cordelia said.

"Yep, but that won't last."

As Dallas helped her clean the child, an ache settled deep within her chest for all the children

Dallas would care for in the future, all the children who would not belong to him. Houston's children. Austin's children. But never his.

How unfair of Fate to give Rawley's father a son he would never appreciate while Dallas would live the remainder of his life with no hope of ever acquiring a son.

Dallas, whose large hands cradled and comforted the child.

Dallas, who looked upon a child barely an hour old, with love in his eyes.

While Rawley's father gave his son nothing but pain, Dallas would have seen to it that his son had all that his heart desired.

When she finished washing the baby, she watched as Dallas patted his niece dry and slipped a blue gown over her head. A gown his son would have worn.

He brought a dry blanket around the baby and cradled her within the crook of his arm. A corner of his mustache lifted as he smiled. "Hello, little December. Aren't you a beauty? You ready to see your ma? Get something to eat?"

He looked at Cordelia, a sadness in his eyes. "Did you want to take her upstairs?"

At that moment she knew she loved him more deeply than she thought possible. "No, you go ahead."

When he'd left, she glanced around the kitchen. Together they had cared for Houston's daughter. They worked well together, they always had. "We would have made good parents," she whispered to the shadows in the corner. "It's not fair that we were denied the chance."

Without knowing her destination, she walked out of the house, her slippered feet leaving a trail in the thin blanket of snow.

The wind whipped around her, and she heard the rapid clackety-clack of the windmill. Then she was standing beside her son's grave—for the first time.

His wooden marker was simple:

**LEIGH
SON
1881**

She wanted to hold him. She wanted to bathe him and comb his hair and watch him grow. She wanted his tears to dampen her shoulder, his laughter to fill her heart.

She wanted all that she could never have—and she wanted it desperately.

The anguish ripped through her chest for all they had lost: their son and the foundation for a love that he might have given them. Dallas would never love her now as she loved him.

She heard muted footfalls, but couldn't bring herself to turn around. She tried to wipe the tears from her cheeks, but others surfaced. She wrapped her arms around herself, trying to hold in the pain, but it only increased.

Dallas placed his sheepskin jacket on her shoulders. His arms circled her, and he brought her back against his chest.

To her mortification, she released a small wail and his hold tightened.

"I never even saw him," she said, her voice ragged.

"He was so tiny, it was hard to tell . . . but I like to think he would have looked like you."

"It hurts. God, it hurts."

"I know," he said in a raw voice.

"We lost so much when we lost him."

"Everything," he said quietly. "We lost everything."

His words circled her on the wind.

Everything.

Chapter Eighteen

Cordelia walked into the entryway and stumbled to a stop at the sight of Cameron and Duncan standing just inside the doorway. Joy swelled within her as Cameron looked up and smiled.

She rushed forward, taking his hands. He brushed a kiss against her cheek. Then she reached for Duncan.

"It's so good to see you," she said.

"Christmas isn't the same without you," Cameron said, and Duncan nodded his agreement.

"I'd hoped to come by today, but"—she pointed toward the stairs—"Amelia had her baby last night, and everything has been so hectic."

Sadness filled Cameron's eyes as he dropped his gaze to her waist. "We heard you lost your baby."

The tears came suddenly, without warning, burning her eyes, clogging her throat until she could do little more than nod.

"I'm sorry, Dee," Cameron said.

She pressed her hand to her lips, wishing she could control the overwhelming grief.

"Actually, that's why we're here," Duncan said. "Boyd wanted to meet with Dallas."

Cordelia swallowed back the tears. "Boyd is here?"

"Yeah, he's in the office talking to Dallas."

"About what?"

Her brothers averted their gazes, one staring at his boots, the other at the ceiling. Foreboding ripped through her. She rushed down the hallway and eased her way past the partially opened door.

Dallas stood before the window, gazing out. Boyd stood beside the desk, a scroll in his hand.

"So that's the way I see it," Boyd said. "The contract says if she gave you a son, you'd deed the land over to us. She gave you a son. It's unfortunate he died, but that doesn't change the fact that she upheld her end of the bargain. Now, I expect you to uphold your end—"

"The hell he will," Cordelia said.

Dallas spun around, agony reflected in his gaze, just before he threw on a mask of indifference. "Dee—"

"This doesn't concern you, Cordelia," Boyd said.

"The hell it doesn't. You and Father bartered me away for a strip of land, and now you have the gall to say it doesn't concern me? How dare you! How dare you come into our home and demand anything of us, anything of Dallas. There isn't a court in the state that will side with you, that will say a dead son is the same as a live son—"

"Dee—" Dallas began.

"No!" she said, hurting for him, the pain twisting inside her for all that they had lost. They would lose no more. She turned her hardened gaze on her brother and pressed a hand to her chest. "We hurt, damn you! We lost something that we desperately wanted, something we can never regain. Where was my family when I was suffering? Where was my family when I thought I might die? Marking off the land they wanted to claim!" She trembled with rage, hurt with disappointment. "I never again want you to step foot in this house. You will never acquire the land because I am now unable to give Dallas a living son. I have a strong need to hit something, Boyd, and if you don't get out of my sight right this minute, there's a good chance you'll be the thing I hit."

Boyd glared at Dallas. "You gonna let her do the talking for you?"

Dallas nodded sagely. "I'll even hold you for her if she wants to hit you."

"You'll regret going back on your word," Boyd spat out just before he stalked from the room.

Cordelia sank into a chair, shaking as though she'd been thrown into an icy river. Dallas knelt beside her.

"I've never gone back on my word, Dee, but for you, I will. I'll move my fence back across the river if you want."

She shook her head. "I don't know what I want right now. Just hold me."

He wrapped his arms around her. She pressed her face to his shoulder and wept: for the family named McQueen that she had lost, for the family named Leigh that she would never have.

SAUNTERING FROM THE back room in the barn, Austin heard the faint harsh breathing, like someone running, fighting for air. He halted and listened carefully. Then very cautiously and quietly, he climbed to the loft.

Rawley was crammed into a corner, his arms wrapped tightly around his drawn-up knees, rocking, rocking back and forth.

Austin eased over the straw-covered floor. "Rawley?"

Austin had never seen raw terror, but he knew he was looking at it now. He touched the boy's shoulder and could feel the tremors racing through him.

"He's here," Rawley whispered.

"Who's here?"

"The man what hurt Miz Dee."

Austin crawled on his belly to the open window in the loft and gazed out. He recognized the three horses tied to the railing, but he couldn't believe one of the McQueen brothers was responsible for hurting Dee. He glanced over his shoulder. "You sure he's here?"

Like a frightened turtle, Rawley drew his shoulders up as though he thought he could hide his head. "He paid my pa."

"What he'd pay your pa for?"

Rawley rolled his shoulders forward. "To hurt me," he whispered in a voice that echoed shame.

Rage surged through Austin. "Can you point him out to me when he leaves?"

Rawley shook his head vigorously. "Said he'd kill me if I ever told."

"Give you my word, Rawley, that he'll never touch you again." He held out his hand. "But I gotta know who it is before I can deal with him. Come on. Help me."

Slower than a snail, looking as though he'd retreat back to the corner at any second, Rawley crawled toward Austin. Austin pulled him down beside him until they lay flat on the floor, their eyes just above the straw.

Austin saw the three McQueen brothers leave the house and mount up. "Which one?"

Rawley pointed a shaking finger. "The one in the middle."

"You sure?" Austin asked.

"Yes, sir."

Austin turned his head and smiled at the boy. "You done good, Rawley. You just leave the rest to me."

TWO HOURS LATER Austin swaggered into the saloon. The smoke was thick, the noise thicker. He slapped a nickel on the counter and eyed his quarry. "Beer."

He took the glass and downed the bitter brew in one swallow. He was the youngest, the baby, the one everyone else always watched out for.

Not this time.

He removed his gun from the holster, took careful aim, and fired a bullet in the wall of the saloon . . . just above Boyd McQueen's head.

Boyd tipped over in his chair and hit the floor with a resounding thud. He came up sputtering.

Austin couldn't believe the calmness that settled over him as he strode across the room. Men jumped out of his way. Men who had been sitting at Boyd's table hastened to move to other tables.

Austin planted his hands on the table and glowered at Boyd. "I know the truth—everything. You stay away from me, mine, and anyone I consider mine or my next bullet goes through your heart."

He spun on his heel.

"You don't have the guts to kill," Boyd taunted.

Austin slowly turned and faced his adversary. "Mark my words, McQueen. Nothing would bring me greater pleasure than to rid the ground of your shadow."

SPRING CAME AS though winter had held no sorrow, blanketing the earth in an abundance of assorted reds, yellows, and greens.

Cordelia sat on the front porch of Amelia's house, watching as Amelia nursed Laurel Joy. The child kicked her chubby arms and legs in rhythm to her sucking mouth. Cordelia did not resent that Amelia held the child to her breast, but she could not help but ache for the children she would never nourish.

Cordelia turned her attention to a lean-to where the men and Rawley were working to help a mare deliver a foal. Always births would abound. Always the pain inside her would deepen, for what she could not have, for what she could not give Dallas.

"You look as though you have something on your mind," Amelia said.

Cordelia averted her gaze from those she loved. She gnawed on her lower lip. "You told me that you and Dallas had acquired an annulment. How did you go about it?"

Amelia shifted Laurel to her shoulder, buttoned her blouse, and studied her as though trying to understand the reason behind the question. "It was really rather simple. We never consummated our marriage."

"Oh." Cordelia felt her heart sink. "That wouldn't work for us, would it?"

"No, you were obviously intimate at one time."

At one time. Dallas hadn't come to her bed since the afternoon they'd shared in the hotel. He watched her with wariness as though he wasn't quite certain what to do with her.

"Then what would a woman do if she no longer wanted to be married?" Cordelia asked.

"Have you talked with Dallas about this?"

"No, we don't talk at all anymore. We are more like strangers now than we were before we got married."

"He's hurting—"

"So am I. But I can end his hurting."

Laurel Joy burped and Amelia scooted up in her chair. "How?"

"By leaving him. By giving him the opportunity to marry someone who can give him a son."

Amelia shook her head. "I don't think he wants that, Dee. When you were losing the baby, he begged me not to let him lose you, too."

"Words easily spoken—"

"Not for Dallas. He's never been one to speak what he feels."

"He didn't know what it would cost him to say them because he didn't know I'd never be able to give him the son he so desperately wants."

Sympathy filled Amelia's eyes. "You love him."

Tears clogged Cordelia's throat. "Help me, Amelia. Help me to give him what he wants."

Amelia sighed with resignation. "You should probably talk with Mr. Thomaston."

"The lawyer?"

Amelia nodded. "There's something called a divorce. I don't know much about how it's done, but I know a divorced woman is looked down upon, so think hard on this before you do it, Dee."

She looked back toward the lean-to. Dallas was hunkered down beside Rawley, pointing toward the mare, his mouth moving, instructing, explaining as she knew he'd always wanted to teach his own son. He deserved that opportunity to teach a child who carried his blood.

"I don't have to think about it," she said softly.

STANDING INSIDE SHAWNEE'S stall, Rawley noticed the stench first, liked boiled eggs he'd hidden once so he wouldn't have to eat them. Then the cold of dawn crept over him much as he imagined a skeleton's bony fingers would feel as they skittered over his neck.

He swallowed what spit he had and crept out of the stall. A barn owl swooped down with a swoosh that nearly stopped Rawley's heart from beating.

Shadows quivered in the corners. He could see sunlight hovering between the crack where the doors to the barn met.

He smiled. The first light of dawn. Mr. Leigh would be waiting on the back steps—

The pain ripping through his chest caught him unaware as something slammed into him and knocked him to the ground. Someone straddled him and wrapped a large hand around his throat. He didn't know why. He couldn't have breathed if he'd needed to . . . and he needed to. He needed to bad.

A face hovered within inches of his, a face that he'd once known. The face now looked like a wooden puzzle that someone had put together wrong.

Black and white dots fought each other in front of his eyes. The black was winning.

"I'm gonna move my hand away. If you yell, I'll snap your neck in two," his pa rasped.

His pa. His insides recoiled at the thought.

The hand moved away. Rawley dragged in a deep breath, swallowing the bile that rose as the stench of his father filled his nostrils.

His pa got off him and pulled him to his feet as though he were little more than Maggie's rag doll. He slung him against the wall, and Rawley wished he were a doll so he wouldn't feel the pain fixing to come his way.

"Living fancy, ain't you, boy?" his pa rasped.

Rawley shook his head.

His pa smiled. He didn't have as many teeth as he'd once had and those that remained were black at the top of his smile. "Well, I'm gonna be living fancy, too, and you're gonna help me."

Rawley listened to the words. He wanted to take himself away to that place inside his head where nothing could hurt him.

But he knew if he did . . . his pa would kill the lady.

THE PICNIC HAD been Rawley's idea.

"A way to make you happy," he'd said shyly, eyes downcast.

Cordelia should have known then that something was wrong, but she was too wrapped up with thoughts of leaving Dallas. Rawley had told her that he knew of a perfect place for a picnic, a place Dallas had shown him.

That should have tipped her off as well. Rawley always referred to Dallas as Mr. Leigh.

In retrospect, she could see that he had given her clues, small hints that something was amiss.

But it wasn't until they had sat on the quilt to enjoy the food—not until the riders arrived and Rawley's eyes brimmed with tears and he refused to look at her—that she came to understand the true reason behind his suggestion for a picnic.

Dear Leigh,
  I am Mr. Cooper's prisoner. You got until noon tomorrow to bring $1,000.00 to the dried well on the north end of your ranch. Wait there alone, without any guns or knives.
  I ain't hurt, but if you don't follow his orders, he'll kill me.

Mrs. Leigh

Cordelia glared at her captor. He snatched the paper from beneath her hands and held it toward the light of the lantern. "Good, good, you wrote just what I said."

She wondered if he could read, if he did indeed know that she had written his words exactly as he'd spoken them. She wished she hadn't written them at all.

She glanced at Rawley, her sole reason for doing as Cooper instructed.

Within the shed, he sat on a wooden crate. Unmoving. His hands folded in his lap, a grown-up posture out of place on a little boy. He seemed to be staring at the flame quivering in the lantern, only the flame, nothing else . . . as though he wished there were nothing else.

As though staring at the lantern, holding himself perfectly still, would make the gun pressed against his temple go away.

"Well?" the man holding the gun asked.

Rawley's father nodded. "Go ahead."

Before Cordelia could react, the man pulled the

trigger. She screamed as a resounding click echoed around the room.

Rawley's father laughed. "You lucked out again, Rawley."

He drew his hand back and slapped Rawley across the face. Rawley staggered off the box and hit the floor.

"No!" Cordelia cried as she hurried to the corner and took Rawley into her arms. He was shaking as though he'd been dunked into an icy river.

"He didn't feel it," his father cackled. "He's tetched in the head; goes someplace far away. He ain't smart like me." He pointed to his temple. "Now, me, I'm a thinkin' man. Always thinkin'." He knelt and brought his abhorrent body odor with him. "Know what I'm thinkin'?"

Cordelia gathered her strength around her as she tucked Rawley more closely against her. "It doesn't matter what you're thinking."

"He'll come, and when he does I'll kill him."

"Why? You'll have the money—"

"I told you I'm a thinkin' man. Your brother paid me to kill him, but I'm thinkin'—Dallas Leigh ain't gonna be an easy man to kill. He'll fight.

"Then I get to thinkin', Dallas Leigh thinks he's smart. Thinks I'm dumb. So I think to myself, I'll kidnap his wife. Make him bring me money. Then I'll kill him. I get money from him. I get money from your brother."

"Dallas won't come. He's not a man to trade something for nothing. He wants a son, which I can't give him. With my death, he will gain an opportunity to marry a woman who can give him a son."

Rawley's father stood. "You'd better pray he does

come 'cuz if he don't come"—he raked his gaze over her body and Cordelia forced herself not to shudder—"I know lots of men what would pay to spend time with you, just like they paid me to spend time with that boy's ma."

"That boy? You mean Rawley? You sold your wife—"

"She weren't my wife. She was a squaw I found." He tapped his temple. "Told you I'm a thinkin' man. Took her in, made a lot of money off her till she died. Give her boy my name, but I don't imagine I'm his pa. He ain't nearly as good-looking as I used to be. And you'll be better than she was 'cuz I won't have to worry about you leaving me any worthless brats."

Chapter Nineteen

Dallas stared through the window of his office as darkness settled around him . . . along with the loneliness. He'd never before experienced loneliness, perhaps because he'd never understood companionship: the comfort of knowing someone was willing to listen to his thoughts, the joy of sharing something as simple as watching the stars appear within the velvety sky.

He wanted Dee to be in his office now, curled up in her chair discussing her ideas, her plans. But she hadn't come to his office since she'd had the confrontation with Boyd in his office.

He crumpled the note she'd left him on the dining-room table.

Rawley and I have gone on a picnic.

Only a few months before, she might have invited him to join them. Now, she didn't even want his company when she rode into town to check on her hotel.

They had become strangers.

After her accident, he had been afraid to sleep in her bed, fearful of hurting her. With each passing day, a chasm had widened between them, a chasm he had no earthly idea how to close.

He wondered if she would even come home tonight. She had begun to spend more nights at the hotel. He bent his head until his chin touched his chest. Damn, he missed her, and he didn't know how to get her back.

Her smiles for him had disappeared, along with her laughter. Sometimes, he would hear her chuckle at something Rawley said. He'd hoard the moment as though it were for him, knowing full well that it wasn't.

It seemed that the night they had lost their son, whatever tender feelings she might have had for Dallas had perished as well. How could he blame her? He hadn't been there to protect her. He had been as useless as a dry well.

He heard the galloping hooves and looked up in time to see the rider bring his arm back. The window shattered as a rock sailed through it.

What the hell?

He found the rock, untied the string that surrounded it, and unfolded the note. He recognized Dee's flowing script long before he saw her signature.

Sitting at his desk, he turned up the flame in the lamp. He read the note a dozen times. The words remained the same, chilling him to the bone.

He planted his elbows on the desk and buried his face in his hands, digging his fingers into his brow. Christ, he didn't know what to do.

The well on the north end was visible for miles—as was everything around it. If anyone followed him to offer assistance, whoever waited at the well would see him.

If Dallas held his silence, told no one about the ransom note, brought no one with him . . .

He sighed heavily. He'd probably viewed his last

sunset, already regretting that he hadn't taken the time to appreciate it, for he had little doubt that a bullet would be waiting for him beside the well.

DALLAS POUNDED ON the door until the hinges rattled.

The door opened slightly, and Henderson peered out into the darkness. "Good God, Dallas, your wife didn't ask for a loan today."

"I know that. I need a thousand dollars—cash."

"Come see me at eight when I open the bank."

He started to close the door, and Dallas slammed his hand against it. "Now. I need it now."

"For what?"

"Business. You can charge me double the interest on it."

Henderson scurried outside, and Dallas followed him down the steps. As Henderson fumbled with the keys, Dallas refrained from grabbing them and shoving them into the locks himself.

When Henderson turned the key on the last lock, he glanced over his shoulder at Dallas. "You stay here while I get the money."

Nodding, Dallas handed him the saddlebag. "Make sure it's exact."

As Henderson disappeared into the building, Dallas walked to the edge of the boardwalk and gazed toward the end of town where Dee's hotel stood before turning his attention to the sheriff's office. He toyed with the idea of waking the sheriff as well, of explaining the situation to him in case Dee didn't return home tomorrow. But if Cooper didn't release Dee, what difference would anyone knowing make? None at all.

He glanced back at the hotel, and the pride

swelled within him. The Grand Hotel. She had envisioned it and turned it into reality. He couldn't remember if he'd ever told her how proud he was to have had her at his side.

For a man who thought he'd lived his life by side-stepping regrets, he suddenly discovered that he had left a great many things undone.

DALLAS ARRIVED AT the well an hour before the sun shone directly overhead. The windmill clattered as the slight breeze blew across the plains. He shifted his backside over his saddle and waited.

He loved the land, the openness of it, the way it beckoned to a man. If treated right, the land returned the favor, but it couldn't curl against a man in the dead of night. It wouldn't warm his feet in the middle of winter.

He saw the solitary rider approaching. He wasn't surprised that the exchange wasn't going to take place here. Still he had hoped.

The man who neared wasn't Cooper. Dallas had never seen the burly man before, and he hoped to never see him again.

"You got the money?" the man asked through a mouth of missing and rotting teeth.

"Yep. Where's my wife?"

"At the camp." The man held out a black cloth. "Put this on."

Dallas snatched the cloth from the grimy fingers and bound it over his eyes. He wasn't a man accustomed to playing by another's rules, but he had no choice. He'd do whatever it took to keep Dee alive.

She'd lost their child because he'd thrown caution to the wind. He didn't intend to be as careless this time.

The dark material muted the afternoon sun's blinding rays, but Dallas used the intensity of the light to measure the passing of the day, to gauge the direction that they traveled: west, toward the sunset.

After what seemed hours, Satan stumbled to a stop.

"You can remove the mask now," his captor said.

Dallas jerked off the foul-smelling cloth. His eyes needed little time to adjust as dusk was settling inside the small canyon.

His gaze quickly swept the area, registering the dangers, the risks . . . the terror in Dee's eyes as she stood with her back against a tree, her arms raised, her hands tied with coarse rope to the branch hanging over her head.

Dallas dismounted, grabbed the saddlebags, and strode toward Cooper, ignoring the man's knowing smirk, unable to ignore the whip he was trailing in the dust like the limp tail of a rattlesnake.

"Cut her loose," Dallas ordered as he neared the loathsome man who called himself Rawley's father, sorry to discover that he'd left too much of the man's face intact.

Cooper spit out a stream of tobacco juice. "Not till I got the money."

Dallas slung the bags at Cooper's feet and stalked toward Dee.

"Stop right there or Tobias will shoot her," Cooper snarled.

Dallas spun around. A man standing to the right of Cooper had a rifle trained on Dee. The man who had brought Dallas to the camp had dismounted and snaked an arm around Rawley, holding him close against his side, a gun pressed to the boy's temple. Dallas would have expected fear to be hovering within Rawley's dark eyes. Instead they only held quiet resignation. Dallas tamped down his anger. "You've got the money. Let them go."

Cooper chuckled. "This ain't just about the money. This is about what I owe you." He snapped the whip and the crack echoed through the canyon. "My face can't even attract a whore after what you done to it. Hurts something fierce. Figure you could do with a little hurt yourself." His lips spread into a smile that lit his eyes with anticipation. "How many lashes you think it would take to kill her?"

Dallas took a menacing step forward.

A rifle fired.

Dee screamed.

Dallas froze. He slowly glanced over his shoulder. Dee vigorously shook her head. He could see no blood, no pain etched over her face.

"Next time, Tobias won't miss," Cooper said.

Swallowing hard, Dallas turned his attention back to Cooper, deciding it was time to risk everything in order to gain all. "Kill her and you'll never get the money."

Cooper's laughter echoed around the canyon as he kicked the saddlebags. "You damn fool. I've got the money."

"Do you?" Dallas asked.

The laughter abruptly died as Cooper dropped to his knees and flung back the flaps on the saddlebags. Frantically, he pulled out paper. Pieces and pieces of blank paper. Fury reddened his face as he glared at the man who had escorted Dallas to the camp.

"Quinn, you fool, didn't you look in the saddlebags before you brung him out here?"

"You didn't tell me to look in the saddlebags. You just told me to bring him."

Cooper glowered at Dallas. "Where's the money?"

"In a safe place. All one thousand dollars, but you don't get it until I know Dee is safe. She leaves with me now, and I'll bring the money back to you. Give you my word."

"Your word. You think I'm some kinda idiot? I ain't letting her out of my sight until I've got the money, and you ain't never leaving here alive."

"Then we can handle this another way. Take her to town, let her check into the hotel. A man is waiting there, watching for her return. When he knows she's safe, he'll give you the money. Meanwhile, you'll have me as insurance."

Cooper narrowed his eyes. "Who is it? One of your brothers?" He rubbed his jaw. "Austin. It's gotta be Austin."

Dallas shook his head. "Nope. Figured you'd expect it to be one of my brothers. You'd never suspect this man."

Cooper struggled to his feet, his knuckles turning white as he clenched the whip. "You'll tell me who has the money, by God. You'll tell me!"

With a quick flick of his wrist, he brought the whip back and snapped it. It whistled through the air. Dee gasped as it sliced through her skirt.

"Damn you!" Dallas roared.

"Tell me who it is," Cooper yelled, "or I'll whip her to death."

When Cooper brought his arm back, Dallas raced across the expanse separating him from Dee. He pressed his body flush against hers, drawing in a hissing breath through his teeth as the whip bit into his back.

Reaching up, he fumbled with the knots in the rope.

"If you untie them ropes, Tobias will shoot her!"

Dallas stilled his hands. He'd never in his life asked or begged for anything. "Christ! You want me on my knees, crawling on my belly? I'll do anything you want, just take her into town. Let her register for a room at the hotel. The man and the money are waiting for you."

"So you say," Cooper yelled. "The law's probably waiting on me."

Dallas heard the whistle and clenched his teeth, but he couldn't stop his body from jerking when the whip sliced across his back. His shirt offered little protection against the razor-sharp tip, and he realized with sickening dread that he had lost his gamble. He'd hoped his change in the plans would have forced Cooper to honor his end of the bargain.

He wrapped his hands around Dee's trembling fists, gasping when the lash hit him again.

"Move away," she whispered hoarsely.

"No." He slammed his eyes closed when the pain ripped through him. When he opened his eyes, tears hovered within hers. "Don't you dare cry," he growled through clenched teeth. "Don't you dare give him that satisfaction."

She nodded bravely, and he could see her blinking back her tears. Dear God, but he couldn't have asked for a finer wife.

"You have to get away from here," she said in a low voice as the whip tore into him. "One of my brothers paid him to kill you."

"Figured it was something like that. That's why . . . tried to force him to take you to town." He lowered his trembling fingers to her soft cheek. "Keep the promise you made to me . . . my land . . ."

The pain intensified, drowning out his thoughts, his muscles quivering as the onslaught continued. He buried his face against her neck, her warmth, her sweet fragrance. He wanted to tell her something else, something important, but it hovered at the edge of the agony.

"I'm sorry," slipped past his lips before the blackness engulfed him.

WITH THE SPUTTERING flame from the stub of a candle casting a fluttering glow over Dallas's back, Cordelia tried to asses the damage.

She had removed what remained of his shirt, the blood-soaked strips that could not even serve as a bandage. Crimson rivulets of torn flesh and seeping blood criss-crossed his broad back. His trousers had grown black and stiff as the blood had flowed more freely with each strike of the lash.

Although unconscious, he groaned and clenched his fists. Her trembling fingers hovered over his tortured flesh. She didn't know how to ease his pain, how to stop infection from settling in, although infection was the least of her worries. They intended to kill him, and with a sickening dread, she knew they intended for his death to be a slow, agonizing affair.

"Why did you come?" she whispered hoarsely as she brushed the black hair from his furrowed brow.

She stiffened as she heard a key go into the lock of the shed's door. It opened and Cooper burst into the room. "He awake yet?"

Cordelia moved so her body partially covered the sight of Dallas's back. "No."

Cooper lumbered across the room and squatted beside Dallas. He grabbed his hair and jerked his head up. Dallas moaned, his eyes opening to narrow slits.

"Who has the money?" Cooper demanded.

"Go to hell."

Cooper slammed Dallas's head against the dirt floor. "I'm gonna take her into town tomorrow. If I don't come back with the money, you're gonna die a slow death. I know how to keep a dead man screaming for days."

He shoved himself to his feet.

"And if the money's there," Cordelia said, hating the plea she heard in her voice, "you'll let him go."

Cooper sneered at her. "If I get the money, then I'll kill him quick. Like I said before, your brother paid me to kill him. I ain't got no choice in the matter except to decide if he dies fast or slow. Now that decision is in his hands."

He left the shack, slamming the door into place. Cordelia heard him lock the door. She leaned close to Dallas's ear. "Does someone have the money?" she asked.

"Yes."

"Who?"

"You're safer . . . not knowing."

"I won't leave you here."

Grunting and groaning, he struggled to sit up, sweat beading his body, his muscles quivering with the strain. Roughly, he cradled her cheek and brought her face closer to his. "You will leave, dammit."

"He's going to kill you," she whispered brokenly.

"Maybe." He dropped his hand to the dirt. "Look, I think we're here."

In the dim light of the candle's glow, she could see his hand trembling as he drew an X in the dirt.

"Well on north end." Another X.

"The house." X.

"Town." He lifted his pain-filled gaze to hers. "Once you get into the hotel, wait in our room with the door locked until a man comes for you. He'll say, 'You hold my heart.' Draw him a map. Go with him to the sheriff. There's a chance they could get back here . . . in time."

She knew from the resignation in his eyes that he thought the chances were slim. His face was a mask of agony as she laid her palm against his cheek. "Lie down. You need to save your strength. I'll see if I can stop some of this bleeding."

His breathing shallow, he stretched out beside her. She imagined each intake of breath was agony as his back expanded. She had no way to cauterize the gaping slashes. She tore off a strip of her petticoat and pressed it against the worst of his wounds, trying to stanch the seepage of glistening blood. The air hissed through his teeth.

"I'm sorry. I don't know what else to do." She glanced at his face. His eyes were closed, his jaw clenched. She touched his cheek, realizing with gratitude that he had lost consciousness.

She trailed her fingers along his sides where the whip had sometimes slithered. The cuts were shallow and had stopped bleeding. She wanted to curl beside him, wrap her arms around him, and take away his pain.

She hadn't planned to fall asleep, wasn't certain when she had, but she awoke to a scratching at the door. The candle had gutted and the small shed was wrapped in darkness.

The scratching intensified, then she heard a click, and the door squeaked open on dry hinges. A small silhouette stood in the doorway.

"Miz Dee?"

Cordelia rose to her knees. "Rawley?"

He took a small step forward. "We gotta go."

"Where's your father?"

"They're all passed out, drunk as skunks, but we gotta hurry."

Cordelia shook Dallas's shoulder. He groaned. She slapped his cheek, alarmed to find it so warm. "Dallas?" She slapped him again. "Dallas, wake up."

Moaning, he grabbed her hand before she could hit him again.

"Rawley unlocked the door. We need to go." She slipped her hands underneath his arms. "Help me. Come on. Get up."

Slowly, laboriously, she got him to his feet. He draped an arm over her shoulder, and she wrapped her arm below his waist, trying to give him some support.

"Horses?" he whispered.

"They never took off the saddles," Rawley rasped into the darkness. "But we gotta hurry. They'll whip my butt if they wake up."

They staggered into the night. Cordelia didn't know how Dallas managed to pull himself into the saddle, but he did.

Then they were galloping, galloping toward freedom.

Cordelia kept the map Dallas had drawn emblazoned in her mind, her gaze focused on the North Star he had shown her one night. She knew they were heading in the right direction, away from their captors, but she didn't know exactly where the house was, or the town, or Houston's home. They could all easily be missed with the vast expanse of land stretching out before them.

She had no way to gauge the time as the steady pounding of the hooves echoed over the plains. Rawley kept glancing back over his shoulder. She didn't blame him. She had little doubt his punishment would be severe if they were caught.

"Dee!"

She jerked her gaze around. Dallas was slouched over the saddle horn, his horse slowing to a trot. She brought her own horse to a stop and circled back as Satan staggered to a halt.

"Dallas?"

His breathing was shallow, his knuckles white as he gripped the saddle horn. "Tie me."

"What?"

"I'm close to passing out. If I fall, you won't have the strength to get me back on this horse." He struggled to loosen the rope from its place on his saddle. "I want you to tie me to the saddle so I can't lose my seat."

She glanced around. "Surely you can hold on a little while longer. We can't be that far from home."

"We have hours yet to ride." A corner of his mouth tilted up. "That's the problem with owning so much land. It takes forever to get home."

Rawley had sidled his horse up against hers, his young face etched in worry.

Cordelia reached out, took his hand, and squeezed gently. "You keep a look out while I help Mr. Leigh. If you see riders coming, you ride fast and hard for town."

He gave a quick nod and settled his anxious gaze in the direction from which they'd ridden. Cordelia dismounted, worked the rope free from the saddle, and glanced up at Dallas, the pain carved deeply into the creases of his face.

"What do I do?" she asked.

"Slip the rope beneath the legging of the saddle . . . wrap it around my leg . . . bring the rope up . . . loop it around my waist and the horn in a figure eight . . . take it to the other side, wrap it . . . secure my hands to the saddle horn . . . give me your word if something happens and I can't ride . . . you'll keep going."

"No."

"Dee—"

"No," she insisted as she wound the rope around his leg and knotted it. "If you want me safe, then you'd best find a way to keep riding."

"When did you . . . get so ornery?"

She knew it was unfair to ask so much of him when he was suffering as he was, but she'd be damned before she'd let him give up. She brought the rope up to his waist, careful not to let the rough hemp touch his bare back.

When she had finished following his instructions, she mounted Lemon Drop and took Satan's reins. "Am I going in the right direction?"

He gazed at the stars before looking out over the land. "Head south . . . east."

She kicked her horse into a lope, ignoring her husband's strangled groans, hoping that home lay just beyond dawn.

Chapter Twenty

Cameron jerked awake, his neck stiff, his arm numb from using it as his pillow. His gaze darted around the lobby of The Grand Hotel.

It was empty, silent. Even the low fire that had been burning within the hearth had died quietly. Through the windows, he could see the darkness of night. It had been night when last he'd looked.

When was that?

He thrust himself to his feet and shoved his hand into his pocket, pulling out his watch. Two-thirty.

Dallas would kill him if he'd been sleeping . . .

He rushed across the lobby and pounded the little bell on the registration desk.

Bleary-eyed, Susan Redd peered out from the room behind the desk. "What do you need?"

"Has Mrs. Leigh registered?" he asked, unable to keep the alarm out of his voice.

Susan sighed and shook her head. "No, but she has a key to one of the rooms upstairs. She could have come in without me knowing."

"What room?"

"Three-oh-one."

"Thanks." Cameron dashed up the stairs and pounded on the door. "Dee?"

With an unexpected burst of panic, he kicked in the door. The room was empty.

Dread filled him. She should have been here by now. Christ, why had Dallas laid this burden on his shoulders? Should he wait . . . or should he leave?

He took a coin from his pocket and tossed it into the air. Heads he'd leave.

It landed with a thump on the floor.

Heads it was.

THE FIERY FLAMES licked at Dallas's back unmercifully. He searched for the peaceful cocoon of oblivion, but it hovered beyond reach as the pain shot through his back and his whole body jerked in rebellion. "Damn!"

"Sorry, son, but I have to get these wounds cleaned."

Dr. Freeman.

Dallas forced his eyes open, only then realizing that he was lying in a bed, his hands fisted into the mattress.

"Dee?"

"I'm here," she said softly as she laid her palm over his hand.

He wanted to turn his hand and intertwine his fingers with hers, but he was afraid he'd crush her bones. He didn't seem to have any control over his body as it flinched with Dr. Freeman's not-so-gentle ministrations.

"Home?"

She placed her cool fingers against his fevered brow. "Yes, we're home. When I didn't show up at the hotel, Cameron came here and told Austin what had happened. Austin had the men out searching for us. Our paths crossed near dawn." She brushed his hair up off his brow. "Why did you trust Cameron with the money?"

"The day you married me . . . he was the only one who cared about you . . . enough to threaten me. What about Cooper?"

"Austin went to town to get the sheriff so they can go arrest them. I drew them a map like the one you drew for me."

"Good. Your . . . other brothers?"

When Cameron had heard the whole story, he'd paled considerably. She'd told him to check into a room at the hotel until the matter was resolved. She knew he didn't have the stomach for the harsh conflict about to erupt. "I'll take care of them. I'll take care of everything. You just need to get well."

"Put out the fire."

She brushed her lips along his ear. "There is no fire. You have a fever and your back . . . your back is a mess."

He thought he felt rain falling along his cheek, soft gentle rain. Then he thought nothing at all as the pain carried him under to the darkest recesses of hell.

Cordelia carefully wiped her tears from Dallas's face, then swiped them from her own. "Is he going to live?"

"Hell, if I know," Dr. Freeman answered, the frustration evident in his voice. "He's lost a lot of blood, he's fighting infection, and there's not a whole hell of a lot left for me to sew up." He turned his wizened gaze her way. "But then, he's a fighter. Always has been so I reckon he'll fight this, too."

He went back to work and Cordelia averted her

gaze from the sight of Dallas's ravaged back. A gentle hand closed over her shoulder.

"I fed and bathed Rawley. He's sleeping now. Let me take care of you," Amelia said.

Cordelia shook her head. "Not until Dallas's fever breaks."

"That could be a while."

"I know."

After Dr. Freeman left, she stayed by Dallas's side, wiping the sweat from his brow, his throat, rubbing ointment over his chaffed wrists, fighting back the tears that threatened to surface every time she gazed at his back.

He was so undeserving of the suffering. Even unconscious, his jaw remained clenched, his brow furrowed, his fists balled around the sheets. His body jerked from time to time. He moaned low in his throat, the sound like the bawl of a lonesome calf lost on the prairie.

It was late afternoon before footsteps thundered up the stairs. She came to her feet as Austin and Houston stormed into the room, the sheriff in their wake.

"How is he?" Houston asked as he ran his gaze over his brother's back.

"Fighting. Did you find the men—"

"We found them," Austin said as he slung himself into a chair beside the bed.

She looked at the sheriff. He seemed ill at ease standing in the room, holding his hat in his hand. "Did you arrest them?"

"No, ma'am. They're dead."

Cordelia stumbled back. "Dead?"

"Yes, ma'am. Somebody got to them before we did. Looks like whoever it was slit their throats while they were sleeping."

Cordelia slammed her eyes closed. "Then you have no way of knowing which of my brothers paid them to kill Dallas."

"No, ma'am."

"Boyd," Austin said.

"Why Boyd?" Sheriff Larkin asked. "Because he's the oldest? Because he shot you? I gotta have a better reason than that to arrest a man."

Austin bolted to his feet. "I can give you a good reason to arrest him."

Houston harshly cleared his throat.

Austin dropped his gaze. "Dallas wouldn't want you to arrest him anyway. He takes care of his own problems."

Houston stepped between Austin and the sheriff. "We're all tired and bickering among ourselves isn't going to help anything."

Sheriff Larkin settled his hat into place. "Let me know when Dallas is up to talking. Maybe he knows something else." He pointed his finger at Austin. "Don't go breaking the law thinking it'll even things out. Two men breaking the law is just two men breaking the law."

"I ain't gonna break the law, but I'm not going to let them get away with it either."

Cordelia put her hand on Austin's arm to restrain him. "I'll handle this." She shifted her gaze to the sheriff. "Thank you, Sheriff. If we should gather any other information, we'll let you know."

"You do that, ma'am. I'm sorry I can't do more."

He walked from the room. Cordelia turned to Austin. "What were you going to say before Houston stopped you?"

Austin looked at Houston, and Houston shook his head. Cordelia dug her fingers into Austin's arm. "You promised to be my friend. What do you know that I don't?"

Austin sighed heavily, his blue eyes filled with sadness as he touched his fingers to her cheek. "Boyd was behind the hotel the night you got hurt."

Cordelia felt the blood drain from her face. "No."

She watched Austin swallow. "Yeah, Dee. Apparently, he enjoyed hurting Rawley, paid his pa to let him do it."

She staggered back and fell into the chair, her hand covering her mouth.

"I'm sorry, Dee, I never meant for you to find out."

"Does Dallas know?"

"No. Houston and I talked about it. We figured Dallas would kill Boyd if he knew."

"That doesn't mean Boyd is responsible for this," Houston pointed out. "We just know he's got a mean streak . . . and apparently no conscience."

Cordelia rose from the chair and took a deep breath. "If one of you can watch Dallas, I need to go speak with my family this afternoon."

"I'm going with you," Austin said.

Cordelia captured his gaze. "I'm taking the men with me. You're welcome to come, but understand that I want no interference."

"Amelia will watch Dallas. We'll both come with you," Houston said.

"All right. Let me make the arrangements."

She walked out of the house to the barn where she found Slim brushing Satan's coat to a velvety sheen. She supposed everyone felt a need to do something for Dallas in their own way. "Slim?"

He turned and gave her a lopsided grin. "Yes, ma'am."

"I need you to gather up the men. I want to go

talk with my family this afternoon, and I have no desire to go alone. Be sure every man is carrying a rifle and a side arm, and that they are prepared to use them if necessary—but only on my orders."

"Yes, ma'am."

"Austin and Houston are coming along as well. I'm certain they'll go into the house with me. I'd like you there as well."

"Yes, ma'am. I'll saddle your horse."

"Thank you, Slim." She walked from the barn, across Dallas's domain, grateful her name was no longer McQueen.

SHE DIDN'T BOTHER to knock when she arrived at her father's house. She simply walked through the door, Houston, Austin, and Slim in tow.

The house was shaped like an *H*. One story with three bedrooms on each side, the main living quarters arranged in the center. She walked through the front parlor, straight into her father's study.

Her father sat behind his desk, nursing what she supposed was a whiskey, Duncan was slouched in a chair, and Boyd was staring out a window.

Boyd turned. Blinding white-hot rage swept through her as she crossed the room, brought her hand back, and slapped Boyd as hard as she could.

He grabbed her wrist, his fingers digging into her flesh. "What the hell?"

Three guns were drawn and cocked.

"Let her go," Austin snarled, "or I'll put a bullet through you where you stand."

Boyd released her.

"What's going on, Dee?" Duncan asked as he came to his feet.

"Boyd murdered my child. How could you?

How could you leave me there? And then to demand that Dallas give you his land—" Bile rose in her throat as she turned away from him. She had never felt such revulsion.

"Well, after that little dramatic display—"

She spun around so quickly that Boyd stepped back.

"You haven't seen my dramatic display yet."

He smiled condescendingly. "Calm down, Cordelia. This behavior isn't like you."

"It's exactly like me . . . now that I'm free of the oppression I lived under in this house."

Boyd walked across the room and took his place behind her father's chair. "You've made your point, Cordelia. You didn't need to air our dirty laundry in front of others."

"My point, Boyd?" Cordelia asked, the quivering in her stomach intensifying, but not yet spreading into her voice. "I haven't begun to make my point. You need to move your cattle away from Dallas's river. In the morning, our men will take the fence back to where it stood the day Dallas married me. Any of your cattle that remain will be confiscated."

Her father struggled to his feet. "Have you lost your mind? Your husband gave his word—"

"Yes, he gave his word that he would pull the fence back if I married him. He kept his word. I just watched him flayed to within an inch of his life because one of my brothers paid Cooper to kill him."

Boyd remained motionless, Duncan lowered his gaze. Her heart sank.

"Oh, Duncan, tell me it wasn't you."

"I don't know what you're talking about, Dee."

He lifted his gaze, and she saw the truth within his eyes. The plan had been Boyd's, and Duncan had known of it.

"You knew," she whispered. "You knew what Boyd planned, and you went along with it."

"I don't know what you're talking about," he repeated. "Cooper was a drunk. Whatever he said was a lie."

"Duncan's right," Boyd said. "It's our word against Cooper's. Who are you going to believe? Family or a drunk?"

"Cooper and his associates are dead," she said with resignation, "so the sheriff won't make any arrests because we have no proof. But let me make something perfectly clear. If Dallas dies, I inherit his land, and unless a blizzard blows through hell, you will never possess that property. So you gained nothing, and lost everything. Get your cattle off our land."

She spun around.

"Cordelia!"

She staggered to a stop and slowly turned as her father's voice reverberated around the room.

"You just accused your bothers of trying to commit murder."

"No, Father. From this day forward, Cameron is the only brother I have. If you allow these two to remain in your home after what I have just told you, then I also have no father."

"You're as high-spirited and stubborn as your mother. I warned Leigh that he needed to keep a tight rein on you, but he wouldn't listen."

"Dallas isn't one to follow in other men's footsteps. Giving him permission to marry me was the finest gift you could have ever given me."

DALLAS GREW WARMER with each passing hour. When he shivered, Cordelia didn't dare bring the blankets up to cover him. Dr. Freeman had told her Dallas's raw back needed air. Even if that weren't true, she didn't think he could have survived anything touching him.

Night had fallen by the time they returned from the McQueen spread. Houston had taken Amelia and the children home. Austin had ridden to town. Rawley slept soundly, not even stirring when she'd brushed the hair back from his brow.

She had taken up her vigil beside Dallas, placing her hand over his. Such a strong hand, with a gentle touch. Such a strong man, with a tender heart.

He would deny it, of course, but she had seen too much evidence not to recognize the truth. For all his gruffness, he had a heart as big as Texas.

She heard shuffling and turned to see Rawley standing in the doorway, his black hair sticking straight up on one side. She held out her hand. "Come sit with me."

He hurried across the room and stopped just short of her reach. "I can't, Miz Dee. I tricked you. He said he'd kill you if I didn't. I didn't know he was gonna hurt Mr. Leigh. Honest to God, I didn't know. I won't do what he says no more. I swear to God I'll let him kill me before I do what he says."

She reached out for him, and although he was resistant, she finally managed to work him into her embrace, onto her lap. She began to rock back and forth, her heart breaking for the life this child had endured.

"He won't hurt you, Rawley," she whispered, stroking her fingers through his hair. "He's gone away. He's gone to heaven."

Rawley jerked back, studying her. "You mean he's dead?"

She hadn't wanted to put it so bluntly, and in all

honesty, she didn't think he had gone to heaven either. Although she didn't think Rawley had any affections for the man, Cooper had been his father. "Someone killed him."

"I'm glad," Rawley said with vehemence. "I'm glad he'd dead so he can't hurt nobody no more."

She pressed his face against her breast and soon felt his warm tears soak through her clothing. She knew he needed to grieve. Even though his father had never loved him, he had still been Rawley's father. Just as she needed to grieve for the family she had said farewell to that afternoon.

She had finally come to realize that with the exception of Cameron, she had never truly known their love, but still it hurt to say good-bye.

THE HEAVY POUNDING on the door awoke Cordelia at dawn. She had put Rawley back in bed and returned to Dallas's side, only to fall asleep in the chair. She placed her palm on his cheek. His fever had risen.

The pounding continued, and she wondered why Austin didn't attend to it.

She rushed into the hallway and began her own pounding. "Austin, can you answer the door?" When he failed to respond, she opened his door. His bed was empty and looked as though he hadn't slept in it. Had he come home?

She hurried down the stairs and flung open the door. Sheriff Larkin filled the doorway. She pushed her way past him. "Slim?"

The foreman turned from the group of men. "Yes, ma'am?"

"Send someone into town to fetch Dr. Freeman. Right away."

"Yes, ma'am."

She turned to the sheriff. "I'm sorry, Sheriff. Did you need something?"

"I need to talk to Austin."

With her fingers, she brushed the stray strands from her face and tried to remember when she'd last taken a comb to her hair. Too long. "I don't think he's here," she said as weariness settled in. "He went into town yesterday evening, but it doesn't look as though his bed has been slept in so you might check the hotel."

"I've already made inquiries around town. No one saw him yesterday evening. He didn't check into the hotel."

Alarm skittered along her spine. "He said he was going into town. Do you think he's hurt?"

Beyond the sheriff's shoulder, she saw Rawley shuffling out of the barn. "Rawley!" She motioned for him and he ran to the house.

"Rawley, have you seen Austin?" she asked.

He shook his head. "Not since I told him 'bout the man."

Cordelia knelt in front of him. "What man?"

"The man what paid my pa to kill Mr. Leigh."

Her heart started pounding.

"Who would that be, boy?" Sheriff Larkin asked.

Rawley didn't take his eyes off Cordelia as he answered, "The man what hurt you."

"Boyd?"

"Don't know his name. Pa always called him 'my special friend.' Only I never thought he was special at all."

Cordelia agreed with Rawley's assessment of her brother. He had not been special, only cruel.

"How do you know that he's the one who paid your father to kill Mr. Leigh?" she asked.

"Pa told me that once he'd killed Mr. Leigh for my special friend, he was gonna give me to him for keeps."

Imagining the terror that the child must have felt upon hearing his father's words and the fate that might have awaited him had they not escaped, she drew him into her embrace.

"And you told this to Austin?" she whispered.

He nodded. "Said he'd take care of everything."

She rose to her feet as the vague outline of a rider on a black horse emerged in the distance. Out of the corner of her eye, she saw Sheriff Larkin rest his hand on the butt of his gun. "There's Austin."

Austin brought his horse to a halt and dismounted, eyeing Sheriff Larkin warily. "What's going on, Dee?"

It suddenly occurred to her that she had no idea what was going on, what exactly had brought the sheriff out to the house. "I'm not—"

"You got blood on your shirt," Sheriff Larkin pointed out.

Austin glanced down and touched his fingers to the slender trail of blood that ran along the side of his shirt. He looked up and met the sheriff's gaze. "Must have scratched myself."

"You got somebody that can vouch for your whereabouts last night?" Sheriff Larkin asked.

Austin took a step back, his gaze darting between Cordelia and Sheriff Larkin. "What in the hell is going on?"

Sheriff Larkin blew out a big gust of air. "Mrs. Leigh, I didn't want to break the news to you like this, but Boyd was murdered last night. We found him out on the prairie. Gut shot."

Cordelia staggered back and wrapped her arms around the beam. She'd been angry at him, quite possibly had come to hate him, but she hadn't wanted that for him. No one deserved that slow agonizing death. "Who do you—"

Her heart slammed against her ribs as Sheriff Larkin turned his full attention on Austin.

"Now, then, boy, you got someone who can swear you were with them last night?"

Austin looked at Cordelia, a silent appeal for forgiveness in his eyes, before he quietly spoke. "No."

"That's too bad," Sheriff Larkin said as he stepped off the porch, jangling the manacles. "Because Boyd wrote your name in the dirt before he died."

WHILE DALLAS'S FEVER raged, Cordelia constantly rained cool water over his body and worried about Austin.

A circuit judge had arrived that morning, and he saw no point in putting off the inevitable until Dallas had recovered.

"Dee?"

She moved up at the sound of Dallas's raspy voice and laid her hand over his where it was tied to the bedpost. They had been forced to bind him, spread-eagle, to stop his thrashing at the height of his delirium.

She brushed her lips over his fevered brow, his eyes glazed with pain. "You have . . . to get away," he rasped.

"No, we're safe now. We're home."

"Home?"

She laid her cheek against his bristly one. "Yes, we're home."

"Bury me beside our son."

The rage exploded through her. "You are not going to die!" She clamped her hand beneath his chin, digging her fingers into his jaw. "Do you hear me? You are going to have a son, but only if you live. Do you hear me? You're going to get what you want."

He looked at her through a pained gaze. "Not . . . what . . . I want."

His eyes closed, and she felt his tensed body relax. She wondered if the fever was damaging his brain. A son was what he wanted. All he'd ever wanted. Why was he denying that now?

Near dusk, she heard footsteps along the hallway just before Houston walked into the room. His face told her the verdict long before he was able to speak the words.

"They found him guilty."

Her heart plummeted. "How could they find him guilty? I should have gone to the trial. I should have testified—"

Houston wrapped his hands around the bedpost and leaned his forehead against the scrolled wood. "It wouldn't have made any difference. Not after it came out that he had threatened to kill both Boyd and Duncan. Damn it all, he even went so far as to shoot a bullet into the saloon wall right above Boyd's head and announce that he wanted to rid the ground of Boyd's shadow."

Cordelia slammed her eyes closed.

"I wanted to shake him when I heard that testimony," Houston added.

"This is going to kill Dallas when he's well enough to understand what happened."

"Yep. The sheriff is escorting Austin to the prison in Huntsville tomorrow."

"So soon?"

Houston nodded. "Think the sheriff is afraid that if he waits until Dallas is well, Dallas will interfere." Houston laughed derisively. "He's right."

"I need to talk to Austin."

"I'll watch Dallas. Amelia's cooking supper. Thought we'd stay here tonight, do what we can to help you because we sure as hell can't help Austin."

THE JAIL WAS built of brick, but it didn't look as grand or as lovely as her hotel. It looked cold, hard, and depressing.

The sheriff's office was small. He sat at his desk, his legs crossed over papers scattered on top. A door at the back stood ajar.

"Reckon you're here to see Austin," he said as he brought himself to his feet.

She nodded, her voice knotting in her throat. She had to be brave, she had to be strong.

He pointed. "You'll find him through that door."

Cautiously, she walked through the door, not certain what to expect. Bars stretching from the floor to the ceiling ran along both sides of the corridor. Other bars divided each side into two. Four jail cells altogether.

Austin was in the last one, leaning against the brick wall, his hands cupping Becky Oliver's face while her fingers clutched his shirt through the bars.

He turned his head slightly and gave Cordelia a halfhearted smile. "Hey, Dee."

The truth of his situation hit her hard. "I'll come back."

"That's all right. Becky was just leaving."

Tears streaming along her cheeks, Becky tilted her head back to look at Austin. "Let me tell them, Austin."

"Shh." He touched his thumbs to her lips. "You just wait for me, sweet thing. Like we talked about."

With a sob, she released her hold on him and skirted past Cordelia. Austin turned his face toward the wall. Cordelia could see his throat muscles straining, working. She gave him time to compose himself before she quietly approached.

"I didn't kill him, Dee," Austin said as he met her gaze.

Reaching out, she trailed her fingers over his bristly cheek. "I know that, Austin. That's the one thing I've never doubted in this whole mess."

He looked as though she had just lifted a weight from his shoulders. "How's Dallas?"

"His fever hasn't broken, but I just left Dr. Freeman. He's going to see what more he can do."

They looked at each other—with so much to be said—but here, with the words traveling between iron bars, too much remained unsaid. Taking a deep breath, Cordelia finally ventured, "You're protecting someone, aren't you?"

Austin dropped his gaze to his boots, the toes sticking through the bars as though searching for freedom.

"Cameron?"

"No."

"If it's the person who killed Boyd—"

"It's not."

"But you were with someone that night, weren't you?"

He continued to stare at the floor, and the truth dawned on her so clearly that she wondered why no one else had thought of it. "Becky," she whispered hoarsely. "You were with Becky."

He lifted his gaze.

She wrapped her hands around the cold bars.

"That's what she meant when she said, 'Let me tell them.' Austin, she can vouch for you—"

He shook his head sadly. "It's just five years, Dee. It's not worth ruining her reputation. It's not worth bringing her shame. We want to live here. Raise our children here. I won't have people whispering behind her back."

"But you've been accused of murder. You don't think people will whisper about that?"

"When I get out, I'll figure out who did it, and I'll handle it."

"But, Austin . . . five years."

"Houston married Amelia five years ago, and it seems like yesterday. It's not that long."

"It's an eternity when you have no freedom."

He wrapped his hand around hers. "You tell Dallas to stay clear of this."

Reaching through the bars, she hugged him as fiercely as she could. "You take care of yourself."

"Take care of my violin and my horse. I'll need them both when I come home."

Chapter Twenty-One

Cordelia wept with relief when Dallas's fever finally broke near dawn. The pain hadn't gone away with the fever, but they were able to untie him. He was incredibly weak, too weak to sit, but he managed to slurp broth from a spoon that she held to his lips . . . over and over . . . off and on throughout the day whenever he wasn't sleeping.

While he ate, she prattled, explaining things that had happened since they'd returned to the ranch, carefully avoiding any mention of Austin. She told him about moving the fence back beyond the river, the death of Rawley's father, her plans to add a theater to Leighton.

Talk of the theater made him smile.

Houston and his family remained at the house and took turns seeing to Dallas's needs. To say he was a difficult patient was an understatement.

The third morning after his fever broke, Cordelia walked in the room to find Dallas sitting on the edge of the bed taking short gasps of air, his hands knotted around the mattress, sweat beading his body.

"You shouldn't be up," she scolded as she hurried into the room and set his breakfast tray on the foot of the bed.

"Where's Austin?"

The moment she'd dreaded had finally arrived. All the words she'd practiced saying suddenly seemed trite, insignificant. She knelt in front of him and placed her hands over his. She could see the pain etched in his features, the strain in his muscles. How she hated to add to his pain.

"He's in the prison in Huntsville."

He blanched as though she'd struck the whip against his back again. She tightened her hold on his hands.

"Boyd was murdered. Apparently, before he died, he scrawled Austin's name in the dirt. They sentenced Austin to five years in prison because he had threatened to kill Boyd. And Austin wouldn't say who he was with the night Boyd died."

"Who was he with?" Dallas said through clenched teeth.

Cordelia pressed her forehead to his knee. "He doesn't want anyone to know." She looked up, her eyes pleading. "Give me your word that if I tell you, you won't betray his trust."

He averted his gaze, and she watched him swallow. "Give you my word," he said with resignation.

"Becky Oliver."

"Get my horse saddled."

Cordelia fell to her backside as Dallas stood. "You gave me your word."

"I'm not gonna break my word, but I'll be damned if I'm gonna let him give up five years of his life for a woman."

He took a step, faltered, reached for the bedside table for support, and sent the table and himself crashing to the floor.

He cried out in pain, rolling to his stomach. Cordelia yelled for Houston. He stormed into the room and dropped to his knees beside Dallas, slipping his hands beneath Dallas's arms, trying to help him get to his feet.

"What happened?" Houston asked.

"I told him about Austin," Cordelia said.

Dallas glared at his brother. "Why in the hell didn't you do something?"

"I did all I could do. The evidence was stacked against him, and he wouldn't open his goddamn mouth. The one time he should have opened it, and he kept it closed."

Struggling, Houston finally got Dallas to his feet. Dallas shoved away from him, staggered, and regained his balance.

"Austin told me to tell you to stay out of this. It's his problem and he'll take care of it," Cordelia said.

"He has a hell of a way of taking care of it. Prison, for God's sake."

Dallas walked stiffly across the room, jerked the drapes down, shoved open the door, and stepped onto the balcony. He took a breath of fresh air, fighting off the pain and nausea. He thought his back had been in agony, but the hurt didn't compare to the anguish ripping through his heart.

"There really was nothing we could do," Houston said quietly from behind him. "The judge was lenient with his sentence because of the antagonism that existed between the two families."

Dallas flung his arm in a wide circle. "Look out there. I own it. Every goddamn acre, but it didn't stop my son from dying. It didn't stop someone from abducting my wife. It didn't stop Austin from going to prison for a murder he didn't commit.

What the hell good is it?" He bowed his head. "I want to see him, Houston."

"I know you do, but he'd rather you didn't. I know we raised him, and it's hard to see him as anything but our baby brother, but he's a man now. He knew what it would cost him if he held his silence, and he was willing to pay the price. All we can do now is give him a place to come home to."

"What in the hell did he think he was doing?"

"Reckon he thought he was following in our footsteps, doing whatever it took to protect the woman he loves."

CORDELIA WAITED UNTIL Dallas's strength returned, until his wounds had healed enough that he could wear a shirt and effectively manage the affairs of his ranch.

Taking a deep breath of fortitude, Cordelia rapped her knuckles on the door to Dallas's office. Her courage faltered when his voice rang out, bidding her to enter.

She would never again step into this room, never again hear his voice booming on the other side. Even as she opened the door, he smiled as he came to his feet. Always the gentleman. Always the man she would love.

She crossed the room as quickly as she could, clutching her hands together. Dallas tapped his pencil on her meticulous notes.

"You took care of a lot of loose ends while I was . . . recovering."

"I tried to manage things as I thought you might. Your men were most helpful." She took a step closer. "Dallas, I've given our situation a great deal of thought—"

"Our situation?"

Her mouth went dry, and she wished she had brought a glass of water into the room with her. "Yes, our situation. Our marriage was one of convenience. The reasons holding it together no longer exist. My family does not deserve, nor will they gain the right to hold your land as their own. And I can't give you a son."

He tossed his pencil onto his ledgers. "Dee—"

"I think we should petition for a divorce," she stated quickly, flatly, before her resolve melted away like a solitary snowflake.

"A divorce? Is that what you want?"

She forced herself to keep her gaze focused on the disbelief mirrored in his eyes, knowing it was the only way he would believe her. "I think it would be best for both of us."

He walked to the window and gazed out over his land. "Do you know what life is like for a grass widow?" he asked, his voice low. Turning, he met her gaze. "No matter what reasons we give, people will question your morals, not mine. They'll blame the failure of our marriage on you, not me. Your prospects for building another business, for finding another husband, will dwindle—"

"Then I'll move to another town, where no one knows me. As long as men continue to lay rails for the trains, towns will flourish along the tracks and hotels will be in demand."

"You're looking at years of hardship—"

"A year ago the thought would have terrified me." Tears rose, and she fought them back. "But I'm a stronger person for having been your wife."

A corner of his mouth lifted. "You were always strong, Dee. You just didn't know it."

At this moment she felt incredibly weak. She

wanted to cross the expanse separating them and let him enfold her in his embrace. Instead, she tilted her chin. "I'll leave in the morning."

"Fine." He turned away from her. "If that's what you want."

She didn't want it, but life gave her no choice, not even the illusion of a choice. She wanted Dallas to be happy, and he would never be happy if she stayed by his side.

"About Rawley. I thought it would be best for him if he could stay here."

"I've got no problem with that. He's already drawing wages."

"I'll explain things to him then before I leave. Will I see you in the morning?"

"Probably not. I need to check on my herd."

"Then I'll say good-bye. In spite of the heartache we've suffered, I'll take some cherished memories with me, and I thank you for that."

"Goddammit! I don't want your gratitude." He spun around, anger flaring in his eyes. "I never wanted your gratitude."

"That's too bad because you have it."

A ghost of a smile flitted over his face. "Whatever happened to the shy woman I married, the woman who cowered when I kicked in the bedroom door? You'd probably throw your brush at me now."

"Yes, I think I would." If her fingers hadn't been trembling, she might have gone with her instincts and reached out to comb the wayward lock of hair off his brow. "On your next wedding night, don't kick in the door."

"I won't."

His quietly spoken words hurt far more than she had expected them to. He would have another wedding night, another wife . . . the son he desired—

all that she wanted him to have. The knowledge should have filled her with joy, not pain.

"I need to start packing." She walked halfway across the office, stopped, and glanced over her shoulder. "Dallas, next time hand your wife the flowers instead of leaving them on the bed. She might discover them too late."

She strolled out of the room while everything inside her screamed to stay.

RAWLEY COOPER KNEW too much about sadness not to recognize it when he saw it.

Miz Dee was about the saddest-looking person he'd ever seen. He thought she might even be sadder than she'd been the night they whipped Mr. Leigh.

She sat on the edge of his bed, wearing a smile that looked like she'd drawn it on a piece of paper and slapped it over her lips. It wasn't warm like her smiles usually were. It didn't reach up and touch her eyes.

At any moment, he expected her to cry, and she was holding his hand so tightly that he was surprised he hadn't heard a bone crack. With trembling fingers, she brushed the hair off his brow. It fell back into place, and she brushed it again, over and over.

"I love you, Rawley," she finally said quietly.

Those were the prettiest words he'd ever heard, and he was afraid he'd be the one who cried. He wished he could say them back to her because he did love her, but the words couldn't get past the pain in his chest.

"I wanted you to know that because I'm going to be leaving, and it has nothing to do with you."

"Leaving?" he croaked.

"Yes, I'm going to build hotels in other towns."

"What about Mr. Leigh?"

"He's going to stay here and take care of you."

"You gonna come back?"

She bit her bottom lip. "No. So I need you to do two very special things for me. I need you to take care of Precious, and I need you to take care of Mr. Leigh. When he has a new wife, I know she will love you as much as I do."

She stood and pulled back the covers. "Now get into bed."

He crawled beneath the blankets. She tucked the ends around his shoulders. Then as always, she leaned down to kiss his forehead. He threw his arms around her neck.

"I love you, Miz Dee. Please don't go."

She hugged him close. "I have to, Rawley. Because I love you and Mr. Leigh, I have to leave."

"He won't let you go. Mr. Leigh won't let you go."

She pulled back, and her gaze roamed over his face as though she were trying to etch it in her mind. "Yes, he will. He always gives me what I want, but I can't give him what he wants."

She pressed a quick kiss to his forehead—a final kiss, the last one he would ever receive—and walked out of the room, closing the door behind her.

A glimmer of moonlight filtered through the window. Rawley could see the key in the lock. He no longer felt a need to turn it.

He rolled to his side, curled into a ball, and watched the shadows dance over the walls. He thought about slipping out of the room, finding Mr. Leigh, and talking to him man to man about Miz Dee leaving, but he didn't see the point.

Mr. Leigh was a man who knew how to fight for what he wanted. Rawley figured sooner or later, Mr. Leigh would decide on his own that he wanted Miz Dee to stay with him.

THE CLOCK DOWNSTAIRS chimed midnight as Cordelia placed the last of her belongings into a box.

Heaving a deep sigh, she stretched to work the ache out of her back. She was incredibly tired, but she knew sleep would elude her. It had ever since Dallas had stopped sleeping in her bed, his body draped over hers.

She had thought about asking him to sleep with her tonight, just to hold her, but she feared it would make her leaving that much harder on them both. The memories of what had been, what might have been, would have been rekindled. As it was, they were slowly fading into glowing embers.

She walked across the room, drew back the drapes, opened the door, and stepped onto the balcony. A million stars twinkled in the black velvety sky. From the top of a windmill, she had viewed the land through Dallas's eyes.

She wondered why she had ever thought it desolate.

She heard a horse whinny and glanced toward the corral. Her heart pounding, she eased closer to the edge of the balcony.

She could see her husband sitting on the corral railing, his shoulders slumped, his head bent.

If she didn't know how strong a man Dallas Leigh was . . . she would have thought he was weeping.

WITH A PAINFUL knot forming in her chest, Cordelia watched as Slim loaded the last of her boxes into the wagon.

She held close to her heart the farewell Rawley had given her last night. It had been so hard to release him, to leave him alone in his room, but her leaving was for the best.

She didn't know what the future held for her, where she would go, what exactly she would do, but she knew Rawley needed stability and he would find it here with Dallas.

Dallas was part of the land, his roots buried deep within the soil.

The bump of the last box hitting the floor of the wagon echoed around her. Her chest tightened in response. Her mouth grew dry, her eyes stinging as she searched for fortitude.

Slim turned and wiped his hands on his trousers. "Well, that's it. You taking your horse?"

Lemon Drop. She had ridden the horse beside Dallas. She nodded.

"I'll get her and your gear, then."

In long strides, Slim began to walk toward the barn. Cordelia heard the front door slam and heavy footsteps resound from the veranda. She had hoped Dallas had gone to check on his herd as he'd said he would last night. She didn't know if she could survive one more farewell.

She pivoted and met Dallas's unflinching gaze. He leaned against the beam, his hands stationed behind his back, his eyes dark, his expression hard. He reminded her of a predatory animal, waiting, waiting to strike.

She intertwined her fingers, searching for the words that would lessen the pain of her departure, but the words remained hidden. She cleared her throat. "Everything is packed. Slim is getting Lemon Drop. I suppose it's all right if I take the horse."

Dallas only glared at her, like a wooden statue in front of a store. If a muscle in his jaw hadn't jerked, she might have thought he'd turned to stone. She took his silence as approval. "Do you want to contact the lawyer or should I?" she asked.

His stare intensified.

"I suppose I should talk with him," she said into the silence permeating the air. "I'll tell him to send word to you regarding the best way to handle this matter. I'm going to stay in our room at the hotel until I decide exactly where I'm going to go. I'm fairly certain that I won't stay in Leighton. I think it would be easier on us if I left. I'll let you know what I decide." The words were running out of her mouth now, and she seemed unable to stop them. She knew the tears would not be far behind. "I wish you all the happiness you deserve."

She spun around and hurried toward the front of the wagon.

"Stay."

The strangled word, spoken in anguish, tore at her heart, ripped through her resolve. She swiped at the tears raining over her cheeks and slowly turned, forcing the painful truth past her lips. "I can't stay. I can no longer give you what you want. I can't give you a son."

Dallas stepped off the veranda and extended a bouquet of wildflowers toward her. "Then stay and give me what I need."

Her heart lurched at the abundance of flowers wilting within his smothering grasp. She shook her head vigorously. "You don't need me. There are a dozen eligible women in Leighton who would hap-

pily give you a son and within the month there will
be at least a dozen more—"

"I'll never love any of them as much as I love
you. I know that as surely as I know the sun will
come up in the morning."

Her breath caught, her trembling increased,
words lodged in her throat. He loved her? She
watched as he swallowed.

"I know I'm not an easy man. I don't expect
you to ever love me, but if you'll tolerate me, I
give you my word that I'll do whatever it takes to
make you happy—"

Quickly stepping forward, she pressed her shaking fingers against his warm lips. "My God, don't
you know that I love you? Why do you think I'm
leaving? I'm leaving because I do love you—so
much. Dallas, I want you to have your dream, I
want you to have your son."

Closing his eyes, he laid his roughened hand
over hers where it quivered against his lips and
pressed a kiss against the heart of her palm.

"I can't promise that I won't have days when I'll
look toward the horizon and feel the aching emptiness that comes from knowing we'll never have
a child to pass our legacy on to . . ." Opening his
eyes, he captured her gaze. "But I know the emptiness you'll leave behind will eat away at me every
minute of every day.

"When I was a boy, I went to war searching for
glory. I didn't find it. I came here, thinking I'd find
glory if I built a ranching empire or a thriving
town." He trailed his thumb over her lips. "Instead
I discovered that I didn't even know what glory
was, not until you smiled at me for the first time
with no fear in your eyes."

His gaze swept beyond her, to encompass all that

surrounded them. "A hundred years from now, everything I've worked so hard to build will be nothing more than dust blowing in the wind, but if I can spend my life loving you, I'll die a wealthy man, a contented man."

Tears overflowed and spilled onto her cheeks.

"Stay with me," he said.

Nodding mutely, she wrapped her arms around his neck. The flowers floated to the ground as he lifted her into his arms and carried her into the house.

"Your back," she said as he started up the stairs. "You shouldn't be carrying me."

"My back's fine."

It wasn't fine. It would forever carry the scars he'd earned trying to protect her. A hundred times she'd wondered what she might have done differently to prevent his suffering. A hundred times, she could think of nothing.

Inside their room, she slid along his body until her feet touched the floor.

With infinite patience and tenderness, as though they had a lifetime to fill, he removed her clothes, pooling them at her feet. His knuckles skimmed the inside swell of her breast as he gathered the heart-shaped locket he'd given her for Christmas within the palm of his hand.

"I didn't know you were wearing my gift," he said huskily.

"I thought wearing it was the closest I'd come to ever holding your heart."

"You've held my heart for so long that I can't remember when you didn't, but I didn't know how to tell you. I thought if I gave you this, you'd figure it out. Discovered today that the words aren't that hard to say. I love you."

His mouth swooped down to covers hers, kissing her deeply, warmly. He had kissed her before, so many times before, but never like this . . . as though her mouth were the only one he'd ever known, as though her lips were the only ones he'd ever teased, as though her kiss were the only one that would ever satisfy him.

He loved her, and as he carried her to the bed, she wondered why she'd never realized it before. He had shown her in so many different ways, enticing her into the sunlight until she cast her own shadow.

He shrugged out of his clothes and lay beside her. She trailed her fingers over his chest and his eyes darkened. She guided her hands to his back and felt the uneven ridges that he would forever carry. Tears welled in her eyes.

He cupped her cheek. "Don't cry."

"I hate that they did this to you."

He kissed her cheek. "You have scars, too. I'd take them away if I could."

But he couldn't. They both knew it. His scars on the outside. Hers on the inside. They had both hovered near death. The scars would serve as a reminder of their triumph.

She braced her palms on either side of his face and held his unwavering gaze. "Dallas, are you sure you can give up your dream without coming to hate me?"

"You were my dream, Dee. I just didn't know it. The part of me that I was always searching for."

His lips found hers, hot and vibrant, full of life, desire. His hands touched and fondled, stoking the dying embers of her passion to a roaring blaze.

She kissed his neck, his chest, running her hands over his chest and lower, boldly stroking, relishing the deep guttural sounds that vibrated within his throat.

They had made love, trying to fulfill a dream. They had made love to celebrate the promise of the dream.

Now, at long last, they were celebrating what they should have gloried in all along: their love for each other.

He captured her gaze as he sank his body into hers. She marveled at the perfection of their joining. Then he began to rock, the brown depths of his eyes smoldering, the fire raging through her, burning brightly until it exploded with a glorious burst of sensations, colors, and sounds, unlike any she'd ever known.

Dallas shuddered above her before collapsing on top of her, his breathing harsh near her ear, his fingers threaded through her hair, gently scraping her scalp.

"I love you," she whispered.

"'Bout time you gave me my Christmas present," he whispered low, in a tired voice.

"Your Christmas present?"

"That's all I wanted for Christmas. Your love."

She closed her eyes, remembering his words in the hotel room that night so long ago. "Something that could only be given it if wasn't asked for."

Something she would gift him with for the remainder of her life.

Epilogue

May, 1884

Dallas heard his wife's scream and bolted out of the chair.

"Sit down!"

With panic raging through him, he stumbled to a stop and glared at his brother.

"Sit down!" Houston ordered again.

Dallas balled his hands into tight fists. "A husband should be with his wife at a time like this."

"You'd just drive her crazy. Hell, you're driving me crazy."

Dallas dropped back into the chair, dug his elbows into his thighs, and buried his face in his hands. "Dr. Freeman said she couldn't have children. Christ, I'll never touch her again."

"You'll touch her," Houston said.

Dallas looked up, determination etched deeply in the lines of his face. "No, I won't."

"Yes, you will. One night, she'll curl up against you, all innocent-like—" Compassion, understanding, and a wealth of sympathy filled Houston's gaze. "You'll touch her."

The door to the office opened, and Rawley slipped into the room as quietly as a shadow. "I thought I heard Ma yell."

Dallas smiled at the boy. His black hair was neatly trimmed, his face scrubbed clean. The dirt and grass stains on his newest coveralls were the only evidence in sight that he wasn't as grown-up as he tried to pretend he was.

They had adopted him in their hearts long before the documents made it legal. Against Dallas's preference, Rawley had kept his last name, mumbling something about not deserving the Leigh name. Dallas hoped with time and patience, the boy would someday change his mind.

Rawley had quickly fallen into the habit of calling Dee "Ma." He had yet to call Dallas anything other than Mr. Leigh. Dallas had a feeling that the boy had a long way to go before he'd trust men.

"Why don't you take Precious for a walk?" Dallas suggested.

Rawley eased farther into the room. "I already took her to play with her friends for a while."

Dallas furrowed his brow. "Her friends?"

Rawley nodded. "Yep. She's got a whole passel of friends out in the meadow. They like to play leapfrog. Only they don't jump over her. They just sorta jump on her. Looks like they keep trying to jump over her, but they just ain't strong enough, I reckon."

"Good God, is she in heat?"

Rawley shrugged. "Reckon she gets hot out there. I do and I ain't got all that fur."

Houston's laughter reverberated around the room. "I'd say before too long, you're gonna be making a whole lot of leashes."

Dallas was on the verge of issuing a threat to silence his brother when Cordelia's scream resounded through the house. Rawley visibly paled and backed into a corner.

Dallas shot out of the chair. "Take care of Rawley."

He rushed out of his office and bounded up the stairs, taking them two at a time. As he neared his room, he could hear a small wail. He staggered to a halt, his heart pounding. He placed his forehead on the door and listened to the lustful cries of his son. A miracle he'd never expected. A child born of the love he shared with Cordelia.

The door opened and Dallas nearly tumbled into the room. He caught his balance as Amelia smiled at him.

"Hello, Papa."

"How is she?" he asked.

"Oh, she's fine."

He peered into his bedroom. Late-afternoon shadows graced the corners. At least his son had the good sense to be born at a decent hour.

"Can I see her?"

"Dr. Freeman is finishing up now."

She took his arm and led him into the room. He felt awkward standing at the foot of his bed, watching his wife run her fingers over their son's head.

Dr. Freeman snapped his black leather bag closed. He gave Dallas a hard state. "Enjoy this child because you aren't getting any more. I guarantee it. I don't know how she managed to give you this one."

He shuffled from the room, Amelia in his wake. She closed the door behind them, leaving Dallas alone to gaze in wonder at his wife.

She cast a glance his way and smiled shyly. Dallas walked around the bed and knelt beside her. He brushed back a loose strand of her hair. "How are you feeling?"

"Tired, but happy. So happy." Joy lit her face, warmed her eyes.

Dallas gazed at the tiny bundle nestled snugly within her arms. A small head, a scrunched-up face that looked as though it belonged on an old man, and black, black hair. "He sure has a lot of hair."

He shifted his gaze to Dee. Her smile withered, and she brought the child closer to her breast as though to protect it.

"What?" he asked. "What's wrong with him?"

She ran her tongue slowly around her lips. "He's fine. Just fine."

Dallas narrowed his gaze. "No, he's not. I've never known anything to be fine when you say it's fine."

She took a deep breath before blurting, "He's a girl."

"What do you mean he's a girl?"

She gingerly folded back the sides of the blanket. "You have a daughter."

He stared at the spindly legs, the tiny toes, the small chest rapidly taking in air and releasing it. Quickly he covered the child to prevent her from getting chilled. His fingers inadvertently brushed against the child's taut fist. She unfurled her hand and tightly wrapped it around Dallas's finger.

She may as well have flung her arms around his heart.

"I'm sorry," Dee said quietly.

"Sorry?" Dallas croaked.

"I know you wanted a son—"

"I have a son, and now I have a daughter." He

trailed his fingers along Dee's cheek. "We have a daughter, and she's beautiful, just like her mother."

Tears welled in her eyes as she laid her palm against his bristled cheek. "I love you so much."

Leaning over his daughter, he pressed his lips to Dee's, kissing her deeply, bringing forth all the love he held for her.

"Will you hit me if I thank you for giving me a daughter?" he asked quietly.

She buried her face against his neck. "No. I was so afraid you'd be disappointed."

"Nothing you give me could ever disappoint me."

A soft rap sounded on the door before it slowly opened. Houston stuck his head into the room. "Rawley's been worried."

Dee waved her hand. "Bring him in."

Rawley shuffled into the room, cautiously approaching until he stood beside Dallas.

"Heard ya scream."

Reaching out, Dee took his hand. "Sometimes, things hurt, but we get wonderful things in return." She turned the baby slightly. "You have a sister."

Rawley scrunched up his face. "A sister?"

"What do you think of her?" Dallas asked.

Rawley glanced up. "Think she's butt ugly."

Dallas grinned. "Give her a few years, and you'll no doubt feel differently."

"What are you gonna call her?"

Dee met Dallas's gaze. "I was thinking of Faith," she said quietly, "to remind us that we should never lose faith in our dreams."

DALLAS AWOKE TO the sound of a small cry. The flame burned low in the lamp as he carefully eased away from Dee. He slipped out of bed and, in bare feet, padded to the cradle where he had laid his daughter earlier—after he had bathed her and marveled at her perfection.

Gingerly, he lifted her into his arms. "Hello, sweetheart," he whispered. She stared at him with deep blue eyes, and he wondered if the color would change to brown.

He glanced toward the bed. Dee was curled on her side, her eyes closed, her breathing even.

Quietly, he crossed the room, pulled the curtain back, unlatched the door, and stepped onto the balcony. The warm night air greeted him.

Holding his daughter close with one arm, he pointed toward the distant horizon. "As far as you can see—it all belongs to you, Faith. Someday, I'll take you to the top of a windmill and teach you to dream. When you reach for some of those dreams, you might fall . . . but your mother and I will be there to catch you because that's what love means: always being there. I love you, little girl." He pressed a kiss to his daughter's cheek. "So much . . . it hurts. But I reckon that's part of love, too."

He stood for the longest time, holding his daughter, remembering a time when he'd been a man of small dreams, a man who measured wealth in terms of gold.

"What are you doing?" a sleepy voice asked.

He glanced over his shoulder as Dee sidled against him. "Just showing her the stars and wishing Austin were here."

Dee slipped her arm around his waist and nestled her cheek within the crook of his shoulder. Carefully balancing his daughter within his embrace, he hugged his wife closer against him.

"He should have been here," he whispered

through the knot building in his throat. He still didn't understand all that had happened, but in his heart, he knew his brother was innocent.

And there wasn't a damn thing he could do about it. The detective he'd hired had been unable to find any evidence to prove Austin's innocence or another's guilt.

Dee laid her palm against his cheek and turned his head, until their gazes locked. "He chose to hold his silence for whatever reason—"

"It was a damn stupid thing to do, whatever the reason."

She smiled softly. "You'd never do something stupid to protect the woman you love?"

He recognized from the warmth in her eyes that she knew she had cornered him. He had done something stupid: going after her alone, knowing death waited for him. And he knew beyond a doubt that he'd do it again, would risk anything for her. How could he condemn his brother for sacrificing five years of freedom when Dallas would gladly give his life to keep Dee from experiencing any sort of suffering?

Shaking his head, he gazed at the canopy of stars. His daughter would be walking by the time Austin came home. His son would be herding cattle. His wife would be building a theater in Leighton . . . and anything else that struck her fancy.

Drawing Dee more closely against him, falling into the depths of her dark gaze, he allowed himself to be lured into the glory of her love.

**Don't miss the next captivating
historical romance in Lorraine Heath's
bestselling Sins for all Seasons series,**

WHEN A DUKE LOVES
A WOMAN

Gillie Trewlove knows what a stranger's kindness can mean, having been abandoned on a doorstep as a baby and raised by the woman who found her there. So, when suddenly faced with a soul in need at her door—or the alleyway by her tavern—Gillie doesn't hesitate. But he's no infant. He's a grievously injured, distractingly handsome gentleman who doesn't belong in Whitechapel, much less recuperating in Gillie's bed . . .

Being left at the altar is humiliating; being rescued from thugs by a woman—albeit a brave and beautiful one—is the pièce de résistance to the Duke of Thornley's extraordinarily bad day. After nursing him back from the brink, Gillie agrees to help him comb London's darker corners for his wayward bride. But every moment together is edged with desire and has Thorne rethinking his choice of wife. Yet Gillie knows the aristocracy would never accept a duchess born in sin. Thorne, however, is determined to prove to her that no obstacle is insurmountable when a duke loves a woman.

Coming Fall 2018 from Avon Books

**Be sure to check out the rest of
Lorraine Heath's captivating Texas Trilogy!**

TEXAS DESTINY

He's fallen for a woman . . .

Anxious to meet her soon-to-be-husband, Dallas Leigh, for the first time, mail-order bride Amelia Carson is en route to Fort Worth, Texas. When she steps off the train and locks eyes with her betrothed, she immediately feels drawn to him. But the cowboy standing before her isn't Dallas. Instead, Dallas's brother Houston has been sent to accompany her on the three-week journey to the ranch where she'll begin her new life.

Who belongs to another . . .

The war Houston Leigh fought has left him with visible scars, a daily reminder of his cowardice on the battlefield. Denying his intense attraction to Amelia, he is determined to deliver her untouched, as promised. But during their long dangerous trip, he can't help but admire her inner strength and fearlessness. And when she looks at him—as if she can see beyond his scarred face and read his innermost thoughts—he loses his heart to her. Now as they near the ranch, Houston must choose to remain loyal to his brother—or find the courage to fight for the woman he's convinced is his destiny . . .

TEXAS SPLENDOR

A man on a mission . . .

After five grueling years in a Texas prison, Austin Leigh is finally a free man. He can't wait to go home and be reunited with his sweetheart. But when he discovers she didn't wait for him and is now married, he becomes more determined to clear his name of the crime he never committed.

Meets the one woman who could
offer him salvation—and love . . .

En route to the state capital, he meets a young woman, Loree Grant, and her dog. When he learns that they have survived a mysterious tragedy, he is moved—and curious. And as he spends more time with the lovely, intriguing woman, he sees glimpses of a future he had thought was no longer possible as they both find a new lease on life—and a love that can overcome any obstacle.